Dirk Eichhorst's

"THE TEMPEST IN GLASS"

★★★★★

Sheena Monnin, Stellar Media Club

"A thrilling adventure story. One of the things I most enjoyed about 'The Tempest in Glass' by Dirk Eichhorst is the unbiased and intellectual way the author approaches spiritual topics. The incredible pacing of this story coupled with characters that act, react, speak, and think with such realism makes this book a treasured read. The steady evolution of the main character and the subtle evolution of the supporting characters is powerfully portrayed... An ironic journey of personal growth, given the delightfully surprising ending. This book is a must-read for lovers of thrillers, mysteries, the possibility of life after death."

From Readers

"An epic adventure that compels you to turn its pages until you reach the end. A must-read!"

"Dirk Eichhorst takes readers on an enchanting and breathtaking journey into perilous places of mystical dimensions, leaving readers in awe and wanting a sequel."

"A fantastic journey into worlds not of our own, where the absoluteness of reality is shattered and replaced by a foreboding spiritual uncertainty."

"The author creates original settings described so vividly you feel you're right in the middle of it all...the protagonist is so well developed it's easy to feel his internal struggle right along with him."

"A spiritual journey towards the power of prayer. The vivid landscapes and lush writing transport the reader into a different dimension all-together. For fans of *Lord Of The Rings* and *Dune*, and those who seek inner clarity of their calling."

This book is a work of fiction. Names, characters, places, and incidents either are products of the author's imagination or are used fictitiously. Any resemblance to actual events or locales or persons, living or dead, is entirely coincidental.

"The Tempest In Glass"
Limited First Edition
www.tempestinglass.com

Interior formatting by Jen Henderson of Wild Words Formatting
Front cover title font by Darrell Flood
Cover Design by Dirk Eichhorst
Images from DespositPhotos.com
Used under standard license

ISBN: 978-0-578-35123-0

Esper Joslyn Publications, LLC

Copyright © 2021 by Dirk Eichhorst
All rights reserved.
Printed in the United States of America at
Gorham Printing, Inc

A very special thanks to

Tobias, Stephen, Tara, David,
Cynthia, Brenda, and Dixie

whose encouragement and shrewd commentary
helped me reach the finish line

For

Billie Rae Miller

May she rest in peace

CONTENTS

PART I 1

PART II 97

PART III 229

PART IV 391

PART V 439

Author's Note 457

About the Author 459

"Call to me and I will answer you,
and show you great and unsearchable things you do not know."

– Hebrew Bible, Jeremiah, Second Book of the Latter Prophets
c. 580 B.C.

THE TEMPEST IN GLASS

PART I

1
TARRAZU

Marvin Fischer had resigned himself to the irrefutable conclusion that Caroline wasn't coming back. That, he had known for a long time, was impossible. Marvin Fischer had grown accustomed to solitude, and while detachment sometimes morphed into the melancholy conditions of lonesomeness and gloom, he had taught himself to be content in his work, which he excelled at, and in the simpler pursuits of life, like his comfortable condominium, an exceptionally luxurious automobile, and a damn good cup of coffee. Marvin had regressed into a monotony of acceptable contentedness and professional challenge, while dismissing the void in his spirit, warding off the unresolved part of his life that loomed around the corner like a bellicose specter.

Marvin's indigo Jaeger suit was perfectly fitted, the knot in the patterned blue necktie perfectly pulled, the black wingtips perfectly polished. The silver Rolex on the left wrist glimmered clean with the assurance that it kept exact time. Marvin was tall and trim; the bristly, overcast hair military short. The sharp jaw was freshly shaven beneath an urbane balm that he had carefully applied thirty minutes before. The stormy blue eyes and constant glower produced the impression he was always deep in thought about something. Approaching fifty, Marvin Fischer did not look forward to turning the decade. But the commanding handsomeness, combined with the smart assemblage of apparel, presented an impressive human being.

And now, as Marvin Fischer entered his favorite morning haunt for his black coffee, he hadn't the slightest inkling that the events about to unfold would send his life whirling like a festival carousel gone mad.

Bustling coffee house staff boomed its greeting as Marvin saluted the hello which was his custom. He chatted over the counter with the sprightly barista while waiting his turn, and didn't mind waiting for the beans to be freshly ground for the delicate pour-over, which would produce the full-flavored brew Marvin had come to savor. Acquainted with his preference, the barista delivered Marvin his jumbo Costa Rican Tarrazu in a glass mug rather than the paper, together with a package of finely salted mixed nuts. He asked the girl how the French classes were progressing, and they smiled their *au revoir*. Marvin forewent the sugar counter, wove his way around the expectant patrons vying for the line, and escaped out the door.

Marvin moved onto the welcoming patio with its cheerful yellow chairs and tables. Amber morning sunlight lanced through the wakening tree branches. Clutching the glass mug with both hands as if it were a delicate Greek cylix, Marvin stood for three minutes beneath a leafy elm, watching the cars and pedestrians zoom past along the streets and sidewalks of North 66th and East McDonald. He took his first smoky pull and savored. He liked the feel of the sturdy crystalline mug in his hand rather than the flimsy cup, the solidity of the smooth glass touching his lips. Marvin liked surety. Predictability. Control.

Marvin drew in a deep breath, held it, and blew it out with a soft whistle. He relished the crisp early morning air of springtime in Arizona. His condo in Paradise Valley was just around the corner from the business district and The Bean Sack, the locally owned coffee house. The stroll around the block to fetch his salted nuts and morning coffee, and the bright chats with the baristas, ignited his mind and charged his body for the day's challenges.

Marvin settled into a bistro chair and savored the rich umber tint through the mug's glass wall. He opened the bag of salted nuts and munched, then chased it with the hot brew, further releasing the spicy aroma. It was a simple and sensuous combination that Marvin anticipated with delight, one of those things that made life worth living. He popped another handful, gazing casually across East McDonald Street at the new little storefront church that called itself Hope Crossing, with its glittering sign of bright LEDs that promised *We're praying for you*. Marvin swallowed the nuts and savored the next sip of perfect coffee.

Marvin enjoyed taking his time. He disliked hustle. Soon he would walk back to the condo garage where he parked the Jaguar, and ride into work downtown. Once he got to the office, he would be occupied all day with puzzles that would activate his mind in ways he could only tolerate for a few hours at a time.

But for these minutes, Marvin was free. He could already feel the rush of caffeine. The first mug always went fast. Soon he'd go back inside for a refill. He closed his eyes, more conscious now of his aural senses. There was the whoosh of a passing car, the clop-clop of passers by, the soft babble of talk, the whiz of a bicycle chain. Marvin closed his mind to the bustle. The breeze felt light across his face.

For a moment he missed Caroline.

Marvin leaned glumly forward. Life was okay, even without her. Every day she visited his thoughts. It was unavoidable. And every day, his heart reached for her. Marvin stared into the mug at the brew, the elm branches above reflecting on its mirrored surface. Caroline had loved coffee too. Back in Detroit. Many mornings were shared reclining lazily in bed before work, sipping steaming coffee over talk of remodeling the entryway, the car that needed new tires, the vacation they wanted to take, those quacky ducks trying to break through the ice on the pond just off the balcony.

Marvin felt profoundly for Caroline. He scolded himself for still missing her, even after all the time that passed. He tried to snap his mind to other thoughts. A ping on his smartphone did the trick. He pulled the phone from his inside breast pocket and opened the new message. There was no text, just an old photo. A portrait of a very young woman.

Marvin frowned. He did not recognize the young woman. She had short brunette hair, dark eyes, a pleasant look on her face. It was a posed shot, black and white, like something from a yearbook. Marvin checked the sender—*Simon*. There was no phone number and no *Unknown* or *Masked Call* message—just Simon.

Did he know a Simon?

2
WOMAN IN A BORDEAUX SUIT

Marvin tapped *call* and put the phone to his ear. He waited. There came only silence. Marvin looked back at the phone. It flashed blank, then returned to the home screen. Marvin blinked away the mystery and tucked the smartphone aside. It was just one more puzzle to add to the long list that would become his day. With his next coffee sip, comfort returned.

Then his gaze shifted ahead and drifted into the morning crowds. Through the crisscrossing of pedestrians, he locked on a well-dressed woman who immediately impressed him. Her burgundy blazer cut into her waist. No, the color wasn't burgundy. Was it Maroon? Claret? The barista learning French might call it *bordeaux*. With that decided, Marvin continued his observation of the woman. A matching knee-length skirt hugged the woman's hips over classic tan tights disappearing into black medium heels. Marvin guessed the woman to be a few years past 30. The woman carried a tiny purse and clutched a small brown briefcase under one arm. She stopped on the sidewalk and looked hastily around.

The woman scanned until her eyes fell to Marvin. She squinted. At once the desperate look on her face melted. At first Marvin thought the woman had just caught his random eye—but no—she was fixated on him. Now the woman turned to someone else whom she waved closer. Through the crowd Marvin saw a boy appear alongside the woman—a boy of maybe 12. The woman gestured and the boy turned his head, looking in Marvin's direction. By their dark hair and sepia complexions, Marvin guessed they were Latinos. The woman walked toward Marvin. The boy followed. Marvin's thoughts raced, trying to place the woman's face. He had no idea who she was, but she was certainly not the young woman in the text message portrait.

The distance closed between Marvin and the pair. He pretended not to notice them.

"Sir!" The woman called. "Are you Marvin Fischer?"

Marvin blinked. "What?"

The woman and the boy reached Marvin's table. "Are you Marvin Fischer?" the woman asked again.

Marvin sat straight. "Who are you?"

The woman swooped urgently and sat across from Marvin, her clear chestnut eyes wide with excitement. Her wavy brunette hair flowed to the shoulders. Straight teeth beamed white through an electric smile. She smelled of sweet vanilla. The woman set the purse and briefcase down on the table and focused on Marvin. "My name is Rubi Valdez. This is my beautiful son, Antonio." The woman's English was confident, with a crisp Latin American flair. Marvin exchanged glances with Antonio. The boy appeared embarrassed.

Yes, a lean 12-year-old. His mal-proportioned body gave the impression of a tree in spring that would burst six inches by summer's end. A backpack hung over the boy's shoulder. Dangling from the neck on a blue nylon cord were binoculars. The boy wore faded blue jeans and a lime green T-shirt bearing the name of a music group with which Marvin was unacquainted. Marvin guessed the boy was smart and full of stored ambition.

"Are you Marvin Fischer?" Rubi asked a third time.

Marvin looked back at the woman. "Yeah, I'm Marvin Fischer. How do you know me?"

"Are you a pastor?" Rubi asked.

Marvin's eyes narrowed. "No. I work for... for the community."

And Marvin Fischer was completely unprepared for what came next. Rubi Valdez took Antonio's hand, eyes fixed on Marvin, and said, "Mister Fischer, I wish you to pray for me."

Marvin sat frozen. "Pray?"

"Yes Mister Fischer. I wish you to pray for me."

Shockwaves of resentment rippled through Marvin like a nuclear blast.

Marvin Fischer hated prayer. It had been a long time since he prayed. Not since Caroline. Years ago. Many years ago. And that had been when everything was nice and tidy and wonderful, before things tipped suddenly and irreversibly askew, and whatever faith Marvin may have developed had spun wildly out of control. He wanted to slam this door, slide the bolt and lock it tight. He wasn't even sure how to explain this to himself, much less to anyone else.

Suspicion. Resentment. Anger. Fear. All mixed in a jumbled mess that Marvin had bitterly avoided. Now the wraith had risen again with an unwelcome fury and Marvin had to temper it discreetly.

Don't have a meltdown right in front of the poor woman!

Marvin's face was stone. He shifted his shoulders uneasily, wincing an eye. "Why do you want me to pray for you?"

Rubi closed her eyes and smiled. Marvin watched her chuckle nervously as she bit her lip. She tipped her eyes to the sky. It seemed to Marvin that the woman was burying some complicated thoughts, but was desperate to convince him. "Please, Mister Fischer—"

"You don't even know anything about me."

"I realize how silly this sounds for some strange woman to ask you this. But I have faith. I have prayed for myself. Antonio has prayed for me. But I need a man to pray for me too. A certain man… A very specific man. And that man is you."

Marvin wondered where the husband was, but decided not to go there. Presently, he turned to Antonio. "What do you think about this, young man?"

"She's starting a new job… it might be dangerous," the boy answered.

"It's with the Arizona Department of Public Safety," Rubi finished.

Marvin's eyes glinted with recognition. "I know people there."

"So that's it!" Rubi smiled. "I knew there was a reason it had to be you!"

"Look Miss…?"

"Valdez. Rubi Valdez."

"Miss Valdez, I don't really do the prayer thing. You should go to some person from the church."

"I have, Mister Fischer. Many people at my church are praying for me. But… I don't have time to explain. My car has a flat tire… I had to wait for a taxi… now I'm going to be late. Please, Mister Fischer. I just wish you to pray for me, for a good first day, and especially for my safety on the job."

Safety.

Marvin looked to the curb and noted the waiting taxi. He took a deep breath. "You know this is nuts."

"Yes, I know it sounds crazy, Mister Fischer. But…"

Rubi paused and leaned in. And through sharp, determined eyes, she said with gravity—"I am certain that it is you that must do this for me."

It seemed almost like a command. She was mesmerizing, unsearchable, magnetic.

Antonio pulled his hand away from his mother and brushed it through his thick brown hair. "Just let me pray again. You gotta go!"

"Wait—" said Marvin, looking at his Rolex. It was 6:25.

Marvin weighed his options. He could just dismiss himself and walk away. Get out of this nonsense quickly and forget about it. Soon he'd be at work and there'd be plenty of distractions. The woman would be fine. Or—Marvin looked at her again. Everything about her was put together and polished. She seemed sensible, despite the unusual request. And someone he knew downtown apparently had the confidence to hire her.

The fact of the matter was that Marvin was terribly apprehensive about the idea. The last time he invested his faith in prayer, it had ended disastrously. He knew what he was afraid of. Could he put aside his reservations and just pray for the lady? Accommodating her would make her day. Just get through this thing and make the woman happy and everyone could move on.

"Mister Fischer... please." said Rubi.

Marvin made his choice.

"I gotta run too," said Marvin, "—but I'll do it. Okay? I'll pray for you, you can be on your way, and you can have a great day. Alright?"

"Thank you Mister Fischer! You don't know what this means to me!" Rubi smiled brightly and closed her eyes. Then she opened again and asked, "You do believe, don't you, Mister Fischer?"

"Hmm?"

"You do believe... in the prayer?" Rubi smiled.

Marvin's lips rounded, but nothing came out. Thinking suddenly of Caroline, he said finally, "Of course."

Rubi beamed again and, reaching out a hand, she took Antonio's palm. With the other, she reached across the table and touched Marvin's hand as he held his coffee mug.

Marvin hesitated awkwardly, then clasped Rubi's fingertips.

He closed his eyes.

Marvin began, "God... this nice woman, ah, miss Rubi Valdez, wants me to ask you to help her have a good first day at work... and that you'd... especially... keep her safe. Amen."

Marvin felt Rubi's fingers tighten around his for a moment. Then she let go.

"Thank you, Mister Fischer. Thank you again!"

"Good luck."

Rubi turned to Antonio. "You can walk to school from here sweetie?"

"Yes!" The boy seemed frustrated.

"Okay. I love you." Rubi kissed Antonio on top of his head. She gathered her briefcase, flung the purse over her shoulder, and smiled again at Marvin. "God bless you."

Rubi Valdez hustled away toward the waiting taxi. Marvin and Antonio watched her scurry off.

"Well, I gotta go. Thanks," Antonio stepped away.

Marvin gave a half-hearted wave and took a long pull of coffee. The brew was already cooling. He rose from the chair, drained the last drop, and was thinking about a refill when he felt something push into his chest. Pressure on his neck shot through as he was swept with abrupt panic. The mug crashed down on the table. The thought of a heart attack bolted through his mind like lightning. But there was no pain—and Marvin became aware that the feeling wasn't internally physical. It was pressure from *outside*. The air around him felt heavy, somehow invisibly falling, like a shift in atmospheric energy, an invisible presence closing in.

Then, through a blur of pedestrians and a passing bicycle, for the briefest of moments, Marvin saw something thick and long and winding and slithering through the street. Marvin shook his head. What was it? A creature of some sort? It glided between cars—or through them?—the appearance of concentrated ferocity in marble-black eyes. A swoop of aqua flickered from the head.

In the next moment, the thing vanished.

Then the piercing screech stung Marvin's eardrums.

The wrenching scrape of steel and the metallic boom ricocheted between storefronts.

Marvin tried to shake off the sensations of the last seconds. Dreamily, he goggled around. Across the street, two cars stood crumpled, their windows shattered, steam billowing. There came gasping and cries of shock from onlookers as they scuffled toward the mangled vehicles. A driver got out and rushed to join the Samaritans already crouching in the street.

On the pavement between the two cars lay a woman, bloody and motionless.

No—it couldn't be…

Yes, it was Rubi Valdez.

3
HALLOWED GROUND

Marvin shook his head sharply.

His environment squeezed into abstraction. The streets and storefronts became a haze of blur and noise; the mesh of people a kaleidoscope of mayhem.

It must have been a dream.

A terrible nightmare.

What happened?

He had prayed for Rubi Valdez, and moments later the cars had smashed her body like rocks in a crusher.

Did he really see that creature slithering through the street?

In foggy astonishment, Marvin shuffled his feet and meandered across the patio like a drunkard, moving closer to the street, trying to comprehend the seeming impossibility of what had just occurred. Still clutching the handle of the broken glass mug, he stepped off the patio, crossed a thin strip of grass, and stopped at the curb. He winced at the blurp of a biting siren. Lifting a hand, he shielded the glinting sun that came blinding off the fire truck, and watched.

Across the street, a police officer guided onlookers further down the sidewalk, away from the scene in the street. Another officer seemed to be interviewing a witness. Marvin strained to watch the paramedics lift Rubi Valdez onto a stretcher. She was not moving. She had already been covered in plastic.

This could not be happening.

But the collapsing reality caved in as Marvin watched the paramedics lift the stretcher onto the backside of the ambulance to the clatter of gliding wheels on metal, and they pushed the body into the tomb.

And when Marvin turned again, he saw Antonio Valdez—the boy—sitting on the sidewalk a few yards down, cowered, knees pulled to chest, a blanket over his shoulders, an emergency responder squatting close by. Marvin froze in bewilderment as he watched the boy. Antonio's eyes remained fixed and stoic on some indefinite spot ahead. Then, focus coming to his eyes, the boy searched until he found Marvin Fischer. Antonio's stare—blank and unreadable—held Marvin captive. Marvin could not shake the boy's look. There was something behind the vacancy that Marvin could not pinpoint. Suddenly Marvin felt vulnerable and guilty, and he tore himself away from the boy's dominating stare.

Was this mess his own fault?

What if he hadn't prayed at all—just left well enough alone—like he'd wanted to in the first place? Would he now be off the hook?

Or would the accident then be even more clearly his fault? The direct result of his failure to pray for the woman?

As the ambulance drove off, Marvin wobbled backward, bumping the curb with his ankle and losing his balance. He managed to steady himself, then settled gradually down to the curb.

Officer Nolan Garrison was a husky, dark-skinned police officer wearing a Brunswick-green uniform and gold-rimmed aviator sunglasses. He stepped off the street and crossed the sidewalk. The police badge glinted gold as the radio on the belt blurted a direction. Officer Nolan Garrison stopped at the curb where Marvin sat and squatted down.

"Sir—hello—I'm Officer Nolan Garrison. Phoenix Police Department. Did you witness the accident this morning?"

Marvin cleared his throat. "Not really."

"Is that a yes or a no, sir?"

In the street, another police officer helped a tow truck driver guide his truck backwards toward one of the crumpled cars. The hiss and click of the radio crackled as more voices chopped over Officer Garrison's radio. Garrison turned the knob to lower the volume. But Marvin heard the voices—official voices, calm and professional and ironically reassuring—the only sanity in this insane morning.

Marvin felt his head tip. His muscles stiffened and he instinctively inhaled, hoping the surge of oxygen to the brain would help him focus. He rapidly felt weary. For a moment it was as if he were looking up into the sky but his eyes remained wide and locked and unregistered on the disaster on the street in front of him. He was suddenly aware of his dry mouth. He lifted his hand to his lips and then realized the coffee mug was no longer present on the glass handle he still clutched. Marvin knew his mind and body were reacting in ways he could not control, trying to flee from this incredible, horrific scene. But he was part of it, stuck in it, intimately connected in ways he could not possibly assemble into anything that made a shred of sense to him.

Marvin forced a cough and an obnoxious sniffle, trying to convince his body to cooperate. "I didn't actually see it happen," Marvin said finally. In a show of control he rose from the curb, brushing a dried leaf off his suit pants.

"But you were in the vicinity?" asked Officer Nolan Garrison, standing up with Marvin.

"Yeah."

Officer Garrison tapped into a digital notepad. "When would you say the accident occurred?"

"Um… a few minutes ago." Marvin absently tossed the broken mug into the grass.

"Did you see any other vehicles?"

"She's dead, isn't she?" Marvin stared frozen at the spot where he had seen Rubi's body lying in the street only minutes before. Now the spot was empty, bloody, the last mark on the planet where Rubi Valdez had been alive. Hallowed ground.

She was dead!

"I'm not at liberty to say," continued Officer Garrison. "May I get your name sir?"

"… Marvin Fischer—uh—S-C-H…"

"And what were you doing here this morning, Mister Fischer?"

"I ah…" Marvin forced his eyes wide open. He tucked the fingers of his left hand casually into his pant pocket while his right hand animated, "I was on my way to work. Stopped at The Bean Sack there like I always do."

Officer Garrison jotted another note. "You seem upset, Mister Fischer."

"Well yeah, it's a terrible thing." Marvin shifted his gaze across the street and found himself again caught in Antonio's shocked glare. What was going through the young boy's mind? Antonio did not break the stare with Marvin, an unyielding fusion as if locked by the poles of magnetic force.

Marvin felt as if he were on trial.

"Did you know the victim, Mister Fischer?"

At last Marvin cracked free of Antonio's spell and said to Officer Garrison, "I talked to her right before it happened."

"You talked to her."

Marvin nodded and gulped another breath.

Officer Garrison put a hand to Marvin's shoulder. "I want you to sit back down, Mister Fischer. You may be in shock."

Buoyed by Officer Garrison, Marvin sunk down to the curb. Officer Garrison sat beside him.

"Are you alright, Mister Fischer?"

"Yeah."

Officer Garrison leaned toward the shiny mic clipped to his shoulder and pressed the button. "Cheri, can I get a blanket and some water across the street please for a witness please? Thank you." A crisp voice crackled acknowledgement. Officer Garrison turned back toward Marvin. "Where did you talk to the victim?"

"Right there … at that table, by the coffee shop."

"Was that boy with her?"

"Yes."

"What happened?"

"Well the boy went that way … he was on his way to school … Miss Valdez, she um … she must have been alone when she crossed the street… I didn't even know them … We had just met … We were strangers."

"Did anything come up in your conversation that might have upset her?"

Marvin's face contracted in confusion. He squinted and licked his dry lips. He watched a police officer assist Antonio up from the sidewalk and move to a police car. The boy walked slowly, head down, the gaze plunging toward the pavement.

"Mister Fischer? Anything that could have distracted her?"

Marvin, his face pale and distressed, turned helplessly to the officer, and piercing into Garrison he said—

"She just wanted me to pray for her safety."

4
THE ACTIC

The bronze door of the Otis elevator whined open. Marvin Fischer breathed in the lingering scent of fresh carpet glue as he paced across the new berber in a vast office. The space was dim and shadowy, where quiet and sometimes excited activity was illuminated only by halogen desk lamps and the soft cast from computer monitors. Even as Marvin strolled coldly through the space, he could appreciate that his request to replace the outdated, isolating cubicles had finally been honored, and now the modern black desks snaked in curved contours, equipped with hard drives fast as lightning. There was no artwork or greenery to distract. The hushed silence was broken only by a whisper, a ringing telephone, or the occasional burst when everyone would crowd and gather around a single screen to celebrate victory, or to commiserate over a deflating setback.

This was the hub of intelligence analysis at the Arizona Counter-Terrorism Information Center in Phoenix. Known by its acronym ACTIC, this was where terabytes of threat-related information poured in daily to be categorized, analyzed, and if necessary, disseminated. The ACTIC was Arizona's fusion center—a creation of the post-9/11 world that sought to maximize information sharing across law enforcement and intelligence agencies to forecast and prevent crime and terrorism, increase global awareness, and distill actionable intelligence from the massive volumes that streamed in from everywhere imaginable.

It was a monumental effort, and as Chief of the Field Intelligence Group, Marvin Fischer was responsible for making sense of it all here at the ACTIC. Most recently, Marvin's team had collaborated with the Arizona Department of Homeland Security and the FBI's Joint Terrorism Task Force in a complex series that led to an arrest and the deactivation of an explosive device in the Desert Sky Mall. The success drew media attention and earned Marvin and his team praise from across the intelligence community.

Marvin had taken the job at the ACTIC after working 30 years elsewhere in law enforcement. He'd started his intelligence career in Detroit, after serving a few years on the police force downtown.

That's where he had met Caroline.

Caroline had been working her way up quickly in the Detroit PD, where fellow officers were both confused and amused by Caroline's tough performance and tendency towards romanticism and classical music. It so happened that Marvin and Caroline were thrown together to work the Detroit beat for two years, during which time their frequent disagreements had turned into romance. They skipped dating and married, exasperating their colleagues even further. Then Marvin's ambitions outgrew the DPD, so he had applied at the Federal Bureau of Investigation, where the vetting process was rigorous. He had been told the Bureau's background checks of applicants stretched back to the fifth grade. Marvin had joked that as long as they didn't go back to the fourth grade, he'd do fine.

~

Marvin nodded quietly to colleagues as he moved past. The fingertips of Marvin's right hand checked the knot in his tie as he wove around desks. He reached a set of taupe double doors and pushed into a room furnished with stainless steel appliances and wood tables.

Marvin was in the break room, alone. He stepped instantly to the cabinet, where he selected a mug. He closed the cabinet and reached for a coffee pot on the counter. As he lifted the pot from its plate his thoughts hovered to Rubi Valdez.

Why did she get hit by the car right after he'd prayed for her?

Marvin flinched when hot liquid seared his fingers. The mug had filled to overflowing. Marvin set the glass pot quickly down, and with the sleeve of his indigo suit wiped his burning hand. His sleeve now stained brown, Marvin grimaced. He stopped still in the familiar room, which suddenly felt strangely hard and cruel.

Marvin tipped his head down and slurped the steamy brew teasing the top ring of the ceramic. He snapped his tongue. The flavor was raw to his liking. Someone had made a pot of the common stuff. Marvin exhaled a sigh and took another draw anyway. Perhaps getting into his personal office would finally calm his twanging nerves.

Marvin turned back to the doors, eyeing the level of coffee in the mug. To his surprise the double doors rocked open, stopping him dead—making a mess of the coffee across his blue silk tie and his neatly pressed, cameo blue poplin shirt.

"Oh Marvin..." said a woman with bright blonde hair, the culprit who had just stormed and knocked Marvin off balance. "Sorry Marvin—I'm sorry," said the woman with bright blonde hair as she moved to the counter, the comet tail of hair streaking under white light. The blonde woman reached and tore the final sheet from a towel role. In her other hand she held a thin red folder. "I ruined your clothes." She crossed to him and began urgently wiping his tie. "I know how you are—crap I'm sorry."

Marvin looked down at his shimmery silk blue tie with its tricky patterns of navy and white, now disgraced forever in brown.

He set the mug on the counter and gently took the towel from the woman. "I got it."

The woman with bright blonde hair gave in and backed off, lifting the back of her hand to her forehead as she watched Marvin attempt the cleanup. "Sorry…." she said again.

The name of this woman with bright blonde hair was Elizabeth Walsh. One year ago, Elizabeth Walsh had come over from FBI's Denver Field Office to assist Marvin as his new lead analyst at the ACTIC. As he continued to wipe the tie, Marvin looked up calmly into her green eyes, and as he held the green eyes he watched the relief wash through her. She was forgiven. It was the silent shorthand they had developed throughout the last year of working together in this office, facing challenges of intelligence that pushed them to their limits, on occasion betraying their emotions, but never their respect. The unspoken sizzle between them beckoned resolution.

"What is it?" Marvin asked, still rubbing the tie.

"Nothing."

"Come on. You came streakin' in here like a Ferrari at Le Mans. What's goin' on?" he winked curiously at the thin red folder Elizabeth held at her side.

"Okay—Yes. This! It's from FBI headquarters. It's hot. Where have you been? I tried calling but you didn't— "

" —I forgot to call." Marvin acknowledged.

He had been sorry to see his previous lead analyst go, and while Marvin had been impressed with Elizabeth Walsh's credentials, he had expressed concern to his superiors that she had just crested 29 years old, and may not have the experience he'd hoped for in a lead. But she had served four years in the army, and from there completed a degree in intelligence studies with honors, before serving three years at FBI Denver, where she had again excelled. Elizabeth Walsh was in top shape physically, which made her a prime candidate for fieldwork, but she preferred the intrigue of intelligence instead, and had convinced the recruiter to give her a shot in the office. So she was hired to the ACTIC, where she conducted priority analysis cases as assigned by Marvin Fischer.

Elizabeth Walsh was also, by nearly any man's assessment, a very beautiful woman. And based on her beauty alone one might never guess that she had a great interest in military and global affairs, and might presume that she could have easily become successful in modeling or entertainment. But Elizabeth would have none of the vanity, and didn't want her good looks to be a distraction to her counterparts. She dressed conservatively with minimal makeup, and wore no fragrances or jewelry except for a single crucifix necklace, which bore certain sentiments for her. Today she presented herself in a very sensible plain white blouse, a knee-length khaki skirt and hose, and dark brown block heels.

Elizabeth held up the thin red folder. "The Bureau finally put Abiku Madaki on the Most Wanted list."

"Abiku Madaki? The untraceable?"

"Madaki the Untraceable. Did you hear about the bombing?"

"What bombing?"

"The Mexico bombing this morning?"

Marvin held up a hand and closed his eyes. "Hold on." He waited for his thoughts to settle, then said, "Gimme ten minutes and come to my office."

"—kay."

Marvin forced a custom made smile for her. He didn't want his rootless mood to come off as a rebuff. "Good morning Elizabeth," he offered.

"Good morning, Marvin. Sorry again, about your tie."

Marvin pushed through the double doors. "Maybe fate is tryin' to tell me something."

5

WOUNDED SILK

Marvin stood alone at the sink in the office bathroom. Water gushed. Steam rose from the basin. With coffee mug next to him on the counter, Marvin scrubbed vigorously at the coffee-stained tie with fresh paper towel.

His blue poplin shirt could be easily replaced. But not this tie.

It had been a Wednesday before a Christmas, with lights glistening and flurries of nighttime snow in the stinging cold air on Beacon Street outside the once-popular downtown department store in Detroit, where Marvin and Caroline had been doing some last-minute shopping for a few last-minute gifts for those last-minute friends whom Caroline had decided really should get a little something. Marvin didn't know it, but it would be the last time they'd go Christmas shopping together. It had been hurried and crowded and frenzied, and Marvin had already rudely thrown plenty of ice-cube prompts of 'hurry-ups' and 'let's-goes' into Caroline's shiny face. But it was 'just this store yet' and 'oh isn't this cute' and 'just in here yet' to find just the right thing. Caroline had relished as Marvin had frowned, carrying the spoils closer to checkout. It was when they had passed the men's clothing that the necktie flashed and caught Caroline's twinkling eye. She'd held it up to her man and insisted on acquiring it for him, as she had never before seen a necktie that matched so perfectly his cobalt eyes, which had proven blustery all evening. Caroline plopped the catch atop the rest of the presents as they waited their turn, and that had been that. She'd softened his heart with the impulse purchase of a new necktie, and especially with that tender kiss she'd placed on his chapped lips at the end of the three grueling hours.

Now Marvin clung to the tie like a soldier to dog tags in the trench. What had been experienced as an evening of impatience and agony had become one of Marvin's most treasured memories of his time with Caroline that he looked back on with romantic nostalgia.

Marvin scolded himself over the sentimentality.

The navy and whites of the necktie crisscrossed in a jagged maze just like his work and his life, interacting beautifully with whatever suit he chose to wear.

Not anymore. Now the tie was a hopeless case.

He should finally let the damn thing go.

But he kept scrubbing and rinsing until his thoughts turned back to the bleak morning that he still could not accept had happened just hours earlier.

Why would God let Rubi Valdez die right after he'd prayed for her?

6
JERSEY GUY

Marvin was now tieless, the top two buttons of his coffee-stained shirt open. He passed through a pool of white light and circled to a desk where a young field ops analyst named Lyle Stratton sat laser-focused on his computer screen as he bit into a breakfast sandwich. Marvin stopped next to the workspace holding the coffee mug and his wadded-up wet tie. He rested his right arm atop the low rising divider and stared with mild amusement at Lyle Stratton. Marvin asked, "And how many sandwiches have we had for breakfast this morning, Mister Stratton?"

"Hhmm?" Lyle Stratton huffed out aloof, eyes never leaving the computer screen. Lyle Stratton was a heavier-set man in his twenties, with tussled brown hair and black-framed glasses, his white shirt struggling to stay tucked into his khakis. Lyle Stratton clicked off Spotify that had been quietly streaming the latest rounds of top singles. "I've got to get this forecast done for Miss Walsh," said Stratton in his thick Jersey way. "It was supposed to be done before I left last night but I couldn't get all the indicators in the matrix the way I wanted. Don't tell her okay?"

"Okay that's fine Lyle, but I need you to take a little break from that and get on somethin' for me first," said Marvin as he slipped his cell from his pocket. "This is my smartphone."

Stratton pushed the last of the sandwich into his mouth and watched the crumbs tumble down the front of his shirt before snapping back to the computer.

"Stratton—over here," said Marvin, waving the smartphone in the air.

"Hhhmm?" Stratton swiveled away from the screen. "What's that?"

"This is my smartphone."

"No—that!" Stratton pointed to the wet tie balled up in Marvin's hand.

"That's my tie."

"Why aren't you wearing your tie? You always wear your tie."

"Never mind that. I received an image message at 6:16 this morning from an unknown sender, but the name 'Simon' showed up as the caller and then disappeared. I tried calling this Simon but I got nothing, not even a ring. I need you to run a back trace or a reverse call backup or whatever you need to do, and see if you can identify a number and who sent it, and if you can get an origination point that would be terrific. And find out who the woman in the image is please." Marvin handed the smartphone to Stratton, who took it, flipped it around and examined its exterior.

"I can only find the origination point if I can identify that phone's IMEI."

"I know. Just try."

"Did you hear about the bombing Mister Fischer?"

Marvin was already walking away. "Just try."

"Yes Mister Fischer I'm on it. What happened to your shirt?"

7
THE UNTRACEABLE

The blazing yellow ball rising high in the eastern sky charged Marvin Fischer's office with energy. To the south across Arizona Route 101 was Buffalo Ridge Park, with the Phoenix skyline and the misty veil of mountain peaks prominently beyond. Marvin stepped to a walnut desk, set the coffee mug onto the glass top, then crossed to the windows and adjusted the blinds, cutting the sunlight to a level that pleased him.

    He returned to the desk and rolled out his chair. He tilted his eyes to the mashed wet tie still balled in his fist, and with a heavy sigh tossed the dead thing into the garbage. He stared at the tie's limp wilted form, clumped at the bottom of the empty can, and momentarily lamented that the prized necktie's glory days were over. Then, sitting down, he sighed, placed his elbows on the desk, and with tense fingers rubbed his temples. Then he rested his hands flat on the desktop and stared at the bright knives slashing through the window blinds. He checked his Rolex. It was just before 10 in the morning.

Marvin snatched his tortoiseshell reading glasses and tapped the keyboard to log in. He sniffled, opened his email and scrolled through the subject lines, eyes glazed and unfocused. As if frozen, he stopped scrolling and stared at the screen. He minimized the email window and launched the Internet browser. The screen burped up the *East Valley Tribune*, but Marvin did not engage in his usual habit of perusing the headlines. Instead he clicked the bookmark for his search engine and typed something into the search field.

How does God answer prayer.

There came a knock at the door. Marvin slipped off the glasses and focused on Elizabeth Walsh, who stood at the open door, washed in diagonal lines of sunlight, her face keen, eyes unblinking, both hands clutching the thin red folder she had fanned in the break room.

Marvin lifted his coffee mug. "You know you can just walk in," he said and sipped.

"I know." Elizabeth marched in, her figure and white blouse bursting through bright bands of sunlight. "Your tie?"

"Goner."

For an instant Marvin saw her eyes absorb his unbuttoned shirt. He rose from the desk and gestured toward four hunter-green upholstered chairs in the middle of the room. Centered amidst the chairs was a large glass coffee table hosting a copy of *Inside Homeland Security* magazine, today's *New York Times*, and last month's issues of *Car & Driver* and *GQ*. Marvin moved to sit in one of the green upholstered chairs and was joined opposite by Elizabeth. She brushed a hand behind her skirt as she established herself into another green upholstered chair and reached across the glass table to hand over the thin red folder. "So, Abiku Madaki brand new on the Most Wanted," Elizabeth said crisply. "He's the prime suspect in the bombing attack in Mexico this morning."

"Get enough sleep last night?" asked Marvin.

"I don't know. Did you?"

"Still reading that novel? Scoundrels at El Dorado?"

"I was researching."

"You know those books are fake, right?"

"The report, Marvin."

Marvin leaned forward and pushed aside the periodicals on the coffee table. "This guy's attacked Mexico now?" Marvin set the thin red folder on the coffee table and opened it. He donned his glasses again and, resting his elbows on his knees, interlaced his fingers and examined the first page of the report. The thin brief outlined all that was currently known about the bombing attack in Mexico and the primary suspect Abiku Madaki, whom someone in the Italian ASAI—after a bombing at Saint Peter's Basilica—had dubbed *Madaki the Untraceable*. "Since when are terrorists attacking Mexico? Is this a drug related thing?"

"I don't think so," said Elizabeth. "It isn't a cartel hotspot. And there's new intel on him. We think he may have run with the Somali pirates. One of them fessed up in Seychelles this week, swears he recognizes Madaki from the file photo. Says Madaki was their leader, then vanished into thin air when the Royal Navy apprehended their dhow in the Indian Ocean."

"How'd he manage this time? To vanish?"

"Don't know. He always does."

"And he hasn't been seen again until these bombings started."

"Right."

"Hmm. What about this latest bombing?"

"It happened near a place called the Pyramid of the Sun, at Teotihuacán."

"Teo—ti—what?"

"Teotihuacán. It's an ancient city in ruins, with pyramid temples and plazas, that sort of thing, and a long street called the Avenue of the Dead. It's been deserted for hundreds of years but now it's a tourist attraction. It's pretty famous."

Marvin scanned the photo of the pyramid, a portion of its front section blown out and crumbled. He flipped the page to an 8 by 10 of the suspect supplied by the Italians. Marvin was familiar with the image. Abiku Madaki's dark skin agreed with the theory that he might be a Somali. The head was bald. The temples were narrow and the umber eyes set close. The face widened to a strong bony jaw. On the chin was a black goatee of tightly curled dense hair. The expression was blank.

"Where'd we get this guy's name again? The Mosque?"

"The Omayyad Mosque in Damascus, yes," said Elizabeth, her blonde hair flashing in sunlight. "One of the worshippers said Madaki attended dawn prayer for two weeks before the bombing there. Pretended to be a devout Muslim, apparently."

"So this Madaki, who's the suspect in the Mosque bombing—and the bombing three months ago at Saint Peter's at Vatican City—this same guy now we're sayin' bombed this pyramid thing in Mexico."

"That's what FBI and CNI are saying," said Elizabeth. "We still can't find him. He's got no social media presence, no known addresses, no citizenship that we can find, no official documentation."

"So why Damascus? Why Rome? Why this Teoti—thing in Mexico?"

Elizabeth leaned back and crossed her long legs. "I'm beginning to form a theory."

"Hit me."

"All three locations hold religious significance, but from different faiths," Elizabeth observed. "The Omayyad Mosque used to be shared by Christians and Muslims until their congregations outgrew the building and the Christians moved out. The Basilica in Rome—Saint Peter's—is significant to Catholics, quite possibly the burial site of the apostle himself."

"And this place in Mexico?"

"A Mesoamerican structure, The Pyramid of the Sun, located at Teotihuacán, which used to be this ginormous religious and economic center in the Mexican Valley. No one knows who actually built it, but eventually the Aztecs used it, and researchers think the place might have been used for some sort of religious custom. Marvin, the explosion was huge. You see the picture. Blew a hole in the side of the pyramid at the entrance to some sort of underground tunnel. No idea why he even chose the place."

"I don't see any of the religious stuff in the brief," said Marvin.

"I did some looking this morning. We've got a Muslim site, a Catholic location, and now this ancient temple in Mexico all linked to the same suspect. It doesn't make sense. Usually if a terrorist attack is religiously motivated it stems from a radical extremist from one religion, but this guy seems to be targeting religion in general. Anyone that believes in some sort of god."

"So your theory is that this Abiku Madaki is just a hater of religion in general."

"Possibly. Maybe an atheist, or a secular extremist. Or—"

Marvin raised his eyebrows. "Or what?"

"Or... maybe there's some weird spiritual angle."

"Hit me."

Elizabeth went silent. Marvin felt her eyes digging into him. Then he said, "C'mon. Tell me what you think."

"You okay?"

"Yeah. Why?"

"Something else is bugging you."

Marvin contained his surprise. Was he really that transparent?

"I'm good. Keep going."

"Why were you late this morning?"

"Just hit me will ya?"

Elizabeth fingered her hair behind an ear. "I looked up the meaning of his name. 'Abiku' is some sort of death spirit, from West African mythology. And 'Madaki' means... warlord. So... *Death Spirit Warlord.*"

Amused, Marvin stared at Elizabeth. "Okay, and—?"

Elizabeth contorted her face in a way that said maybe she didn't want to go here, but now it was too late. "Maybe Abiku Madaki is working for the other side."

8
SILVER CRUCIFIX

Marvin took off his glasses. "What do you mean, the other side? What other side?"

"I mean, *the other side*."

Marvin opened his mouth for an instant, and then the implication of what Elizabeth had said jumped all the necessary synapses deep in Marvin's brain, and he could not contain the hearty laugh that burst forth. It felt good, to laugh after the gut-wrenching morning he'd had. It was a short but full laugh and then it carried into a prolonged chuckle. Marvin's smile was handsome and full of life, his crystal-blue eyes glinting, and he could not stop chuckling. Finally he stopped and sniffled and rubbed his eyes and leaned casually back in the hunter-green upholstered chair. He gazed into the spangled green of Elizabeth's shiny eyes and, rubbing his index finger across his clean-shaven chin, was for a moment distracted. Elizabeth sat silent and confident. Marvin's gaze shifted down to the necklace with the silver crucifix dangling around Elizabeth's neck. The emblem strangely impressed him in a way it had not before. Then he turned away to look into the sunshine burning through the window blinds. He took a deep breath and exhaled.

"What?" asked Elizabeth after a long pause.

"You're right, I doubt these are random bombings," Marvin said finally. "There's got to be a commonality. All these religious sites are somehow connected." He turned back to the table, perched his glasses onto the bridge of his nose, and studied again the file photo of Madaki. "I've got a funny feeling about this guy. What are we tangling with here?" Marvin peered over the top of his specs at Elizabeth Walsh. "The other side, huh?"

"What happened this morning?"

Damn, she was persistent. Marvin took off his glasses again. He chewed the inside of his mouth and sniffled, avoiding her gaze. "What else ya got?" he said.

Elizabeth uncrossed her legs and leaned forward, looking solemnly across at the man. "Marvin—Dominic at DHS called this morning. He wants assurance that we re-checked all of our leads on Abiku Madaki after Damascus."

"We did that, and we did that again after the blast in Rome. We did all that."

"I know," Elizabeth's eyes went to the glass tabletop, where she studied Marvin's face reflecting in the crystal smooth surface. "He just wants to make sure we're looking everywhere. Especially now. After Mexico. We don't want this guy showing up in the states."

"I get it."

Marvin winced and his shoulders slumped and he felt his heart sink to his stomach. He wanted to fight terrorism more than anyone. He and his team had done their best and now he was determined to knuckle down and do the best again. But it was different now. He was fighting a new battle. Fresh combat that had started this morning the moment he had met Rubi Valdez.

Marvin stood up and brushed a hand across the top of his extra short hair. "Alright Elizabeth, thank you, pull up all the interviews from Damascus and Rome and get a couple of people together and make sure you check and recheck 'em and look again for associations this guy might have. Revisit those Somalia connections too. If you don't find anything new, I'll check 'em myself." Marvin walked to the window, laying twenty feet between him and Elizabeth. He put his hands in his pockets and looked out towards the skyline of downtown Phoenix. His eyebrows creased with a refusal to lose, but inside the atoms of his being were blowing apart, bouncing in aimless confusion. "Maybe we missed something. I wanna know who this Abiku Madaki is connected with."

"Okay," said Elizabeth. She hesitated, as if waiting for more. Marvin knew she was on to him, she had sensed his quandary, she knew there was something else going on, something other than Abiku Madaki, something other than Damascus, and Rome, and Mexico.

Finally Elizabeth stood and abruptly began the walk to Marvin's office door. But she paused and turned, took two small steps back toward Marvin and stopped again.

Marvin's face was stone. He was thankful for the ten feet that still remained between them and pushed off the magnetism.

Then came the soft voice. "What happened?"

Marvin's face melted in her tenderness. Gone in a vapor were the professional tone and the business at hand. He hated making his personal life a part of the office, but his colleague was now the caring friend. He inhaled deeply, opening his eyes wide and blinking rapidly, still staring out the window without reason. Then he gave in. "Bad accident. I was a witness, so I had to stick around."

"How bad?"

Marvin's eyes sank to the brand new carpet and he licked his lips. He glanced up and focused again on the silver crucifix hanging on the smooth pink upper part of Elizabeth's chest, and deep inside he gave up on propriety and nodded a gesture.

"You're Catholic?" asked Marvin.

Elizabeth let out an unfiltered, petite chuckle, perhaps relieved that maybe she had gotten through to him. Her natural lips parted in a wide smile, exposing a row of white teeth that were not quite perfectly aligned. "I've been here a year, I've worn this necklace every day, and you've never asked me that." Her shoulders lost their tension; the stiffness in one knee relaxed. "Yeah," she answered.

"Sorry I don't mean to get personal. I just noticed your necklace. No—that's not true. I noticed it on your first day."

The morning sunlight glinted off the bright polished metal. Elizabeth looked down at the beautiful piece of jewelry but it rode so high on her chest that she could not see it herself under her chin. "Let me tell you something Marvin, if I'm wearing a necklace it's fair game. You're allowed to ask. I've had it since I was 12. It was a gift from my mother at Confirmation."

Marvin nodded and looked again through the bright slats of the window blinds, hands still in his pockets. "So I've heard..." he started.

"Heard what?"

"I've heard that people of the Catholic faith—they pray to Mary? Is that right?"

"I know Mother Teresa used to. But, it's for veneration, not like praying to God. Usually we just pray to God."

"Mm hmm," Marvin nodded. "How about Mother Teresa? Did she ever get any good results when she prayed to God? That you know of?"

Elizabeth blinked and looked outside. She opened her mouth, but words did not come immediately, until she said, "I would think so."

Marvin felt the ping of discomfort. "Sorry," he said, hating himself for falling into the personal trap. "It's none o' my business."

"It's ok."

Marvin took his hands out of his pockets and turned into his office.

"Hey," Elizabeth said, "Can I get you a cookie or something?"

Marvin smiled. "I just need to snap to it here. Sorry about the questions, you know, about the necklace… and…" Then he said without looking at her, "You're doing an excellent job, Elizabeth. Please keep up the good work."

Elizabeth nodded, grabbed the brass handle and pulled the door quietly closed as she stepped across the threshold into the dim shadows of the giant cave where the blinking computers churned and the analysts mused.

Marvin's desk phone buzzed. He stepped over and scooped up the receiver. "Yeah."

"Lyle Stratton at your service, sir." The cheerful tenor of Lyle Stratton's voice lifted Marvin from his gloom. "I checked out your smartphone. That contact you told me about, the Simon guy, it came back a zero."

"Are you sure?"

"It's a spoofed number. This 'Simon' is essentially a masked call, no caller ID."

"Can you get the info from my carrier? I can get a warrant—"

"Your carrier wouldn't even have a record of the call, or message in this case. You see Mister Fischer there is no sender. It's like he doesn't exist. There's no IMEI. It's like a ghost number. I mean it can't even be a spammer from one of the places you buy your nice clothes from even."

Marvin swayed his head side-to-side in frustration. "You're tellin' me you don't have the technology to find out who sent me this message? Is that what I'm hearing? Really?"

"I've never seen anything like it, Mister Fischer."

"What about the picture?"

"That's a really weird one too sir."

"Who is it?"

"It's an old photo."

"I got that. Hit me."

"She came up in the database. She's famous."

"Hit me."

"It was taken in 1928 when she was eighteen."

"Come on!"

"She's Albanian."

"Out with it already!"

"It's Saint Teresa of Calcutta... Mister Fischer—it's Mother Teresa."

9
HOUSEHOLD NAME

The ultra-blue Jaguar F–Type coupe didn't glide smoothly as the yellow Audi R8 Marvin had owned since two autumns ago. But speed and agility mattered most, and on these counts Marvin was bemused to discern a notable difference between the two. And in Marvin's opinion the Jaguar's inescapable sleek looks outran the Audi's by many miles. Marvin drove skillfully fast without being reckless. It was about preparedness and being in tune. He was no racecar driver and he knew it, but he pretended to be, and right now he was doing 130 down Arizona Highway 51, leaving the ravages of the day in the dust behind him.

The testosterone of Dire Straits' *Heavy Fuel* pounded the speakers. Peripheral view rushed by in a blur as the super-car blew through almost invisibly, devouring the curves in the road past the Phoenix Mountains Preserve. Marvin preferred the 51 to Interstate 17, which he found undesirably congested, and so he routinely went out of his way for the better ride. He was pleased with how the Jaguar handled the flat and dry Arizona roads, not like the washboards of Detroit he had left behind long ago.

Marvin's shock over what happened in the morning had at first numbed him and then percolated into frustration. He cursed himself again for giving in, for praying against his better judgment. He'd sworn off prayer, after it had stopped making sense. Now he had opened a psychological Pandora's Box with no way to contain it.

He should never have prayed for Rubi Valdez.

He should have said *sorry, thanks for asking*, and sent the woman on her merry way. But no, something inside of him had nudged him into complying.

Why?

And who was that damned Simon?

Marvin pushed hard out of the apex of a curve, then hit the brakes for a truck. He downshifted and slammed the pedal again to pass the annoyance. He'd risked his luck for the last several miles, and didn't like using his position at the ACTIC as an excuse for breaking speed laws. Frowning, Marvin allowed discipline to return, took his foot off the gas, and let the car slow to an easier 85.

Marvin had been almost embarrassed with himself for how little he had known about Saint Teresa of Calcutta. He had known of her fame, but never the details.

And now a phantom named Simon had sent him an ancient photo of her for an inexplicable reason.

Following his meeting with Elizabeth Walsh that morning, Marvin had locked himself in his office and asked not to be disturbed for 30 minutes. Those 30 minutes had become two hours as Marvin spent a long lunch scouring the Internet for everything he could find on Mother Teresa. There was plenty to absorb, and he was astounded at what he found.

Marvin didn't know that Mother Teresa had been born in North Macedonia in 1910 and baptized a day later. In Bengal India, tales told by missionaries had gripped her, and by age eighteen she'd devoted herself to religious service, left her mother and sister, moved to Ireland, and joined the Sisters of Loreto at the Abbey in

Rathfarnham. Marvin guessed that it had been around this time that the mysterious photo had been taken.

A year later Teresa moved to Darjeeling in the lower Himalayas, where she'd learned the local language and took her first religious vows. She then moved to Calcutta, where she lived and taught at a convent school for 20 years. Mother Teresa had felt a deep desire to serve those who were sick and unloved and unaccepted by society. She'd gained notoriety first with the Indian officials, then at the Vatican, and over the next decades would become a household name, revered and respected by people the world over, crossing religious divides through her inarguably positive social impact.

She had been awarded the Nobel Peace Prize in 1979. By the time she died at the age of 87, her *Missionaries of Charity* in Calcutta was managed by more than four thousand sisters who oversaw orphanages, worldwide charity centers, care for refugees, victims of floods and famines, and the poor and homeless. The mission she'd founded now operated 600 facilities in 120 countries. Pope Francis had canonized Mother Teresa in 2016 at Saint Peter's Square in Vatican City, with tens of thousands in attendance.

As Marvin navigated off the highway and onto the side roads, he slowed to posted speeds and contemplated the accomplishments of this remarkable saint. What struck him most was that for most of her life, Mother Teresa had experienced doubt in her beliefs, describing in letters to her advisor a spiritual dryness, and of a longing to feel close to God. She'd often felt her prayers went unheard, and she did not commonly feel the presence of God, yet she'd continued the work she felt called to.

Here was a woman—now deemed a saint—who had led a life dedicated to the service of others, who'd believed in Jesus and the holy work, but who had not felt close with the God to whom she prayed.

Marvin veered onto Tatum Boulevard, still having no idea who had sent him the photo of Saint Teresa of Calcutta, or why. What he did know was that Mother Teresa had prayed, and that she had managed to press on, despite her doubts.

Marvin's thoughts circled back to his own doubts about prayer. What is prayer anyway?

10
PAST THE YELLOW LANTANAS

The Villas of Stone Creek were a pleasing buttery yellow and lush tan, with towering bold cornices above the second floor windows. The iridescent blur of Marvin's Jaguar floated past the junipers along the dusty sienna driveway. The evening sun flashed off the lifting garage door as Marvin steered past a row of finely pruned yellow lantanas and into the drive. It was a well-maintained community, which suited Marvin's penchant for all things clean, tidy, and organized. The living engine's growl calmed as he drove into the white and uncluttered garage, activated the brake, and shut the car down.

One minute later he was inside the condo and past the mirror in the foyer and moving into the kitchen. Marvin clicked on the light, awakening the color in the tropical islands calendar, the only decoration in the kitchen other than a small vase of fake pink wildflowers from a place he'd once shared with Caroline. Feeling dehydrated, Marvin opened the cupboard and selected the nearest bottle of Acqua Panna from a collection of about 40 of them, unscrewed the cap, and downed the bottle. He crunched the empty plastic, opened a cabinet next to the stainless steel dishwasher that he never used, and tossed the waste into a recycle bin. Marvin closed the cabinet door without slamming it, took off his suit coat, draped it in half, and set it lightly on a barstool by the counter top.

Marvin looked out into his plain living area with its generic white walls which he had thought of repainting but never did, and noticed again the bareness of the place. A pair of easy chairs and a fine leather couch took up most of the space in front of the fireplace, which he also never used, and there was not a single piece of artwork or pottery or sculpture or decoration or character or warmth. Caroline's touch had not followed him. A rush of his wife's presence filled the emptiness as Marvin imagined what his days would be like were Caroline still with him. For a moment he saw the smile and heard the voice that had first charmed him. Her short and stylish and irresistible jet-black hair drew him as he watched her position decorative greenery on a bookcase beside a rare facsimile of the Geneva Bible of 1560. Another memory flashed—when she rearranged some pictures that she had framed after their visit to the California coast. Then came the candles and the snow in the dark and the Terpsichore with its guitar and violins, and a shared evening of romance over wine, and in an instant Caroline's spirit was gone, the place empty, void of her scent, or of any sound that brought him joy.

Marvin sniffled and shook his head quickly and violently from the scene he could no longer have, only to return to the day behind that still did not release him. He could not help but wonder what effect his prayer had on the fate of Rubi Valdez. Turning it over and over in his mind, he wished that he'd never met the woman— that he had sat inside the coffee shop instead of outside, that he had left earlier for work. Anything would have avoided dragging him into this most uninvited torture. In those fateful moments sitting at that yellow table under the elm, he had somehow let himself be persuaded into praying for Rubi Valdez, against all his prior choices to avoid prayer and religion and—he admitted—to avoid God. Maybe his prayer hadn't been good enough. Maybe he had prayed without faith.

Had God even heard the prayer? Had God heard it and ignored it, with the full and complete understanding that his own intervention could have kept those cars from colliding, and prevented the accident? Had God heard Marvin's prayer but let Rubi Valdez die anyway, in some sort of sick joke? Was God toying with him? Was this God's revenge against Marvin for shutting him out all the years since he'd lost Caroline? Was this all to make Marvin feel powerless and worthless, like a stupid fool for even thinking for a second that God cared what happened to him, or to this woman Rubi Valdez?

If he had not prayed, if he had just left it alone, maybe Rubi Valdez would still be alive.

Marvin placed his palms open and flat on the granite counter. He felt used, tricked into something he had not wanted to do, and now someone was dead, and a young boy with a bright and promising future was without his mother.

Marvin lifted his arms one foot off the counter top and with the strength and might of an angry lion slammed his hands forcefully down on the counter top and blurted out a single, seething obscenity, then stared motionless into space.

11
ALBIREO

Twinkling stars by the millions withheld their secrets from the young boy far beneath the deep black dome of the Arizona sky. Antonio Valdez peered through the eyepiece of his Celestron telescope and focused the lens. He was only twelve, but his striking young face foreshadowed the coming of a handsome man. He had been reading Carl Sagan's *Varieties of Scientific Experience*, a book Antonio found fascinating. It detailed characteristics of the planets and moons of the solar system, the possibilities of extraterrestrial life, and Sagan's personal search for God. Antonio had been fascinated with outer space and life on other planets since last year, when his sixth grade teacher, Mrs. Carswell, had taught an extended lesson on the solar system and encouraged him to participate in the school's science fair. Mrs. Carswell had talked with energy about the differences between the planets, the many years it takes for the light of a star to reach the earth, and had speculated about what might lie beyond.

Now more than ever, Antonio was thinking about what might lie beyond. He wondered where his mother was now. He was lost without her physical presence, grasping for her spirit. He wondered if everything she had believed about life after death were true. He hoped so, and he felt that he believed it too. But Antonio already missed his mother terribly, and he wished she hadn't been taken away so suddenly. She had wanted to live to be a hundred! Antonio's dreams of traveling to outer space were fast becoming an obsession—a necessity to find his mother—to see what might lie beyond, if what she had believed about God were true. But Antonio couldn't get there. He had no rocket, no spaceship; he was no angel. He was stuck, powerless to do anything or to chase away the numbness in his heart.

    As he panned the telescope left, Antonio's thoughts went back to his sixth grade class. What had he learned there that could serve him now? What had Mrs. Carswell said that had impressed him so? Alpha Centauri is the closest star to earth. Andromeda is the closest galaxy. Earth is not the only planet with a moon. Neptune has 14 moons. Jupiter 49. Saturn 62. Antonio thought about the diorama of the solar system he had constructed, crafting the sun and 183 planets and their moons out of styrofoam balls that hung with black thread in a giant cardboard box he had painted to look like space. Antonio had thought it looked stupid; a poor attempt at capturing the glory he knew was the creation. But he had taken home the first prize blue ribbon in that science fair, and in celebration his mother Rubi had bought him this telescope.

Today had been a horrible day. In the morning at the corner of North 66th and East McDonald, Antonio had heard the terrible screech and turned disbelieving to see his mother smashed on the street. Only moments before, Marvin Fischer, a total stranger, had prayed for her safety. It was supposed to be an exciting day for Antonio's mother, a day she had studied for long and hard. Antonio had been happy for her, and now he could not believe that she was gone.

Antonio had been taken to Paradise Valley Hospital to be treated for shock. It was there he had received the official word that his mother Rubi Valdez had been pronounced dead. Since Antonio had no next of kin—and no designated legal guardian—Tom and Tiffany Tindal from the Agape United Methodist Church had met the paramedics at the hospital to help Antonio through the ordeal, and to cope with the initial anguish and tragedy of losing his mother. The nurses and doctors had been charitable and empathetic. As Antonio had lied there in the warm hospital bed with the lights dim and the TV turned low and fluids flowing into his body, he could not shake the image of Marvin Fischer staring in bewilderment at the blood and crushed bones in the street. It had all played out like a movie before Antonio's eyes as he had watched the cars destroy his mother's body, and yet he felt like he was not even one of the characters, but here he was, true and real as any other day, the son of the woman who would now appear on the evening news as the tragic victim of an unfortunate coincidental crash under a bright blue sky.

Tom and Tiffany Tindal had known Rubi and Antonio Valdez ever since the single mother and her son first visited the church when Antonio was just three years old. Tiffany had worked the nursery and cared for Antonio while his mother Rubi taught Sunday School. Antonio knew Agape United Methodist as a safe and gracious community of people, a tight knit group that seemed to spend most of their lives together in some sort of social activities whenever not at work or at school.

Rubi Valdez had formed an immediate bond with Tiffany Tindal, and Tom had been helpful.

Antonio had never known his own father.

After Antonio's discharge from the hospital, the Tindals had taken him to their home in Mesa to care for him during what would be a very difficult next few days. Tomorrow they would be at the funeral home making arrangements for visitation and a service at the church.

~

Antonio tried again to distract himself with his favorite hobby. He zipped up the orange hoodie his mother had bought him from Old Navy, reached beneath the telescope, adjusted a knob on the mounting, pitched the tube up five degrees, and looked again through the eyepiece. The Tindal's deck in the backyard gave him a sturdy platform for the tripod and an open view of the stars above. He had turned off the patio light to create as dark a makeshift observatory as possible, having to be careful as he carried his precious tool across the deck while his eyes adjusted to the darkness.

Tiffany Tindal opened the sliding door and stepped onto the deck. "Hey," she said softly.

"Hi."

"I made mac 'n' cheese."

"Okay," Antonio looked back through the telescope and swiveled the head.

Tiffany asked, "What are you looking for?"

"Albireo… but I think it's too early in the spring."

"What's Albireo?"

"A double star. One of them looks blue and the other one's yellow. About three hundred and ninety light years from earth. My Mom really likes it. She likes the colors. But we only saw it in books."

"You'll find it," Tiffany consoled.

"No, not tonight." Antonio settled onto the soft blue cushion of a wicker deckchair. "Maybe if I had my computer." Antonio had changed his clothes since the morning at the hospital, after Tom had made a quick trip to Rubi's apartment for some of Antonio's more important items, and had the foresight to grab Antonio's science books and telescope.

"We could go back to your Mom's place and get your laptop if you want," Tiffany offered. "But why don't you come in and eat something first."

Antonio backed away from the eyepiece and looked up into the sky, scanning the heavens. He was still disoriented to the reality of what had happened. Despite the kindness of the people in his life, he felt alone and orphaned. Where was his mother?

She wasn't really gone. *It didn't happen.* He'd wake up tomorrow and find this had all been just a bad dream.

Antonio rose from the wicker chair and treaded toward the house. Tiffany forced a smile and opened the sliding door for him. Antonio stepped inside the dinette, wondering if Marvin Fischer had seen the strange creature right before the accident.

12

FOUR VIEWS ON A SCREEN

The jade bodycon dress was the only clean outfit left in Elizabeth Walsh's dusty closet when she rose early for work. She'd been putting off laundry, so the dress would have to do. She showered hurriedly, tied back her hair, slipped into the ivory tights with the hole in the toe, skipped the breakfast of yogurt, threw on a pair of black Cole Haans and was out the door. Halfway to the office she winced that the deep green dress would accent the emerald in her eyes, presenting allure rather than professionalism. But she didn't turn back. She wanted a jumpstart on the day, anxious for any new leads on their new most wanted man, Abiku Madaki. No one had contacted her during the night, but who knew? Maybe something awaited her at the ACTIC.

Elizabeth's unpolished nails flickered across the keyboard as she reviewed the daily bulletins from FBI field offices, her desktop a tangle of papers, open books, sticky notes, and granola crumbs.

She had already checked the hourlies and phoned Arizona DHS and the Phoenix PD. There had been nothing new. Several members of her team were casting for intel from other agencies hoping to reel in a new puzzle piece. She would sift through that material later with Lyle Stratton after Marvin got in.

Elizabeth finished scanning the bulletins and clicked back to her emails for the tenth time in 15 minutes.

She rechecked her phone. Maybe she'd missed a text.

Still nothing.

No one had reported any new information on Abiku Madaki.

Disappointed and stumped, Elizabeth put an elbow on the desk and rested her chin in her palm. Staring at the computer screen, she nibbled the tip of a blue Montblanc.

"Elizabeth, get with the Arizona DOT," a voice called. "I need to look at something from the traffic cams." Elizabeth snapped up straight. It was Marvin Fischer, tall and prim in a natural tan linen suit, edgy woven tie and Utah brown wingtips, a take-out cup of Bean Sack coffee in hand, zipping through the snaking aisles between desks. Elizabeth hadn't even noticed Marvin come in. Without missing a step, Marvin nodded hellos to the staff and Elizabeth caught the spicy scent of the Tom Ford eau de parfum as he passed. Marvin slowed, turned, and said, "Corner of North 66th and East McDonald. Yesterday morning between six and seven. All views, please."

"Do you want Stratton to—"

"What'cha dressed up for? You got a lunch date?"

"I don't know. Do I?"

"Do you? And no Stratton for this—" Marvin said, then pointing —"Just you."

"Yes sir." Elizabeth scooped up her desk phone and punched a key. "Nice tie!" she shouted.

"And you're not gettin' anywhere near it!" said Marvin, disappearing into his office.

~

Marvin popped the plastic cover from his coffee and slurped before setting the vessel down on the glass-topped desk, tossing the lid into the trash, and stepping to the window to yank up the blinds. The room exploded in light. There was excitement and energy in Marvin's step as he paced, left index finger to chin and right hand on hip. He had been awake most of the night, brooding over the slithering creature he'd thought he'd seen just before the accident that killed Rubi Valdez. He'd postulated that maybe a caffeine rush had caused the hallucination, or maybe a light refraction. He couldn't attribute it to shock, because he'd seen the thing before the accident, not after. At two o'clock in the morning as he'd thrashed in bed, it had suddenly dawned on him that he could check the traffic camera network to see if anything showed up that would confirm or deny the presence of the reptilian beast, and he'd been cursing himself for not thinking of it yesterday.

Elizabeth chirped into her desk phone. "Marvin, I got it."

"Coming."

Elizabeth punched off, jumped out of her chair and rolled it aside. She adjusted the monitor's brightness as Marvin rounded the corner.

"What'cha got?" Marvin asked, resting a hand on her desk. He slipped on his readers and leaned in to the computer screen.

With the Montblanc Elizabeth pointed, indicating four rectangular traffic camera views on the desktop. "North, South, East, and West views, starting exactly six yesterday morning."

"Alright good," said Marvin. "Fast forward to about six twenty-five."

Elizabeth pressed a key and observed the time burns as the video blurred by on all four views. "Okay, six twenty-five and forty-six seconds." She watched Marvin scrutinize the mechanical footage; the bland and the boring bustle of the everyday, the secret lives of each mind undisclosed in the black and white artless frames. She sensed Marvin's eyes flicking from one angle to the next and back again, judiciously spying the cars in the streets. She noticed in one view Hope Crossing Church and its sign, *We're praying for you.* Marvin held unmoving and silent. She wished he would say something. Her lips parted to say, "This is where it happened, isn't it?"

"Yeah," said Marvin without looking at her. "I know this doesn't have anything to do with what you're workin' on. I just need to check somethin'."

"Okay."

She continued to watch the video times.

6:27.

There was a dog on a leash, crossing the street with a pedestrian.

"Are you looking for something in particular?" Elizabeth asked.

"I just thought I saw somethin' out there. Wanted to check it out... Wait—"

A woman entered frame on the east view camera. Elizabeth leaned in beside Marvin and watched as a car on North 66th seemed to hit the brakes, and another accelerated. In the silent and telling image, one of the cars struck the woman at high speed. The body crumpled and tumbled and tore beneath the vehicle as its hood collided hard into the trunk of the car ahead, the body rolling mangled and bloody and crushed on the pavement behind.

Elizabeth gasped and put a hand to her lips, horrified.

Marvin closed his eyes. "Sorry, I shoulda warned you."

"My God..."

"Stop the video."

Elizabeth drew the hand from her mouth to click pause.

Marvin turned away, removed his readers and looked up at the ceiling, shaking his head and rubbing his face.

Elizabeth folded her arms and tried to purge the images from her mind. She let Marvin stand silent and process the event all over again, and putting a hand back to her mouth, she dared to look again at the screen. She stood silent, watching the frozen images for a long moment, and then blinked. Her head tilted, her eyelids squeezed. She uncrossed her arms and leaned in again to study the images. What was that in the frame? Elizabeth advanced the views forward, stopped, then tracked backward.

"Oh my God."

Marvin looked back at the monitor. "Now what?"

"Marvin—the east view." Elizabeth pointed with the pen. "In this crowd."

"What am I supposed to be seeing? The dog?"

"No! This guy! Look at him! He looks like Abiku Madaki!"

Marvin's eyes narrowed. He put his glasses back on. "You've got to be kidding."

"Marvin I think that's him. That's our guy."

"Get Stratton over here."

The large round oak table stood solidly in the center of the conference room where Marvin had gathered Elizabeth Walsh, Lyle Stratton, and other key staff members to discuss action points in lieu of the indication from video surveillance that Abiku Madaki had been at the scene of the accident involving Rubi Valdez. In the 15 minutes since the discovery, Marvin had alerted FBI, while Elizabeth had contacted Arizona DHS and the Phoenix PD, who passed the information elsewhere across law enforcement. Lyle Stratton had verified with NSA that the surveillance footage had not been tampered with, and was thus deemed one of the most authentic and important pieces of intelligence on Abiku Madaki to date.

Members of public safety had come up from the lower floors to join the meeting, the Phoenix Chief of Police had shown up, and FBI Phoenix Division had streamed in two agents via the secure interagency network.

THE TEMPEST IN GLASS

With ceiling lights dim, a giant image of the best freeze frame of Abiku Madaki splashed across the canvas of a wall screen, washing the team of professionals in reflected tones of gray. The projector fan whirred quietly overhead as task forces were assigned to scour greater Phoenix for any sign of Madaki. The group wanted to review all witness interviews from the accident. Elizabeth suggested a new round of questions might be needed. Marvin agreed, then announced he would contact transit authorities between Mexico City and the Arizona Border Patrol to find out how Madaki—fresh on the new Most Wanted list—could possibly have made it across the US/Mexico border without detection.

What puzzled them all the most was why Abiku Madaki would show up here? Why appear in public? Was he somehow involved in the crash, trading bombs for cars? The other three cases in which Madaki was a suspect had all occurred at religious sites. Did the nearby presence of Hope Crossing Church have anything to do with it? Except here, there had been no bombing, no terror attack, just a heart-rending car accident.

Was there more to this crash than met the eye?

Marvin thanked their guests for attending, dismissed the group, then bolted to the break room for more coffee.

13

IN BRASS AND MAHOGANY

Marvin Fischer walked moodily through the large wooden double doors of the funeral home, wearing a tailored navy suit paired with a black shirt. The triangle of the double Windsor in the Italian silk tie was crafted to match the collar, with not a spot to be found on his black royal Oxfords.

 Marvin passed the welcome sign directing him down the hall where Rubi Valdez lay in repose, and briefly felt like he were invading a tomb. His footsteps fell soft on the thick carpet. The chambers echoed with the solemn tones of voices fraught with their losses, or catching up with friends they hadn't seen in many moons. Marvin moved through the warm wallpapered hallway with its incandescent sconces, up to the doors of the room filled with people. Bathed in soft light, Marvin crossed the threshold and stopped to calculate how he could best navigate the crowd. Scanning the room, he didn't recognize a single face. It was a room full of strangers.

 To the left, a large collection of flower arrangements lent their colorful serenity. From between two visitors Marvin spied a glint of

THE TEMPEST IN GLASS

brass hardware and then the deep red grain of the mahogany casket. Marvin inched slowly in that direction. He made his way through the pack, gently nodding to those he passed, wishing he could close his nose to the mixing scents of fragrances and hair products. Turning on his heels to allow two guests to pass him, Marvin realized he had come upon a long table with an elaborate display of photos representing Rubi Valdez and what had been her life.

Marvin paused by the display and forced himself to glance at the photos. He recognized many of the locations as areas local to Arizona and the surrounding states. He supposed that Rubi had lived most of her life right in this place. There were other pictures with Rubi and groups of people in what looked to be far away places, tropical and jungle-like. So she had traveled, Marvin surmised. Another collage showed Rubi smiling with a baby boy, then with a young toddler, and finally a handsome boy. This kid had to be her son Antonio.

In the center of the display was a larger portrait of Rubi herself. She had been a beautiful lady, her energetic smile and bright brown eyes beaming with life, full and deep brown hair curled to the shoulders. From the tent card beneath, Marvin discerned that Rubi had been born 35 years earlier.

Marvin looked away and shook his head.

Another amazing life snuffed out, gone too soon.

Marvin lost his breath as a spear of guilt penetrated his gut. He turned back toward the casket and made some progress toward it. Looking around as he tiptoed forward, he did not see Antonio. Marvin craned to see around the heads of guests, when a voice behind him cut through the heavy air.

"Marvin?"

Marvin turned to see a bald head with a deep round black face and wide white eyes. The face was familiar, but the name escaped him.

The man spoke. "Nolan Garrison. I was the officer at the incident." Nolan Garrison, dressed in all black with a missing top button, held his hand out to shake.

"Of course," said Marvin, managing to get a hand between guests to firmly grasp Nolan Garrison's hand. "I didn't recognize you without the uniform."

"It's all good." Nolan Garrison squeezed between the people to get closer to Marvin, and now the two men were so close that Garrison's belly pressed into Marvin's side. "You okay?" Garrison asked.

"Better. Did you know her?"

"Oh yes, Rubi was everywhere."

"Ah," said Marvin, not really sure what Garrison meant by that.

Nolan Garrison continued, "You know, after all my years on the force, it never gets any easier to see the people you're supposed to protect, get killed. No matter how hard you try, you can't save 'em all. It's even harder when you know the person, and I don't know how much more of it I can take. I was here just two weeks ago to bury my own nephew."

"Oh—I'm really sorry to hear that."

"Got himself mixed up with the wrong crowd. We kept prayin' and prayin' for him, but he wouldn't come around. The kid just wouldn't come around."

Marvin scowled. Garrison too? An unanswered prayer?

Garrison said, "Well it's nice that you came. Take care." He placed a hand on Marvin's shoulder and pushed through the crowd.

"You too," said Marvin, watching Garrison disappear into the mass. Marvin released a long sigh and turned back toward the red mahogany casket and finally saw an opening in the mourners. Marvin took four quick steps and abruptly found himself under the same warm lights that cast their glow over the casket. Marvin tried not to look obvious as he took a deep breath.

He stepped closer and looked at her. There she lay in a beautiful floral dress, eyes closed, motionless, arms crossed over her waist. Rubi's head had survived demolition in the crash, and her face was as perfectly made up as could be done, and somehow the people in charge of her postmortem had managed to reassemble her broken body in such a way as it was impossible to see that under the dress she was broken and shattered.

But there was no mistaking.

Rubi Valdez was dead.

Marvin's lips tensed and he inhaled deeply through his nostrils. He felt powerless.

He stood there for another moment, looking into the face of the lifeless body.

Marvin leaned in and whispered softly into the unhearing ear, "I'm sorry."

He rose slowly again and noticed the people right behind him, waiting their turn. Marvin moved on, giving the people behind him their opportunity. As he stepped away, Marvin stared blankly at the carpeted floor, at the feet of all the people who had come to bid their farewells. He lifted his head sharply to snap himself out of the gloom. Then he saw a group of people not far away, gathered near a set of couches.

Standing among the group was young Antonio Valdez.

Marvin froze, unblinking and confused about how he felt as he saw Antonio. Was Marvin afraid the boy would see him? Antonio was dressed in a black suit and white dress shirt and black tie, with black shoes. His thick brown curly hair was groomed with a shiny gel that made the boy look older and sturdy and strong. Marvin observed a handsome young couple, strangers to Marvin, standing with Antonio.

But Antonio was listening to another man talking to him, facing him, an older man in a gray suit, glasses, and gray hair. The man had a hand on Antonio's shoulder, and was speaking intently. Marvin guessed this might be the clergyman.

At that moment Antonio's gaze shifted away from the older man in the gray suit with glasses and landed on Marvin. Marvin felt caught staring, but he kept looking at the boy, locking eyes again like they had done at the scene of the accident. After a moment that seemed like about a minute to Marvin, Antonio's eyes turned expressionless back to the older man in the gray suit. Marvin debated walking over to express his condolences, but hesitated.

The kid probably didn't even want him there.

Finally the older man in the gray suit with glasses and gray hair stepped away from Antonio, and another group of people slid into his place and begin talking with the boy.

Marvin looked around the room one more time, then made his way toward the exit. He pushed through the crowd and left the room, feeling like a coward.

14

SWIRLING VESPERS

Pastor Deckland Smith, his gray hair neatly combed, swiped a wooden matchstick against a checkered matchbox. The brilliant ball of white flared before it calmed to a wavering yellow. Pastor Deckland Smith turned toward an ornate dark wooden desk, where a fresh pale-green incense stick waited in its cradle like a tiny Nordic javelin. Pastor Deckland positioned the tiny flame under its tip, and after a brief exercise of his patience, the tip of the incense began to glow. Deckland removed the match flame, waved it out, leaned closer to the incense, and puckered his lips to exhale a focused gust of air. The tip of the incense glowed orange and then dimmed to emit a thin wisp of gray smoke that rose silently upward. A smile flashed across Pastor Deckland's craggy face as he stood up and dropped the extinguished match into a glass bowl. The thin wisp of smoke grew into a swirling thread, gracefully widening as it escalated higher and higher into the surrounding air until it began to lose its shape and dissipate into the room.

"This is sweet incense," explained Pastor Deckland as he closed the matchbox and set it on the desk. "The fragrance is probably a lot like the one experienced by the Israelite priests in the wilderness tabernacle, back in the day, except theirs was a very special mix burned at the altar of incense. The smoke was a picture—a symbol you could say—of the people's prayers making their way up to God."

Marvin Fischer, eyes empty and miserable, was sitting in an old, creaky walnut chair in front of Pastor Deckland's desk, which was equally old and dark but didn't match the chair. Marvin's pitch dark Vantablack suit and tie absorbed every color in the room. His elbows dug into his knees, hands in front, the tips of his fingers joining and tapping skeptically. Marvin's face was troubled, his head and body stagnant as the deep blue eyes tracked the smoke rising from the fragile stick eight feet in front of him. The living smoke merged with rays of the grinning sun as it streamed in from a tall arched window high in the auburn brick of Pastor Deckland's large study. "So that's what happens? The prayers rise to God?"

"Well not literally," smiled Deckland, reclining into another squeaky dark wooden chair identical to Marvin's, positioned at a comfortable angle for talking and sharing.

Marvin had decided to get the pastor's views on prayer, in hopes that a conversation might shed some light on the dilemma. Marvin had never thought much about God while growing up, having been raised by French-German agnostics who'd emigrated from East Prussia on the Baltic, after the big war. But after Marvin married Caroline, he had become a regular church attender. Caroline had invested much of her time in devotion to God, to prayer, and to a resurrected Jesus Christ, and had lovingly coaxed Marvin into joining her for services at the old Episcopal Church in downtown Detroit. So Marvin had fallen into it and become a part of it, not against his will or against his liking. In fact, after a time he had grown rather fond of the peaceful comfort the church experience brought to him and his relationship with Caroline; but he himself had never developed the passion that Caroline had for church involvement. Marvin had followed along and prayed like everyone else, thanking God for this or that, asking for this and that. But he had never really asked a lot of questions, or paid much attention to the simple and daily and seemingly ordinary prayers that were offered as a matter of routine in the social circles of people of faith.

The morning after he'd attended the visitation for Rubi Valdez, Marvin had called the funeral home to inquire if there had been a pastor there. The gentleman who answered the phone had freely supplied Marvin with the name of Miss Valdez' home church—Agape United Methodist—whose senior pastor was Deckland Smith. Pastor Deckland was in his seventies, had served in the Methodist tradition for all of his life, and was well loved by his congregation of almost three hundred weekly attendees.

Today, on the day of Rubi Valdez' funeral, Deckland had been kind enough to give Marvin a few minutes of his time a couple of hours before the service. When Pastor Deckland opened the heavy wooden door to the church that morning, Marvin had immediately recognized him as the man in the gray suit from two days before, whom he had seen speaking with Antonio at the funeral home. Today Deckland wore blue jeans and sneakers with a clean white T-shirt over his scrawny frame.

At the first instant Marvin had stepped into the church and smelled the mixing scents of candle wax with old wood and fresh plaster, he had been struck with a blast of sentiment that carried him back to his church days with Caroline. He had not expected it nor prepared for it, but he suddenly again missed her. It occurred to him that he had not set foot in a church since, and despite Pastor Deckland's welcome, Marvin had felt uneasily out of place in this sacred building.

Pastor Deckland had guided Marvin through a newly remodeled foyer, past a quiet and cavernous sanctuary, and then through a maze of twisting and turning cement hallways that left modernity behind, giving way to the musty, older part of the church that Marvin guessed had to be over 100 years old.

Marvin had followed the pastor into a brick-walled wing of the building that Deckland explained had once been a small chapel, but had been converted into a generous space for studying and counseling. As the two men marched into the historic chapel-now-office, Marvin's gaze followed the brick wall high up into the cathedral ceiling with its pecan-colored wooden beams and modern track lights, some of which had burned out, collecting dust and cobwebs. Large palms stood like quiet observers beside the arched window. Bookshelves lined the room, hosting a sizeable collection of books, many with their paper spines cracked from heavy use.

These details had registered only vaguely with Marvin Fischer as, coming to the center of the study, he had settled gloomily into the creaky chair. Now, as the smoke from the incense continued to rise mystically toward the rafters, Marvin observed a framed Rembrandt-esque painting on the wall of the Etruscan Saint Francis of Assisi in a posture of prayer. Marshaling his thoughts, Marvin said, "I had a bad experience with prayer a few years ago. I couldn't believe what happened. It was... a real disappointment. Since then I've stayed away from the prayer thing. I haven't been able to bring myself to it again. Until..."

"Until Rubi Valdez," Deckland finished.

Marvin drooped backward in the squeaky wooden chair, stared into the glare of sunshine through the smoke and put a finger to his chin, forlorn and desolate. "I should never have prayed for Rubi Valdez."

"That prayer from a few years ago, when you had this disappointment. It was a request of some kind?"

Marvin nodded cloudily, "Yes."

"As with Rubi Valdez."

"Yes."

Deckland scratched the back of his ear and sat back, crossing his left leg over his right. "Not long ago, my wife Shirley became gravely ill. Pneumonia. She'd always had asthma so we were careful, but it snuck up on us after a trip to some rain forest. A remote spot. Long story." Deckland paused and continued, "Shirley was 71 at the time. The doctor did what he could for her, with what minimal equipment he had. And I thought, 'Well, it'll be okay, because God knows and he's here.'" Deckland swallowed and went on. "So I prayed, and I prayed, and I prayed for Shirley's recovery. I got on the wire and this entire congregation prayed for her recovery. But nothing happened. She got worse. In less than a week, my wife was dead. That was hard, very hard." Deckland wiped a misty eye. "A disappointment, just like you."

"But… you still pray."

"Yes, I do." Deckland rested one hand on the denim knee of his crossed leg, the other on his sneaker. "Marvin, we can be sure that God does hear our prayers. When he responds, and how he responds, is not always to our liking. But that's where faith comes in. If we believe in God, in his purpose, we have to know that there is design and structure in everything that happens. There is a reason for the ultimate good, for the final outcome of what God has planned for humankind. Every detail we experience, no matter how insignificant or unpleasant it might seem to us, plays some small part in the grand plan."

It was a common platitude that sunk to the floor after Deckland's emotional story. Marvin fiddled with his tie clip. He focused again on the smoky incense rising from the stick. Following its slow ascent upward toward the beams in the ceiling, Marvin watched the smoke vanish indistinguishably into the air. Suddenly conscious again of the fragrance, he tried to find comfort in its pleasing scent. But his face betrayed him and his eyes dropped low, away from the smoke, glossing over again into dreariness. His mind struggled to grasp any kind of hope in the situation.

Deckland tilted his head. "What I'm trying to say Marvin, is that it's not up to us what God does with our prayers. He will catalog and orchestrate and respond according to his will. It's out of our control."

"Then why pray?"

15

GRAND PLAN?

Deckland's eyes shifted down to the worn brown carpet below Marvin's shoes, and then with some effort he uncrossed his leg and rose from the chair. "Why pray… Because it's the only avenue for communication with heaven that God has given us in this present age." Deckland circled the desk and moved toward the window. "If you want to have any meaningful relationship with God, any closeness, prayer is it. Some people might call it meditation. But whatever. The point is, our mind and our hearts are engaged with God, a power much greater than ourselves, acknowledging our dependence on him and his sovereignty over humanity, and our trust that all things work together for good. That he's got things under control." Deckland turned to a bookcase and rested a hand on a large thick book lying center on the shelf. "In Bible times," Deckland continued, "the scripture records that God visited his people in various ways, and communicated with them personally. Through the burning bush with Moses in the desert, for example, God talked directly with Moses from the flames and commanded him what to do, and Moses could respond." Deckland put his hands in his pockets. "At other times, God would send a messenger, like an angel, to deliver a very specific message, such as the angel that visited Mary to tell her that she was with child and would bear a son. The angel would travel somehow, to the earth from the heavenly realms—wherever that is—and meet with people face to face. It's incredible really, when you think about it. But after Jesus' ministry on earth, he sent the Holy Spirit to guide us in our hearts and minds, and instructed us to pray continually to maintain that link of communication with God. We pray, he responds, either with a literal outcome to our prayer, or by gently guiding us in our hearts through the Spirit. Sometimes the Spirit intercedes for us, prays for us, in ways our own words could never express." Deckland stepped toward Marvin and leaned forward, placing his hands on the desk. "Does this make sense to you?"

Marvin chuckled and shook his head. "It's just not that easy, pastor." Marvin squeaked up from his chair, tapped his fists together thoughtfully, and began his usual habit of pacing. "And it still doesn't answer my question. I'm supposed to just believe and accept that okay—I pray, and when it doesn't go my way, it goes badly—it's just somehow part of God's big idea for something I can't see or understand? So Rubi Valdez comes to me, firmly convinced that I—a total stranger—am supposed to pray for her safety. She's so convinced that she makes me feel like I *have* to, or something bad will happen. So I pray for her and then within a matter of seconds, she's dead. How does that make sense?"

Deckland's eyes slid to the scratchy desktop. There was no easy answer, no explanation for the circumstances Marvin described. Several silent moments passed before Deckland reflected, "I've known Rubi Valdez and her son Tony ever since they joined this church nine years ago after Tony's father left. Rubi was jubilant. Always optimistic. But also very level-headed and sensible. She had a strong awareness of the supernatural, but she wasn't crazy. So I can't explain why she came to you that morning Marvin, or what may have happened to her that convinced her that she needed *you* to pray for her. She had a strong, simple faith, and she believed in a God who loves her. She believed in Jeremiah 33:3, *'Call to me, and I will answer you'.*"

Marvin stopped pacing. "Well she got her answer all right." The accident rushed through Marvin's mind again and he thought about seeing Rubi at the cheerful yellow table in front of the coffee shop, and he remembered Rubi's bright brown eyes full of hope, and suddenly Marvin clenched his teeth and stepped in front of Deckland's desk and squatted down on one knee, and with one arm resting on the desk, he stared derisively at the silly stick of incense still sending up its smoke signals, and then Marvin gushed like a fountain.

"So what happened, Pastor Deckland? Can you help me understand? When I prayed years ago, I prayed *believing*. When I prayed for Rubi Valdez, even though I didn't really want to, I prayed believing. What happened to that prayer? Hmm? How do we know that that prayer even made it to God's ears? Because if God is a God of love, and he cares about humanity, then how is it that he can let us sit down here and pray and ask and seek and beg, and then just decide he's not gonna bother answering? Or he's just gonna say *NO* even though it's gonna be devastating and it's gonna destroy somebody's life? Because if that's how God operates, then how are we as humans supposed to go on and have faith? You see I'm not so sure those prayers really always get to God like we think they do, because if they do, then that God up there doesn't give one care or another about how his supposedly *grand plan* is going to terminate people who reach out in faith! So I ask again, how do those prayers reach God? The spiritual mechanics. What actually happens to those words? Those thoughts? Those hopes? Somebody—somewhere—has figured this out, right? There's a verse or a text, or a document or a brilliant thesis or a secret tablet buried in Egypt somewhere that tells us how it happens, and we know for sure that the prayer makes it up there to God, right? He hears us crying for help, doesn't he?"

Deckland's eyes blared wide, taken aback at this sudden burst of feeling, this dramatic theological implication. Marvin watched desperately as Deckland stood speechless.

Finally Deckland said meekly, "Nobody knows."

Marvin blinked. "What? What do you mean nobody knows? After all these centuries, after all the thousands of human years of existence, nobody has figured out how prayer reaches God?"

"It's a mystery, Marvin," said Deckland quietly. "A great mystery. I can only say that the holy scriptures tell us that we can have confidence in approaching God. That if we ask anything according to his will, he hears us. I don't know what else to tell you."

"According to his will," Marvin winced and wagged his head, trying to shake off the unbearable quandary.

Then came an awkward pause. Feeling badly about the aggressive nature of his questioning and the accusatory tone, Marvin rose up finally off his knee and stood up from the floor. He put a hand to his temple and rubbed his face. "I'm sorry, pastor. It's just that..." Marvin's words did not finish because the thought did not finish, lost in an impossible tangle of theology and a spiritual cloak that he could not see through and for which he had no solution.

Deckland said, "For some unknown reason, Rubi Valdez came to you. We may never know why. Have you talked to her son?"

Marvin turned away, shaking his head, remembering how he'd chickened out at the funeral home two days earlier. "No."

Deckland still hadn't moved since Marvin began his rant three minutes before. "I empathize with your frustration, Marvin. You've rattled me. I haven't thought much about this, since Shirley died. Your questions are only human. And the loss of Rubi Valdez from my own congregation, and Tony being left without a mother, are devastating realities." Finally Deckland leaned forward, his own eyes despondent, and in a display of total submission to his own humanity, Deckland said, "Our ability to understand God, and the acceptance of death, are two of the hardest things for humankind to do."

"Yeah," responded Marvin faintly.

So that was it. A lot of good talk that amounted to really nothing at all. No solution or direction that Marvin could go with confidence. There was nothing left to say, nothing left to ask, no stone left to overturn. "Well, I know you've got to get ready for the service." Marvin reached out a hand. "Thank you. I do appreciate you taking the time, pastor."

Deckland smiled weakly and grasped the hand in a firm shake. "Visit anytime, Marvin. I can lead you back to the front, or actually there's a door just around the brick corner there, the sidewalk outside will take you back to the front."

"I'll do that, thanks."

"And Marvin, remember…"

"Yeah?"

"For those who are called, all things work together for good."

16

STANDING ROOM ONLY

Against the sonic rhythms of Pink Floyd, Marvin sat edgily in the leather bucket that was the driver seat of his Jaguar, watching the cars stream in to the church parking lot like ants to the hill. With the lot filling up, cars looped to exit and park in the street. The steady line of visitors entered the building: couples, young and old, some with kids in tow, individuals of all kinds, in all manners of dress and in all colors.

How many people were coming to this funeral?

The service was scheduled to begin in 15 minutes. After his meeting with Pastor Deckland, Marvin had driven to the nearest gas station for a cup of junk coffee, then decided to head back to the church and wait for the funeral to begin. He had debated getting a donut, but stuck to his rule that eating in the car is a no-no. He allowed himself the coffee, being careful not to dribble, especially not on his tie. He knew he was taking a chance and would have to deal with the consequences if he was clumsy enough to spill.

Marvin checked his Rolex. Ten minutes. He suddenly realized how stupid he'd been to wait in the car all this time. With this many people cramming into the building, he'd be lucky now if he even got a seat. He set the coffee cup in the holder, made sure he had his keys, and hurried out of the car.

The place was packed. It was standing room only. The air resonated with the long tonal notes of an organ playing tenderly, and the soft voices of guests greeting one another and searching for an open pew. Marvin elbowed his way into the sanctuary and up the stairs to the balcony, which looked to Marvin like the upper deck at the World Series—packed elbow to elbow. As he climbed the steps he cursed himself for lingering in the car.

Now he was stuck along the distant wall in the balcony. Fortunately, the cavernously wide and modern design of the space gave him a good view of the stage. Giant chiffon plaster walls on either side angled steeply down from each side of the room, leading the eye down to the center platform, where a single glass pulpit stood before a tall brick wall with a large and beautiful stained glass cross twinkling with color. The casket holding Rubi Valdez' body stood open and prone in front of the broad carpeted platform below the pulpit.

A tall black ghostly shape proceeded effortlessly from the wings and stepped to the casket. This funeral home staff member reached for the cover and relaxed the hinges and slowly and gently and calmly lowered the mahogany lid shut, and that was the last the world would ever see of Rubi Valdez.

Marvin stood on his toes and craned to look around the balcony, then down again to the main floor. He didn't know the seating capacity of the building, but he guessed there must be over five hundred people jamming for a spot. Marvin hoped Deckland wouldn't light up his incense and set the whole place on fire.

The organ piece came to a close and the air waited for new sounds to fill the room. Marvin watched a quintet of brass players take the stage and arrange themselves. Golden light glinted merrily off each instrument as the musicians raised their horns, poised for performance, and opened into a melody that Marvin immediately recognized. He wasn't sure the name of the piece, but he knew it was something he had heard at the church he'd attended with Caroline. Not sad or melancholy, but pleasant and soothing.

And now as the horns played, Marvin spotted Antonio Valdez below, in black suit and tie, walking up the aisle to front row center, accompanied by the same handsome couple he'd seen with the boy at the funeral home. The woman led the trio and took a seat, followed by Antonio and the man beside him. Marvin wondered what the boy must be thinking, how unexpected this all had been for him, how utterly surreal it must seem.

The final note from the horn players dissipated into the rafters and the musicians stepped off the stage, walking single file to the far side of the pews and took their seats. Dressed in a flowing black robe, Pastor Deckland Smith emerged from somewhere in the front row and climbed up the three steps to the transparent podium. Deckland placed his hands on either side of the podium, glanced briefly at Antonio, and looked out into the crowd before him. The air dropped every remnant of sound and the room fell into solace before Deckland's amplified voice cut the silence. "Great is the Lord and greatly to be praised, and his greatness is unsearchable." Deckland paused, then said, "In the current order, things are the way they are, and they are out of our control. But we are grateful for the one who is in control, and he is our Lord, Jesus Christ."

Marvin stood and listened as Pastor Deckland began the most moving and touching eulogy he had ever heard. Rubi Valdez had been an icon in the church. Her bubbly personality had lit up the rooms she'd entered, bringing joy to everyone she met. As a single mother, she had raised a beautiful and intelligent son named Antonio. And at 35 years old, she had recently graduated from

Grand Canyon University with a degree in Public Safety and Emergency Management. Rubi had wanted to take her passion for the welfare of others to the professional level and serve the community. She had just been hired at the Arizona Department of Public Safety, and was on her way to her first day on the job, when the unthinkable happened.

The accident that had taken her life.

Rubi had touched many lives through her service in the church as a Sunday School teacher, a leader at Vacation Bible School, as a member of the Outreach Team. It was Rubi Valdez who cheered on the young people's club here at the church to run the annual car washes, so the kids could raise money for summer camp. It was Rubi Valdez who helped organize a short-term missionary trip to the Bandiagara Escarpment in Mali to bring the gospel to the Dogon tribe. It was Rubi Valdez who, five years ago, had introduced a local program aimed at helping the poor and needy, a program sponsored by this church, which had fed over 100 people in the Phoenix area every week.

Marvin was reminded of Mother Teresa, of her efforts at serving those in need... and it struck him: Rubi Valdez had been not just another church attender, not just another taxpayer, not just another person starting a new job. Rubi Valdez had been exceptional. She had been dearly loved by hundreds of people who had come to this service today to mourn her, to celebrate her, to say goodbye to her.

The service continued with a piano solo, then a choral number, and finally a short closing prayer.

Marvin watched the pallbearers step to the casket, turn it, and roll it slowly down the carpeted aisle toward the exit. When Marvin saw Antonio rise to his feet and follow with the handsome couple, the winds of feeling gusted in his heart at the impact of the profound loss. As Antonio disappeared from view, Marvin wondered how all of this could possibly be part of whatever purpose Deckland had been talking about. It made no sense. But right now, Marvin Fischer was determined to make his way down through the crowd and talk to Antonio Valdez.

17

SKETCHBALL

Coming down from the balcony, Marvin felt like a penned cow as he swayed impatiently on the stairs behind the slow descent of people, until finally reaching the main level of the church. Still trapped in the sanctuary, Marvin was desperate to catch the boy before he left for the cemetery. Marvin scanned the aisles between pews looking for an opening, but the mass of human obstacles was like a traffic jam on Interstate 17. Marvin geared his brain into driver mode. Tracking the flow of humans, he anticipated a gap, and made his move. Lurching forward and lifting his hands, Marvin twirled to slip between a pair of couples, then wove past a group of women and cleared the pew just before another couple blocked his way. Marvin had only a few feet of clearance now before another blockade would thwart him. If he could snake his way around, he'd be home free for the French doors leading out. He saw his chance and hit the accelerator. It was a rude move that sparked a rebuke from an old lady who had overdosed on Liz Claiborne. But it was worth the offense as the move won Marvin his freedom and now he was out of the sanctuary and into the lobby.

Marvin searched above bald heads and curls and updos. No Antonio. The boy was probably already out of the building. Once again Marvin went into passing mode and wove to the front. He pushed past a cluster of college kids chattering about something that amused them, and then crisscrossed through another gathering until finally making it into the concrete breezeway, through the front door, and out into the day with its fresh and clear warm air.

Marvin paused on the sidewalk, squinting in the daylight. His eyes tracked with a long line of cars that was already forming along the curb of the sidewalk. He spotted the black Hearse at the front of the line twenty yards down. Behind the black Hearse, a clean white Jeep waited with engine idling. Marvin guessed Antonio would ride in the Jeep behind the Hearse, and that's when Marvin's eyes landed on the handsome couple that had accompanied Antonio in the sanctuary. Marvin stepped decisively along the sidewalk and the lineup of cars toward the Jeep.

Over the hum of the Jeep's engine, Marvin pitched his voice to the pretty woman opening the Jeep's back door. "Excuse me Miss... my name is Marvin Fischer. I know you don't know me, but I saw you with Antonio Valdez—"

The pretty woman paused by the open door and turned to oblige. "I'm Tiffany," said the lady.

"Hi, ah, Tiffany, um—I was there the day of the accident, with Rubi Valdez, I saw it happen—May I please talk to Antonio real quick before he leaves?"

Before Tiffany could answer, Antonio leapt out of the Jeep and called across the hood to Marvin. "Mister Fischer!"

Marvin turned and met eyes with Antonio. "Antonio, hi— Could—can I talk to you?"

Antonio nodded readily and circled the Jeep. "I'll be right back," he said to the pretty woman.

Marvin moved to the edge of the sidewalk beside a row of bay leaf shrubs, trying to create a bubble of privacy amidst the nearby people streaming out of the building. He rubbed his hands tensely together, his eyes flicking about. Antonio moved quickly to join him, his clear brown eyes wide with anticipation. The boy put his hands in his back pockets and looked eagerly at Marvin as if there were no one waiting, seemingly welcoming this intrusion. "Hi Mister Fischer," said the crackling voice. "I saw you at the funeral home. I was hoping you'd come talk to me. Did you see it?"

Marvin stopped rubbing his hands, staring anxiously. "What?"

"That thing, that creature!"

Marvin froze solid. "You've got to be kidding."

Antonio persisted, "You saw it, didn't you?"

"Yes, I did. So—I wasn't seeing things? It was there?"

"Yeah it was there. I definitely saw it. I've been wondering if you did. There's something sketchball about all this. My mom saw something else the day before she met with you."

Marvin was caught in the magnetism of Antonio's statement.

What was this new secret?

Antonio took his hands out of his pockets, stepped closer to Marvin, huddled by the bushes and whispered, "My mom said she saw Saint Peter. And Peter told my mom to come find you."

What?!?

Marvin's reality was coming apart. "Saint Peter? The apostle?!" Marvin asked, incredulous.

"Yeah," Antonio said.

"Are you sure?"

"Well that's what she told me. She said Peter was real. She thinks it was a vision!"

Marvin's mind whirred with events and feelings colliding in unresolved havoc. He needed facts to analyze, solid intelligence to corroborate. There was something highly unusual about this particular boy, about this particular funeral, about Rubi Valdez, and about his own involvement. "Alright," said Marvin, "something very strange is going on here, Antonio. I don't know what it is, but we're gonna find out."

"Call me Tony. Everybody calls me Tony."

"Okay Tony, I know you've got to go," and seeing Tiffany waiting patiently at the Jeep, Marvin asked, "Who are these people you're with?"

Tony glanced at Tiffany, who smiled back expectantly. "That's the Tindals. Tiffany, and her husband Tom is going to drive us. They're just helping me out until—you know—I figure out what's going to happen now."

"So you're stayin' with them?"

"Yeah. My mom is besties with Mrs. Tindal."

Marvin slipped a business card from his suit pocket and handed it to Tony.

"Tony, if it's alright with you, I'd like you to ask Mister and Mrs. Tindal if I can get together with you again, at their earliest convenience. Text me at this number."

"Okay." Tony looked at the card. "Arizona Counter Terrorism Center?"

"Yeah."

"Wow."

Marvin forced his anxiety aside and said earnestly, "Tony, I'm very sorry about what happened. I'm very sorry that you lost your mother."

Tony's eyes left Marvin's and drooped to the ground, but only for a moment, before quickly lifting again and returning stoutly to Marvin, "Thank you, Mister Fischer."

Tiffany called, "Tony, we have to get going hun."

"Okay!" Tony called, and then nodding to Marvin he said, "I'm glad you came, Mister Fischer."

Marvin sensed the comfort in Tony's face and watched as the boy circled back to the Jeep's open passenger door.

Marvin stepped away and quickly decided to opt out of riding along in the procession. His mind was working furiously, and he was in desperate need of a hot coffee.

~

As the Hearse drove off to lead the procession of cars and the Jeep began to roll away, Tony watched Marvin through the window, pacing on the sidewalk, hand on his chin. Tony didn't know much about this Mister Fischer, but he felt like he could trust him. Tony appreciated Mrs. Tindal; she had always been very kind to him, and her help now brought him great comfort. But he wasn't sure about Tom. He was mostly nice, but sometimes the man didn't seem to want Tony around. Sometimes Tony felt like an intruder.

And there was something about Mister Fischer that made Tony feel that maybe this man could help him in ways that the Tindals could not.

Tony couldn't wait to talk to Mister Fischer again.

18

SAINT ON THE INNER CIRCLE

The ping from Antonio Valdez came just prior to five o'clock that same afternoon. Within a minute, Marvin Fischer was on speakerphone with Tiffany Tindal and the seemingly quiet husband Tom. Marvin quickly learned that the Tindals had been the pair that had welcomed Rubi Valdez and young three-year-old Antonio when they had first visited Agape United Methodist nine years earlier. Tiffany had already visited the ACTIC website noted on Fischer's business card, and consumed his picture and bio. Tiffany thanked Marvin for his contributions to National Security, complimenting him for the honors he had received while in service to the country.

But Tiffany and Tom were curious about Marvin's intentions with Tony. They understood that Marvin had been present at the accident, that he had prayed for Rubi just beforehand, that Tony seemed to trust this Mister Fischer, and wanted to speak with him. But what was this really about?

Marvin respected their questions and expressed praise for the steps taken to ensure the boy's well being. Marvin explained that he was deeply sorry for Tony's loss, and that there might be some healing aspect for them both to talk things through, since they were the last two people on earth to speak with Rubi before the accident. A conversation might settle some questions and calm some anxieties.

This made sense to the Tindals. Tiffany invited Marvin to their home in Mesa where they could have a more proper introduction, and Marvin was welcome to talk with Tony there.

Marvin assented. He was given the address, and the call ended agreeably.

Marvin tucked his phone away and sipped from the glass mug which he nurtured, sitting deep in thought outside The Bean Sack under the same elm tree and at the same yellow table he had sat four days earlier, where he had met Rubi and Tony Valdez the morning of the accident. Marvin left the coffee mug on the table and stood up. He had changed out of the black suit he'd worn to the funeral and into a breezy white seersucker shirt, lava brown chinos and cognac Derbys. The lighter colors filled him with much-needed cheer. He thumbed a light scuff from the toe of his shoe, then passed beneath the shadows of elm leaves and stepped to the intersection, pressed the silver button on the light post, and waited for the pedestrian signal. He glanced a block away where the dreaded accident had occurred, and then to the spot where he had seen the strange creature. Marvin hadn't told the Tindals anything about the creature, and guessed that Tony hadn't either. It was also probable that Tony hadn't mentioned Rubi's visit from Saint Peter. The signal turned and as Marvin crossed the street to his Jaguar, he questioned his own judgment. A creature? Really? A saint long dead appearing in some vision? Marvin felt foolish for playing along with the fantasy.

The Jaguar chirped. Marvin gripped the latch and opened the door, evaluating how much of this he and Tony were going to keep to themselves.

~

THE TEMPEST IN GLASS

The GPS led Marvin directly to the Tindal's house without a single wrong turn. Marvin was glad the technology gurus had finally gotten it right. He'd been led down rabbit trails plenty of times during the technology's infancy, and had once popped a tire on a dirt road in Rio Verde while hunting down a suspect. It had been an enormous inconvenience. He was glad now for the clean smooth pavement that welcomed his high performance tires as he pulled up. He hoped they wouldn't mind the imposition of parking in the drive behind the white Jeep, rather than the street.

Marvin stepped out of the car and into the welcoming scent of desert peonies drifting across the rocky yard. He stepped up the drive of the peach sorbet house and rang the door chime. Tiffany Tindal quickly opened, joined then by Tom. It was a pleasant introduction. They welcomed Marvin into the small tiled foyer with its tall walls, and young Tony appeared from the living room. Tony was barefoot, having changed into a pair of striped sports shorts and a tank top bearing the number twelve, with the binoculars on the blue cord around his neck. His lean athletic frame contradicted his moderate movements as he leaned pensively against the wall with arms folded behind his back, brown eyes fixed on his visitor. Marvin could not help but notice the bloodshot eyes and red face, the clear indication of bereavement, as could be expected from any child who had lost a beloved parent. Marvin suddenly felt sadness instead of anxiety, and empathized with the boy.

How will the child cope with losing his mother?

Soon the four were seated on plush gray couches around a slate table in the airy living room. A ceiling fan spun gently overhead. Tiffany set a tray of white mugs and fresh coffee, which she poured and Marvin gratefully accepted. He complimented the couple on their very large and colorful *Jean-Claude Picot* while the three adults shared coffee and Tony gulped a Mountain Dew. They talked about how well the funeral had gone, and about the many people in attendance. Tom indicated it had been a funeral record for the church. The trip to the cemetery had gone well, but had been rough on Tony.

Marvin said, "I know it's been a tough day, and I do appreciate you allowing me to visit." Turning to Tony, who had been quiet for most of the discussion, Marvin asked, "You ready to chat?"

"Sure," said Tony, trying to smile, but pursing his lips tensely. He stood up.

Marvin asked, "Is there someplace private we can talk?"

"How about the study," Tiffany offered. "You can close the French doors."

Marvin left the French doors ajar an inch, hoping not to appear too dismissive to the couple. Tony sat down in a wooden chair near a large paned window. He drained the Mountain Dew and set the empty bottle on a long narrow table in front of the window bearing a single bunny ear cactus in a terracotta pot. Marvin took hold of another wooden chair and settled into it.

"They seem like nice people," Marvin said softly.

Tony looked distantly out the window. He whispered, "They were supposed to go to France this week. This messed it up. I don't think Tom wants me around. But don't tell them."

This came unexpected to Marvin. "Ok," he said, but decided not to pursue it for now. He finished the coffee and set the mug near the cactus, put his elbows on his knees, folded his hands, and looked remorsefully at Tony.

"I'm sorry about the prayer," Marvin offered.

"Why didn't you want to do it?" Tony asked.

Marvin had not anticipated the question. It struck him like an accusation, but Marvin guessed that was not the intent. He struggled for an answer. The reasons were complex.

"I could tell," Tony continued, "by the look on your face. You didn't want to pray."

"No I didn't," Marvin confessed. "But your mother was insistent."

"She can be that way," said Tony. "She was worried about not finding you."

Marvin was immensely curious about that. But instead asked, "You holding up?"

"I still can't believe it happened."

"Why did your mother feel it had to be me?" Marvin asked.

Tony touched the needles on the cactus, delicately enough not to get pricked. Marvin sensed that the boy wanted to be very careful with his answer.

"I know it sounds crazy," Tony began, "but my mom said she was visited by Saint Peter. It was the night before her first day—you know—at the new job. She said it was in her bedroom. She always leaves the window open because she likes the breeze." Antonio paused. Marvin remained silent as the boy continued. "She said a voice called to her, and she looked around, didn't see anyone. So she got out of bed, went to the window, and there was nobody there. So she went back to bed, and heard the voice again. So she went out into the hallway and looked around, and then came to my room and asked if I was calling her. I said *no I wasn't*, so she went back to bed—I guess—and after a few minutes she heard the voice again, and this time she sat up and saw a man standing by the window."

Marvin's eyes narrowed. It was extraordinary. It sounded like a ghost story, something he was not prone to believe quickly, but he had to admit he was intrigued. "Keep going," he said.

"The man told her not to be scared, and she asked him who he was, and he said *I'm Saint Peter of Galilee*. He said that she was in danger or something, and that she needed to meet this man in a suit, *a man named Marvin Fischer*, at this coffee shop before she went to work. And then, he just disappeared. I was like, *mom are you sure you weren't just dreaming* and she said *no…*", Tony paused in thought, then concluded, "She said she trusted Peter because he was part of Jesus' inner circle."

Now Marvin had an elbow on the narrow table, his eyes slim, a finger rubbing his chin, his mind reeling in the information. He strained to recall what he had heard about Saint Peter from church sermons he had attended with his wife Caroline. Peter had been a fisherman on the Sea of Galilee in Israel, Marvin remembered, and one of the first to be called by Jesus to follow him. For the time being, Marvin decided to accept the story as told by Tony, assumed the truth of it, and allowed himself to continue down the road of possibility. "And what were you thinking, when your mom told you all this?"

"I just kind of thought, *whatever*. Because she was always really spiritual. And close to God. And prayed a lot. So I thought, *well, maybe Saint Peter really did come*. And she believed it. So maybe it was true."

"And now what do you think?"

19

WHAT HAPPENED IN NEW YORK

"If Saint Peter wanted you to pray for my mom, to keep her safe, then why did she still die?" Tony asked. "If she was in trouble, why didn't Peter just help her himself?"

Marvin pondered. "Maybe he couldn't."

"What do you mean?"

Marvin shifted his jaw, trying to find logic in the matter. "Maybe Peter could communicate with your mother, but couldn't actually do anything for her." Marvin reached into his pocket. "A few days ago, I received a text message from somebody named Simon. It was really weird, we couldn't trace it. It was a picture of Mother Teresa. You know who that is?"

"I've heard of her. Someone famous."

Marvin located the black and white photo of the young Teresa on his phone and turned the screen to Tony. "She's a Catholic saint. A person who accomplished great things for God, despite her doubts." Marvin tucked the phone away. "Now you're tellin' me some other saint—Peter—tried to reach your mom. I'm a realist Tony, but I think something out of this world is goin' on."

"Like the creature," Tony said.

"Yeah, right. The snake thing."

"With bluish-green feathers coming out of its neck."

"Is that what those were?"

"Feathers, yeah, behind its head. I'm positive."

"Big black eyes?"

"Like marbles," Tony agreed. "And then it was gone."

The two of them sat in silence, staring out the window, answers eluding them. Tony took hold of his binoculars and peered toward the sky. "I've been reading this book about the solar system. Space exploration. Whether God exists. I don't understand it all. But it's really interesting." Tony lowered the binoculars, letting them hang in front of his chest. "So, do you believe that life really exists in other worlds? Like in other planes of existence? Or in outer space? Or in other dimensions?"

Marvin looked squarely at Tony. The boy was straight serious. Marvin thought of Caroline, how her belief in the afterlife had been a central part of her faith in the doctrines of the church. "I do think there's somethin' out there, yeah."

Tony fiddled absently with his empty soda bottle. "So why didn't you want to pray for my mom?"

Marvin cleared his throat and sat back in the chair. He felt he owed the boy an explanation. "You've heard of the terrorist attacks on the World Trade Center, on September 11, 2001?"

Tony nodded quizzically, "Yeah."

"Tell me what you know."

Tony dismissed the empty bottle and looked up toward the ceiling. "These guys from—somewhere, from the Middle East—they hijacked some planes and flew them into buildings in New York, and a lot of people died."

"That's right. I was workin' in Detroit at the time, at the FBI office, but there wasn't enough intelligence—not enough information—to know when or where or how, or even if the attacks would actually happen. I know all this was before you were even born, Tony, but I remember it like it was yesterday. My wife,

Caroline, she was a police officer working downtown in New York City that day. She had gone over there for some specialized training. I stayed in Detroit, at the FBI office. We both lived there, in Detroit. Anyway, she was in New York when the planes hit the buildings, and she was one of the first responders at the scene."

"Wow." Tony pulled his knees to his chest and wrapped his arms around his shins.

"A lot of people at the office where I worked knew people who were way across the country, over there in New York City, where this was happening, and at the Pentagon, because we all work in security and law enforcement and such. You get it, right?"

"Yeah."

"So we were all worried. We had friends, family, loved ones who were in harm's way, tryin' to help the people who were stuck in those buildings. But I was helpless at the office, six hundred miles away, and there was nothin' I could do except one thing."

"Pray," said Tony.

"Exactly. Me—and everyone in my office—stopped what we were doing. The whole country stopped. We watched those news reports on TV, and we worried, and we hoped, and yeah—we prayed. We huddled and we put our arms around each other, and we prayed. The whole country was praying. I tell you Tony, that was a day this country came together like I can't remember ever before, because we were all terrified, and all we knew how to do, despite our training, armed forces and technology, all we knew how to do was reach out to God and pray. It was instinct."

"Did you know where your wife was?"

"I talked to her on the phone while it was all goin' on. Breathing in the smoke, she was right there at ground zero."

"Right where it happened."

"Yeah. This was before the first tower fell. I don't know how many details you know about the attack Tony, but nobody guessed that the towers would fall. Everyone was worried about gettin' the people out of the buildings before they suffocated or got burned to death. Well I hung up with Caroline…"

Marvin stopped, the feelings clawing deep, threatening to unravel him. He composed himself and continued. "I prayed for Caroline. In fact—she didn't know it—but I used to pray for her every single morning. After she was out the door to police headquarters, while I drove to FBI—every morning—said a little prayer for her safety. But on this day, 9/11, I prayed for her extra hard. And I believed it. All my prayers would count. I honestly believed that God would rescue her."

"But he didn't," said Tony.

"No. The tower fell and my wife was gone. Crushed in the rubble. And I was powerless to do anything." Marvin stared out the window.

"That's really sad, Mister Fischer."

Marvin's fingertips went to his forehead. "Sorry Tony, you just buried your mother and I'm unloading on you."

"It's okay."

"What I'm tryin' to say Tony, is that when I last prayed, on that horrible day in September, I prayed and it didn't matter. My wife died anyway. So that's why I didn't wanna pray for your mother. I was afraid the same thing was gonna happen again. And it did."

"Wow...' Tony's eyes drifted.

"After New York, I couldn't pray anymore. But now I *have* prayed again, for your mother, and this happened, I feel powerless." Marvin tapped his fingers on the arm of the chair. "You know what? This time I'm gonna do somethin' about it."

"What can you do?"

Marvin hesitated. He felt he needed to take action, but he had no clue how to proceed. "I don't know," he said, falling into defeated silence.

And then, breaking the despondence, came a ping from Marvin's smartphone. "Now what?" Marvin yanked the phone from his pocket, held the screen to his face, and frowned. "Another one?"

"What is it?" asked Tony.

"It's another picture."

"From Simon?"

"Yeah. Of some other woman."

Tony got up from his chair and circled beside Marvin. "Who is it?"

The picture was a color portrait of a rather appealing woman with round high cheekbones, brown hair styled in a classy updo, and commanding hazel eyes in an obvious pose for the camera. Marvin guessed the woman hovered not much beyond 40 years.

"I don't know," pondered Marvin, staring at the image. "It looks like somebody's profile picture. From that Simon again. I don't even know a Simon."

"Wait a minute," said Tony thoughtfully. "Simon... Simon Peter... Simon was another name for Saint Peter!"

Marvin lowered the phone, eyes narrowing and mouth hanging open as he considered Tony's comment. "Are you tellin' me you think *Saint Peter* sent me this picture? And the other one? Of Mother Teresa?"

"Well it fits with all the other craziness we've been talking about," said Tony. "It could be. Couldn't it?"

"I did try to return-call the number, and couldn't get through." Marvin stood and circled the room. "So here we are sayin' that Simon Peter is somehow communicating with me... on my cell phone... from where? From heaven?"

Tony giggled.

"Ha!" Marvin shouted in amusement, smiling at the absurdity of the idea. "How could it be... they have smartphones in heaven?" Tony laughed and Marvin couldn't restrain a chuckle. He continued to pace, his thoughts swirling. He hit the return call key on his phone and waited. "I can't get through. No ring... Nothin'... Okay—" Marvin tucked the phone back into his pocket. He put a finger to his chin, thought deeply for a moment, then said, "I want you to come with me to my office at the ACTIC. We're gonna look up this picture and figure out who this woman is. You and me. We have to do this together."

Tony was transfixed. "That is straight fire!"

Within the minute they were in the foyer, seeking permission from the Tindals to go out for awhile. Tom, reclining with his laptop on the sofa, gave his thumbs up. Tiffany was concerned the boy had not had anything to eat, and invited Marvin to stay for a late dinner of *croquet monsieur* she had quickly whipped up.

"I'm still not hungry," said Tony.

Marvin checked his Rolex. It was almost seven o'clock. "I'll have him back by nine. You've got my number," Marvin reassured her. Tiffany waved them off, and Marvin and Tony torpedoed out of the house.

20
STRATEGEM

With the staff gone for the day, the ACTIC was quiet and sleepy, with only the hum of database fans and the dim blue glow of security lights along the floor's perimeter. While the giant room slumbered, flashing green lights on computer towers silently collected data that was still streaming in from everywhere, ready for tomorrow's analysts.

Then in the center of the long wall, the bronze elevator door whined open, and Marvin Fischer and Antonio Valdez stepped into the ghostly atmosphere. Tony tore open a Snickers and munched into it while following Marvin between workstations.

"Don't tell them I gave you that," Marvin warned.

With bright eyes Tony absorbed the flashing lights dancing in the dark and knew he was in on a trove of secrets.

Marvin leaned in to Lyle Stratton's workspace, tapped the space bar on the keyboard, and logged in with his own credentials. "Let's see if I can remember how to use this thing," he said and plugged his smart phone into the hard drive.

"Do you have some super secret database or something? Stuff on everybody in the world?" Tony asked. He finished the candy bar and dropped the wrapper on the desk.

"Not exactly, but I'm gonna upload this image and see if the facial recognition system pings anything unusual." Marvin swept the candy wrapper into the garbage and referenced the computer screen again, clicked through a series of windows, dropdowns, and folders, then clicked an innocuous green icon. "If the database doesn't find anything, then the system will scan open sources. Everything on the Internet that's searchable publicly, unless it runs into a firewall, in which case we could be here all night."

"Dope," said Tony as he watched a gray progress bar creep across the screen. The gray bar finished, then a blue bar popped up and began to travel.

"So nothing in our database, checking open sources to find a match…" said Marvin. Glued to the screen, he watched the blue bar with Tony until it stopped. A split second later, a new window launched in the browser. "It found somethin'."

The same photo from the text image Marvin had received popped up onscreen—the woman with a brown updo, the high cheekbones, the hazel eyes, and now, a bio. "No kidding. Here she is," Marvin scanned the text. "Doctor Amina Karimova. University of Edinburgh. Crap."

"What?" asked Tony.

"She's in Scotland. Or at least—that's where she's currently tenured. Amina Karimova, professor of Religious Studies. No kidding."

"Maybe she's an expert or something. Maybe she can help us!"

Marvin scrolled down, scanning the bio. "Born and raised in Kazakhstan… instilled with a sense of the divine since her youth… only child… graduated Northwestern… Tony look at this—She's a medium."

"What's a medium?"

"Someone who contacts the dead."

The electric tingle of nerves shot between them. Tony shared his mesmerized glance with Marvin. "It seems," said Marvin, "that Saint Peter wants us to find this Doctor Karimova."

Marvin closed out the browser, cleared the history, and logged off the computer.

"You ever been on an airplane, Tony?"

"Yeah, I went with my mom to Mali last year, for a mission trip."

"So you have a passport. You like flying?"

"Sure."

"How about a trip to Scotland?"

Tony's eyes lit. "To find Doctor Karimova?"

Marvin snatched his phone from the hard drive and the computer screen went black. Then the demons of doubt seized him. Marvin ground his teeth. Wild ideas and unlikely possibilities were suddenly filling his mind. This plan was going against logic, against reason, against solid evidence. Much remained up for analysis. His brain erupted with rebellion. But he turned, rested a hand on Tony's shoulder, and leveled his gaze into the boy. "Tony, we're gonna find Saint Peter. And we're gonna bring your mother back to life."

PART II

21

ITINERARY

Marvin's first personal encounter with Doctor Amina Karimova came during a phone call he placed to the University of Edinburgh, where an operator put him straight through. Doctor Karimova picked up, citing Marvin's good fortune at having caught her in the office, as she was hardly ever actually there. Marvin found her voice crisp, cool, and businesslike.

"Ah! An intelligence commander," said Doctor Karimova after Marvin introduced himself. "What a grounded profession."

Marvin explained the tragic and mysterious circumstances surrounding Rubi Valdez' death, and that he had received Doctor Karimova's profile picture in a text message that he believed came from Saint Peter. Marvin wanted to bring Antonio Valdez from the United States to meet with the doctor, in hopes of contacting the saint.

Doctor Amina Karimova expressed immediate intrigue with the story, confessing it unusual, and forewarned that it may be difficult to contact someone with the eminence of a saint. She agreed to a meeting, affirming her willingness to discuss the details of a séance once they arrived in Edinburgh. Marvin confirmed his satisfaction with the arrangement, they exchanged smartphone numbers, and Marvin promised to make contact upon arrival in Scotland.

Marvin Fischer spent the next morning arguing with his superiors and making up excuses for why it was important that he depart unexpectedly for a few days. He did not disclose his reasons for the sudden requirement, other than describing it as 'personal.' With the new case on Abiku Madaki hitting so close to home, his bosses wanted him in Phoenix. Marvin argued he had already assembled a stellar task force, and the case was in the capable hands of Elizabeth Walsh. Marvin would be available via technology and be back in a week's time. Everything would proceed in an orderly fashion without Marvin Fischer for a couple of days.

The higher-ups vehemently denied the request. They wanted Marvin present for every development, every conversation, every possible scenario that might play out in these next critical days in the Madaki case. Marvin walked out of the meeting red-faced and tight-fisted. He was one of the top members of the state IC and had never asked for any special favors.

Incensed, Marvin would have to spin things his way.

It came as a surprise to Tiffany and Tom Tindal that Tony wanted to get on an airplane and fly halfway across the world with a man he had only met a week prior. They listened as Tony insisted on going, clinging to the hope of finding his mother. Tony believed his mother still had big plans for life on earth, and had in no way expected to be taken away. Primary at the forefront was that Tony himself loved her and needed her and wanted her back. She was his anchor, and in these last few days Tony had felt adrift and frightened of the future. Tony was determined with all fortitude in teaming with Mister Fischer to recover his mother.

In their little home study with the French doors closed, Tiffany and Tom had their own private squabble. They believed Rubi's soul had already reached heaven, and that she was now in the presence of God for all eternity. They agreed the thought of bringing Rubi back to life was ridiculous. But on the point of the trip to Scotland, Tom argued in favor. Tom reminded Tiffany for the tenth time that as Rubi had left no will, it would be up to the court to decide who would become the boy's legal guardians. They were caring for the kid now out of kindness, but the kid could do what he wanted. Fischer could be trusted. He was a well-honored member of the United States intelligence community. There was nothing to worry about, argued Tom. Let the kid go. The experimental journey with Fischer would satisfy the curiosity. Tony would go and pursue and be disappointed, but at least it would be out of his system.

Tom's reasoning had been swiftly rebutted by an accusation from Tiffany that this was really about their lost trip to France. Tom stormed out of the study and left Tiffany standing as the only resistance. After a quick prayer in front of the window, she felt relieved and immediately called Marvin Fischer offering the consent of both she and her husband. She would negotiate an excused absence from Tony's school, and insisted on periodic contact with the boy along the journey. Marvin soundly agreed.

Three days after the funeral, Marvin and Tony packed their bags for the trip across the Atlantic. Marvin would fund the entire journey out of his own pocket. The boy, at only twelve, couldn't be expected to dip into his savings. Marvin had been smart with his money—having tucked away a percentage of every paycheck since he was 18—so he could afford to travel in style. He recruited his trusted travel agent to secure a rental car, hotel accommodations, and two first-class tickets aboard Lufthansa, Marvin's preferred airline—the biggest and classiest of Europe.

The day before the trip, Marvin donned his readers and reclined at his condo over a cup of freshly brewed Tarrazu and reviewed the itinerary. The 3,700-mile flight would depart Sky Harbor International Airport the next morning at 9:22. After the first leg of the voyage, they'd have a three-hour layover at Chicago O'Hare, where Marvin would procure an aromatic cup of his favorite Ethiopian blend from Metropolis Coffee. Then they'd hop the connecting flight for another seven-and-a-half-hour journey across the ocean before landing at 7:50 the next morning at Edinburgh Airport in Scotland, where they'd pick up a luxury car for the drive to The Balmoral Hotel, a five star classic built in 1902 by the British Railway Company on the edge of old-town Edinburgh. They'd be just a short drive from the University where they would meet Doctor Amina Karimova.

22

PARTING GIFT

The waxing crescent moon was already slicing the indigo dusk of the evening sky. Elizabeth Walsh was unaccustomed to feeling nervous and did not know quite how to deal with the uneasiness. She wound the steering wheel of the green crossover onto the cobbled sienna drive at The Villas of Stone Creek and began to scan addresses. It would be her first time seeing Marvin Fischer's condo. She hoped the man wouldn't scold her for showing up uninvited, not to mention for invading his privacy and smuggling his address from office records. Elizabeth found Marvin's driveway, quietly pulled up the drive, and evaluated.

A warm light emanated from the front window. Inside, a shadow passed, and Elizabeth's stomach did a summersault.

Maybe he had already noticed her car in the drive!

Elizabeth pursed her lips and tugged air through flared nostrils. Peeking in the rearview mirror, she quickly examined herself. She rubbed something from the side of her nose, and fingered the waves in the freshly-curled bright blonde hair. She had chosen silver stud earrings to match the silver crucifix necklace, had lightly penciled her thin brows, applied a reserved amount of rouge with purple Anastasia Beverly Hills to the eyes, and had finished with a splash of rose to the lips. Elizabeth was suddenly afraid she'd overstepped, and blushed in a brief squall of panic.

Placing both hands in her lap, Elizabeth looked again at the light pouring from Marvin's front window.

Did he already have a guest?

Decidedly, Elizabeth swiveled and from the passenger seat plucked a small thin package. She opened the car door, stepped out onto the drive, and closed the door. Without further hesitation she tucked the small gift at her side and approached the front door. She had decided on white jeans and brown leather boots with belt, and a loosely-tucked white V-neck cotton T-shirt with short rolled sleeves. She stepped onto the porch and stood with ankles together and pressed the door chime. A welcoming jingle echoed from within. Elizabeth stood confidently and waited. She heard footsteps on wood. The lock clicked and the door opened.

Marvin stood still, soaking her in, his face plain.

"What the hell are you doin' here?"

"Ha!" Elizabeth blurted. Her eyes involuntarily scanned the man. "Wow. T-shirt and jeans. Who would have thought." He was barefoot, in dark jeans with a navy blue tee.

"This better be good," said Marvin.

"Where are the wingtips?"

"Shut it."

"What if I don't?" she said playfully, feeling out of character—like she had already blown it.

"I've got an early morning," he said.

"I know—sorry—Just wanted to wish you well," Elizabeth said, still fighting the nerves. It was far too late to deny her attraction to him. That she had made the drive and had the guts to ring, and was now standing in front of Marvin at his place of residence, was proof enough. She knew that the personal visit would be a dead giveaway. "And I got you something," she finished, holding out the giftwrapped package. Now there could be no doubt.

Marvin squinted and smiled reservedly, reaching to take the package from Elizabeth. It was nicely and neatly wrapped in paper of silvery blue, with a white ribbon crisscrossed into a curly bow. "That is very thoughtful, Elizabeth. Thank you," he said genuinely.

"You're welcome."

"I can't invite you in."

"I know I've gotta go… I want to get in early… and you're leaving early…"

"Okay."

"Sure you can't tell me what this trip is about?"

"No. Shoo."

"Okay," Elizabeth said, turning away. "Have fun."

"Wait…" Marvin closed his eyes. "Actually, there is somethin' I need to tell you."

Marvin's tone signaled that something was askew. Elizabeth spun on her toes and tipped her chin down. Her forehead puckered between the green eyes. "What?"

"Yeah well, Dominic doesn't exactly know that I'm leaving. In fact, nobody knows, except you."

"Why not?"

"They wouldn't give me the time off."

"So it's not business."

"No."

"And you're going anyway."

"Yeah."

"When were you going to tell me this?"

"After I got to where I'm going."

"You devil," Elizabeth said, fearing suddenly that he was heading off on some impromptu rendezvous with a woman. "Must be pretty important."

"Yeah." Marvin sealed his lips and looked at her silent.

Elizabeth crossed her arms and stared him down. "You're still not going to tell me."

"I'm sorry I can't talk to you about it now."

"A woman?"

"No."

Elizabeth didn't quite believe him. But ok, so what if it was? There was so much she didn't know about the mysterious creature standing before her. "So they're going to be breathing down my neck asking about you, and I'm going to have to cover for you."

"No you're not, because you don't know anything. But, yeah, the case—Madaki—it's in your hands. Unofficially. Until I get back. You can call me of course, and I'll call you, just like we agreed. Keep tabs on the case."

"Secretly, and hope they don't trace my calls and find your location. That's okay I'll just sit on the toilet in the women's bathroom and call you from there." Elizabeth's cheeks formed deep caves on the sides of her face. She hoped her glaring eyes would have the desired effect of inflicting a spear of guilt into Marvin's chest.

Marvin continued, "Everything's gonna be fine."

"Dominic's going to kill you."

"No, he won't—"

"You could get fired."

"Yeah I know."

"And that's fine?"

Marvin held up a hand. "It's not gonna happen. You got this thing covered. I have the utmost confidence in you, Elizabeth. You and Stratton. Look, I'm sorry for buggin' out on you, and for not tellin' you sooner. I should have. I should have talked to you sooner. But I'll be back as soon as I can. I promise."

Elizabeth released a gust of breath and glanced off the brick of the condo. Her eyes went back to Marvin. Her resentment had more to do with being left out of the loop than it did with being left in charge.

"I'll call you when I get there," Marvin promised.

Elizabeth looked at him again with her chin up and sighed through her nose. "Well don't have too much fun." She turned and stepped off the porch, feeling like the jealous college girl, wishing already that she could retrieve the stupid remark.

Marvin Fischer denied himself a glance at Elizabeth's caboose as she paraded away, and closed the front door.

The visit had been a complete surprise, a warm gesture of friendship and maybe a bit more, and Marvin had returned the signal with a sledgehammer blow. Why not just go along with it? No—keep it cordial. Professional. Platonic. Cold. He didn't want the woman tangled in his own mess any more than necessary. He had known he could trust her to keep the knowledge of his trip from Dominic, even though he hadn't let her in on his deviance until now. Why hadn't Marvin just been up front with her previously? He could have—and he should have. Dammit, he was using her, and for the moment he hated himself.

Marvin shook off the feeling. He stepped to the foyer table under the mirror and paused to gaze at the beautifully wrapped gift. After fully appreciating the reflective paper and the effort behind it, he pulled the string on the perfectly tied white ribbon. The ribbon dropped away, and Marvin carefully tore the silvery blue from the thin white box. He set the box on the table and removed the lid. He pulled back the leaves of white tissue paper and revealed a jet black shimmery necktie, with waves of lime green and bold blue flowing through the length of the silk, like ebbs of water along a tropical river.

Marvin lifted the necktie from the box and held it up, examining it with both hands. His eyes became glistening discs. The tie was exquisite. His fingertips graced its surface. He held it to his neck and turned to the mirror. Briefly he imagined making the tie his new favorite. It certainly could have been. It would go well with many of his suits. But his smile dulled. He lowered the tie and leaned forward to the mirror. Staring into his cobalt eyes, his heart went cool. Something was missing.

23

SATELLITE RADIO

Marvin had stuffed his suitcase into the tiny container called the trunk in the back of the Jaguar. He was concerned about his suits getting crushed, but was left with little choice in the matter. He fretted there wasn't much room left to squeeze in Tony's luggage. The F–Type was a two-seater designed for beauty and speed, not comfort or practicality. But when Marvin arrived to pick up Tony from the Tindal's house, lack of trunk space was not an issue. Tony traveled light.

"All I need is a change of underwear," Tony joked.

Tony was treated to a series of oldies on a satellite station Marvin had programmed into the Jag's dash. As a fan of classic rock, Marvin attempted to instruct the young man on the qualities of Chuck Berry, Aerosmith, and Led Zeppelin. They were classics, Marvin insisted, deserving of recognition by all generations. Tony enjoyed the melodies and lyrics, though he promised to introduce Marvin to the music of his own generation, like Esta and Green Day. Marvin baulked at the proposition.

As Marvin and Tony debated the merits of melody versus message, an old spiritual by Elvis Presley caught their attention. It was a fun and peppy tune about the biblical prophet Joshua at the battle of Jericho. As the lyrics went, *Jericho, Jericho, Joshua fit the battle of Jericho, And the walls came tumblin' down*. The song referenced the story of how God had commanded Joshua to capture the city of Jericho as part of the Israelite's conquest of the Promised Land. It was a certain victory—since the conquerors had God on their side—so the towering stone walls that fortified Jericho came crashing down at the blowing of trumpets, allowing the Israelites easy entry into the city.

…*The trumpets began to sound, Old Joshua shouted glory, And the walls came tumblin' down.*

The topic shifted the pair into a theological discussion about the probabilities of Old Testament miracles like this having actually occurred. Tony had been taught the fundamental stories since his youth in Sunday School. As Marvin drove, Tony Googled the Jericho story on his phone, discovering that archaeological evidence had affirmed the discovery of ancient Jericho in Israel north of the Dead Sea, and that remains of substantial walls are still visible in the present.

"I'm not denying the existence of the city," said Marvin. "I just have a hard time accepting that high walls of stone six feet thick could just tumble down with a cry of glory."

"Oh this is dope," said Tony, referencing another online article. "It says one of the early cultures at Jericho used to plaster the skulls of their dead relatives and paint the features of their faces on the plaster."

"Oh I've done that," Marvin kidded.

"They kept the skulls in their houses!" said Tony through a fascinated smile.

"How do they really know that? These experts, they tell us so much about what they think they know about this stuff, but really, how accurate can they be?"

Tony scrolled further into the article. "So they think the walls were built in the fourth millennium B.C., and it was in 1400 B.C. that the battle of Jericho happened. It says the walls were destroyed when Joshua's army walked around the city seven times carrying the Ark of the Covenant. On the seventh day they blew rams horns and the walls fell down."

"So all it took was a bunch o' guys blowin' rams horns to make those walls crumble? You sure they didn't throw boulders at the walls, or hit 'em with somethin' hard like battering rams, or cannon balls?"

"They didn't have cannons then, Mister Fischer."

Marvin smiled.

Tony kept reading, "Excavations reveal that the most likely cause of the wall's collapse was an earthquake."

"So there's a natural explanation."

"Yeah but it was at the exact time that Joshua's army blew the rams horns and shouted," Tony defended, unfazed by Marvin's skepticism. "And I don't remember an earthquake in the Bible story. I don't think it was the trumpets that knocked the walls down anyway. It was God's power doing it, and he was just using the Israelite army for... well something. I don't know." Tony had talked himself into a corner.

"Well, what we know for sure is that the good guys won, right?" offered Marvin. "The walls came down, and it was a win."

"Yeah," Tony chuckled. "I still think God did it. Somehow."

They both concurred that there was something unique about Jericho. Marvin thanked Elvis for the discussion starter, then steered the Jaguar into long-term parking at Sky Harbor International.

24

THE SCOTTISH KAZAKH

After the Chicago connection, the Boeing 737 cruised high above the Atlantic Ocean bound for Edinburgh, the beige and blue cabin diffused in sunlight sneaking in around the drawn shades of passenger windows. Marvin was pleased with the wide and comfortable seats of first class, he by the aisle, Tony next to him by the window. After exploring the inflight radio stations, Tony began surfing television channels. Marvin refrained from insisting he collapse into his homework, as Tiffany had arranged with the school. He would get to that in due time. Right now he let the boy watch TV and enjoy his Mountain Dew.

Marvin had opted for a Sprite instead of coffee. He had surprised himself with the choice, but had felt dehydrated so chose something wet. He tilted the seat back, crossed his legs, and rested his head against the cushioned backrest. He forced himself to thoughts of Doctor Amina Karimova. While waiting in the airport lounge, he'd pulled up her bio again to educate himself.

Amina Karimova had been born and raised near the mountainous region of Tian Shan in southeast Kazakhstan. It was her proximity to the mountains that Karimova credited with instilling a sense of the divine within her since youth. She was an only child, fluent in Kazakh, Russian and English. She had experienced the dissolution of the Soviet Union in 1991, before moving with her parents closer to the capitol city of Astana. Anima had been raised Christian by her parents, and though she believed in God, maintained an open mind. Her parents took issue with Amina making friends with her Muslim and Russian Orthodox schoolmates. But Amina had been adept at finding common ground between herself and people of other faiths. By the time she graduated Primary School, Amina had taken an interest in esoteric religion, a topic she studied on her own before being accepted at Northwestern University in the United States, where she finished with honors. It was while in the US that Amina had taken up spiritualist mediumship, having started out doing sittings for friends before launching a service for paying clients. Over the years Amina had become a premier on the subject, highly sought after by celebrities and political figures who wished to remain anonymous. Doctor Karimova now held an international reputation as having an uncanny ability to communicate with the other side.

The other side. Whatever that really meant.

Doctor Amina Karimova had allowed her mediumship practice to diminish recently, so she could focus on the University's School of Divinity, where over the last five years she had become an accomplished professor for the Religious Studies program. She had been invited to teach courses in Christian history, ancient mythology, and East Asian traditions, which then expanded to include New Age. Marvin reflected that as a Christian in Kazakhstan, Amina had been in the minority, and now as a Kazakh in Scotland, she was again in the minority. Marvin guessed her to be a strong woman. He wondered if he would find Karimova firmly grounded in rational thought, with merely a great interest in religious subjects, or if she might be an eccentric. Marvin had chosen to accept her role in whatever personal story was unfolding in Marvin's own life. After all, Saint Peter was considered a pillar in the Church, and it was Peter that had connected Marvin with Tony, and now with Doctor Karimova.

Was it really Saint Peter that sent him those texts?

What if this was all just a hoax?

Marvin recalled his conversation with Tony on the drive to the airport, about the walls of Jericho crashing down after the beckoning of Joshua's army. Marvin had never been much interested in archaeology, let alone biblical history. But he had to conceive that the walls of Jericho must have been made of very heavy stone, and yet the city was famous for its tumbling walls. Marvin smiled. It sounded like a child's fairy tale. He felt his own doubt resurface. It was all ridiculously improbable. Yet a part of him wanted to believe it to be true. Marvin had to admit that he contradicted himself with his own reasoning. On the one hand, he questioned the veracity of the Jericho story, and yet here he sat, sipping a fizzy soft drink on a plane bound for Scotland, ready to lure some screwball shaman into communicating with a dead apostle, in the hopes of resurrecting a deceased woman. Marvin wondered if instead he ought to volunteer himself to the asylum to be locked away.

Everything that had challenged Marvin in the past few days gave him reasons to doubt. The death of Rubi Valdez after the prayer, the alleged visit from Saint Peter, the anonymous text images, the strange creature, the pursuit of a medium. But in Marvin's world of the analysis of competing hypotheses, he had to admit there was at least some chance that the collection of strange events may point to something bigger. The probabilities had to be explored. To fail in following up on the indicators would be akin to ignoring glaring pieces of intelligence that could link terrorist cells or members of an organized crime group.

Marvin had to follow this course, or these events would haunt him for the rest of his life.

~

Marvin finished the last of his Sprite. The attendant came by after a moment and collected his can, then Tony's. Service in first class was nice indeed. Marvin tilted his head and watched the images flash on the in-seat TV monitor that kept Tony glued. It seemed the boy had settled onto some program about outer space.

Marvin turned and looked at the seat in front of him and plunged into thoughts of Elizabeth Walsh. He still felt like an ass for leaving her in the dark. He had yet to thank her for the necktie. Perhaps it was because he wasn't sure just how to do it. And perhaps that was because he was now forced to confront the pestering fondness he felt towards the lady. A phone call would be too much, unless he shoehorned a *thank you* between business discussions. But he could think of no excuse to force a business call. If there was news on the Madaki case, she herself would call. And he was in the middle of a flight so the call would not go through anyway. But it would seem rude of him to ignore her friendly gesture.

Is that what it was? An innocent gift to replace the tie she had messed up?

No, Marvin was certain it went beyond that.

The special trip to his condo.

The makeup and smashing clothes.

What to do? What to say?

Marvin decided to compose a brief text. The message wouldn't go through until landing, but that was ok. He reached for his smartphone and launched the app. The screen yawned open with its blank box, waiting for words.

Marvin was stumped. He admitted again that this meant something to him, but he wasn't sure how he really felt about her. There was electricity, yes. But what was it? Just casual flirting?

He hated the ping-pong in his mind.

Finally he made a decision and typed.

Flight took off ok. Thanks for the tie. It's marvelous.

That should do it. Marvin tucked the phone away and suddenly realized how exhausted he was. It had been an early morning following a series of short nights. Marvin closed his eyes. Within two minutes came the tunnel of sleep.

Marvin's travel agent had booked him a Range Rover Sport for getting around Scotland. Upon arrival at the pickup counter, Marvin was told the vehicle was not available, but they could get him into a Bentley Continental GT for the same price. Marvin was delighted. He crossed the street with Tony to the rental lot where they found the brand new satin silver beauty. Tony didn't even know what a Bentley was, but once he plopped into the cozy leather seat and began playing with the hi-tech dash and interior mood lighting, he was in a video game. Marvin plopped their luggage into the boot, and the two travelers were on their way to the Balmoral within less than 30 minutes of landing on this April day in Scotland.

Marvin was impressed with the Bentley's smooth purr and silky steering. It would have been pleasurable to take the car soaring through the Scottish hillsides for a few minutes of high-speed enjoyment, but that could wait. First he wanted to beam to the Balmoral and get on to the University. Tony activated the dash GPS and assigned himself the duty of onboard navigator. Tony started them out on Glasgow Road, which became St. John's, then Western Terrace and A8, before confusion set in as they approached old town Edinburgh where the thick and tumbling gray clouds gave way to patchy beams of sunshine spilling into the streets. On the 26-minute drive they passed a modern shopping center, the Edinburgh Zoo, and the Consulate General of China.

Marvin suggested that Tony re-compute and take them down the Royal Mile. It was only slightly out of their way. Tony's attention was drawn to the towering architecture in shades of brown stone. It was beginning to look much different than his

Phoenix neighborhood and Tony was filled with a sense of dreamy agelessness, as if he had traveled through time, and then began to feel like he was in a Harry Potter movie. They drifted past the world famous Edinburgh Castle atop the rocky cliff, the shops and restaurants tucked into bulky stone and wood storefronts, followed by the towering spires of Saint Giles Cathedral with its medieval stonework and stained glass windows, then the strikingly modern Scottish Parliament building. Their sightseeing ended at the Queen's residence at the Palace of Holyroodhouse on Canongate Road. Tony had forgotten all about the navigator. Marvin took the roundabout to Calton Road past Waverly Station, to Princes Street and the extravagant Balmoral.

Marvin found a parking spot and popped the boot to retrieve their luggage. Tony opened the passenger door and stepped out, looking up at the grand building with its 200-foot Victorian clock tower. A kilted doorman greeted the pair at the main entrance and assisted them with their bags. They passed into the grandeuresque reception area, warmed by cream-colored walls and an elegant beamed ceiling. Floral accents on jet-black tables decorated a long, swathing rug of bold earth tones. Marvin passed beneath a twinkling chandelier and inquired of the concierge about getting his suits steamed, then texted Doctor Amina Karimova about meeting up at the University later that afternoon.

After gaining permission from Mister Fischer to bill the room for use of the hotel's glossy black antique rotary guest telephone in the lobby, Tony put in his first overseas call to the Tindals to inform them that he and Mister Fischer had arrived safely in Scotland, and would soon rendezvous with the infamous medium. Tiffany reminded Tony not to neglect the homework, but the clunky receiver had already cozied back to its cradle, and Tony dashed off to see the room with Mister Fischer.

25
SHARP AS A KNIFE

After a sweet snack of short bread and a refreshing nap, Marvin and Tony stepped out of the Balmoral, climbed into the Bentley, and drove seven blocks to the University. Marvin parked alongside a stand of trees on Mound Place, shut down the car, and ducked to get a better view out the driver window of the 400 year-old, grand-looking School of Divinity building. The place was immense and commanding.

"Here goes nothing," Marvin said as he swung the silver car door open. The breeze was chilly, so Marvin had donned his navy peacoat over his suit jacket, while Tony dressed in his best white shirt under a dark green wool sweater. They waited for a car to pass, crossed the street, and approached the building's front entrance.

Like two reserved Jedi knights, Marvin and Tony ascended the wide concrete stairway between the gray blocks of two rook towers, moved past a pair of iron sconces, and stopped at two large wooden doors framed by stone archways. It almost seemed the doors were awaiting some password. Marvin took a moment to absorb the atmosphere and ground himself.

"Are you nervous?" asked Tony.

"About goin' through the door?"

"About doing the séance."

"No. You?"

"Yeah."

"Yeah me too. Let's do this." Marvin put his hand on the cold black iron handle, pushed through the ancient door, and they were in.

Marvin glanced around to get bearings, referencing a map he and Tony had printed at the hotel's guest computer. The lobby was giant, the floor of black and white block tile, latte-painted walls with heavy dark wooden doors and trim. Crisscrossing timbers watched curiously from above.

Doctor Karimova had instructed Marvin to meet her by a blue desk at the top of a short flight of stairs at the far end of the library. They found the cavernous library without difficulty, but after several minutes there was no sign of Doctor Karimova. Marvin checked his phone. No message or incoming call. He checked his Rolex and fired off an inquisitive text.

The University ghosts laughed as Marvin and Tony wandered the elegant halls like two lost puppies, Marvin's fancy dress shoes clicking embarrassingly across the tile floor. He and the boy peeked into empty classrooms and saw only abandoned desks, dark wall monitors, and scribbled chalkboards. Marvin doubled-checked the map and then tossed it perturbedly, beginning to wonder if the mystic was even on campus.

It was the distinct sweetness in the air that gave Marvin his first clue that they were finally close.

"Mister Fischer... you smell that?" whispered Tony.

"Yeah... it's incense."

With Tony at his heels, Marvin stepped to a door and paused. He lifted a hand, pushed the door a few inches, stuck his head into the opening, and peered into the room with Tony.

Marvin felt an immediate and invisible draw to the large and rectangular room, the ceiling high and tall, everything dark except for soft daylight glowing from three windows high above. There were no large furnishings. The floor was solid wood.

Beside two amber crystalline lights on the far side of the room, Marvin could see the telltale wisps of incense smoke rising from two sticks. Directly between the two amber crystalline lights sat a woman dressed in a long-sleeved, dark bodysuit, her erect back facing the door. The woman sat on the floor completely still with legs crossed like a Tibetan monk, elbows gently out to the side with hands resting on each knee, the hair tied up in a bun. The head faced sturdily forward.

Marvin watched with Tony, frozen in the doorway, eyes wide and unblinking.

The place was like a vacuum, not a sound to be heard from anywhere.

Then the woman turned her head slightly in the direction of the door.

Marvin backed away with Tony.

"Wait," the woman called, the voice echoing strong in the void.

After some hesitation the two adventurers peeked back into the sanctuary.

The woman bowed her head at something unseen, then stood up. She lifted her hands stylishly skyward and stood on her toes, held the position for four seconds, then lowered and twisted side to side.

From a small table nearby, the woman plucked a small rod with a cup on the end, stepped to one of the incense sticks, and extinguished it. She moved across to the other stick and doused that one. The woman set the tool back on the little table, stepped to the wall, and clicked a switch. A single chandelier in the center of the ceiling bloomed to life, filling the room with warm yellow.

The woman swanned gracefully across the space toward her visitors. "Please come in," she said. Tony followed Marvin three steps into the room. As the woman came closer, Marvin could see that her hair was light brown. The athletic feet were bare. The singular black sheath of clothing clung to her figure like a diving suit. The shoulders were round and strong, arms and legs very thin, the hips narrow and bony. She was much shorter than Marvin's six-foot frame. There was something appealingly animalistic about her presence. Despite her petite size Marvin sensed the strength and stealth of a leopard. Cautious, Marvin tried to read the woman's sharp, piercing hazel eyes, which he swore glinted with flecks of gold. Her facial structure appeared Asian, but her skin was creamy white, the lips full and natural. On her lobes dangled large gold hoop earrings that reminisced of wings on an Egyptian goddess.

"Welcome. I am very pleased to meet you," the woman said. "I am Doctor Amina Karimova. You must be Marvin Fisher." The accent was Asian, with some British influence. She extended a hand in welcome. Marvin reached out and grasped it. Her grip was cool, dry, and strong. "And you," said Doctor Karimova, looking at Tony, "must be Antonio Valdez." She took the boy's hand. Her speech was crystal clear, sharp as a knife.

"Yes Doctor Karimova," said Tony, shaking her hand with respectful awe.

"I am truly sorry for your loss."

"Thank you, Doctor Karimova."

"Please, call me Amina. Let us dismiss formality."

"Okay. Then you can call me Tony."

"Ah! But why not the more grand *Antonio*? Did you know, that in the ancient Greek, the name Antonio means *priceless one*?"

Tony's eyes beamed. "Priceless?"

"Oh yes. A most fitting title for you, I am sure."

"Wow..." Tony smiled and looked at Marvin.

Impressed, Marvin said, "Hey thanks for takin' the time to see us. I know you're busy."

"What does your name mean?" Tony asked Amina, still fascinated with the discussion.

Amina placed her palms together in front of her. "Amina is of Arabic origin. To most, it means *trustworthy*. Some consider it also an allusion to the *Amen*, as spoken at the conclusion of a prayer. *Let it be so.*"

It was immediately clear to Marvin that the boy had been sucked in. Admittedly, there was something intensely mesmerizing about the woman.

"How about his name? Marvin?" Tony pointed.

"It's okay—" Marvin held up a hand.

Tony grimaced while Amina chuckled. "May I call you Marvin? I recognize you have traveled a great distance to see me. I do apologize for overlooking the time. I was in deep conversation with Shada."

Marvin blinked. Tony stared around the room. There was no one else there.

26

SPIRIT GUIDE

"Shada is my spirit guide," Amina explained. "It is important I maintain close contact with her, especially given the challenge the two of you ask of me."

"Okay…" said Marvin.

"Have you ever seen her?" asked Tony.

"Shada? No, I have never seen her," said Amina casually. "I befriended her while in meditation. She was once a powerful Navajo Indian. A warrior."

"What does *Shada* mean?" the boy asked.

"The name *Shada* is of Native American origin. It means *pelican*."

"Like the bird?"

Marvin felt his insides cringe and his teeth clench.

"Does Shada travel to you?" asked Tony. "From other worlds?"

Amina put her hands flat on her narrow hips and smiled with pleasure. "You are a curious young man, are you not? I like that! And very smart."

Marvin squinted at Tony and could almost see the wave of glittery warmth passing through the boy's body as he smiled awkwardly, probably embarrassed by the unexpected compliment from the lady.

Marvin cleared his throat.

"I digress," Amina winked at Marvin. "Shada is my best friend on the other side. She is my gatekeeper."

"Gatekeeper?" asked Tony.

"Shada is like my spiritual agent. When I want to talk to someone from the other side, Shada helps me find them."

"How does she tell you? How does she find them?"

"It is a tricky thing, Antonio. I believe Shada has lived several lives on earth through reincarnation, and has learned some valuable earthly lessons. That is why she can help me. Her last physical life on this earth was as a Navajo Indian. She was deeply devoted to the Great Spirit and remains so. She is very close to the Great Spirit. A good spirit."

"Is the Great Spirit God?"

"You are asking me some very difficult questions, young man."

"I just want to find my mother."

"Yes, I know." Amina put an arm across her waist and a hand thoughtfully to her face. "I ask Shada for guidance. I have sensed that her job has become more difficult recently."

Marvin watched Amina's eyes carefully and sensed something behind them that he could not place. He wanted to trust this woman. But it was all sounding weird and impossible, and he wondered again about the feasibility of it all.

Amina shifted her position and put her hands together decidedly. "But we will get into all that later. Did you have a good flight? Get into town okay?"

"Yes we did, thank you," said Marvin absently.

"We rented a Bentley," said Tony.

"Very nice," Amina smiled. "I am glad you are pleased. I want us to get off on the right foot. I do apologize for my appearance, I had intended on changing before your arrival."

"That's okay," said Marvin. "We're lookin' forward to your expertise."

"Ah! There's that dirty little word, *expert*," Amina said, straight faced. She took a step toward a flowery purple satin robe hanging on the wall nearby. She removed the robe from its hook and slipped into the shimmery garment as she continued, "I dismiss my expert status. I am not a fan of the word, really, or of the concept. The term *expert* denotes a certain finality that denies further learning. As if one has reached the pinnacle of achievement in a given discipline. The study of religion contains too many unknowns for anyone to consider oneself an expert. My opinion." She finished tying the satin belt around her waist. "Nobody really knows anything. I rather consider myself an explorer."

Marvin wasn't quite sure how to handle the unexpected take at humility. "Well, I'm sure you're very good at what you do," he offered. "Many people think so."

"Thank you," said Amina. She slipped her bare feet into two black flats by the door. "I suggest we continue in the morning."

"Tomorrow?" Marvin looked at Tony in surprise.

"Yes," answered Amina. "You have been traveling. Take the remainder of today to settle in, get some rest. We can start the day bright and early when we are all fresh. I have had a bit of a busy day myself."

"I thought we were gonna do the séance? Contact Saint Peter?" Marvin quizzed.

"Mister Fischer—I told you I would talk to you. I did not yet promise the séance."

"You mean we're not gonna do the séance here?"

"Heavens no. This is not the place," said Amina, grabbing a tiny black purse and a bag from a narrow shelf. She paused and looked directly at Marvin to make her point.

"And we are not ready," she said.

Marvin glanced uneasily. "Okay. Yeah we can meet tomorrow. Whatever works."

"Splendid," Amina smiled, the hazel eyes glistening. "We will discuss our goals, and the results of our conversation will determine whether or not I choose to accept the challenge."

"Fair enough," said Marvin tentatively.

"You are staying at the Balmoral? Let us agree to meet at the hotel for a light breakfast at the Palm Court where we can get further acquainted. They serve absolutely delicious Viennoiseries. Fine tea. The best of coffees."

Marvin's face brightened at the mention of fine coffee. "Alright, sure."

"What are Vienneis…?" asked Tony.

"Viennoiseries are a flaky puff pastry. Originating from Austria and later becoming popular in France. Rich and sweet. You will love them!"

"Straight fire!"

"Okay then," said Amina, ushering the two to the door. And for a moment Marvin felt she might be checking him out. "I will get on with some further preparations. See you both tomorrow morning at the Palm Court. Seven o'clock."

Marvin nodded. "I better make a reservation."

Amina denied the necessity of a reservation on a weekday and much to Tony's amusement, the adults squabbled about it as they stepped into the hallway.

"See you tomorrow. I shall not overlook the time again," Amina promised. She pulled the door closed, locked it with a key, and dropped the key into the tiny black purse and smiled at the two. "The adventure begins." She turned and walked off. Her flat shoes made no sound on the black and white tile floor as she floated away.

Marvin and Tony remained standing alone in the hall, watching Amina disappear around the corner like a ghost. Marvin put his hands on his hips and looked at Tony. "What do you think?" asked Marvin.

"I think she's pretty."

Amina's nerves sizzled as she rounded the corner into the next hall, the prospective challenge charging her with a moment of excitement and not a small amount of fear. Contacting Saint Peter would be a grand experience; the pinnacle of achievement in her already successful career.

But she was afraid. Deeply and gravely afraid.

This worry she wanted to keep hidden, especially from the man. Her fingers rubbed harshly together. She shook her hands vigorously to stop herself from the habit. Her stomach prickled again. She remembered the awful night of eighteen months ago, when she had sat on the sand near the Pillar of Vasco da Gama at the Indian Ocean, along the shores of the popular tourist town of Malindi, performing a midnight séance for a prestigious African townsman who had summoned Amina Karimova from her Scottish abode to call out to his dead wife of six months. The wife had been deeply religious, a devout follower of Jesus Christ. The man's sister and the brother of the man's wife had also been in attendance. Something about the man had left Amina unsettled, but she had proceeded with the séance anyhow. Amina knew at once, when she couldn't sense Shada, that she should abandon the ritual. But the African townsman had paid her bountifully, and had insisted on continuing. Then Amina remembered feeling the air fall around her, the sudden change in atmospheric energy. And that was when the wind had hit. Hard and cold and roiling off the surface of the sea. An unexpected and vicious monsoon had crashed onto the shore and sent Amina and her clients tumbling across the sand and into the rocks.

And Amina had sworn that she had heard through the raspy sand in her ears, the whisper of an ominous voice saying three times, "*Erzok... Erzok... Erzok.*"

That was the last time Amina had attempted a séance.

The experience had so terrified her that she had chosen to abandon the practice, and it was then that she knew something had gone terribly wrong on the other side. Things had shifted. Darkness was overtaking the After Worlds, she was certain of it. It had taken three more weeks after the event in Malindi before Amina finally sensed once again her friend Shada, who had still seemed distant and unclear. Keeping the experience to herself, Amina had quietly retired from the business of performing sittings, and resolved into the more comfortable routine of teaching full time at the university.

And yet here she was, about to do it again. Was she crazy? Did she dare? Why return to it? Why now? She felt somehow called. Perhaps she felt she must achieve this for her own satisfaction? Was it to overcome her fear? Was it the hope that she would once again sense the Light? Yes, it was some of that.

And the boy needed his mother back! She must help him!

Amina stopped walking. She stood alone in the center of the hall in bewilderment. She had been paying no attention to her path and now found herself at the opposite end of the university.

Marvin could not appreciate his deluxe hotel room with its splashy mauve carpet, cozy lighting, tartan drapery and satin pillows. He was too busy huffing over what he took as a dismissal from Amina Karimova. He stood firm and stiff and tense in front of the giant window, looking out through the glass at the stone building across the street from the Balmoral. With his forehead in a wrinkle, Marvin stared out with hands together in front of him, literally twiddling his thumbs. He took a deep breath, continuing to glare at the building across the street as if it held some comfort or answer.

She wasn't an expert?

Marvin turned abruptly to look over his shoulder at Tony, who sat in a giant lush chair across the room, arms on the rests and legs crossed. Tony snapped his eyes to Marvin, with much less concern than the adult by the window.

Tony said, "That short bread was stupid good. Wanna get some more?"

Envious of the boy's patience, Marvin creased his brow and turned back to the window.

27

VIENNOISERIES

At 6:35 the next morning, while Tony brushed his teeth and dressed in the bathroom, Marvin Fischer, wearing his favorite medium-gray windowpane Hugo Boss, opened a dresser drawer in his room at the Balmoral. From beside his carefully rolled socks, he withdrew a small gift box. He opened it, revealing a new black tie with fiery lime green and blue swishes—the brilliant gift from Elizabeth Walsh. It shimmered clear even in the filtered light blooming from the window. But Marvin did not remove the tie from the box.

Making up his mind, he set the box back in the drawer. He reached instead for another box—of wood, finely decorated in gold and scarlet decoupage—and opened it. From this he withdrew the jazzy navy-white tie—the old tie from Caroline—that Elizabeth had destroyed with a splash of violent coffee. He had salvaged the old tie from the waste can in his office. Marvin had tried again to clean the tie, but it still bore the conspicuous stain, an oblong circle with spatters of brown, like drips of chocolate ice cream slopped on pavement in hot summer. No matter. Decidedly, Marvin stood in front of the mirror, hurled the stained tie around his neck, and knotted it expertly. Even so, he thought himself something of an idiot. Wearing it went against all his style sense. But he stood straight, facing himself and nodding with confidence that yes, he would wear the old tie from Caroline, stain and all. It wasn't that bad. No one would notice.

Forty minutes later, beneath the bulbous blue clouds of the Edinburgh morning, Marvin stepped out onto the sidewalk and looked up and down Princes Street. He checked his Rolex. A quarter past seven. Where was the woman? Approaching now from behind a rattling tour bus came a long saloon taxi, its doors beckoning guests to visit the glass houses downtown at Royal Botanic Gardens. The saloon steered close and pulled to the curb. When the door swung open and a periwinkle leg stepped out onto the sidewalk, Marvin's frustration briefly atomized.

As Amina Karimova paid the fair and thanked the driver, Marvin quietly absorbed her. The periwinkle slacks flowed below an avocado coat and met with low heels. The curled brown hair formed a posh loose bouffant. The saloon zoomed off.

"Good morning, Marvin!" The makeup was light and classy. There was an invisible cloud of fine perfume. "A bit chilly is it not? I trust you slept well?" Her ears were adorned with the same large golden hoops of the previous day, teasing the gold out of her eyes.

Marvin could not help but appreciate the attractive package in front of him, the perfectly thought-out combination of style and color. Did she always look this fine, or was this extra effort to make up for the bungled meeting yesterday? "We almost ate without you," he said.

"So early in the day and you are already frustrated," said Amina. She looked him up and down, then patted his chest, at the stain on the necktie. "I see. It seems we have had a little accident this morning. It is okay Marvin, it is only a necktie. We have more urgent matters to concern ourselves with." She pushed past him. Marvin grimaced and followed.

The Palm Court was nearly empty, proving Marvin's reservation unnecessary. The translucent dome above glimmered with soft daylight. Marvin and Amina were escorted by an attractive and finely dressed host, past the latte-colored columns to a table covered in white cloth, and fine leather armchairs the color of fresh peas. Tony was already seated, looking at the menu, in his best jeans and favorite tan denim jacket, binoculars around his neck. The adults plunked into the luxurious seats beside walls of hand-painted scenes of Scotland's opulent landscapes. Exchanging places with the host, the waiter arrived, collected beverage orders from the trio, and floated away.

Amina picked up the menu and tilted her eyes to Tony. "Your binoculars are a constant companion, Antonio."

The boy's eyes twinkled. "I can get closer to things I want to see better, and check out the sky. It would be dope if I could have brought my telescope."

"Ah!" said Amina. "A student of astronomy."

"I think there's life on other planets," said Tony firmly. "And maybe when we die, our souls join that life on the other planets—planets we haven't even discovered yet—and we get to live with them, on those beautiful perfect planets, like the earth was when God first made it. I know my mom is out there."

Tony continued, "Maybe heaven is on another planet, or even on lots of planets, way beyond what we can see with telescopes like the Hubble, and way beyond what we can find with space probes, like Voyager. It's still floating out there, you know? Like 13 billion miles away. Maybe eventually it will find the heaven planets."

"The heaven planets. An interesting theory, Antonio. Perhaps it is one of those planets that has been referred to as the third heaven."

"Third heaven?" asked Marvin.

Amina set down the menu. "I believe there exist various levels of heaven—planes of existence, if you will. Since it is Saint Peter that we are concerned with, a biblical character, I am approaching our challenge from the perspective of the Christian teachings. The basis for the Christian faith is a series of recorded stories and events, which took place over a 2,600-year period and culminated in a book, which we call the Holy Bible. Agreed?"

"Yes," Marvin scratched his nose.

Amina continued, "The Christian scriptures speak of a man being caught up to the *third heaven*, where he was told secrets, 'what no mortal is permitted to speak'. This man eventually returned to earth in the body, though we do not know the identity of this man. But I digress. The point is that, the Bible's reference to the third heaven provides a great clue into the structure of the afterlife. Based on the testimony from Antonio's mother, we believe Saint Peter recently visited this plane to some degree. It is possible the saint may still be close by. But if the saint has already returned to the third heaven, it may be extremely difficult to contact him."

"Caught up to the third heaven." Marvin gestured. "So what's the third heaven?"

"That is a matter of great debate," admitted Amina.

The beverages came. Marvin savored his first sip of the peppery *Café Touba* while Amina was served a woody oolong tea, and Tony a tall glass of orange juice. Tony took a draw and licked his lips. "Some people think that the sky we can see from the ground, from the earth—including clouds and storms—are *heavens*," said Tony. "And then after we leave the earth's atmosphere, about 300 miles up, it's space, and we can see a lot more clearly because there's no atmospheric haze. Some people think that space is like heaven, but a different part of heaven. Like another level."

"Antonio you are absolutely right," said Amina. "What you refer to is a common religious take on ancient cosmology. It is a common Christian view, as well as the view of the Holy Koran and some Jewish Merkavah texts, implying the existence of various heavenly levels. As you pointed out Antonio, the sky that we see with our naked eye is commonly deemed the first heaven. Space—as well as outer space and the expansive universe—is the second heaven. Beyond that—far beyond anywhere that even the Voyager has traveled, beyond the edge of the universe—is the *third heaven*."

Hearing Amina Karimova talk sounded to Marvin like listening to a live textbook reading, and Marvin had to remind himself that he was engaging with a professor of religion at one of the most prestigious universities on the planet. She probably always talked this way. At least she was informed. "So," Marvin pondered, "this guy that the Bible says was caught up to the third heaven, you think he was taken somewhere beyond the measurable universe."

"Most certainly," said Amina.

"And is that heaven? THE heaven, where God is?"

"And where my mom's soul is?" asked Tony.

"Perhaps, unless she has not yet arrived there," said Amina.

The pastries arrived on white dishes of the finest china. Marvin thanked the server, who bowed graciously and dismissed himself. Soon the trio was enjoying the finest Viennoiseries they had ever tasted. Marvin and Amina had chosen the plain glazed, and Tony the cinnamon. The boy went all in, coating his pastry with a generous swath of butter and sticky strawberry jam.

"So wait a minute," Marvin dabbed his lip with the cloth napkin. "So what about that? You think Tony's mother might not have arrived to heaven yet?"

"Where is she?" asked Tony. "Can Saint Peter still bring her back?"

"That is difficult to ascertain," said Amina, setting down her tea mug. "Spiritual interference may be a factor. But we will get to that. Perhaps Tony's mother is in a holding place for the soul. In Dante's classic work *The Divine Comedy*, he describes his journey into hell, and then into purgatory, and finally into heaven. Dante describes purgatory as one of three levels of spiritual existence, a place to make amends for past sins, before the soul can be released to God, to paradise, to the third heaven."

"But it's not Rubi we're tryin' to contact, it's Saint Peter," said Marvin.

"Correct," said Amina. "But Rubi's whereabouts may have bearing on whether the miracle of bringing her back is feasible. The Bible describes another reference to the underworld—Sheol—a resting place for souls. And there are other possibilities we must consider. Some belief systems describe what is called the astral plane, a field of energy that may be populated with immaterial beings. Is the astral plane a place for the dwelling of conscience? For the soul? Hinduism and Buddhism use terms like Bardo and Samsara as references to a *between state*, a realm where spirits sojourn between destinations. The texts of the Abrahamic religions describe from three to seven layers of heaven. The Indic religions describe anywhere from zero to six. Mesoamerican cults have as many as thirteen levels. There are so many names for heaven. Nirvana. Elysium. Topan. Paradise. Olympus. Are these all just different names for the same place?"

Amina bit her pastry and licked the sugar from her lip. "What I am saying is that for as many religious texts that we have, collected over centuries from all parts of the world, in many languages and from many different points of view, and taking into account all of the death-and-return experiences, nobody really knows anything for certain about what is on the other side. After millennia of study and contemplation, it still remains a mystery."

Marvin stuffed the last bite of pastry into his mouth. He shook his head and rubbed his fingers on the napkin. The concepts seemed impossible to comprehend, and he hated the uncertainty of it all. It was sounding an awful lot like Pastor Deckland's speech about the mysteries of prayer. "So what can we be sure of?"

"You can only be sure of what you believe," answered Amina. "Whether it is the truth or not, you will not know until you die."

The ominous statement weighed heavily over the table as the group finished up the last of their decadent treats. For a moment,

Marvin dismissed the weight of the conversation and found himself silently admiring the way the locks of Amina's luminous brown hair tumbled gently near her golden hoops. Marvin asked, "And what do you believe, Doctor Karimova?"

Amina looked at Marvin in a way that he found curiously prophetic. She set down her napkin and folded her hands softly on the table. "I believe in a great realm of possibility."

28

PENELOPE'S

The navy peacoat with black leather gloves gave Marvin a rather Bondian look as he motored through Edinburgh in the Bentley. Amina sat shotgun. Tony rode in back, leaning eagerly between the headrests so as not to miss the conversation. After breakfast, Marvin had hoped to move on to a location where the séance would be performed, but Amina had insisted on making "a little stop." Passing Calton Hill and its unfinished monument, the conversation about heavenly levels was migrating into specifics of the other side.

"Any details of what exactly it's like on *the other side?*" Marvin asked as he veered left.

"Marvin you are going left. I said stay right."

"You said go left."

"She said stay right."

"Dammit."

"Take this to the next roundabout. Then right on London." Marvin growled.

"The other side, yes, what is it?" said Amina. "There are various claims from many people who have had death experiences and returned with descriptions of what they saw. These individuals claim to have died, and while they were dead and crossing to the other side, they saw light, they saw a tunnel. They saw deceased members of their family awaiting them. But that is really it —Turn right here. Then look for Annandale."

Marvin veered through the roundabout and straightened onto London.

"I heard someone on a TV interview once," said Tony. "She said she saw grass and trees before she woke back up in the operating room."

"There are many such stories," affirmed Amina. "Most accounts seem to agree that there is the experience of bliss and relief on the other side. Exactly what the other side is—and where it is—nobody really knows. Concepts of the afterlife vary greatly across time and religion. There are many commonalities, but no single, central point of agreement."

"There's Annandale!" Tony pointed.

"Yes make a right here Marvin. It will take you back to Elm Row and you will have to jog across to Montgomery. Then look for Penelope's, the black and red storefront. On the left."

The Bentley howled as Marvin gunned it across to Montgomery.

"The best we can say is that most religions acknowledge the reality of physical death," Amina continued. "Even the idea of a passage to the afterlife is not shared across every belief system. What the afterlife looks like is anyone's guess. We have only a few clues to go by."

"There it is!" Tony pointed.

"I see it," grumbled Marvin.

"You can park at curbside. There's a spot."

~

The tinkling glass bell upon opening the door signaled entry into a place of enchantment. Following Tony and Amina into the little shop, Marvin was smacked with the jumbled scents of sage, thyme, and rosemary. There was not a wasted spot in the place. Nooks and shelves were occupied with all things metaphysical. Candles. Herbs and teas. Oracle decks. Celtic figurines. Jewelry. Little glass jars of who-knew-what. There were books, vessels of iron and clay, wood boxes of polished stones, crystals, and shimmery metals. From somewhere above came the moody notes of a Gaelic psalm.

"What we have to go on gentlemen, is recorded history, coupled with current study," said Amina as she floated past the healing rocks display toward the back of the shop. "By recorded history I am talking about written records that have been corroborated by discovered fact. By current study, I am talking about new knowledge that is being gained in the present, which adds to what has already been recorded. Current study, like recorded history, must also be corroborated to be valid." She paused by a wall of candles. She first selected a click lighter, then three white pillar candles of medium size. "And when it comes to religion, we have few facts to go on, because so much of the evidence we seek exists in other realms, which we have yet to travel to. This makes it very difficult to offer proofs. So you see, much of what we believe about the afterlife is based on theory."

They passed a shelf of essential oils. Tony snatched one, opened it, and sniffed.

"Put it back," said Marvin.

Emerging now from a door jam of hanging beads hobbled a medium-sized round woman with skin pale as an oyster. Dressed in all black, the round woman with her spiked hair and lances of piercings reminded Marvin of a sea urchin. At the sight of Amina, the round woman beamed a welcoming smile. "Miss Amina! How are you my lovely?"

"Penny! So good to see you!" Amina handed the three white candles off to Marvin. Frowning, Marvin cradled them in his forearms like firewood, and watched the two women embrace like long lost friends. "I've missed you," Amina smiled. She introduced the woman as Penelope, the shop's proprietor.

"A pleasure, gentlemen," said Penelope.

"Hello."

"Does all this stuff in here have mystical powers?" asked Tony.

"Well," said Penelope with some glee, slanting an eye toward Amina. "In the possession of the gifted and trained, they can be useful tools." Penelope raised an eyebrow to Amina. "Are you…?"

"We shall see," answered Amina noncommittally. "Have you moved the salts?"

"Yes my lovely," Penelope pointed. "By the herb rack."

The urchin moved to answer a ringing telephone. Marvin and Tony followed Amina to the wall of small glass jars of varying colors. "Antonio, choose one of your favorite color." Tony reached for an orange vessel with enthusiasm. "Marvin?"

"Blue," he sighed. Amina selected blue and plopped the jar into Marvin's arms with the candles. Crossing the shop, she came to a display of incense sticks. Marvin and Tony followed like ducklings.

"Do I get to pick one?" asked Tony.

"Not this time. We shall all go with Frankincense." Amina plucked several sticks and a couple of holders.

"What's all this shit for?"

"Don't ask questions Marvin. Just go with me."

The Bentley blew past the Bellfield Brewery and a string of apartment buildings. After leaving Penelope's, Amina had instructed Marvin in the direction of Holyrood Park and Arthur's Seat, for another "little stop". From the A1 the car motored along and swerved a hard right onto Queen's Drive. Amina had apparently become more curious about Marvin's spiritual center, and had deftly cornered him into a situation that demanded explanation.

"I rely on common sense and guesswork," said Marvin, holding the leather steering wheel at 10 and 2. "I'm good at gathering facts, analyzing facts, coming to some sort of projection. The world of intelligence, as you may know, is all about knowns and unknowns. I take what I know, compare it against what I've learned, form competing hypotheses relating to a current predicament. I weigh each hypothesis against the indicators, present several possible outcomes."

"That all sounds quite logical," said Amina. "How about in here?" She tapped her chest. "What is in your heart, Marvin?"

Marvin didn't glance at her.

"He used to be married," Tony blurted. Marvin gave him a look in the rearview mirror.

"May I ask what happened?" asked Amina.

"She died."

"She was religious like my mom," said Tony. "Her name was Caroline. She got him to go to church."

"Tony—zip it."

"So you are familiar with the spiritual realms, with a higher power," said Amina. "God, Jesus, stories in the Bible."

"The walls tumbling down at Jericho," said Tony.

"Yeah but…"

"But what?" asked Amina.

"What does this have to do with contacting Saint Peter?"

"I am intelligence gathering," said Amina. "You can relate, can you not? I have some specific thoughts about the creature you said you saw…"

"You know what the creature was?!" asked Tony with excitement.

"… and about Saint Peter's visit to Antonio's mother." Amina continued. "Do not make it difficult for me, Mister Fischer. I am still undecided about the venture."

"Then why'd I buy all that stuff?" Marvin parked the Bentley with his two passengers along Queen's Drive. He shut the car down and peeked out the windshield at the side of the 800-foot hill. "We have to go up there? This is an expensive suit," he said. "We gonna do the séance here?"

"Antonio, please wait for us at the start of the path. We will be along shortly."

"Okay." Tony exited the car and shut the door. Marvin wrinkled his lips and watched the boy walk toward the hill. He felt Amina's stare and turned to her. "What?"

"From Antonio, I have not seen looks of doubt or skepticism. I see acceptance and eagerness, the vigor to explore. In you, I sense deep reservation."

Marvin sucked in a breath.

Amina tilted her head. "We must—all three of us—be in concert, sharing the same energy, the same mindset. Are you willing to set aside whatever inhibitions you may have so that we may proceed?"

"I'm doin' my best," Marvin defended. "This is new to me."

"Understandable," said Amina. "But spirits can sense doubt, and they may be less likely to correspond if they do. Have you prayed about this?"

Marvin could not help a sudden chuckle. He shook his head.

Amina frowned. "What is funny?"

"Prayer hasn't exactly worked out for me."

"But your wife prayed."

"How'd you know that?"

Amina studied Marvin attentively. "Antonio said Caroline was religious. That implies a belief in a higher power. I presume she prayed. But you stopped. Something happened. There is bitterness in you."

Now it was getting too personal. Marvin felt suddenly invaded. He was impressed as well as baffled at how well the woman could read him. How quickly she drilled down to the core of things. Of course he had doubts about what he believed.

"You traveled all the way from the United States with the boy to see me," said Amina. "You must believe something. Have faith in something, in the afterlife, that this will all turn out for the good."

There it was again, that statement—*all things work out for good.* Marvin sat stone still, staring blankly at his hands resting on the black leather of the steering wheel that had become his comfort zone. He had thought much about Rubi Valdez in these last days. But it was the whereabouts of his own wife Caroline that he suddenly realized he had not thought about in a long time. Finally Marvin took his hands off the wheel and turned to her. "I do believe in God. Of course I do. I believe there is a higher power. I believe in Jesus. I wouldn't be here right now if I didn't."

Amina smiled. "Very good. You must believe in a power greater than yourself, before you can believe in yourself. Trust in the higher power, and in yourself. Believe, and pray."

"Right…" said Marvin vaguely. He looked again out the window. Tony was tossing pebbles into the sky. "So—Is this where we're gonna do the séance?"

Amina opened the car door and began to remove herself. "Don't ask questions Marvin. Just experience."

29
THE CHAPEL

Arthur's Seat was so named because some thought that this very hill atop the 600-acre park might have once been the site of Camelot from the Arthur Legend. No such proof existed, but the name took, giving rise to many a conversation among tourists of whether or not King Arthur himself had actually existed, and if so, where. Almost certainly not here, but it remained an engaging and entertaining topic. The hill was a popular escape for both locals and tourists, not far from the Queen's Palace. A number of winding trails led up the sides of the hill, some of them steep and craggy.

The trio ascended the grassy knoll along the trail from north to south. The clouds had begun to break, proving the sky blue, but the wind had begun to nip.

Amina turned up the collar of her avocado coat. "I brought you here because it is the highest point in Edinburgh, almost a thousand feet above sea level. Here you can see far and wide, and get a sense of watching what goes on below. The higher up one climbs, the less one feels part of the earth, and more a part of the heavens."

They passed a swath of rugged dolerite rock jutting from the grasses. Amina walked the center of the wide path, flanked by Marvin and Tony. The boy asked, "Amina, instead of trying to contact Saint Peter, why don't we just talk to my mom? Maybe she can tell us where she is, and how we can find her?"

"A good question, Antonio," answered Amina. "Most mediums agree that it is best to wait awhile—weeks or months in fact—before attempting to contact a departed soul. The reasoning is that the soul is still new to the other side; that it may be best to let them acclimate before attempting to reach them from their former home. Think of it like moving from one city to another—except for your mother, this is more like moving to a foreign country. Perhaps your mother has already met with some loved ones who have previously made the journey to the other side, and who are giving her the grand tour, so to speak. It is like she has moved not just into a new house or a new city, but to a whole new way of being."

"But if she's coming back here, why would any of that matter? What if she wants to come back and just can't find a way?"

"I can understand why that makes sense to you, Antonio, but I do not feel that to be the proper course. I believe it is best to start with what we know, and that is with Saint Peter. He is our first point of contact, a much more experienced spiritual traveler."

The group was getting higher up. It was a prime vantage point. Marvin turned for a view of the city below, then glanced to the east across the arm of the North Sea. Tony pitched his binoculars west toward Edinburgh Castle, perched a mile away on the cliff beyond the city. "That is dope."

Continuing up, the group veered left. "What's that?" asked Marvin.

"The chapel," said Amina. "Let us settle there. It will provide shelter from the wind."

Standing sentry on a grassy outcrop overlooking St. Margaret's Lock, the "chapel" looked more like the skeletal ruins of a medieval castle than a religious structure. All that remained was a rugged wall of stone, some 30 feet tall, with a single opening—presumably the door—and two openings further up that must have been windows. Tony scrambled through the "door", looking up at the wall and scanning the distant lock below with his twin specs. Amina sunk to the grass, crossing her periwinkle legs. Marvin stood silent as Tony finished rounding the wall, completing his makeshift inspection. "Did they have church services here?" he asked.

"Not much is known of the chapel, but I would think certainly, yes."

Tony ambled beside Amina and plunked down, following her example by crossing his legs. Marvin frowned, inspecting the grasses.

"We really do need to select you some clothing more appropriate to our adventures." said Amina. "Did you bring any sportswear?"

Marvin bent to flick away a dried leaf from the grass, then sat down to complete the triangle. He crossed his legs obediently and set his hands on his lap.

"Very good, Marvin."

"You know what that creature was?" asked Tony.

"I have some ideas," said Amina. The breeze swooshed her brown bangs against her cheek. "When we first spoke by telephone, Marvin, you mentioned that you experienced some sort of shift in energy right before the car accident that killed Rubi Valdez."

"Right."

"And you and Antonio both assert that you saw some sort of creature right before the accident. Something neither of you could identify."

"Right," Tony affirmed.

"So let us talk about that," said Amina. "Let us talk about the creature. From what you described to me Marvin, it sounds like a version of a famous deity of Mesoamerican origin. As far as I can ascertain, the creature may have been *Quetzalcoatl*."

"Kwet—a what?" asked Marvin about the jawbreaker.

"Quetzalcoatl. Like this Marvin: 'Kwet'—say it with me."

"Kwet—"

"Kwetsal—"

"It's Kwetsal Coat-ahl," said Tony perfectly.

"That is right, you see, Antonio's got it. Try again, Marvin."

"Kwetsal Coat-ahl."

"You have got it, Marvin. Quetzalcoatl is a fascinating creature from the myths of ancient Mexico and Central America. A mythic deity that may have originated with the Olmec thousands of years ago, and was later embraced by other cultures like the Toltecs and the Aztecs. Quetzalcoatl appears in many of the drawings and paintings in ancient Mesoamerican codices. His likeness in stone statues adorns some of the ancient temples even today in Central America."

"What does his name mean?" asked Tony. "Quetzalcoatl?"

Amina smiled. "A *quetzal* is a beautiful bird with bright and colorful plumage, and a *coatl* is a snake. In mythic and spiritual terms, Quetzalcoatl was thought to be a snake-like creature with obsidian eyes, large teeth, and bright colored feathers growing from behind its head. From your description, Marvin, it is hard to imagine you saw anything but Quetzalcoatl. Antonio, does this fit?"

"Yes!"

"Okay," said Amina. "So let us go with that. Understand—and this is very important—just because I use the terms *myth* or *mythic*, please do not assume that I am referring to fictional stories. I believe there is truth to be uncovered in ancient myth. Many myths have at least a tangential link to history, archaeology, and known fact. Suffice it to say, this supposedly mythological creature—Quetzalcoatl—may be a glorified version of a real person, in the person of *Topiltzin*, a priest-ruler of the Toltecs."

"Who were the Toltecs?" asked Tony.

"Wait a minute," Marvin interrupted. "Has anyone ever seen this *quetzal* thing before? Any documentation that it's ever been sighted? In real life?"

"Not in recent memory Marvin, no. Your sighting is highly unusual. As I was trying to say, it is a creature from mythology that may be a deified version of Topiltzin, who was an actual, historical man. If Quetzalcoatl actually appeared to you and Antonio, even if it was just for a moment, it lends credibility to ancient myth, and validates the spiritual realm."

Tony tugged Amina's sleeve. "Who were the Toltecs?"

"The Toltecs were one of many early people groups from Mesoamerica. Warriors that predated the Aztecs. Topiltzin is believed to have been a good man, a noble leader. The first Toltec ruler to abolish human sacrifice and appease the gods with natural resources instead of human blood. He was well liked by his people for obvious reasons, but later shamed by his nemesis and driven from the land."

"And Topiltzin really existed? He was a real person?"

"As far as I know Antonio, yes it seems so. But written accounts from Mesoamerica are rare. Much of what we know about Topiltzin has been passed down to us through oral tradition, the myths, artwork, what we have learned from archaeology."

"But why did Topiltzin appear before my mom died? Did he kill her?"

"I prefer to think that Topiltzin may have been trying to protect your mother from an adversary. If the stories about Topiltzin are true—if he was a just and righteous man—then Topiltzin may have appeared there in the form of Quetzalcoatl to fight the presence of evil. But, unfortunately, he failed to reach your mother in time to save her."

"Adversary?" Marvin said. "You think this quetzal guy was a good spirit, tryin' to fend off a bad one?"

"I believe the accident that killed Antonio's mother may have been a spectral clash between good and evil, manifesting itself in the physical realm. And that is why we must talk immediately about Saint Peter."

30
ASCENDED MASTER

Amina leaned forward with a wily stare. "You have asked me to reach out to Saint Peter, in the hope that he will assist us in bringing the deceased woman Rubi Valdez back to life." She paused, her golden eyes flicking between Marvin and Tony. "These are lofty goals, gentlemen. But are we agreed, this is our desire?"

"Yeah," said Marvin. "But what's this about an adversary?"

Amina leaned back. "Well, many spiritualist mediums are lately experiencing difficulty in communicating with the dead. If there is an increase in spiritual interference that contributes to that, it may affect the ability of spirits to travel. That interference may be coming from an adversary."

Marvin had forgotten all about sitting on the grass in his nice gray windowpane suit. His teeth clenched as his mind traveled back to what Elizabeth Walsh had said about Abiku Madaki working for *the other side*. Marvin had laughed it off, surprised that Elizabeth's normally sound and professional mind would even go there. But now Amina Karimova was suggesting the very same kind of thing. "So what's this interference? You mean like from evil spirits?"

Amina's eyes went to the grass in the center of their little triangle. Now Marvin noticed the woman had begun to fidget discreetly with the fingertips of her left hand. "There is risk involved in communicating with the spirit world," she said. "We do not know which spirits can be trusted. The prospect of evil misleading us is real. However, together with Shada, while in sitting, we can work together to best navigate our minds spiritually. This is not for either of you to worry about, but for Shada and myself."

"But we can trust Shada," said Tony hopefully.

Amina smiled. "Shada is determined to break through the interference."

Leaning forward, Marvin was fully engaged. "Tell us more about this interference."

"Normally, when I make contact with a deceased person, I may receive a message back in images, flashes in my mind. A deceased spirit will make his or her presence known to us by moving an object in the room, by blowing out a lit candle, or by some other supernatural phenomenon. Should we decide to move ahead with our reach to Saint Peter, I have no idea how he may choose to manifest his presence, although I confess to being abundantly curious. In any event, all the signals I have just indicated have been, at least in the last several months, difficult to perceive."

The woman paused and again looked blankly into the grass. Then, as if making a choice, she squared her shoulders and looked at the wall of stone that was the chapel. "Perhaps my theory of interference will be easier to explain in the context of Saint Peter." Her eyes fell to her two listeners, her hands went to her knees. "What do we know of this Saint Peter?"

"He was an apostle," said Tony quickly. "In the inner circle of Jesus."

"Indeed," said Amina. "A powerful figure from the first century of our modern calendar who is credited with having had a significant role in the formation of the Christian church following the ascension of Jesus Christ into the heavenly realms. Saint Peter is known to have had a strong and bold will, a man who held a very close relationship with the Christ—the Christ, who by the way went by many names according to the ancient texts—and whom Peter believed to be the son of the living God."

"Isn't Peter the one who walked on water?" asked Marvin.

"Very good Marvin. According to one account, Peter attempted a walk on a stormy sea, where he lost faith, and was rescued by the Christ. Peter later denied knowing the Christ, but was restored to power upon the recorded resurrection. Perhaps most significant of all, gentlemen, as it pertains to your case, the good Saint Peter himself performed several miracles during the founding of the early church. It is for this reason that I have clarity that your request may not be an impossible one."

Amina breathed and continued. "But it is not often that I am asked to contact someone of a saint's prominence. Saint Peter could be considered by some—I certainly do—as an *Ascended Master*. It has been reported that Ascended Masters are sometimes visible to a person as one is dying, as one begins to pass into the next life. This is rare, mind you. To witness an Ascended Master during the dying phase can be considered a great blessing to the one dying, a special recognition you might say, from the Higher Power, from the Creator, from God, favoring the person at death with the reward of attendance of an Ascended Master during the transition to the afterlife. As rare as such an appearance is, rarer still is for an Ascended Master to appear to a human being at a time *other than* at the time of death, as professed by your mother, Antonio. It is phenomenal that your mother reported to have *physically seen* Saint Peter. The rarest of rare—is your request, to actively seek out and contact an Ascended Master, our Saint Peter."

Amina settled her chin into her fists. "Antonio, let us talk about your mother, and what she said about her encounter with Saint Peter. How did she describe him to you?"

Tony described everything as he had for Marvin in the Tindal's study, about his mother's open window, the voice calling, the thought that it might be a neighbor or someone from out on the sidewalk, and that suddenly there was a man in her room, standing by the window."

"How did your mother know it was Saint Peter?" asked Amina.

"Peter told her who he was."

"How did your mother describe the saint's appearance?"

"He was an older guy, probably older than you Mister Fischer. She said he was dressed in loose clothes, maybe a robe. I'm sorry I can't remember exactly what she said, but I think that's pretty close."

"It sounds like your mother had a remarkably clear vision. Did she describe him as transparent, or as a solid mass, like an actual person standing there?"

"She didn't say," Tony said thoughtfully. "I should have asked her. Why is that important, if Peter was transparent or not?"

"Well," Amina rubbed the cloth of her periwinkle pants between her fingers. "How Saint Peter appeared to your mother could tell us much about how he was able to visit her, how much spiritual interference he had to overcome to cross over. I have a theory about spiritual transport. It may be difficult for spirit beings to reach certain realms from different planes of existence, especially if there is interference. For example, think about a radio transmission. The analogy is imperfect, but it will suffice. Certain atmospheric conditions contribute to the clarity of sound waves traveling from transmitter to receiver. Distance also plays a factor—that is, how far is the transmitter from the receiver—as well as topography. Is the signal being blocked by objects? Does the signal have to bounce between buildings or mountains? Is someone else attempting to scramble the signal? All of these are contributing factors toward the resulting quality of the received signal. In terms of Saint Peter, if he was traveling to your mother on a straight line from the third heaven, with no interference, his likeness may have been opaque. An actual materialization of the saint's spiritual body. A clear, complete transmission, so to speak. Or, if he were beyond heaven, existing in some different dimension, or plane if you will, or even another planet as you suggest, Antonio, and there was spiritual interference of some sort along his journey to visit your mother, Peter's likeness may have appeared transparent, hazy or foggy. The clarity of his voice may also be affected by these factors. You see what I am getting at? Again this is just a theory of mine, but we need to consider it seriously as we determine how to make contact with Saint Peter, and what degree of success we may or may not achieve. You see, spirits are not just hanging out in the room waiting for us to call. If our call is heard, the spirit must come to us, or signal to us from perhaps a great distance, or through some great tumult."

Marvin and Tony locked eyes. Then Tony addressed Amina. "I have one more question."

"Of course."

"What if too much time goes by before we find Saint Peter, and it's too late for my mom's soul to come back?"

Amina pulled her knees to her chest and wrapped them in her arms. "Do you recall the biblical story of Lazarus?"

"He was raised from the dead."

"Yes. The Bible records that Jesus of Nazareth raised Lazarus from the tomb after four days. I for one believe the account to be true. It was a miracle. The event gives us some assurance that at least within the time frame of four days, it is not unprecedented that the soul can return to the body. For your mother, my young Antonio, it has been already more than a week."

"So what are our chances?" asked Marvin.

"Slim."

Amina felt her heart slamming in her chest and was grateful for the thick coat that she hoped would conceal the deep inhalation of breath. She was smothered with anxiety over what she was feeling ready to give in to. Her face did not betray the slightest clue of the secret fear within her spirit. Neither had she been aloof to the tall man's presence and the unexpected draw she was beginning to experience toward him.

Amina rose from her spot and brushed her coat. She held her palms up, directing her companions to stand. Marvin and Tony rose and brushed their clothes. Amina fought to retain her poise as Marvin took a determined step toward her and she became suddenly aware of the chilly wind in her face. In a gesture of confidence Amina settled her hands into the pockets of her coat and met eyes with Marvin.

"Okay Doctor," said Marvin. "We've sat through your philosophies, we've heard your theories, you've addressed our questions, and we've answered yours." Now Marvin's clear blue eyes blazed steadfast into Amina's. She stayed firm and focused and professional, but she knew the question was at hand and could no longer be avoided.

"Are you gonna do this for us? Please? Are you gonna contact Saint Peter?"

"Yes Marvin, I have decided. I will attempt to contact the saint."

She watched his stone face soften. "Okay," said Marvin. "Thank you. Where?"

"It will require a special place of high ethereal energy. A remote place, away from people, where we can be assured the saint will not be shooed away by mortal disturbances. I am zeroing in on a location. And it will require a bit of travel."

Amina detached herself from Marvin's look and for a moment gazed out to sea. She withdrew her hands from her pockets and stepped closer to Marvin, reeling Tony in for a small huddle. "Gentlemen, I must be utterly transparent with you." As if to hide from eavesdropping spirits, her voice took on a hushed and secretive tone. "No one knows how long the soul can be absent from the body before it is impossible to reunite them back to the physical life. This is not a Saturday movie, or a video game, or Tolkien's Lord of the Rings. The challenge we face is real, something that no medium has ever attempted. There are no magic keys, goblets, artifacts, or swords." The gold flecks in Amina's hazel eyes glinted with warning. "What you are asking for, gentlemen, is not just a miracle—but an exceptional miracle."

31
SALT JARS AND A NAKED WOMAN

The Bentley rounded into Saint Patrick Square and slowed to drop Amina Karimova at her flat. After a quick wave and a smile, Amina ascended the steps and five minutes later closed her bathroom door.

She slipped the periwinkle slacks down to her ankles and kicked the garment toward a wicker laundry basket. She reached behind her head, grasped the purple blouse, yanked it off and hung it on a hook. Her slim figure and bare skin looked tan in the warm light that emanated from a set of black pillar candles she had ignited on a thin iron pedestal. Amina floated past the shimmer of candlelight to the white Cambridge bathtub on bronze claw feet, where she knelt down, reached for the imperial knob, and turned it with a squeak. She passed her fingers through the gushing water until it was hot, then put the stopper into the drain, the homemade waterfall rushing to please her senses.

Small and pale yellow jars stood waiting beside the bathtub, amidst a collection of other jars and glass vials of differing sizes, colors, and contents. Amina selected one of the pale yellow jars, unscrewed the cap, and generously poured the concoction of odorless salts into the bubbling basin.

She stood up and stepped across the bathroom to the modest vanity, where she removed her large gold hoop earrings and placed them on the stone surface. Next to the vanity stood a small iron table, with only an incense burner atop, ready with a fresh stick of frankincense. Amina struck a match and lit the incense. Watching the tip glow, she puckered her lips and blew gently on the stick and let the smoke rise into the room. She selected a playlist from her tablet and the air filled with the Celtic vibes of Moya Brennan.

Amina's bathroom was simple but spacious. A place where she came to refresh not only her body, but also her mind and her spirit. She liked to unwind like this regularly, but today was unique. Today was much more than a ritual of unwinding. Today was a special cleansing, an intense focusing on the task she had decided to perform later this day.

As the water level rose in the tub, the room hung with steam, and the wisps of incense formed their smoky layers. Amina clicked a wall switch to engage a quiet ceiling vent, just enough to provide circulation, and to suck fresh air in from the wall grille. Amina reached behind her back to unclip the bra, slipped out of it, laid it gently on a wooden rack, then bowed to glide out of her panties, and tossed them toward the corner basket. Amina loved the primal sense that her nakedness gave her, the feeling of oneness with creation, with not an ounce of shame, though she'd always wished she'd had more meat on her hips.

Amina stepped onto a circular powder-blue rug with fringes on its edges, positioned in front of a cheval glass. She put her small feet together and looked down at her toes that were overdue for a pedicure. She lifted her head, took a breath, and stared at her face in the tall and narrow mirror. The wind on the hill had made a tussle of her bouffant. She stood close, her face only inches from the reflective glass. At 41 years old, Amina appeared deceptively young. Her skin was smooth and free of blemishes. She kept her eyebrows plucked and narrow. She disliked her bony body. But she had always been thankful for the striking round cheeks high on her face. Her glittering hazel eyes were a gift from the gods.

The soothing atmosphere Amina had created for herself collided with the apprehensive energy rocketing through her nerves. Holding her gaze firmly on her face, Amina thought about the evening ahead. She had always been confident about contacting the dead. She knew she had the gift. She knew her spirit was free and capable. She knew she'd had much success in her career as a medium. People the world over had come to her for help and guidance. Amina could receive messages from other people's loved ones and give hope to their living relatives that they were safe on the other side.

But who did she think she was to reach out to Saint Peter?

The great saint himself. An Ascended Master!

What if she failed?

Amina purged the thoughts from her mind. She closed her eyes and inhaled the fragrance of the frankincense. She exhaled slowly. She inhaled again, and exhaled. She inhaled a third time and held the air in her lungs for as long as she could. Finally she burst the wind from her mouth and opened her eyes into a hard stare at her own reflection.

She could do this!

She would not let the dark spirits frighten her away or gain victory over her. She would brave it and break her pact of *never again.* Today Amina would reach out to someone with centuries of history. A man whose fame had grown immensely since his life as an apostle of Jesus Christ in the first century. The legend of Saint Peter's miracles spanned the ages and filled people of the Church with awe and renewed faith.

Amina turned to the bathtub. It was almost full. She stepped to the faucet and turned off the water, then lifted her foot over the edge of the tub, dipping into the steamy water. She brought her other foot in and slowly submerged into the hot bath, her skin searing as she became engulfed, and she sank up to her neck. Almost instantly, the relentless nervous energy in her limbs scurried away into nothingness. Amina closed her eyes and began to relax. Her lips opened into a calm smile. The soft whir of the vent and the mystical music were the only sounds to be heard while the candlelight and the incense worked their magic. Amina's spirit calmed, her mind unwound, her breathing slowed. She dozed briefly.

Then out of nowhere the enemy returned. Fear suddenly rushed through her veins once again as her thoughts turned to the boy. Amina opened her eyes. She must not let Antonio down. She already felt an attachment to the boy, a deep sense of wanting to help him. She hoped against hope that she would be able to reach the saint and find some way to achieve the impossible. Could they really request of Saint Peter the resurrection from the dead of this boy's dead mother, Rubi Valdez?

It had never been done, not like this, not across dimensions. She must try. She must succeed.

When Amina lifted the hot water to her face and let it dribble down her cheeks, her thoughts rolled to Marvin Fischer. She hadn't found a man to be this distracting in quite some time. She found him maddening but convincingly attractive. His musky after-shave was killer. She had noticed it when she'd gotten close, on Princes Street as he met her, and down-wind from him on the hill. She admired the casual walk, the confidence, his place in life, his style. His movements displayed the calm deliberateness of a man who knows what he likes and what he wants. The Bentley. Picky about his clothes. She smiled. And the man spoke his mind. Nothing woosy about him. Seemed to know his way around the world. And he had a sensitive side too—looking out for the boy, and God was the man good looking. Maybe a bit tall for her but oh well. She was good in heels.

She took pleasure in thinking about him and allowed her thoughts to drift closer to him. She pictured herself alone with him, outside at a table for two on a warm summer night by a giant lit fountain, outfitted in her finest dress, fully made up and adorned with her fanciest jewelry, smiling at each other over glasses of chianti.

Then her forehead tightened and her mouth curled into an unhappy crescent. She presumed Marvin Fischer considered her merely as a necessary evil, one that had to be tolerated in order to satisfy the boy's need to get his mother back, and would gladly deposit her back to the university once they were all finished with the adventure.

And there was little chance he found *her* attractive.

She hardly dared to think it.

Amina had never known what to do with men. All too many times she had cried secretly to herself on her favorite divan for being too formal, thinking her own personality as off-putting.

A waste of her physical beauty.

She was too weird. Too academic. Too formal. Too cold.

Frigid as ice!

No wonder she had never been with a man. She'd never known what to do. She'd never gotten past this point of thinking and dreaming. She'd always waited for the man, but the ask rarely came, and when it did, she had lied and feigned indifference when in fact she wanted to say *yes*, and the few men over the years that had caught her eye had always made their excuses.

She herself had chased men away.

Amina's mind raced in search of something to replace this distracting argumentation and quickly focused on the much more pressing decision of which distinctive location to hold this special séance.

A single location had made its way to the top of her attention and become her first choice, and she would no longer negotiate with herself over the selection.

Yes, it would be Castlerigg Stone Circle, in Cumbria. They would have to travel to England. Marvin would want to drive, but she would insist on taking the train.

Amina had always been gripped by the mystic feeling she experienced when visiting Castlerigg Stone Circle, an ancient loop of 38 large boulders, set in a valley amidst the tranquil hills of Skiddaw and Derwent Fells. Prehistoric stone circles like Castlerigg existed all over Britain, but Castlerigg Stone Circle had never been extensively studied or excavated. Historians and archaeologists believed that Castlerigg had been used as a place to trade tools, and as a forum for sacred customs. The hands of the faithful had likely erected the circle during the Neolithic period, and Amina believed in the unique spiritual potential of the mesmerizing place.

Castlerigg Stone Circle was sure to meet with the approval of Marvin Fischer and his young sidekick Antonio Valdez. But even if it didn't, that was beside the point. This was Amina's call—and call it she would—and with firm conviction.

Firm conviction? Yes indeed, Amina was convinced, and she would focus on her spirit guide, Shada. The first thing she would do when they got to Castlerigg would be to summon her.

Shada would come. Together they would discover Saint Peter.

Amina reached for another small pale yellow jar of salts, opened it, and dumped its full contents into the bathwater.

32

ORCHESTRA HALL

Marvin locked the panel door of his heavily marbled bathroom that he shared with Tony at the Balmoral. Stripped down to his shirt and underwear, Marvin looked at the wet towels Tony had left on the tile floor, shook his head lightly, picked up the towels, and draped them on a rack by the counter. Marvin wasn't displeased with the boy; in fact he found that he experienced a sense of fulfillment in being a sort of father figure to him. Tony had completed his spiritual saltwater bath cleansing as ordered by Doctor Amina Karimova, and had retired to the adjoining bedroom for an afternoon rest—another order from the Doctor.

Now it was Marvin's turn for the ritual.

He scowled and unbuttoned his dress shirt.

Spiritual cleansing? Was it really necessary? Marvin wondered what purpose it could serve, but had been assured by Amina that it was a necessary step to their success. Marvin wished he could bypass the child's play and get on with the séance. Deviant thoughts entered his mind. Perhaps he would skip the bubble bath. Go have a coffee. Maybe there was a car race on television. No,

Amina would find him out, it would become a controversy and she'd call the whole thing off. Alright then, he'd be a team player and jump in the playpen.

Amina had been precise about how the men were to spend the afternoon. They were to go back to the hotel, each take their saltwater cleansing bath and remain soaking until the incense stick had completely burned out. They were to use the prescribed salts dissolved in the hottest water they could tolerate. They had been instructed not to eat anything. They were to train their thoughts entirely on their forthcoming journey to the secret and sacred location where they would travel later this evening, and the subsequent séance wherein they would reach out to Saint Peter.

With face drooping, Marvin dutifully hung his shirt on a hook by the door, tripped out of his underwear, dropped them into his portable laundry bag, set the bag on the floor, and stepped to the white and gray stone bathtub. He turned the glass knob and let the tub fill. He hoped there'd be enough hot water left after Tony's bath.

Marvin grabbed a fluorescent green paper bag with a white lotus flower printed prominently on its side—the bag of goodies from Penelope's. Marvin reached into the bag and snatched a frankincense stick. He set it into the burner on the counter where Tony had let his stick burn out, struck a match from the enclosed matchbook, and lit the stick. Marvin sat patiently still for the minute it took for the tip to glow orange, then blew it and watched the smoke lift into the room. For a moment the silliness of the ritual vanished, as the smoke reminded Marvin of his meeting with Pastor Deckland, when they had talked about prayer, and how it works. Marvin observed the smoke waft up to the ceiling, as he had done at the pastor's study. He wondered again what really happens to those prayers, where they go, and what God really does with them.

There had to be some truth to it. Don't ask questions, Amina would say.

Marvin stepped back to the tub and felt the water. It was hot. He reached again into the lotus bag and removed the blue jar of salts. He opened the jar, tipped it, and watched its crystalline contents cascade into the water. He leaned over and swished the water around for a minute. He stood up again, crumpled the little bag, and tossed it toward the garbage can in the corner of the bathroom. Score.

Marvin stepped to the mirror and checked his face. He had shaven early this morning but now it was after one o'clock in the afternoon and his facial hair was already starting to show. He decided not to worry about it. The wrinkles under his eyes and the crow's feet at the corners by his temples caught his attention. Time was passing. His life was more than half over. He took an evaluating glance at his naked form, and acknowledged with a sigh that if he didn't get back into the gym soon, he would lose whatever tone he had left. He told himself he would snap to it as soon as he got back to the United States, and finally gear up and get social again, maybe even meet someone and move past Caroline. Maybe even break protocol and swoop Elizabeth Walsh out on that secret date. He could use the gift of the necktie as a convenient excuse for the outing. Forget platonic. He'd already confessed to himself that he cared for Elizabeth. She matched him intellectually and for goodness sakes, she was a bombshell. Especially when she got all made up, like she'd done when she had come over to give him the necktie. The hair. The makeup. Those jeans and the boots. Damn her. Did she have any tattoos? Were her breasts a C-cup? Maybe even a D? If any other man his age could be so lucky. Okay so they'd set aside the age difference. Kids? He doubted it. He would enjoy her on every level, she'd look good on his arm, and she'd be happy in love.

Marvin frowned at his make-believe. The whole idea was preposterous. Elizabeth Walsh still had her whole life ahead of her, and Marvin was fast marching towards retirement. Before long he'd be home nursing a sore back or recovering from a hip replacement, while she would still be out swinging a tennis racket and mountain biking. It was absolutely out of the question. Besides dammit—he still missed Caroline, and he felt connected to her in ways he could not explain or rid himself of.

Marvin remembered how tantalizing Caroline had looked wearing the jet black sheath dress to the holiday fundraising event for the symphony at Detroit's acoustic gem—Orchestra Hall—shortly after they'd married. Caroline had served on the committee that had arranged the event, and as Marvin had caught her in his sight line from across the room, with all its golden carvings and ornate woodwork, in the warm friendly glow of the dim light, Caroline had looked absolutely smashing while she chatted up the patrons and dazzled them with cheer.

Marvin remembered Caroline's face, the fair skin smooth and white almost as snow, the glistening black hair, the red lips of Marilyn Monroe, parting when she laughed as her eyes went bright. He remembered the dangerous slit in the dress flashing the porcelain thigh that went on for miles and how the men were all sneaking their glances, like she was the very finest in a box of bon vivant chocolates. Caroline was a social magnet, someone who made everyone feel esteemed and appreciated. Marvin could never figure out where Caroline had found the energy to sincerely invest in her acquaintances. She'd made every man crazy with envy without realizing it, and they all secretly wanted her. But they always knew she was going home with Marvin Fischer. He'd felt incredibly lucky to have found a woman with whom he'd had such an innate chemistry.

As part of the fundraiser that day, the orchestra had performed a number of the classics for those in attendance. Caroline had been particularly fond of the interpretation of Ludwig Van Beethoven's *Fantasia in C Minor*, a 20-minute piece the composer had rushed to finish for an 1808 benefit concert in Vienna. Over glasses of 1924 double-black cabernet during the intermission, next to the wide dark windows wet with rain overlooking Woodward Avenue two stories below, Caroline had detailed for Marvin her pleasure over how the composer had used each section of the orchestra as children in a playground. The piano had been messing around getting into trouble, the woodwinds and the strings gently reminding the piano of the task at hand, until the brass interceded and ordered everyone to get down to the business of actually developing the theme for the finale. '*Okay, I've got this,*' said the piano, and the auditioning ensued with variations on the theme, until the horns 'approved' the appropriate tune and the full orchestra was permitted to burst into melody as one, in a grand display of emotional vivacity and musical unity. It had all been in preparation for the last section of the piece, where the choral members on stage went into the lyrics, singing of beauty and of peace, of grace and of the gifts of high art, in the resounding finale. Caroline had marveled that the ending would never have attained its effectual power without the previous themes working out their zenith in advance. The piece was a perfect union of development, a masterpiece of experimentation in melody, culminating in joyful finality and celebration of life.

Marvin had sipped his cabernet, looking through the rainy glass at the passing cars on Woodward, his eyebrows rising in wonder at Caroline's analysis of the piece. He himself had arrived at no such fulfillment. To him the piece had been nothing more than a jumble of mixed up chords and notes and trills, punctuated by an occasional moment or two that had caught his attention. And the lyrics of the finale had been in freaking German. He had almost dozed off somewhere in the middle.

They'd wandered downstairs for another drink, and in the midst of the discussion with Caroline as a raffle was about to be drawn, a little boy of four years old had wandered into the hall from Woodward Avenue, soaked in rain from the storm outside. Caroline had rushed to the young boy and learned immediately that the boy had been separated from his mother in the hall, and the boy had wandered outside in search of mom. Marvin had watched as Caroline had comforted the little boy and hoisted the nipper onto her shoulders, so that the little blue eyes could search the crowd for the mother's face. As the rain from the wet boy's clothes dripped down into Caroline's hair, makeup, and dress, Caroline had not minded in the least, instead laughing and encouraging the little one until finally the little boy exploded with glee as he'd spotted his worried mother across the room.

Caroline had been one in a million, Marvin's unrepeatable catch.

And the couple had been madly in love. On occasion they'd fought like pirates but soon made up for it with fiery lovemaking.

33

MAN IN HOT WATER

Marvin drifted back from his fond recollections and returned his mind to the task at hand. By now the bathroom had filled with the frankincense aroma. The water in the tub had reached its fill line. Marvin had almost forgotten to dim the lights, as Doctor Karimova had instructed if there was such a feature at the hotel. There was, so Marvin dimmed the lights down to a warm glow, moved to the bathtub, turned off the water, and stepped into the hot liquid. Sinking deep into the tub, he smiled. It felt so much better than he'd imagined. In fact, it felt so good that Marvin began to chuckle. He could not remember the last time he had taken a bath. Amina had been right after all. It was a tranquil, calming event. Marvin closed his eyes. He had to give the woman credit. This spiritual cleansing wasn't so bad after all.

Marvin wondered if Tony had fallen asleep, or just lay in bed thinking. He wondered what Amina was doing. He imagined her naked body in the bath. He thought back to the moment he'd seen her this morning on Princes Street. She had looked fetching in her avocado tweed coat, periwinkle slacks, gold hoop earrings, and messy updo. But it was as much the smile, the scent, the graceful movements, her voice, and the alluring accent that he could still not place. What was it? The Asian influence was present, but the life in Scotland had burned its effect on her speech.

Marvin caught himself smiling and quickly shook his head to clear his mind. He wasn't supposed to be thinking about any of this anyway. He did not want to allow any of these ideas to be a distraction. It was nonsense, anyhow. He still had a strong sense for Caroline, no matter that she was no longer with him. He was content being single, and he reverted to his conviction to avoid complications with a new woman. Certainly not with Amina.

Marvin's thoughts jilted as his smart phone blared. His eyes shot open as his head turned in the direction of the gray suit pants hanging on the wall twelve feet away. The phone rang incessantly. Really? Now? Marvin sloshed out of the tub, streams of salty water dripping down his body. He scrambled across the marble tile, holding for balance to the edge of the counter and the metal towel bar. He reached his pants and fumbled with a wet hand to yank the phone from the pocket. He checked the caller ID.

It was Elizabeth Walsh.

Crap! He was supposed to call her!

Marvin punched on. "Elizabeth, I was just about to call you."

"Yeah? I was getting worried. You okay?"

"Yeah! Yes, I'm uh… I'm in the middle of something. What'cha got?"

"I'm glad you like the tie."

"Yes! Yeah it's great," said Marvin with energy. "I love it."

"You wear it yet?"

"Um… Yeah I'm wearing it today in fact... Actually no, I was gonna wear it…"

"Something wrong with it?"

"No."

"It's not detective is it?"

"No no."

"Well when you get back I want to see you in it."

"Definitely. Yes." Suddenly he felt chilly and tiptoed back to the bathtub.

Elizabeth said, "You ready to tell me where you are?"

"Never mind that. Any hassles from Dominic?"

"He doesn't even realize you're not here. Not yet anyway."

"Good. What's goin' on with Abiku Madaki? Any developments?"

Marvin was pleased there was no tension in Elizabeth's voice. The hard feelings had blown over. Drama averted. He lifted his lean leg over the edge of the tub and plunged back into the warm water, feeling silly for talking with Elizabeth Walsh over the phone while in the nude.

Elizabeth reported, "Well yeah that's why I called. I've conducted new interviews with the witnesses from the scene at 66th and East McDonald and turned up nothing new."

"Bummer."

"I checked out that church too, Hope Crossing. I don't think there's anything fishy about it."

"Okay." His arm squeaked against the side of the tub.

"I hear water."

"Hhm?"

"Are you hot-tubbing it with the lucky lady?"

"I am not hot-tubbing it."

"I knew it. You slipped away for a quick romantic getaway, you lucky stud. Who is she?"

"I am not in a hot tub, and I am not on a getaway. What else on Madaki?"

"Uh huh. Well, the FBI team is wrapping up in Mexico City with their investigation into the bombing at Teotihuacán. Benjamin Taft is leading the team. They met up with a group with the Federal Ministerial Police at Teotihuacán and got up to speed on what they've found so far. I thought about tagging along but since I'm point over here with you gone, I decided to stay back and wait for Taft to report his findings."

"Alright Elizabeth good work. I gotta run, but call me the minute you get an update—No, on second thought, I'll call you."

"Of course. I wouldn't want to interrupt anything."

"Goodbye, Elizabeth."

Marvin clicked off and blew out a deep sigh. He knew Elizabeth wasn't going to let this go, and at some point he'd be cornered to explain himself. He shrugged off the mess, set his phone aside, and sunk into the water up to his chin. This was not how the cleansing was supposed to go. He was certain that the call from Phoenix would be forbidden by Doctor Amina, against her strict cleansing policy.

Not to worry. There was no reason he'd ever have to mention the call.

34

CASSINI DIVISION

Before Tony had settled down for a rest on his Queen size bed at the Balmoral, he had opened the window across the room just a crack. It was chilly outside but he didn't care. Somehow in his heart he hoped the open window might summon the saint who had visited his mother Rubi Valdez only a few days before, through the open window in her bedroom.

Maybe they wouldn't even need the séance. Maybe Peter would come to him here.

The morning had come early for Tony. And all the input from Doctor Karimova had drained his mind of energy. He had found the cleansing bath fun and relaxing, having dunked himself all the way under in the tub. He had tasted the salts and blown bubbles under the water and squeaked his toes against the polished white stone. Then he had become bored as he waited for the incense to finish and had sat and thought and had been pushed toward sleepiness.

Tony plopped now onto the navy blue comforter and rested his head with damp hair onto the soft white pillow. He lay on his back and put his hands behind his head, staring at the perfect white ceiling. Through the closed door of the shared bathroom he could faintly hear Mister Fischer's water swishing.

The ceiling blurred as Tony thought about his telescope. He wished he could spend a night stargazing. His mind began to replay scenes from his favorite movies and TV shows. He had fallen for *E.T.*, and *Contact*, and *Close Encounters*, the three films that had gotten him hooked on outer space. Recently he had snuck to streaming *The Expanse* against his mother's wishes. Traveling within the solar system was dope—he hoped it would become a reality during his lifetime.

Tony's eyelids became heavy. He turned on his side and curled and within two minutes drifted to sleep.

The strange thing was that Tony felt no wind across his face as he floated toward the moon. He had already left earth's atmosphere without realizing it, maybe because he had been so enthralled with the extra bright moon, and with the hope of finding his mother there. As his body drifted through space, Tony turned around to look at the earth. It was quite a distance behind him now, but Tony felt no fear, and calculated that by now he was probably about halfway to the moon. He felt no chill even though all he wore was a T-shirt and blue jeans as he propelled through the vacuum of space without effort. No flapping of the arms or breaststrokes.

Tony didn't feel he was moving very fast, yet his progress must have been more than was evident, because now he was hovering over the crust of the moon, close enough to touch it. A beam of sunlight reflected brightly off the silvery-gray moon dust and up into Tony's face. He smiled, reached down, and ran his fingertips through the smooth and light dust on the surface. It felt familiar to him, like the white powdered chalk the gym teacher had asked him to bring to the baseball diamond. So that's what moon dust feels like! Tony wanted to stop floating and get down there to walk on the moon dust, but his body did not obey his commands.

"Mom?" called Tony. "Mom?"

No answer, and he did not see her. But Tony was sure he could find her here.

An instant later the moon and the earth were far behind him. Tony floated deeper into the solar system, deeper into space, approaching Mars.

Perhaps his mother would be exploring Mars.

"Mom?"

Tony passed the red ball that was Mars, and must have somehow buzzed past Jupiter without noticing because now the orange giant Saturn was beneath him. Tony knew he was now almost 900 million miles from earth and he began to hear the eerie sounds of a space probe transmitting the piercing whoosh as it traveled through the yellow-blue haze of Saturn's moon Titan, even though Titan was still a great distance away. Tony floated toward the rings of Saturn and still did not see his mother. But in his dream Tony reasoned that she must be close by, since she likes the yellow and blue atmosphere of Titan as it reminds her of Albireo, the double star.

But no, she was not here.

He was not far out enough. She was not even in the solar system.

She was somewhere else.

Tony hovered over the gap between Saturn's two largest rings—the Cassini Division—and was now floating directly over the largest ring of the gas giant, and he could see the gray and rusty rocks and space dust that made up each of the strange bands around the planet. Then he felt something like sand swishing past his face. Instinctively with his hand he brushed it away, but more small particles came, then bigger ones—from Saturn's rings—they came and began to pelt Tony's face and his clothing. The sound was like raindrops hitting his jeans but they were small pebbles and stones and they were getting thicker and denser—the remains of comets and asteroids.

He was drifting into the rings!

The particles became chunks the size of golf balls, then tennis balls, and they began to hurt. Tony reached out with his hands to block the incoming pieces of space rock. Some of them he deflected aside. Others got through and hit him in the face.

Fear and panic took over. He was going to get smashed by space rocks!

Tony flailed, kicked and waved. He wanted to be out of there, to move past the rings, to search the planet's orangey surface gases. But he could not!

Then he saw it, past the mass of pelting space rocks. The yellow blazing ball, larger than Jupiter, calling to him from deep space.

A distant exoplanet!

Somehow, Tony knew he had to get to the yellow planet. It must be where his mother is! Tony groped and pushed and flailed as the space rocks knocked him and spun him until he lost control and lost sight of the hazy yellow planet.

Then came the piercing ring...

Tony was jolted awake when he heard Marvin's smartphone blaring through the bathroom door. Tony blinked and sniffled as his mind cleared and registered where he was. He had been so far away... no, it was just a dream. That's right, he was in Scotland, at the hotel, with Mister Fischer, and they were getting ready to meet up with Doctor Karimova again.

Tony rolled onto his back as his pulse calmed. He felt his face, but there was no evidence of having been hit by space rocks. What about that strange giant yellow planet he had seen? Then he remembered the window, and jerked his head to the right. The window was open, just as he'd left it, the white frame clean and the glass clear, the navy blue curtains hanging still and unmoving.

But no Saint Peter.

Tony let his head rest back down and pulled one of the soft pillows to his chest and curled up. He didn't feel he'd nap again, but it felt good to rest.

As his eyelids became heavy they jolted open again and fixed wide on the clear window. Had he just seen a dark figure passing outside?

35

THE TRANSPENNINE

The Nova 2 was the TransPennine's five-carriage electric bullet that the Brits had recently launched as part of a new fleet, having successfully arranged a financing deal with Eversholt and Beacon. The brand new beauty boasted speeds of over 120mph, faster and more efficient than the Class 350, and the even older 185s that had recently been taken out of service. The plan more than doubled the capacity of intercity railway routes and provided enhanced services into England. The new carriages featured state-of-the-art comforts including free Wi-Fi, power sockets for mobile devices at every seat, air conditioning, and bicycle storage.

Mister Fischer had put in a quick call to Tiffany Tindal, informing her that plans had elaborated to include a jaunt into England. He'd put Tony on the phone, who set Mrs. Tindal at ease, telling her he was having the time of his life. Had he worked on his homework? Some. A little. No. Be sure to work on it. Okay.

Antonio Valdez sat by the window on the Nova 2's Coach E, across a faux wood grain table from Mister Fischer and Doctor Karimova. They had the carriage to themselves, riding in first class per Mister Fischer's insistence after his desire to drive the Bentley had been shot down by Doctor Karimova in favor of saving his energy for the evening. Tony wasn't sure what energy they'd need just sitting for the séance, but Mister Fischer had bowed to the wishes of the Doctor and left the Bentley parked at the Edinburgh Rail Station.

They departed at half past four, and would make a stop after 90 minutes, where they'd hop a bus that would take them deep into the remote land of Cumbria, via the little town of Keswick. Tony looked out the window and watched the sylvan hillside roll by. They were already out of the city. The backpack rested in the unoccupied seat beside him, but he was having difficulty concentrating on the homework spread out on the table. Lifting the binoculars to his eyes, Tony glanced through the lenses. The scenery whooshed past in a dizzying rush of three-dimensional earthen color. There was something calming about the gentle green fields dotted with trees and stones and grazing cows. Even the train car itself was reassuring. Tony lowered the specs, swiveled in his seat, and absorbed the soothing light gray interior with blue accents and matching diamond carpet. Tony had been tuned out to the adult conversation until there was complaining about the dirt.

"You're gonna make us sit on the ground again?" asked Marvin. "How 'bout we stand?"

"I told you to wear something more appropriate."

"I didn't have time to go shopping." Marvin scowled, taking a sip of coffee from a large paper cup. He looked at Tony, and the boy returned the sour look with a smile. Marvin continued his defense. "I didn't bring any jeans and T-shirts. I thought we'd be in your office at the university, or—What was wrong with that big room where you did the yoga?"

"The meditation."

"Yeah that. You already had the incense going and everything."

Amina shared a wink with Tony. The boy had come to enjoy the entertaining squabbles between the grown-ups.

Marvin said, "Well okay then Doctor, tell us about the stones. This Castlerigg thing. All you've said is that it's a big circle o' rocks built three thousand years ago."

"I prefer to call them monoliths, Marvin. I chose the site for its inexplicable supernatural phenomena. Some visitors claim to have heard music resonate off the surrounding hills, seeming to emanate from the stones themselves."

"So we're gonna attend an outdoor concert."

"Marvin, you are forgetting to dash the negative energy. I will tell you more when we get there. Right now I'd be more concerned about scuffing your shiny shoes."

Tony snickered and Marvin said, "You know Johnston and Murphy has been around since 1850. They've made all the shoes for the Presidents of the United States since Abraham Lincoln."

"They are very nice shoes. We shall do our best to keep them as clean as possible for you." Amina's lips broadened into a smile. "I do enjoy our kidding, gentlemen." And then with mischief in her eye she snatched her little black purse and rummaged until she revealed a single piece of string cheese wrapped in its plastic sheath. She began peeling.

"I thought we weren't supposed to eat anything," Tony challenged.

"I experienced a sugar crash after the Viennoiseries."

"I'm sitting here starving and you're downing cheese?" said Marvin. "Seriously?"

Amina finished peeling the plastic and then stripped the cheese into strands. She handed one to Marvin, another to Tony, and kept one for herself. "I am happy to share," she said, and then nibbled.

Tony ate, but Marvin sat and looked at the woman with curiosity. "This isn't gonna mess up the séance is it?"

"I feel confidently grounded. Our afternoon cleansing has served its purpose, and I believe we are safe to eat."

Marvin squashed the soft milky material into his mouth. "Got any more?"

~

Several minutes passed in silence. Abandoning his homework, Tony had gotten up out of his seat and gone to the window at the other side of the carriage to get a look at the flat green farms in the east, which Marvin had told him would soon give way to the rolling hills of Glenkirk.

Now Marvin sat quietly thinking, his coffee cup half empty. He was trying to make it last. It was cold now, but the flavor was still there. He checked his Rolex and estimated they'd passed Symington by now, and would soon be speeding through Crawford. He had studied their route in detail before they left, to be assured there'd be no surprises. He'd made all the reservations himself on the hotel computer. They should make Penrith Railway Station at just after six, just in time to catch the 6:21 bus for the 27-minute ride to Keswick.

Marvin found his eyes drifting to the woman seated next to him. Amina sat stiff and upright, her shoulder blades an inch off the back of her seat. Her eyes were closed, hands flat on top of the table as if she were holding it down. It didn't seem to Marvin that she was even breathing. Marvin decided she was lost in some sort of mental preparation again. The same gold hoop earrings dangled from her lobes, her brown hair still tied up, but tighter now and more kempt, as if she'd taken more time with it. Marvin wondered if she ever wore her hair down. He glanced at her hands. The nails were polished shiny purple. She wore no ring. She hadn't mentioned a husband or a man of any kind, and Marvin wondered if she was even interested in such pursuits.

Marvin's reveries were snapped by a sudden inhalation from the woman as her eyelids popped open in wide surprise. The reflex was accompanied by a violent shudder of her shoulders that startled Marvin. "Everything okay?" he asked.

Amina swallowed and moved her head as if searching for herself. She gasped and put a hand to her heart and on her left hand her fingers fidgeted. "I felt something," she said.

Now Marvin's eyes were laser focused on her face. "Like what?"

"A shift in energy."

Their conversation scattered when Tony's elbow jolted Marvin's shoulder. Coffee sloshed over the lip of Marvin's cup, splashing his necktie from Caroline with another generous brown stain. Marvin could already feel the cold brew seeping through his shirt but hardly reacted. He was fixed instead on the frightful look in Tony's eyes as he felt the boy's fingertips dig into his shoulder. "What's the matter?" asked Marvin.

Tony's eyes were transfixed on the window by the seat across the aisle. "Somebody just looked at me through the window!"

Marvin and Amina followed the trajectory of Tony's pointing finger. There was nothing visible through the transparent high-impact glass except the hills rolling by under a partly cloudy sky. Marvin turned quickly to Amina for an explanation, but there came only the silent shaking of her head with a look of distress.

Marvin set his cup down and brushed his splattered hands. "Are you sure?" he asked Tony.

"Positive. I was looking out the window and this guy popped up from nowhere and then just disappeared."

"A man? What did he look like?"

"Bald… a dark face… how could he just hang on the outside of the train? We're moving like a hundred miles an hour."

"What else can you describe about the guy?"

"I think he had a beard, or hair on his chin. He looked… Mad."

Marvin glared at Tony. The man Tony was describing sounded alarmingly like the new most wanted man that Marvin and his team had been tasked to find—

Abiku Madaki!

"You're sure you saw this person."

"Yes!"

"You weren't half asleep or something."

"No!"

Marvin stood out of his seat and scanned the carriage. He rested a hand briefly on Amina's shoulder, pushed past Tony, and slowly moved across the aisle to the window.

Amina tugged at Tony's shirt. "Did you feel anything?" she asked.

"What do you mean?"

"Like the air moving… like pressure."

Tony shook his head. "No," he quivered, then found Amina's hand with his own and grasped it tight. Turning to Marvin, Tony asked, "Mister Fischer do you have a gun?"

Marvin inched closer to the window. "No. Did the guy have a gun?"

"I don't think so."

Marvin tried the window. "It won't open."

"Are you sure you should do that," asked Tony, "when the guy's trying to get in?"

Marvin pulled away from the window. Amina squeezed Tony's hand in a gesture of comfort, then stood up from her seat and gently pushed past him into the aisle. "Marvin? Do you see anything?"

Marvin shook his head, but his eyes never left the window. "No."

The three of them stood as if waiting for catastrophe. There came no sound but the faint and gentle hum of the train's wheels gliding along steel rails.

Marvin looked again to Amina. "Well?"

"I fear that whatever is outside does not need the window to get in."

36
ENERGY SHIFT

And in the midst of the ominous mood as the train coasted innocently through the landscape, a single cheerful chime from Marvin's smartphone seemed completely unexpected and out of place. Marvin knew by the chime that it could be only one thing—an incoming text. He glanced at his fellow travelers who watched with anticipation. His companions said nothing, but he sensed their fear. And why was there also fear in Marvin's heart over what message his phone beheld? In any other moment it would have been second nature, a casual check that meant nothing more than a new item on his agenda or an answer to someone's question. But now, in this moment, Marvin felt threatened. Then with resolve he finally plucked the phone from his breast pocket and checked it. He punched his security code and opened the message. "It's from Simon Peter."

The three of them stood like statues.

"What does the message say?" asked Amina.

"It's a picture of Abiku Madaki." Marvin turned the phone towards Amina and watched her face for any sign of recognition. There was none.

"Who is that?" she asked.

Marvin decided on full disclosure. "It's the name of a suspect. Abiku Madaki has bombed several religious sites and I have a team gathering intel on him."

"So you are already aware of this Madaki," Amina confirmed.

"Yeah. So why would Peter send me this? There's nothing new here."

Amina's eyes drifted into cloudiness, her mouth dropped. "Abiku Madaki…"

"It means *death spirit warlord*," said Marvin.

"I know…" Amina clasped her cold fingers around Marvin's wrist. "I am afraid the good saint is trying to warn us."

Before Marvin could respond, he felt an intense and invisible push from above, as if the air were somehow falling. He felt pressure in his chest and his eyes went wide. "Do you feel that!?!"

"Yes!" shouted Tony.

"It's the energy shift!" said Amina.

Marvin felt the weight of the air press down against him and then suddenly lift, as if an invisible force was crushing him, and then an instant later he felt weightless. Marvin noticed Tony sitting down and clutching the armrests of the seat.

When Marvin's wrist was torn from her grip, Amina felt as if a part of her arm had gone with him. The invisible power had lifted Marvin off his feet, the terrifying wind now hurling him across the seats and into the aisle of the train car. Homework went flying and the carriage creaked. Marvin crashed to the floor and rolled until his body hit the back wall by the exit door. Amina and Tony watched in horror as Marvin reached for a chair to hoist himself up—only to be yanked off his feet again! The air carried his twisting body and smashed it into the windows across the aisle.

Amina stood frozen, watching helplessly.

"Mister Fischer!!" Tony lunged to help, but then himself became a victim of whatever terrible force had taken over the carriage, and the boy was hurled through the air at lightning speed. Tony's body did a mid-air summersault, his forehead crashing into the overhead luggage rack before slamming against the back of a passenger seat. Tony winced and lifted a hand to the gash on his forehead.

Amina, in wide-eyed terror but still on her feet, braced for the worst, thinking she was surely next. She clenched the back of a passenger seat and remained spellbound. Her mind flashed back to the beach in Malindi, when she herself had been hurled mercilessly, and she knew instinctively this wind must be coming from the same source—a source from beyond, from the other side—controlled by a sinister and formidable foe.

What could she possibly do now, to protect herself, and to help her new friends?

And she remembered immediately a Chantway—the *Wind Chant* of the Navajo—a chant that called out to the good powers beyond, the powers of light. She would call to Shada and to the Great Spirit!

Bravely taking her hands off the anchoring seat and spreading her arms wide over the area, palms facing downward, Amina shouted in a commanding voice, chanting loudly into the air—in the language of the Navajo—the language of her only close friend on the other side. And what sounded like repeating babble, she chanted over and over, with increasing intensity and emphasis on a phrase—the phrase she hoped would counter the turbulent and stormy disaster unfolding before her eyes.

But Marvin lifted off the floor again. His body crashed up into the roof of the train car and fell flat onto the pale diamond-blue carpet in the aisle.

Amina again called out the Navajo Wind Chant with increased passion.

And then as suddenly as it had begun, the air pressure lifted.

Gasping to catch his breath, Marvin lay on the floor, his shirt and tie soaked with spilled coffee. Tony leaned against the back of a seat, his forehead dripping red.

Amina stood motionless.

Everything was still.

Just the sound of the steel wheels on tracks.

Amina lowered her arms and rushed to Tony's side. "Antonio! Are you okay?"

Tony nodded painfully. Amina turned. "Marvin!?"

Marvin rolled to his side, propped himself on an elbow, breathing heavily, sweat dripping from his chin. He shook his head and managed to get on all fours, his hands flat on the carpet. He turned to Amina, and through blazing blue eyes said with grit, "We have to stop the train."

37

EVACUATION

Like a lobster tiptoeing across a coral scarp, Marvin crept groggily on all fours, pausing to claw under a seat where he retrieved his smartphone. Flipping it over, he frowned at the long crack zigzagging across the dark screen. Waking the phone and clicking through a few buttons confirmed the phone seemed in working order. He tucked the thing away, grasped the headrest of a passenger seat, and wobbled to his feet. His mind and vision were a scrambled haze. He shook his head, blinked wide, and blew out a deep breath as if it were smoke. He put one foot forward to take a step and stopped again. One hand still clasping the seat, he lifted the other to loosen the knot in his tie that he suddenly found stifling. Looking for the woman and the boy, he focused on Amina taking a tissue from her purse, then dabbing what looked like drips of blood from Tony's forehead.

Marvin extended a shaky hand. "Stay put," he ordered. "I'm gonna see if there's any security around here." Marvin stumbled his way through the aisle, reached the end of the carriage, opened the door, and moved into the next passenger car.

"You are going to be fine, young man," Amina told Tony with confidence as she gave him control of the tissue.

The words from the pretty lady brought immediate reassurance to the boy, who had every desire to play down his injury. "It doesn't hurt," he said, even though it did. He saw her smile.

"Just rest a minute," she said.

He liked her paying him such close and personal attention. It wasn't quite a motherly attention, but it was sensitive, and for a moment he fantasized making her his girlfriend. Shaken but confident, Tony lifted his eyes to Amina. "What was that wind?"

"This was a spiritual encounter, Antonio," she said. "Something came to strike us. To strike at you, and at Mister Fischer."

"Who?"

"Tell me again what you saw out the window."

"It was a man. Or at least it looked like a man."

Now the tense look on Amina's face worried Tony. Amina took short breaths. "Sometimes a spirit will take human form," she said.

Tony looked out through the windows, scanning each one of them. "He must be trying to stop us from finding Saint Peter. And from finding my mom."

Marvin Fischer had undone the rest of the knot in his tie and was letting it hang loose around his shoulders. He spoke in shaken but firm words with a railway security official in Coach A whose nametag identified him as 'Middleton'. Middleton had introduced himself to Marvin as Officer Scott Middleton, of the higher-ups on the English Territorial Police Force. Marvin had been lucky enough to run into a man who was not just rail security, but a senior law enforcement officer headed to Penrith with a colleague named Scott Jenkins. Officers Scott Middleton and Scott Jenkins were affectionately known back at the station as the Scottish Scotts, and to avoid confusion over their names went simply by Middleton and Jenkins—or after a few drinks at the pub, Middy and Jenky. The two men had worked together for two years and had been instructive consultants during the TransPennine overhaul, with the older Middleton serving as a mentor to the much younger but ambitious Jenkins.

Middleton's involvement onboard the TransPennine had been created in recent years following a stream of threats to public safety stemming from terrorist attacks across the UK. When Marvin discovered who Middleton was, he was swept with relief. Although Marvin worked with some of the largest law enforcement agencies in the world, he was not a field agent. It had been decades since Marvin had served on the Detroit police force, and he was less than confident in his street smarts, especially in a significantly unusual situation on foreign soil. Having Middleton on his side now was like having the Dalai Lama on his team. Marvin introduced himself as the Chief of Field Intelligence at the ACTIC in the United States, and both men shared an instant bond.

Officer Scott Middleton was ready to fully assist Marvin with his request to stop the train and obtain the manifest. Marvin wanted to see if by some luck the name Abiku Madaki appeared on the passenger list. He doubted it, but it had to be checked as a matter of protocol.

Directly to the train's engineer, Middleton commanded into his radio that the train be brought to an immediate stop. An unknown assailant had physically attacked two passengers and remained an imminent threat to passenger safety. After receiving confirmation from the engineer, Middleton barked orders to Officer Jenkins that he wanted the passenger manifest promptly. A safe and orderly evacuation procedure would be conducted once the train came to a full stop.

~

Marvin returned to Coach E, where he slid through the door. He was relieved to find Tony safely seated with eager eyes, and Amina bending to collect the boy's strewn homework. Seeing Marvin return, Amina asked, "What is happening?"

Marvin reached them and put a hand on Tony's shoulder. "You okay? Can you walk?"

"Yeah."

"We're stopping the train and everybody's gettin' off," said Marvin. "Come on, I'm taking you up front. There's first aid there. And I want you with security. There's a guy named Jenkins."

Marvin helped Tony out of the seat as Amina stuffed the homework into the backpack. "I hope we can keep going," said Tony, still holding the tissue to his forehead. Marvin kept a hand on Tony's shoulder and locked eyes with Amina as they moved to the door.

Officer Scott Middleton hung up the onboard communication transmitter in Coach A behind the engine. He had just contacted the territorial police with a description of the suspicious man described by Antonio Valdez, and of the strange events that had unfolded onboard. Police along the nearby highways were being notified of a possible suspect at large, and had been instructed to block routes surrounding Moffat, north to Elvanfoot, south to Johnstoneridge, and west and east between Durisdeer and Garwald.

"The buggar's got to be on foot. We'll nab him," Middleton said to the engineer as he climbed down the steps of Coach A and onto the grassy fields along the railway tracks. It hadn't rained in four days, so the ground was firm. The sun dominated the sky since the puffy gray clouds had given way to its light, its shafts dabbing the countryside like color from an artist's brush. The breeze carried echoes of skylarks from the moors across the distant fields. In all natural respects it was a beautiful crisp day in the Southern Uplands.

Amina and Tony stood near Officer Jenkins in the ankle-high grass. Tony pressed his back into Amina, who had her hands on his shoulders in a posture of mother-like protectiveness. She'd taken him to the first aid cabinet on the train where she had applied some disinfectant to Tony's head wound and carefully bandaged it. The white patch looked clean on Tony's forehead so Amina felt confident the bleeding had stopped, and as long as it was kept protected it would heal up fine without stitches. Amina was feeling more and more responsible for the boy and his safety. She wondered if Marvin might be feeling similarly, if he might even be considering backing off, and abandoning the whole idea following the harrowing attack.

Seventeen other passengers were disembarking along the length of the train, wandering listlessly into the fields. The engineer had made the announcement over the carriage speaker system informing the passengers of the emergency stop, instructing them to take their belongings with them and to stay not more than 50 yards from the train. So far, the emergency evacuation had proceeded without incident.

38

UPLANDS HUNT

Officer Scott Middleton's boots crushed through a patch of spindly wildflowers as he met with his colleague Scott Jenkins in the field. "Jenkins, I'm going to get with Fischer and see if we can't find the buggar hiding onboard somewhere. Keep channel one hot. I don't want him to get by us."

"Yes sir," Jenkins promised. Middleton wandered off to rendezvous with Marvin Fischer while Jenkins clicked his radio to the electronic voice confirming he was on the right channel. Jenkins stepped over to Amina and Tony, who were scanning the hills and mountains for any signs of trouble. "Don't you worry Miss," Jenkins said to Amina, nodding to Tony. "We'll find this fellow. One way or another."

"Thank you," Amina responded, but she knew they were dealing with something that was probably not human, and probably not going to show up here again in front of everyone to make a spectacle. This had been a personal attack—a secret—something to be kept hidden in the shadows. Someone or something was after Marvin and Tony, and Amina was now deep in the middle of it.

She wondered about the plans for the rest of the evening, about getting back on the train, about getting to Penrith and Keswick, and the walk they'd have to make to Castlerigg. By the time they got there it would be dark. She wasn't about to ask Officer Scott Middleton to send security to accompany them, as she wanted the séance to be low-key and free from any such distractions which could ward off the spirits she wanted to contact. At the same time, she knew she would have to figure out a way to keep the dark spirits away. The ordeal would be much more significant than she had at first imagined. There was some sort of primordial shift occurring on the other side, and she was just as curious about it as she was afraid.

She must maintain focus. She must not let the dark spirits know that she was afraid.

Amina put her arm around Tony and checked the bandage on his forehead. "It looks dry," she offered in comfort. "The pain pills kicking in?"

"It's throbbing a little but I can handle it," said Tony.

"Of course," Amina nodded, then looked off into the hills. "Where are we?" she asked Jenkins.

"Officially we're in the middle of nowhere, Miss. Southern Uplands near Moffat. Nobody here for miles I'm afraid. Haven't quite crossed the border into England yet. We've still about forty minutes to Penrith Station. Are you comfortable? Would you like to sit down? Can I get you some blankets?"

Tony shook his head. Amina smiled at Jenkins, "Thank you Officer, we are fine."

"Very good," Jenkins nodded, then lifted his hand to his eyebrows and scanned the countryside. Alert to the cue, Tony raised his binoculars and joined Jenkins in scouting.

Marvin Fischer and Officer Scott Middleton had systematically scoured Coach E, where the strange attack had occurred. They had doubled back to Coaches D and C and found nothing. Now they began to check Coach B, and would then inspect Coach A, working their way up to the engine. They searched for clues under the seats, checked for traces of forced entry around doors and windows, and scanned the ceilings and storage compartments for signs of tampering. All the while Marvin's brain raced to make sense of the mysterious attack.

Outside, a territorial police officer, who had been just nine minutes away, arrived at the scene and now searched below every car looking for clues.

By now Marvin and Middleton had reached Coach A and were finishing up their search. Marvin had dialed Elizabeth Walsh back at the ACTIC as he held the manifest in hand, and was speaking in frenzied tones. Presently it was 5:11pm UK time—seven hours ahead of Phoenix, where it was only 10:11 in the morning. Elizabeth Walsh had just returned from a brisk walk, and was back at her desk frantically conducting a data search. Marvin had briefed her on the strange events on the train, and that a passenger had reported seeing someone that sounded an awful lot like their suspect.

"The name Abiku Madaki does not appear on the manifest," Marvin said to Elizabeth into the phone as he continued to look behind seats. "Are you sure he doesn't have any aliases?"

"I'm doing another compilation as we speak," said Elizabeth. "But Stratton and I already did this when we started the investigation and we didn't find anything. As far as we can tell this guy is known only as Abiku Madaki."

"Okay. Get a hold of British intelligence. Make sure they're current on everything we have on Madaki." Marvin wandered slowly through the aisle on Coach A one last time, trying to talk over the radio chatter from Officer Middleton, who was jabbering something to Jenkins. Marvin spoke louder. "I'm working here with Officer Scott Middleton of the Territorial Police and he's got the word out to his force. Got it?"

"Yes sir, Officer Scott Middleton. Territorial Police."

"You and Stratton stay on this. Nothing else. This is your priority. Clear?"

"Absolutely," said Elizabeth firmly. "So much for your vacation, huh?"

"I'm countin' on you."

"I know," she said. There was a pause, and then, "Anything else?"

Marvin reached the train's door and leaned on the jamb. He wasn't going to let her in on the fact that Simon Peter had sent him a text image of Madaki. He hadn't revealed anything specific to Elizabeth about Rubi Valdez, or his insane quest, and he wasn't about to open that door with her now. "No. Call me with any news. If I don't pick up, leave a message and I'll get back to you. I may be off the grid for awhile."

"Okay. Just be careful."

Marvin clicked off and tucked the phone back into his pocket. Officer Middleton approached from the other side of the carriage. "I'm afraid we've got nothing sir," he reported. "Not in here, not outside."

Marvin squeezed his lips and sighed. He stepped out the door and down the two-step ladder, into the outside air and onto the grass. Officer Middleton followed. Marvin walked a few yards where Amina and Tony waited with Jenkins.

"Did you find anything?" asked Tony.

"No." Looking up into the sky, Marvin scanned the heavens, watched the gray clouds roam across the solid blue, and wondered what secrets lay hidden beyond.

Amina stepped behind Marvin and followed his gaze skyward. So did Officer Middleton, then Tony, and then Jenkins, until all of them stood looking aimlessly upward with blank faces.

"Watcha lookin' for up there sir?" asked Officer Middleton.

"I don't know," said Marvin quietly. "Anything. Something. Anything at all."

~

Five minutes later, Marvin stood limply with hands on hips, ten yards away from the Nova 2 with its electric engines humming back to life, the coffee stain dry on his once perfectly-pressed white shirt. Marvin had un-tucked, still trying to loosen up. He stood alone with Amina amidst the grasses and wildflowers, discussing the wisdom of continuing to Castlerigg given the recent encounter with the invisible force.

"Is this because we ate the cheese?" Marvin jabbed.

Indignation darkened Amina's hazel eyes to russet. "I should slap you!" she said. "The spiritual realm is highly unpredictable. But Shada saved us. I called out to her, she must have heard me and was able to get here quickly. Despite the interference."

"So all that wind. The attack. That's what you would call *interference*? From the other side?"

"Yes, interference of some form, yes," Amina's eyes were unsettled, flitting about the grassy fields aimlessly. In one more minute the train would continue to Penrith. The other passengers had already re-boarded, and the engineer was ready to resume the journey. Officer Middleton had decided to ride in Coach E with Marvin and his party, placing Jenkins in Coach A near the engineer.

"And what if this thing attacks us again?" Marvin postured.

Amina bit her lip, looking at the ground, as if she might find an answer in the soil or blades of grass. She looked up again into Marvin's eyes earnestly. "Your suspect," Amina said. "The death spirit warlord. Marvin I believe your suspect is not human. He may be a spiritual force of reckoning from the other side."

Marvin put a hand to his chin and inhaled. "You think Madaki is from the other side."

"Yes, I do. He is chasing us. Chasing you!"

Marvin looked at her through squinting eyes, still trying to rewire his mind to accommodate this supernatural perspective. It could not be true! Yet everything seemed to be pointing in that direction. And it was exactly what Elizabeth Walsh had speculated. Outside of his connection to the church through Caroline, Marvin was completely unaccustomed to thinking in spiritual terms, let alone contending with forces that went far beyond the norms.

"Come on!" Tony called from the train. "They're ready to go!" Marvin turned toward Tony, who stood waiting on the steps of Coach E, looking impatient. Marvin knew the boy wanted to keep going, that he wasn't about to turn back, no matter how badly his head hurt, or what else they may encounter. The kid just wanted to see his mom, for God's sakes. Now Officer Middleton joined Tony, climbed the last step, and disappeared into the carriage.

Impulsively, Marvin turned to Amina and looked into her face with determination. "We have to do this. We've got to get his mom back. It's us or nobody."

Amina nodded. "I have to admit to you Marvin that… I am a bit afraid."

He could see it in her eyes.

To go forward, or to give up?

To let it go, and just get the hell out of here?

Marvin put a hand on her shoulder now. Then, more gently, he said, "We can do this, Amina. Together."

Marvin's smartphone blared.

Decidedly, Amina nodded and turned for the train. Marvin watched the woman walk away, her back straight, head high, shoulders firm. He snatched his phone and saw the incoming call from Elizabeth Walsh. "Watcha got?" asked Marvin.

"I put a call in to MI5. I'm waiting to hear back," said Elizabeth.

"Okay. That's it?"

"While I was on the phone, Dominic showed up."

"Shit."

"He asked where you are."

"And?"

"I told him you went out for coffee. But he wants to meet with the group tomorrow morning. He wants you to head up the summary. Marvin you need to get back here!"

"I can't."

"He's going to find out you're gone!"

"I'll be back as soon as I can. I gotta go."

Marvin hung up. He had no intention of returning to the States before this was over. Right now he only hoped they'd make it to Penrith.

39

CASTLERIGG

The glistening 5-car tube zinged like a missile across the English border at Gretna Green with the three pilgrims huddled in silent angst. It wasn't much further to Penrith, where they'd hop the bus to Keswick. The 27-minute bus ride through another rural stretch of country was the last thing Marvin wanted to sit through. The wind—*the thing*—whatever it was, might try another attack en route. He imagined the bus spinning out of control, rolling over on the road and tumbling down some forgotten ravine, where their decomposing bodies would be discovered among the tall weeds after a month's time. Marvin shook off the image. They would just have to sit and sweat it out. He checked his Rolex. They would miss their originally scheduled time at the bus stop and not arrive until eight, just in time for the last bus to Keswick. Marvin crossed his fingers. He wanted to make the walk to Castlerigg as quickly as possible, get in touch with Saint Peter, and get this all over with.

~

The walk along Eleven Trees Road from Keswick to Castlerigg was becoming downright spooky. Marvin's nerves were on edge because of what had happened on the train, and as he walked beneath the dusky blue sky along the deserted road with Amina and Tony, he felt constantly as if someone were stalking them. He glanced over his shoulder for the twelfth time in ten minutes.

Their train had arrived safely at Penrith. They'd had only minutes to catch the last bus to Keswick. Tony had led the jog to the bus station, followed by Amina and Marvin, who'd huffed to make the bus, wishing they'd spent more time exercising and less time sitting at desks.

None of Marvin's fears about a disastrous bus trip materialized. It had been an easy ride through grassy hills spotted by trees and deep forests. They'd arrived at the A-framed Keswick bus station shortly after 8:30 and begun the one-and-a-half-mile walk to Castlerigg Stone Circle. It was this walk that made Marvin most jittery of all. Eleven Trees Road was a straight, two-lane asphalt road with the occasional gentle bend, flanked by shallow rolling hills on either side, the shapes of mountains in the distance. They were alone after they passed through town, left to nature, and vulnerable to whatever was out there waiting for them.

This lonely country road would take them all the way to Castlerigg.

The three travelers hiked elbow to elbow, Marvin near the road's shoulder, Amina beside, with Tony walking the painted line in the center like a gymnast on a balance beam. It was a chilly night with a tricky breeze, generally calm and then fanning into agitated flutter. Drifting clouds played with the first quarter moon in the otherwise clear sky, where the brightest stars were already beginning to bloom. The trio's long sharp shadows led their way ahead. It was eerily quiet but for the sounds of shoes scuffing pavement, and the chirping of bush crickets in the nearby fields.

Marvin felt the wind tickle his ear. He turned up his peacoat, buttoned the collar, and reproduced the black leather gloves from his pockets. Tony zipped his denim jacket which he'd layered over his hoodie, and Amina adjusted the small pack of supplies dangling from her shoulder and draped her head with a purple scarf.

"We are fortunate it is not raining," said Amina. "The weather can be quite fickle. This is England, remember."

"No kidding." said Marvin. "Right now I feel like I'm in a Stephen King novel."

"Marvin."

"Right. Positive energy."

Like magnets to metal, Tony's eyes were drawn to the captivating night sky. As his visual senses soaked in the cosmic tapestry revealing itself above, something caught his eye that seemed strange. He lifted his binoculars and focused the lenses, but the bounce in his steps prevented him getting a solid look. He stopped walking, focusing on the irregularity.

Noticing they'd lost a companion, the adults paused and turned to Tony.

"What are you doin'?" asked Marvin.

"There's something up there I don't remember seeing before."

"Like what?"

"I see a bright shape—it shouldn't be there. I mean, it's not supposed to be there." Tony panned left and refocused the lenses. "That's weird. I wish I had my telescope." He lowered the binoculars and pointed. "To the left of the moon, that bright light. It's brighter than the rest of the stars."

Marvin and Amina peered upward where Tony was pointing.

"A satellite?" suggested Amina.

"No, it's not moving," said Tony. He lifted the binoculars. "It's yellow... Mister Fischer I think we're supposed to go to that planet!"

"Get out," said Marvin. "How could you possibly see a new planet without a telescope?"

"The Dogon found a new star," Tony argued while refocusing. "They didn't have a telescope either... Oh poo! The clouds are in front of it now..."

"Come on let's keep goin'," Marvin prompted.

Tony skipped a few steps to catch up with the grown-ups. "It's like the Dogon tribe in Mali. Where I went last year with my mom," Tony pondered. "A long time ago the Dogon people found a star next to Sirius. A new star that's impossible to see without a telescope. But they said they knew about it for like hundreds of years. Before anyone else in the world knew it was there. They named it *Po Tolo*."

"Sounds like a European swim team," Marvin quipped.

"I wonder if I just discovered something new? That must be the planet we have to get to!" Tony mused, looking up again with his binoculars.

"Well you'll have plenty of time to stargaze if Saint Peter doesn't show up tonight," Marvin lobbed. "So Doctor, what else do we need to know about this Castle place? Unique spiritual potential, tool trading, musical choruses, what else?"

Amina smiled at Marvin's review. "Yes, Castlerigg Stone Circle. It is not a castle, it is an ancient circle of large stones," Amina answered.

"You mean *monoliths*," Marvin corrected.

Amina snarled and went on, "It is known more in esoteric groups than to the world at large. Stonehenge gets all the attention."

"Oh yeah, that thing in…uh…"

"—Wiltshire, yes. That *thing*. Castlerigg however dates from Neolithic times. So, newer than Stonehenge, but still plenty old. Older than the Knights of the Round Table, older than the Christ, older than the Buddha. It may have been used at one time as an astronomical observatory, and I believe it may also have been used for supernatural purposes."

"So you really think this place is our best shot at getting in touch with Saint Peter?"

"Yes. I believe that today—this day—Castlerigg is meant for us. For our purpose. For us to join with the hereafter. To somehow make contact, to make the connection we must make. Castlerigg carries great energy, powerful spiritual energy. We must tap into this energy. I believe Castlerigg may be—shall we say—a soft spot in the universe that makes it easier for spirits to communicate with us humans here in the physical realm. I believe it will teach us something that we must know."

"Have people made contact with the dead religious here before?" asked Marvin.

"Unknown."

The sky had grown dark as evening had fully given way to night. Marvin tried to distract himself from a growing skittishness. He observed a fence along the side of the road now that he hadn't noticed before—a fence of thick white posts spaced about eight feet apart. The white posts popped like glow sticks against the darkening grasses and roadside ditches.

"Are we almost there?" asked Tony.

Amina fanned her arm to their right. "We are here."

Castlerigg Stone Circle stood majestically 200 feet off the road in a flat green plateau beyond the white fence posts.

Marvin squinted. As the deep gray shadow of a giant drifting cloud rolled away, he could see under the sharp moonlight the giant stones standing hard and solid and rigid and tall, silently awaiting their arrival. He followed Amina and Tony through an opening between the white posts and stepped onto the field leading to the circle.

There was no distinguishable path.

Amina approached the circle slowly but confidently, flanked by Marvin and Tony, all eyes on what lay ahead of them. With each step they walked deeper into the past, closer to mystery, and into uncertainty. The moon dangled low in the sky, craning in like an emperor to watch his games, its bright beams splitting between the tall stones which cast their spears of indigo shadow. The breeze continued to whisper in unannounced gusts. A setter barked a mile away. Not another person was in sight, no house, no other structure of any kind. And somehow, there were no longer sounds of bush crickets.

The world fell into quietude.

When they were thirty feet away from the ancient stone circle, the brave and venturing trio stopped walking and stood like three marble effigies.

Marvin didn't know why they stopped. It seemed they had all stopped in unison. Maybe they stopped because they didn't know what to expect. Maybe they stopped because none of them were really sure what they were walking into. Marvin looked at each stone in turn. Most of them were somewhat tall and elongated, smooth but irregularly shaped. To him it appeared they all had invisible faces—or was he just imagining them?—looking inward toward the center of the circle. Maybe they were talking to each other. Maybe they were expecting their guests. Maybe they were alive. Maybe they used to be people. Most of the stones were taller than he was. Marvin listened for the mysterious music that Amina had spoken of, that had been heard here long ago by a man and his wife in an inexplicable event that had become legend.

But tonight there was nothing.

Not yet.

After what had been at least a minute, Amina braved the next step forward. Tony followed, then Marvin. He could feel his heart thumping in his chest, the air passing through his nose as he breathed. Amina walked them about a quarter of the way around the outside of the circle, then approached it more closely when she came to two stones that seemed to be set a little farther apart than the rest, and maybe a little taller. Marvin guessed the tallest boulder to be about 8 feet high, and that this must be some sort of formal entrance to the place. Amina stepped between the two large pillar stones and entered into the ring. Marvin and Tony entered with her.

"Castlerigg Stone Circle," said Amina reverently, her head still, eyes flicking left to right as if seeking something invisible, as if gauging a presence she expected to sense. As the enormousness of the moment reached her heart, Amina was overtaken by a deep breath. "Gentlemen, we have arrived." Her formality back in this moment of awe, she continued into the center of the circle. The circle itself was 100 feet across in diameter, comprised of 38 stones, metamorphic giants that had stood watch over whatever had happened here in the last 3,000 years. The circle echoed the shape of the surrounding landscape of distant rolling knolls and mountain peaks hiding in the moonlight.

The place was as glorious as it was ominous, living and breathing history.

"They are singing," said Amina, her heart lifting with courage as she sensed her clairaudience skills coming to her aid. "The spirits are singing. Do you hear them?"

Marvin and Tony listened, and shook their heads.

"No," said Marvin quietly.

"We should not tarry," said Amina. "Let us begin."

Amina led them across the grassy center of the circle to another set of smaller stones aligned near the inside perimeter of the circle. Here, these smaller stones were set in a rectangular pattern, forming an imaginary room without walls, on the very inside edge of the circle.

"Welcome to the sanctuary."

Amina stepped into the imaginary 'room'—the sanctuary—outlined by the smaller stones. Marvin and Tony followed her 'inside'. Amina stopped several feet away from one of the large stones that marked the outside of the greater circle, and turned to face Marvin and Tony. She took her small pack off her shoulder and set it gently on the ground. Bending her knees, she sat down gracefully onto the earth, crossing her ankles in front of her, gesturing for her companions to join her.

"Closer," she said.

Marvin and Tony took two steps each, then sat down opposite her, Marvin to her left, Tony to her right, close enough to touch each other. Amina unzipped her pack and withdrew one of the white pillar candles they'd acquired, and handed it to Tony. Amina dug into her pack again and retrieved the other two candles. She handed one candle to Marvin and set the third on the ground in front of her. The men followed her lead and set their candles down in front of them. Amina reached into her bag a third time and produced the click lighter. She ignited the flame and held it to the virgin wick on the candle in front of her.

"We belong today to the earth, and tomorrow to the heavens," Amina began.

The wick brightened with life by the wax of the white candle. Amina passed the lighter to Tony. He feared the breeze might blow out the candles, but, choosing not to question Amina, obediently ignited the lighter.

Amina continued. "Today we seek those in the heavens, those who can teach us great and unsearchable things which we do not know."

The wick on Tony's candle flared. He passed the lighter to Marvin. Marvin took the lighter, snuck a glance to Amina that fell somewhere between trust and suspicion, and ignited the lighter. He held the flame to the wick.

"We come in peace, love, and harmony," said Amina.

She was already transitioning, Marvin guessed, her mind traveling to some other place. The wind toyed with the flame as Marvin held the lighter, bending it this way and that, but the breeze lost out to the wick as it glowed to life. Marvin released the lighter trigger and handed it across to Amina. She set it quietly back into her pack, then set her hands palms down on the ground on either side of her.

"Feel," she said.

Marvin and Tony placed their hands on the ground beside themselves.

Amina closed her eyes.

She sat still.

The lights of the candle flames matured, burning brighter, strong but flickering in the night breeze.

For at least a minute, Amina sat silently with her eyes closed. By now it was completely dark outside, but for the moonlight that peeked between the passing clouds.

Finally Marvin ventured, "What are we doing?"

Amina opened her eyes to half-mast. "I am summoning Shada." She closed her eyes again. She began to speak in Navajo, like she had on the train, but calmly, slowly, softly.

As she spoke, Tony watched the stones, looking between them, at them, over them. On the top of one of the stones something caught his eye. He lifted his binoculars for a tight close-up. He noticed that the top of one of the stones seemed to align with a bright object in the dark sky above—the same bright yellow object he'd seen on the road on their walk earlier. Tony still could not conclude what the bright yellow object in the sky might be, and with the full moon it was strange to see other celestial objects so clearly and brightly. It excited him, and he wondered if it might have anything at all to do with what they were attempting here at Castlerigg.

Tony wondered if God could see them—if he might be signaling something?

Tony's attention was brought back to the circle when Amina stopped speaking Navajo. She opened her eyes.

Silently, Amina's eyes went to the earth, but they were not focused there. Her concentration was in her mind. She looked to Marvin like she was in some sort of trance. Marvin wanted to say something but held his tongue.

"Shada has not seen the saint," said Amina without emotion.

Marvin sat frozen and silent upon hearing the unwelcome news, eyes locked wide with trepidation on Amina.

Amina spoke again, "We will continue nevertheless."

She lifted her hands off the ground. Her eyes calm brown discs. She held her left arm up, hand open, palm facing forward.

She placed her right hand flat across her stomach. She took one slow, calm breath, and exhaled.

"Breath with me," she prompted.

Tony lifted his left hand up like Amina, palm facing forward, and also placed his right hand across his stomach and inhaled.

To Marvin it was starting to feel a little too much like some weird ritual, but he wasn't about to break this up. He positioned his arms and hands as Amina had, and inhaled.

After three deep, long breaths, Amina said, "Who will echo the prayer with me?"

Marvin's eyes darted to meet her. "What?"

All three of them remained as they had been, seated cross-legged, hands poised.

Amina's head did not move, but her eyes slid to meet Marvin's surprised gaze. "We must ask the favor of the gods before we continue. If the two of you repeat the prayer back with me, it will increase the power."

"Okay," said Tony.

An unexpected level of uneasiness suddenly flowed through Marvin, striking him deep inside his subconscious, down to his very soul.

Pray?...

A prayer was what had gotten them here in the first place!

Prayer was the very thing that had failed him when he desperately sought divine intervention to save Caroline on 9/11. In a microsecond, Marvin's most recent experiences flashed through his mind. He thought of Pastor Deckland Smith who'd prayed for his wife's recovery. Of Officer Nolan Garrison who had just lost his nephew only weeks earlier. Of Mother Teresa's doubt.

And of Rubi Valdez.

How could he possibly…?

"You two do it," Marvin decided.

Tony looked at Marvin. Amina gauged the man. He was looking down at the earth like a trapped soldier. Amina did her best to conceal a scowl.

"Very well," said Amina, and again closed her eyes. "Antonio Valdez, join me in seeking permission and guidance."

Tony nodded. He was afraid, but he was all in. He closed his eyes.

Amina began, "Thank you Lord and Creator and Master, Angels, Ascended Masters…"

"Wait a minute," Marvin interrupted.

"Yes?"

"If I don't pray—if I don't participate—and somethin' goes wrong, it'll be my fault."

"You mustn't think such things, Marvin. It does not work that way."

"Really?"

"You must remain optimistic Marvin. You are participating. Your positive energy will be sensed by the spirits, despite your reservations to recite the prayer."

Marvin's face was placid. "Okay I'll leave you to the prayer."

"Thank you. Antonio?" Tony nodded his readiness. Amina closed her eyes again, and started over. "Thank you Lord and Creator and Master, Angels, Ascended Masters…"

"Thank you Lord and Creator and Master, Angels, Ascended Masters…" Tony echoed.

"Protect all those here today from any negativity," Amina led.

"Protect all those here today from any negativity."

Marvin shifted position slightly. As he listened to the prayer he felt like a coward, like he was not part of the process.

Amina continued, "Thank you Creator and Master for assisting us in our seeking of higher knowledge and wisdom."

Tony echoed, "Thank you Creator and Master for assisting us in our seeking of higher knowledge and wisdom."

"Thank you for helping us to find and act upon our divine life purpose."

"Thank you for helping us to find and act upon our divine life purpose."

THE TEMPEST IN GLASS

Amina continued, "Help us to stay optimistic, calm, and enthusiastic."

"Help us to stay optimistic, calm, and enthusiastic," said Tony.

"We step forward to connect in truth and in love…"

"We step forward to connect in truth and in love…"

"…for the highest and greatest healing of all involved."

"…for the highest and greatest healing of all involved."

"And so it is, Amen."

"And so it is, Amen."

"I will take it from here Antonio," said Amina smoothly. "You may both open your eyes as we call for the saint."

Marvin and Tony opened their eyes, looked briefly around, and then centered again on Amina.

This was it, the moment of truth.

The event they had all prepared for.

The time had finally come.

And so Amina began, "Simon, Saint Peter, apostle and disciple of Jesus Christ, we come in peace. We ask that you communicate with us, here, tonight."

Tony felt a soft breeze against his cheek as the candles flickered. Marvin felt a stone underneath him that made sitting on the ground uncomfortable. Again he shifted position. Amina didn't move a muscle.

Nearly a minute passed.

Amina spoke again. "Simon, Saint Peter, apostle and disciple of Jesus Christ, we know and understand that you have sought us before, through Rubi Valdez. Please come to us now, so that we may hear, and so that we may inquire of you. We seek your wisdom and your counsel."

Another moment passed without any signs of anything changing. Then Amina cringed, as if a cramp had suddenly impacted her stomach. "Mmmmm…"

"What's wrong?" Marvin whispered.

"I have lost contact with Shada," Amina winced. "I no longer feel her presence." Amina leaned forward and grasped her stomach as the pain pierced her inside.

"You okay?" Marvin craned forward, extending a hand to Amina. She grasped his hand and in that moment her eyes lit, and she paused. The pain vanished within her! A soft and faint smile came to her face as she felt something positive—an energetic light beaming from within her spirit.

"Someone else is here!" said Amina. "Someone else is coming! Someone else is coming to see us!"

"Who?"

"I sense goodness... And peace!"

40

IN A WASH OF LIGHT

Marvin felt a gust from the cross breeze and all three candles blew out. Tony's curls rustled in the wind and with a quick jerk of her arm, Amina reached to catch her purple scarf as it blew from her head. At first Amina thought this might be the peaceful signal of a spirit coming to join them, but as the wind velocity quickly increased to a cold and angry push, she knew this was something different.

The force grew so powerfully that the three sitters found it impossible to sit straight without bracing themselves.

Marvin shot a fearful look to Amina just as a bright and piercing blue light blazed straight down on them like a pillar from high in the sky. Tony thought the moonlight had suddenly burst with intensity by a thousand times. Everyone shielded their eyes from the blinding blue light and ducked their heads, but the wind knocked them on their sides.

And if they could have had the privilege of witnessing this phenomenal and supernatural and historic event at Castlerigg Stone Circle from some distance, they would have seen that the entire inner circle had became awash in the bright blue light beaming down from the starlit sky and reflecting so powerfully off the stones that they seemed to glow white hot!

Tony braved a peek, shielding his eyes from the light by forming his hands into a small tunnel around his left eye, so he could see just a pinpoint of his surroundings through his circled palms.

But all Tony could see was a wash of light.

And suddenly there came a crunching CRASH.

Like a lightning impact.

But it wasn't.

To Marvin it sounded like a boom in the center of the circle behind them.

And the blinding light dimmed in an instant like someone had thrown a switch.

Everything went dark as before.

Once again only the moonlight bounced off the stones and the earth.

Startled and shaking, the travelers opened their eyes and looked around.

"What happened?" asked Marvin.

They turned and craned to see what had crashed into the center of the circle.

And there—in the very center of the circle—lay a man!

"There's someone there!" Tony pointed.

Jumping to his feet, Tony rushed over to the man lying on the ground.

Amina gracefully rose from her sitting position.

Marvin winced as his stiff legs awoke. He plodded behind Amina towards Tony and the man.

Tony kneeled down excitedly onto the grassy earth next to the mysterious visitor laying in the center of the circle and put his hands on the man's shoulder. "Mister! Are you okay?" Tony began to help the man sit up. "Mister! Hey—dude! Are you Saint Peter? Are you Saint Peter sir? Saint Peter the apostle?"

Marvin and Amina arrived and crouched next to Tony beside the man.

The man sat up, leaning with both arms behind him to support his torso. He blinked and shook his head, dazed. As the man gathered his composure and awareness came to his eyes, Marvin and Amina observed this newcomer that lay before them. The man wore a rich deep red, thickly woven medieval robe with a narrow collar, with its hood pulled over his head. The man's forehead was strong. He had large, wide-set eyes and bushy eyebrows. A large pointed and crooked nose dominated his face. There were creases along his cheeks that started at the sides of his nose and traveled down to his jowls. The man looked to be about 35.

The man peered at the three people around him and focused his eyes.

"Where am I?" the man asked.

"You are at Castlerigg Stone Circle, in Cumbria, England." Amina answered.

"On the planet earth," Tony added.

"Nice touch," Marvin winked.

"Who are you?" Amina asked the man.

"I am Dante... Dante Alighieri."

Totally confused, Marvin and Tony looked to Amina for clarification.

"Dante Alighieri, the Italian poet." Amina explained.

"Yes, yes that is I," said the man.

Marvin looked quizzically at Amina. Tony's face opened wide with puzzled excitement.

"Dante is Italy's most famous poet," Amina addressed Marvin and Tony's curious looks, and with a look of incredulity herself she went on to say, "Dante wrote *The Divine Comedy* in the fourteenth century. It is his epic poem. We talked about it at breakfast, do you recall? It is about his journey into hell, and into purgatory, and finally to heaven. It is a classic of high medieval Catholicism!"

Marvin leaned forward and pierced Amina with a stare. This was not happening.

"You've got to be kidding," said Marvin. "A poet?"

"Gentlemen this is unprecedented!" Amina continued.

"This guy's from Italy? Then how is he speaking English?"

"Don't ask questions Marvin. Just listen!" Amina was transfixed at the man Dante before her. "It is so, so very rare for someone from the other side to appear in his corporeal state, such firm physical properties, bringing such direct speech to the diviner!" Amina reached out and touched the man's ankles, touched his red cloak. It was breathtaking. She had to feel for herself, to confirm—"Not since ancient times—never in this present age—has it ever been recorded! This is maybe once in a millennium! Guys—somebody sent Dante to us!"

Marvin would have enjoyed calling Amina out for her use of the word *guys*, a clear departure from her professionalism and completely out of character. He chose to say something else but he was interrupted by—

"Wait wait…" Dante uttered. Sitting up straighter, Dante brought both hands to his lap. Feeling his energy return, his focus sharpening, Dante asked, "Who are you people?"

"Forgive me," said Amina. "I am Amina Karimova, professor of divinity and spirituality at the University of Edinburgh. This is Mister Marvin Fischer. He is an intelligence commander—for the government. And this is Mister Antonio Valdez. A student and close friend of ours."

"I see," said Dante. "Edinburgh has a university…?"

"You wrote the *Inferno*, the *Purgatorio*, and the *Paradiso*," Amina confirmed.

Dante smiled, pleased that this stranger was familiar with his work, but he shook his head. "Yes, yes I did. But that was before I knew what I was talking about. It is much more complicated than that, much more complex, much more involved…" Dante squinted and reached out to touch the zipper on Tony's hoodie. "Your clothes?" Dante asked.

"You are in the twenty-first century," Amina informed Dante.

Boggled, Dante's jaw dropped. He sat silent for a moment as his mind worked through the scenario. He shuffled his position, trying to stand up. Realizing what he wanted, Marvin and Amina grabbed Dante's arms and hoisted him to his feet. Tony placed a steadying hand to Dante's waist in case the man lost his balance. Dante looked around. "Such a unique place. There are many such monoliths in England, yes?"

"Yes," said Amina. "Can you walk?"

Dante looked down at the ground and took a careful step, then another. "I am okay," he said. Marvin and Amina let go of the man, still looking at him in somewhat of a state of shock. Dante brushed his robe with his hands and took his first deep breath since his crash landing. "I have not been back to earth since I died," he said.

The statement of the obvious suddenly jolted all three earthly travelers but that they had all momentarily forgotten.

That yes indeed—this Dante Alighieri was a dead man, of deep religion.

Amina knew that Dante Alighieri had been a supporter of the Papacy over the Roman Emperor, and had been exiled from his hometown of Florence and cast out of Italy for being on the losing side of a political crisis. Dante had written his magnum opus over a period of many years, having been strongly influenced by his contemporary, the poet Virgil. Dante's inventive writing style had altered the course of literary development for all time to come, and he had introduced strong theological ideas in his work. He had died centuries ago, but yet here he was—alive in his corporeal state—having come to them from some spiritual realm through some sort of gateway.

Had Dante been transformed from another bodily form so that he could meet with Amina and her companions in the flesh? Amina had no idea. But here was Dante Alighieri, with Marvin and Tony and herself, talking under the starry and moonlit sky.

Amina had been right to come to Castlerigg after all!

Marvin set aside his surreal feelings, tucking them away into a separate compartment in his mind. Here was this unexpected visitor whom he did not know and could not explain. But he finally got in his question. "Who sent you?"

"Nobody sent me," Dante answered.

"What?"

"I received a signal and I came." Dante was still sorting it all out himself.

"What signal?"

"A distress call, something urgent. I was told to come here... I think."

"You just said you weren't sent."

"Well..."

"So someone did send you." Marvin hated the mixed intelligence.

"Well I guess. You see—it is complicated—as I said. Very complicated." Dante walked away from the three, stepping closer to the perimeter of the circle, his heart and his mind and his feelings overtaking him as he absorbed his environment. The crew of three stood motionless and patient as they watched Dante approach one of the giant monoliths on the circle's perimeter. Dante lifted a hand and gingerly placed his palm onto the stone. He ran his hand across the hard surface and studied the rock, captured in awe.

"Magnificent... It is true. I am really here!" Dante stepped to the next stone and examined it. "I never thought I'd be back on this earth again." Then he carefully pointed at each stone in turn, as if counting them.

Marvin slowly stepped from the center and toward Dante, studying him. Amina and Tony followed until they were all beside Dante once again.

As memories of his old and former world cascaded into Dante's mind, he sprang into a verse from his most famous poem—"*And light I saw in fashion of a river, fulvid with its effulgence, 'twixt two banks depicted with an admirable Spring.*"

"That is it!" said Amina. "The Paradiso!"

"*Out of this river issued living sparks,*" Dante continued. "*And on all sides sank down into the flowers, like unto rubies that are set in gold.*" Dante faced Amina. "Yes—the Empyrean."

Amina leaned and whispered to Marvin, "He is describing his vision of heaven." And then to Dante she asked, "You have seen it Dante? You have seen heaven?"

"In a manner of speaking—" Dante answered.

"Hold on!" said Marvin, holding up his hand. "The Empyrean is heaven? Then where's Saint Peter? You must have seen Saint Peter, right Dante?"

"Now wait a minute…" Dante said.

"Did you come here from the Empyrean?" Amina asked.

The question did not register with Dante, who had locked on what Marvin had asked, realizing it was the same thing Tony had first questioned. "Is it Saint Peter you are after?" Dante asked. "Is that whom you were expecting to drop in? Is that why you are all so bewildered to see me?"

"Have you seen him?" Amina asked.

"Saint Peter? No, I have never met him."

"But you wrote about him in Paradiso. Did you not want to meet him, after you died?"

"Well sure I did, but just because you are dead doesn't mean you just automatically know everyone else who is dead too. It just doesn't work that way. It's very big over there—very, very, very big. And it's very complicated."

Tony stepped forward in front of Marvin and faced Dante. "Mister Dante, thank you for coming to see us. I have a question for you. Wherever it is that you come from, have you met anyone named Rubi Maria Valdez?"

Dante took his hand off the rock he had been admiring and paused. "Rubi Maria Valdez…" Dante mused. "No young man, I'm sorry. Doesn't ring a bell. Who is she? Has she been dead long?"

"She's my mother," said Tony hopefully.

"I see. I am very sorry, young man," said Dante, putting a hand on the boy's shoulder. "I hope she is okay."

Amina's eyebrows rose as she asked, "What do you mean you hope she is okay?"

"Well you see, it's very complicated," said Dante. "This person—your mother—Rubi, is it?"

Tony nodded. "Yes."

"Mmm, very pretty name. Rubi. She may be on her way to heaven—to the Empyrean—but there is much turbulence right now. It is very difficult to travel. Getting around is very, very, very complicated."

"You said you wrote your poem before you really knew what you were talking about," Amina sought to understand. "You wrote about the three dimensions a soul could travel to after death—hell, purgatory, and heaven—each of them having various levels of existence. Were you right about anything? Are there levels of hell and heaven?"

"There are no levels. There are no levels of anything. Levels of heaven, celestial spheres surrounding the earth, they do not exist in actuality. This was only our understanding of the earth and the heavenly realms at the time of my writing."

"Righteous!" Tony interjected. "Amina, you said Dante wrote his poem like in the fourteenth century?"

"That is correct."

"Then he wouldn't have known the earth isn't the center of the universe. Back then everybody thought the sun and the planets orbited the earth. They thought the earth didn't move. They thought there were layers around the earth…"

"Yes," Dante confirmed.

"… and they didn't know it was actually the earth and the planets that were orbiting the *sun*. That the sun is at the middle. It wasn't until Galileo who figured all that out. When he invented the telescope!"

"That sounds—err—*righteous*, young man," Dante agreed, putting a finger to his chin as his thoughts unfolded. "You are right. We all thought—since the days of Plato and Aristotle—that the earth was in the middle, hell was below, and heaven was above, and everything was divided into layers, or levels—globes around the globe of the earth so to say—and upon the death of the body each and every soul would travel through those levels and ultimately end up on one of those levels according to what he had done—or, according to what he believed."

"So—" Amina begged the question, "—if there are no levels, what is it really like on the other side?"

"There are different worlds—huge, expansive worlds—throughout which the spirits travel and wherein the spirits dwell," said Dante. "It's like—going to a different place on this planet, on planet earth. Yes? You want to go here, so you just go. You want to go there, you go. But you do not travel through different levels. Different planes. You see?"

"I see," answered Amina thoughtfully. "So, Saint Peter—where is he? Where might we find him? Why did he not respond to me calling to him tonight?"

"There is much turbulence in the spirit world right now," Dante repeated. "Much turbulence." He thought again for a moment, his finger returning to his chin in thoughtful repose. "What is it you seek to achieve?"

Marvin, silently listening to this discourse, realized that for whatever reason, it was now this Dante that was here, however unexpectedly, and he was apparently willing to listen to them and to help them. Marvin wanted to leverage Dante in whatever way he could, and so it would be necessary to reveal what this was all about, and how they had come to be here. "A few days ago," Marvin began, "Tony's mother Rubi Valdez…"

"Yes Rubi Maria Valdez…" Dante uttered.

"… came to me asking for prayer for her safety as she started a dangerous new job. Rubi told me it *had to be me* that prayed for her, because Saint Peter had visited her the night before, instructing her to find me. Saint Peter told Rubi exactly who I was, and where to find me the next morning. So I prayed for her. Tony was there.

And within a minute of that prayer, Rubi was killed in an accident. We want to find Saint Peter so he can bring her back to life."

Dante stood motionless and awestruck. He lowered his finger from his chin. "I see…" he said. His eyes looked around this way and that, moving in every direction and not stopping. He began to pace in wide circles. "So… Somehow, despite the turbulence, the good Saint Peter was able to cross over to warn Rubi Valdez of the coming danger—some complicated danger that would require the intervention of God himself to prevent—and Rubi was to seek you out Mister Fischer, for the prayer. But it didn't work." Dante looked at the three traveler's troubled faces. "The prayer. It didn't work. Your prayer for her safety. Perhaps your prayer did not reach God. Or, perhaps God silently let it pass. The point is, you prayed and Rubi died anyway. Her body was left on this earth and her soul began to travel to the other side, presumably where Saint Peter also dwells, and now you wish to locate the Saint so he can intervene and return Rubi to her physical life on earth, so that she may be reunited with her young son."

"Yeah, that's basically it," Marvin nodded, grimacing again at the seeming absurdity of the idea.

Dante continued, zigzagging now and gesturing with both hands as he spoke. "Yes, I see the logic of your quest. Saint Peter, disciple of Jesus Christ, is known to have performed many miracles after the departure of his Master from the earth. So you believe Saint Peter can perform such a miracle and return Rubi's soul to her body."

"Can it be done?" asked Amina.

"Is it possible?" Tony added.

Dante rubbed his hands together and continued to pace. "Let me think, let me think… Time does exist in the After Worlds, because the After Worlds still exist within the confines of a semi-physical creation, but time is not governed by luminaries orbiting a sun, it is governed directly by the Creator, and it moves nonlinearly and it moves much more quickly. It is difficult to understand and explain. It is very, very complicated."

"Yeah you've said that," Marvin quipped.

"So we can still be affected by time in the After Worlds?" asked Amina.

"Yes," Dante said, and he stopped, facing the three travelers. "There has been a misunderstanding among mortals that time and physical matter are properties of the earth and the created universe alone, and that these properties do not extend into the realms beyond. This is not correct. The Creator, to his delight and to our benefit, has amplified and extended such elements as time and physical places and pleasures, while at the same time adding a spiritual element, offering the ability to travel more quickly, sometimes instantly—ideally instantly—but that has become difficult, and many, many other amazing possibilities beyond the earthly experiment. How else are departed souls to enjoy themselves in the After Worlds? It makes sense, does it not? In any case, what I am trying to say, the souls of the departed, their spirits, their transhumanized forms, are able to interact with the After Worlds in ways that I find difficult to explain. Traveling has become troublesome, as I have already mentioned. Rubi—that is, the boy's mother—may or may not reach her destination."

"What are you gettin' at?" asked Marvin, growing tired of the rambling.

Dante tapped his fingers together. "I seek to explain the situation in a manner that still offers a degree of hope."

Tony took a step forward, afraid of what he was about to hear.

"Is my mom lost? Lost forever in the After Worlds? Can she never come back?"

"That is the question, my boy," said Dante. "Some time has gone by since her passing from this earth. Yes? How long?"

"Eight days," said Marvin.

Dante's jaw wrenched and his eyes pointed skyward as his thoughts raced to assemble a solution. "Even if you enter the After Worlds immediately, Rubi's soul may have already reached the point of no return," Dante said, his voice quivering. "You see, something has gone terribly wrong, and I do not fully understand it, but I do believe that in recent times God has found it necessary to contain and corral and confine as many souls as possible in the ultimate Empyrean—where God himself dwells, to protect them you might say—until such a time as they are ready for safe release and true freedom throughout the marvelous cities and mansions of the After Worlds. I do not believe that even Saint Peter can bring Rubi back once she has reached the Empyrean. You must intercept Rubi's spirit before she enters the Empyrean … Before she reaches God!"

The three adventurers stood still and mesmerized by Dante's words.

This all seemed so unreal.

So impossible.

Most disturbing of all was something Marvin hoped he had not heard or understood Dante to say. Surely Marvin must be mistaken; surely he did not hear what he thought he had heard. Marvin blinked and blinked again, feeling his heart sink and his forehead sweat despite the chill in the breeze. He felt the moonlight spill over his face and after what seemed like a minute but was only a nanosecond, Marvin asked only because he had to—"What do you mean, even if *we* enter the After Worlds?"

"You cannot reach Saint Peter from here," Dante explained. "There is too much interference. Too much turbulence. You must find Saint Peter *there*, in the After Worlds. You must go to the other side! And you do not have much time!"

Marvin could not believe his ears.

How would such a journey be even remotely possible?

"Please tell us, how do we find Saint Peter!" Amina begged.

"It will be very dangerous," Dante warned. "I cannot help you any further from here. You must find another helper in the After Worlds. Someone else who has already died and knows a better way!"

"Who?" asked Tony.

"Ah!" Dante beamed. "I know just the one. Yes, yes, he is most honorable, a mighty warrior, well acquainted with travel in the After Worlds and who knows many great men and women who have joined us beyond, someone who can help defend you against the enemies you will surely face! And I know where you can find him!" By now Dante had paced himself nearly to the center of the stone circle. He turned to face his new friends, eyes gleaming with an adventurous smile, arms spread out wide at his sides.

"You must go to *the clover*!" Dante exclaimed.

The words had hardly left Dante's lips when the wind pushed like a wall, abruptly and violently. Marvin stumbled backward and almost fell over. Amina dipped her head and held out her hands, trying to block the invisible force, but she was pushed back and held firm against one of the tall stones. Tony pressed his foot into the dirt at the base a stone, steadying himself, looking up in search of a source for the sudden increase in wind velocity.

Dante stood firm near the circle's center, his feet apart, red robe whipping and flapping and beating in the wind. He shielded his face from the wind and the wind did not move him.

"You have to get to the clover!!" Dante repeated.

"What's the clover?!" Marvin shouted back. Marvin was down on his knees with his knuckles pressed into the grass, his other hand shielding his face. By now there were at least 30 feet between he and Dante. Over the wind's increasing power, a loud rumbling sounded off, like a locomotive in rolling thunder. Bursts of what seemed like lightning began to flash, illuminating the interior of the circle for just a second or two at a time.

"It's happening again!" Tony shouted.

"It's an attack!!" Amina yelled.

Now Dante looked up and around, fear in his eyes. But he wasn't looking at Marvin or at Tony or at Amina. There was something else—some *one* else—a terrible dark presence, something that terrified Dante. "You stay away from me!" Dante cried into the wind—to a foe that he knew was there—but that he could not see. "Stay away from me!!"

It seemed calm outside the circle and Tony tried to step outside the stone circle. But all the wind concentrated inside the circle and it was so powerful that it kept Tony from exiting the arena of stone. The wind belted around the entire perimeter of the stone structure, encircling and trapping everyone inside. Marvin grasped at the blades of grass and weeds, struggling to crawl toward Dante, shouting above the deafening and thunderous wind.

"What's the clover!?!" Marvin shouted again, cheeks rippling in the wind, hoping Dante would hear him.

But outside the stone circle, where it was still calm, something else—something just as ominous and dangerous—emerged.

Something was happening in the flat green fields surrounding the circle of stones.

And it was not going to be good.

Blades of grass began to push up out of the ground.

Dirt crawled aside.

A fieldstone the size of a golf ball popped forth from the earth.

The stone hurtled toward the circle.

And in the following moments, like prairie dogs peeking from beneath the southern plains, other spots in the field began to pop and open up.

The fieldstones were yanked from the earth and hurled toward the circle as if by an invisible pitcher, passing through the circulating wind and whipping into the circle like line drives at a baseball game.

"Look out!!" Marvin shouted. Amina ducked as a rock hissed past her head and exploded on the monolith behind her. Tony leaped aside to avoid being hit by a rock the size of a tennis ball. Marvin covered his head, peeking toward Dante. Dante stood alone in the middle of the circle, wind now whipping around him like the tentacles of an octopus. Dante batted away rocks with his hands and arms as he began to lift off the ground and into a swirling cloud of wind, light, and gray smoke. "Stay away from me!!" Dante screamed.

"Dante!!" Marvin shouted.

Tony saw it too. "Mister Dante!! Come back!!"

And then—POW!

A flying stone struck Tony in the temple.

Tony crumpled to the ground in a heap.

"Antonio!!" called Amina.

Desperately she tried to move to him.

But the wind was too strong a foe.

Amina could not move.

Marvin saw Tony lying motionless on the earth across the circle. Marvin's forehead wrinkled in anger as he felt his heart race. His face burned hot red as his blood boiled through the veins in his temples. Marvin reached and grabbed and dug into the grass, into the earth, pushing with his feet as he crawled across the ground with every ounce of strength he could muster.

He had to reach Dante!!

The wind whipped and the flashes of light burst and the thunderous noise roared around him. But Marvin pushed and pulled and tugged and crawled his way closer… closer… closer to Dante.

But no… Marvin was powerless, useless to do anything against this impossible enemy.

He couldn't make it!

He couldn't get there!

Marvin looked up again at Dante through the blast and blur of soaring leaves and debris.

Now Dante flipped head over heels, hanging upside down in the flashing air!

The hand of gray smoke engulfed Dante at the very center of the forceful wind.

"Erzok!" Dante shouted. "Erzok! Erzok NO!!"

Amina's eyes bulged at the mention of 'Erzok'.

Dante struggled and groped, trying to get a grasp of the ground. "Help me!!" he shouted.

Marvin screamed a desperate cry as he crawled toward Dante. Marvin reached out a hand.

"Marvin no! You'll be sucked away!" Amina shouted.

Marvin did not listen.

He stretched out his hand as far as he possibly could to Dante's outstretched arm. "What's the clover!?!" Marvin shouted again.

"The clover!! Dante shouted. "It's at the center of the—"

WOOOSH!

Dante vanished in a rush of wind and power, pulled up into the evil cloud.

In the next instant, the wind stopped.

The flashes of light dimmed.

The thunderous roar ended.

Rocks that had still been flying through the air dropped harmlessly to the ground.

Marvin crumpled to the earth and rolled over, exhausted.

Amina staggered to Tony's side.

She reached the boy and turned him over onto his back.

"Antonio! Antonio!" she cried.

No response.

Amina pulled the boy up to her chest and embraced his wilted body.

Marvin lifted himself to his knees and looked helplessly up into the night sky.

A cloud drifted past the quarter moon.

There was no sign of their friendly visitor.

Castlerigg plunged back into darkness.

And Dante Alighieri was gone.

PART III

41

ELEVEN TREES ROAD

The scuffed toe of his dirty wingtip faltered on a protruding stone as Marvin crossed the chasm of gray grass under the moonlight, carrying the unconscious boy back toward Eleven Trees Road. Marvin wanted to get as far away from that dreaded stone circle as possible, and as quickly as he could. Tony's body lay sprawled in Marvin's arms, droopy and limp, head propped in the bend at Marvin's elbow. The only assurance Marvin had that the boy was not dead was the weak pulse and the breath he had felt coming from the boy's mouth, when he had pressed his ear to the lips as the body lay prone under the dark sky in the sanctuary.

Amina followed close behind, her face full of fret and worry and fear, her head turning constantly and frantically behind and before her, as if that were some defense against whatever may come next.

Marvin passed between two white posts and reached the roadside, bent to one knee, and gently let the boy slip out of his arms and onto the grassy earth. Marvin leaned in again to the boy's lips and confirmed the presence of breath. The stone that had knocked Tony had thankfully not cracked him wide open. There was no blood in the hair, no open wound. Even so, the stern crease in Marvin's brow exposed his apprehension. "He may have a concussion."

Marvin stood up and hovered over Tony. The boy lay still on his back with one arm at his side, the other crossed over his waist, head tipped to one side, his binoculars lying between arm and body, its blue nylon cord curled and touching the chin.

Marvin cursed himself for agreeing to the damn train ride, for having left the Bentley back at the Edinburgh rail station. He swept the condemnation aside and snatched the smartphone from beneath his peacoat. Removing one of his leather gloves, Marvin punched a button and waited.

"Scott? It's Marvin Fischer."

Marvin explained to Officer Scott Middleton their desperate situation, and asked if a police car could be sent to retrieve them and get the boy to a hospital.

"By all means, sir," Middleton responded with gravity. "I'll get someone out to you straightaway."

Relieved that help was coming, Marvin tucked his phone away, refit the glove, and turned to Amina. She was standing by one of the white posts, both hands resting on top of it, her face gazing back at the tranquil and innocent stone circle 200 feet off the road.

Marvin stepped behind her, arms at his sides. His voice cut the cold air like a laser. "What's the clover?"

The question prompted an impulsive intake of breath into her lungs as Amina felt her veins rush with nervous blood. She turned around towards the man, crossing her arms defensively. "Marvin…"

"Tell me. What's the clover?"

Marvin squinted, probing deep into Amina's hazel eyes that were avoiding his gaze, and he wondered why she had even turned around if she wasn't going to look at him. Searching, evaluating, speculating, Marvin tried to read the thoughts behind the dodging eyes that looked everywhere but at him.

And now Marvin crossed his arms. "You *do know*, don't you?" he asked. "You know what the clover is. And where it is."

Amina let her arms go free and she swayed as she shook her head. She put her face in her hands, then dropped them suddenly and looked up and drilled her eyes into Marvin's.

"I am protecting you!" she spurted.

"Where is the clover?" Marvin asked again.

"What about Antonio?" she said, her face crumbling.

"I need to get Tony's mother back." Marvin stood firm and unmoving.

"Did you hear what Dante shouted as he was being sucked away?"

"Yeah, he said we have to find the clover."

"He also shouted 'Erzok'. Did you hear that?" Her eyes darted. Her fingers fidgeted.

"So where's Erzok?"

The black memories assaulted Amina with torpedoes of horror. The sandy and rocky shore of the Indian Ocean in Malindi. The Pillar of Vargo da Gama. The African townsman. The séance. The falling air. The wind.

"Erzok is not a place," Amina began. "It is a name, Marvin. It stems from ancient Babylon."

Marvin inhaled. The air seemed instantly colder. He watched the strength and confidence melt away from her. Something was different, something had changed. This was not the woman he had come to know. He softened. "Okay. Whose name?"

"Erzok is the name of a god," her voice quivered. "A powerful and evil god. Perhaps the most powerful. It has always been just a myth, Marvin… just a myth…" Her voice faded. Her nostrils flared in tension. She made her mouth small and tight.

"What else?"

Amina tried to look Marvin in the eyes, and she did when she could. But her nerves were unraveling and she could not stand still. She swallowed and went on. "About a year and a half ago I had a terrifying experience. I was doing a séance for someone in Malindi.

The dark magic interfered. Dark spirits. There was wind, Marvin. It rushed at us from off the water. It threw us into the rocks and I heard the name '*Erzok*.' It ripped me to my core. I have not done a séance since. I have been too afraid."

"Then why did you agree to do this?" He was trying to empathize, to understand.

Amina clenched her lips again and her eyes welled. "Because I wanted to help the boy. And… and I didn't want my own fear to win out." Amina put a closed fist to her chin and swallowed. She breathed heavily and then put both arms down straight at her sides to compose herself. "Many mediums have had difficulty reaching the dead in these last months, I told you that."

"Yes, you did."

"I sense the spiritual turbulence between higher powers is escalating, Marvin, and I am afraid that you and the boy are caught right in the middle of it."

Marvin dropped his arms to his sides and tipped his head up, his eyes still looking knowingly now at the woman. "So that's it," he said. "That's why you didn't show up at the library at the university, when we first came to meet you. That's why you've been so cautious. You've been terrified of this."

"I would be a fool not to be! If you go to the clover Marvin—if you cross over—everything as you know it is going to blow up in your mind. No one has ever tried to go to the After Worlds in-body, and expected to come back. It cannot be done!"

"What about that guy that you said got '*caught away*' to the third heaven? And heard those secret things he couldn't tell? Didn't he come back?"

"No one knows what happened to him. No one even knows who he was!"

They stood there for a half a minute in silence, pondering and breathing. Marvin looked down again at Tony's unconscious body. Amina watched him survey the boy.

"Marvin, please listen. We are dealing with spiritual forces too powerful for humans to contend with. You must stop, Marvin.

You must not go! What happened in the circle changes everything. You will die! And the boy too!"

"What about Shada? She helped us on the train. She'll help us again, won't she?"

"I told you, I lost contact with Shada. I do not know where she is!"

"Don't you have a crystal or somethin' you can give me? A lucky charm?"

Amina scowled. "Mister Fischer don't you dare."

"We're back to Mister Fischer now."

"It is too dangerous!"

"So you're givin' up on that boy?"

"That boy? I am doing this all by myself!" Amina fired back. "At the moment of truth, you sat there in front of *that boy* and did not pray, because of your own rickety lack of faith! How dare you accuse me of giving up!"

She was right, and he knew it. The accusation pierced and stung and Marvin clenched his teeth, ignoring the truth of it. "So what now?" he asked.

"I am sorry Marvin," Amina said, stepping blindly past Marvin and past Tony lying in the grass, and onto the paved road without a backward glance.

"You're just gonna walk away?" said Marvin, arms out to his sides. "Alone? In the dark? The middle of the night?"

Amina turned around, facing him, walking backwards along the road, "Think about it Marvin. Do not go." And she turned again away.

"Amina! Don't!" Marvin pulled out his smartphone, frantic, quickly opening the image of Amina's profile picture, the one sent to him by Simon Peter. He held it up high over his head. "You remember I told you, right? This image—of you—it came from Saint Peter! It has to be you! Just like it had to be me!"

Amina ignored him.

"You've got to be kidding!"

Amina disappeared speedily into the darkness.

Marvin shouted, "Where's *your* faith?!"

Marvin released a disgusted grunt and turned back to Tony who still lay motionless. Marvin checked his Rolex, then squatted down next to Tony.

Marvin resolved he'd just have to find Saint Peter himself, even if it killed him.

42
WHERE'S THE LADY?

The next fifteen minutes seemed like an eternity. The crickets slept. No dog barked. All was quiet. Marvin sat with knees up and heels digging into the grass, resting his elbows on his knees with clasped hands in front. He sighed deeply. He watched a cloud pass in front of the moon. He looked around into the dark hills and felt the breeze lick his cheek. It was gentle but cold, the only sound, as the wind tickled his earlobes. Marvin checked his Rolex yet again, conscious of the sound of the rubbing of the fabric of his own clothing as he shifted, a sound he normally never even thought about, but strangely amplified in this quiet world. Then the sounds of his heels digging into dirt, the breath through his nose, reminded him of his physical self. He lifted the Rolex to his ear and listened to the soft click of the movement. Life was ticking away. His life. Tony's life. Amina's. What would Marvin do next? What would time tell?

He wondered how long it would take Middleton's man to get here. Marvin felt completely out of his element, alone and suddenly angry. He gritted his teeth and clenched his jaw. He knew he was a fool for trying to assure himself that he was tougher than whatever waited for him out there, whenever it would strike again.

And for the first time in quite some time he wished he'd had a gun. He hadn't carried much since he'd left the force. The uniform had offered the obvious excuse to pack. But once he'd donned the daily suit and tie, he'd wrestled with fitting a holster that pleased him. He disliked the bulk of the ankle. The inner waist was uncomfortable, as was the small of the back. The shoulder holster had proved most comfortable, but the bulge ruined the fit of his favorite slim suits. Eventually the sidearm faded from use. He owned only one now anyway, since he'd left the force, a Walther P99 compact, locked in a safe at his condo in Paradise Valley, a souvenir trinket that did him little good. Marvin pondered he hadn't even been to the range in three years, and would probably miss Abiku Madaki if he weren't ten feet away.

Marvin shuffled himself down to listen again to the breath coming from Tony's mouth, and sighed in anxious relief that the boy seemed stable.

And then he thought about praying for the kid.

Amina was right. Marvin had been a pathetic, faithless idiot.

Marvin put a hand on Tony's shoulder. He clenched his jaw again and drew in a breath through tight nostrils, eyes locked on Tony's unconscious face. Marvin wanted to pray, and almost felt like praying, but could not bring himself to it. What good would come from a prayer now? Or worse, what more horror? He would just be talking to the wind, jabbering to dead air, to himself, to closed ears. He decided it would be no use. He chased off the bitter feeling with a quick shake of his head and a cynical glare into the darkness.

The matter was best resolved himself.

No way would he pray.

Help was already on the way.

Marvin kept his hand resting gently on the boy's shoulder and felt himself losing control of his breathing as he choked down another swell deep in his chest. What was it now? Grief? The realization of failure? Guilt over refusing to pray for the poor kid?

Marvin pulled his hand away from the boy and sniffled, wiping his nose in the air that grew colder by the minute. The boy's low pulse would cause his body temperature to fall rapidly. Marvin reached over and gently lifted the boy's head, then yanked the hood out from beneath the shoulder. Marvin worked the orange hood around Tony's head and drew the cords of the cowl tight around the cheeks. Marvin unbuttoned his peacoat, slipped out of it, shook it open, and used it as a blanket to cover the boy. He tucked the coat beneath Tony's arms and under his thighs until Marvin was satisfied with the wrap.

The kid looked like a giant burrito.

A brief comforting laugh escaped through Marvin's lips.

Feeling the cold, Marvin rubbed his hands across his chest and his arms. He pulled his legs in closer to his chest and wrapped his arms around his legs again to keep warm. He thought about retrieving a couple of the candles from the stone circle, but he wasn't about to leave the boy, or go back in there.

Marvin began to worry about how he could possibly continue on without Amina. He knew that at some point Abiku Madaki would attack again, and there was no way he could forecast when or where that might occur. He had no defense, no counter-evil strategy that could thwart the next attack.

It was the hard white light fading up into Marvin's face that jarred him from his thoughts. Far down Eleven Trees Road, from the east, a car was approaching.

The car had just turned the bend and was heading straight for Marvin and Tony. Marvin swiveled on his bottom to observe the incoming vehicle.

Surely this must be Middleton's guy.

Thank God.

Marvin's stiff legs groaned as he stood up, facing the car. The headlights grew brighter as they cut through the cold dark air and Marvin had to squint. His exhaled breath froze in a cloud.

And then, Marvin's body stiffened and his eyes went foggy.

What if it wasn't the cops? What if was Abiku Madaki?!

The thought invaded Marvin.

Fear shot through like a javelin.

He and the boy were alone and defenseless.

Madaki could take them out right here, easily and quietly.

And the world would never know.

Oh shit.

The car came closer.

Marvin spread his feet shoulder width and stood tall and confident, ignoring the cold, standing guard above Tony on the grass. He sniffled and shook his head, tipping his forehead to the sky in a show of strength, and glared at the windshield through the flaring white lights of the headlamps.

The car slowed and rolled up, twenty feet away.

Ten.

Five.

The car stopped.

Marvin still could not see the driver.

He took a breath and stepped bravely to the window.

The pane of glass rolled down and Marvin bent and looked into the cockpit.

Middleton.

"Sorry it took me a bit, sir. We're mighty thin tonight, searching for that suspect."

Marvin's mouth dropped and his eyelids closed as a breath of air gushed from his lungs in release. "Good to see you."

Officer Middleton opened the driver door and stepped into the road. "Let's get the boy into the back." Middleton looked around. "Where's the lady?"

Marvin shook his head and frowned. "She—"

"Oh there she comes," said Middleton, gesturing down the road the opposite way.

Marvin's eyes opened wide, his lips frozen open. He watched Middleton's face looking at something, then Marvin turned to see Amina Karimova walking back up the road.

How far she had gone before she had turned back, Marvin had no idea.

Officer Middleton crouched over Tony on the grass and checked his vitals.

Marvin, a flutter of hope lifting his heart, held up a finger and said, "I'll be right back."

Marvin's dirty wingtips clicked in the night as he quickstepped along the pavement and met Amina face to face in the center of the quiet and dark road. He tried to contain the brightness in his soul as he reigned in an expression of relief. "Did you forget to slap me?"

Hands in the pockets of her tweed coat, Amina's eyes were steady and focused. "Mexico City," she said.

"What?" Marvin's relief snapped back to uncertainty.

"We have to get a flight to Mexico City."

"Because...?"

"Because you are right, Marvin. You are right about everything. And I *do* know where the clover is." She took a step closer to him, locking on his expectant eyes. "The clover is underground. In the tunnel beneath the Pyramid of the Sun. At Teotihuacán."

43

CONSTABULARY

It might have been the rising voices of conversation that finally woke Tony out of his deep period of unconsciousness. When his eyelids first cracked open, he saw an upholstered surface above, and dark windows. There was the hum of an engine. Something bright zipped past one of the windows. He realized he was lying flat in the back seat of a moving car, his head on someone's lap. The scent belonged to Doctor Karimova. Tony's eyes focused on the bottom of her chin. The gold hoop earrings wobbled on her earlobes as she spoke with energy, and Tony could feel one of her hands resting on his chest.

"We're not going home, are we?" Tony's voice creaked.

Amina's face brightened. "Antonio! So nice to see you are awake."

Marvin, riding shotgun next to Officer Middleton, twisted to see the boy returning to the night. "Hey buddy. You okay?"

"I saw that yellow planet again. While I was asleep. I think we have to go there."

"You really do need your head examined."

"Where are we going?" Tony tried to sit but winced in throbbing pain. He settled back into Amina's lap and put a hand to his forehead. Marvin explained that Officer Middleton was driving to the Cumbria Constabulary—that's the nearest police station in Penrith—where the paramedic on duty would examine Tony and evaluate whether or not his head injury required serious attention. If at all possible, for security reasons, they wanted to avoid a trip to the hospital and keep everything low-key. Marvin asked a few diagnostic questions. Tony gave the correct answers, further relieving his companions. Tony knew his name, what year it was, who the President of the United States was, and what country they were in.

In the remaining minutes of their journey to the Constabulary, Marvin explained what had transpired in the time since Tony blacked out. Dante Alighieri had vanished, but had told them they needed to go to someplace called *the clover*. Amina was familiar with Teotihuacán and some of the history and mythology surrounding the clover, and was formulating a theory about its spiritual significance and how it might fit in with their own mission. Marvin explained that Amina's belief was that Dante's reference to the clover was probably an underground formation beneath the Pyramid of the Sun—a 2,000 year-old archaeological site located at Teotihuacán, Mexico. The ancient Mesoamericans believed it to be the birthplace of the gods.

"The clover is situated at the end of a naturally formed cave," said Amina, taking over the conversation. "The Mesoamericans believed the clover was a symbol of creation, a gateway to the underworld. Based on excavations at the site in the 1970s, and early writings in the Huehuetlatolli codices, historians believe there was once a shrine, built directly above the underground clover, which the locals deemed sacred. And with the abundance of rare green obsidian in the valley, the place grew to become an economic metropolis. The shrine above the clover was a magnet of pilgrimage for religious rites and the worship of the deities of water, sun, and moon. As the city grew, residences were erected, and the Pyramid of the Sun was built atop the clover, replacing the original shrine."

Mister Fischer had already made airline reservations via his smartphone while en route. Tony's countenance lifted and his heart raced with excitement as Marvin explained that they had decided to continue their journey and explore Teotihuacán, somehow get down into the tunnel under the pyramid, and find out what this clover was all about.

Officer Scott Middleton navigated the roundabout on A66 that spilled his blue and white police car into the Fire and Rescue Station one block away from the Constabulary. Thankfully, Tony checked out fine with the medic. The man replaced Tony's forehead bandage, which had become loose during the turmoil at Castlerigg, and while he recommended that the boy get an MRI as soon as convenient, he felt confident the boy was okay.

Officer Middleton suggested they all bunk at the station for a few hours before their departing flight from Newcastle in the morning. They'd have to share a room, but at least it was convenient, and perhaps the safest choice. Marvin thanked Officer Middleton profusely and promised him a case of the best California Pinot Noir as soon as he returned to the states.

"Better make it two cases, sir," Middleton joked. "I'm also driving you to the airport in the morning!"

44
CONNECTING THE DOTS

Her birthday was a week away when she would turn 30, and she dreaded the prospect. She was glad that no one besides her sister would even recognize the occasion. As she sat with bare unshaven legs pulled to her chest, lounging on a soft reading chair in her apartment, Elizabeth Walsh felt old.

She was drinking it down fast, so the last sip of pink Zinfandel was still cool to the tongue. Her blonde hair tumbled down unkempt. She sat in loose shorts and a man's T-shirt, from the hot barman whom she'd slept with four weeks earlier and hadn't seen since. It had been an unusual night when she'd gone out on the town alone while in a personal state of anarchy. Now she felt guilty, like a bad Catholic. She did not even know why she had kept the shirt. He hadn't been that nice of a guy, and the shirt still carried the man's scent.

Thinking she might get up for a refill, Elizabeth instead turned the page of the latest romance novel she'd picked up with a dozen more a few weeks prior. The fantasies distracted her from her own pursuit, which had remained stagnant and uncertain in the few days since she'd gifted Marvin Fischer with the necktie. Still she doubted herself, wondering if she'd gone too far.

The novel was making her steamy. Elizabeth set the book face down, snatched the empty wine glass, and strolled barefoot to the kitchen. Her place was a cluttered studio, clothes strewn about, a tiny eating table, a pile of unwashed dishes in the sink, a large framed black and white Eifel Tower on the wall. Elizabeth set the glass on the counter next to the chilly boxed Zin and stripped off the T-shirt and tossed it into the kitchen garbage. She cupped her breasts with her hands, then wished she had never given them to that man. She tugged a sweatshirt from the back of a chair and dove into it. Turning to the wine she refilled her glass, took a large sip, savored its fruitberry notes, and began the short walk back to the chair.

Then her smartphone sprung to life with Norah Jones. Elizabeth reached the table by her reading chair and picked up the phone and checked the caller.

It was Marvin Fischer.

An electric rush streamed from heart to fingertips, but Elizabeth did not want to come across excitable. Excitement became a flash of nerves, and now she wished she hadn't been drinking. It would be okay, she told herself. She was buzzed, but not drunk. She suddenly felt vulnerable. Plopping down in the soft chair, she crossed her chest with a forearm and tucked the phone to her ear. "You're up late," she said matter-of-factly.

"Yeah."

"You back in town?"

"No."

Elizabeth hid the disappointment in her voice when she said, "We've got the meeting with Dominic tomorrow."

"You busy?"

"Just reading."

"Rustlers Under The Texas Moon?"

"None of your business." Elizabeth reached for the wine. She was playing the same game of avoidance with him that he played with her all the time. She didn't know why. What did she hope to gain by the tactic?

There was silence for a few seconds before Marvin offered coldly, "You're not gonna find your knight in shining armor in the pages of a novel."

"Then where am I going to find him?"

"You'll find him."

That was it. He was telling her there was no future for the two of them. The tie hadn't worked, and he'd made up his mind. Was that the intended analysis she was to glean from this vague intel? Elizabeth frowned. Something sank inside of her, and again the spiking fear of another woman stabbed into her chest. She suddenly resented that Marvin was giving her personal advice in the tone as her boss. "Why did you call?" she asked.

"Did you say the Bureau wrapped their investigation at Teotihuacán?"

"Oh you can pronounce it now. Yeah. Why, you got something else?"

"What's the gist of the Bureau's findings?"

Elizabeth sighed, stuffing her fingers into her tussled hair. "Well the official report hasn't hit, but I talked to Benjamin Taft. The kill zone is a crater. Some of the residue from the bomb materials turned up in the intermediate zone."

She reached and took a generous sip of the wine. The glass was already half empty.

"And?" she heard Marvin say.

Elizabeth finished swallowing and said, "It matches the stuff used in the Roman cathedral and the Mosque in Damascus. Bottom line, it's more evidence that ties Madaki to the incident. We need to figure out why the guy set off that bomb right at the open spot to the cave, ya know, leading under the big pyramid. Why that spot. Why that place?"

Now she was really feeling the buzz. That last big sip had traveled fast. There came another silence between them. She wanted to ask him again if there was someone else, but she didn't.

Elizabeth swirled the wine in the glass. "Marvin?" she prompted. "Are you working this case from another angle?"

After another pause, she heard him say, "We got hit again. The invisible force, the wind."

"Like on the train?"

"Yeah."

Elizabeth gulped the last of the wine and set down the empty glass. She leaned forward in the chair, her feet spread wide and flat on the floor, elbows on her bare knees. "What happened?"

"We were at this place called Castlerigg—"

"—Marvin who's *we*? Who's with you?" She couldn't stand it any longer, and the conversation had presented an opportunity to ask the question logically without making her look like the jealous college girl.

And after a few more long pauses of avoidance, Elizabeth finally wrenched the story out of him. Marvin Fischer finally told Elizabeth Walsh about Rubi Valdez, and about what had happened on that fateful morning when he had prayed for her, that Rubi had died in that car wreck immediately after Marvin's prayer.

"Oh my God." said Elizabeth.

Marvin went on. He told Elizabeth about Rubi's son Antonio, about Rubi's visit from Saint Peter, and about the crazy connection with Doctor Amina Karimova that seemed to have been linked to the saint. And then Marvin told Elizabeth details of the encounter with Dante Alighieri at Castlerigg, how the wind had sucked the poet away, and about the imminent trip to Teotihuacán. "We're flyin' into Mexico City tomorrow," he said, "and then we're headed to that pyramid so we can find this *clover* and get to the After Worlds."

Elizabeth was stunned. It was a supernatural quest for an impossible miracle that was leading them all into chaos and disaster. Twice now this man had come close to being killed. Marvin admitted to Elizabeth that the likelihood of Abiku Madaki being human was fading fast in favor of her own crazy theory that Abiku Madaki was from *the other side*.

"And you didn't believe me!" Elizabeth scolded.

"I do now."

Elizabeth shot up from the chair. Suddenly the walls wobbled. The buzz was strong now, but after a second she felt her mind clear and she was still sharp and laser focused. It was the sweet spot of the buzz, her favorite part, when she felt light and great and happy and firm, before the alcohol inhibited her from functioning reasonably. "Wait a minute…" she whispered.

"What?"

"It does make sense in some weirdo way. Why Madaki attacked Teotihuacán."

"Hit me."

Elizabeth sauntered through the apartment. "Madaki attacked Saint Peter's Basilica in Rome, the Omayyad Mosque in, ya know, Syria," her speech was starting to slur. "…the Pyramid in Mexico, and then he killed Rubi Valdez after your prayer."

"I don't get it."

Elizabeth moved past the big picture on the wall and circled the little kitchen table now, chatting excitedly. "Marvin you goof, we were right! These weren't random attacks. Ya know? Madaki is destroying portals leading to the After Life, so that *you* can't get there!"

"What?!"

"Rome and Damascus must have been portals that Madaki was trying to close. That clover at Teotihuacán must be another portal! Maybe the last one!"

"That means he probably sealed Castlerigg too…"

"You better hurry! Ask your new doctor friend! Rubi Valdez must be important to Madaki, that's why he took her out. There's something crazy special about that doctor… I mean, Rubi Valdez."

Marvin went quiet. Elizabeth stopped circling the kitchen and waited, putting a hand on the back of a chair, standing and tucking a foot behind her heel. "Hello? You still there?"

"Yeah yeah still here. I just don't like the sound o' this."

"Don't make the mistake of not believing me again."

"It's just the opposite."

"Marvin I should join you in Mexico. I can help. I can be there tomorrow."

"No no…. Get off the case."

"What?"

"I want you to stop working Abiku Madaki."

"Why?!"

"You heard me. No more research, no more questions. Get out of Phoenix. Take a week off and go to Jamaica or wherever. Do it."

"Are you crazy?"

"And don't tell anybody about any of this."

"You need me working this intel!"

"Elizabeth you're in danger!!" Marvin shot back. "If what you say is right, then you are a target now. Until I finish this, you stay away. Hear me? No more involvement."

"What about the meeting tomorrow?!"

"There won't be a meeting."

Elizabeth put a hand to her head and clenched her hair. Her eyes were starting to well up. "Who's gonna take over?"

"There is no more case. I'll call Dominic in the morning and make up some excuse. But you are released."

"Marvin wait a minute…!"

"That is an order!" Marvin clicked off.

"Damn you Marvin!"

She hurled the phone across the room, and the glass pane shattered and splashed from the Eifel Tower.

In a vacant and dim office at the Constabulary, Marvin Fischer tucked his phone back into his pocket and scratched his forehead with his thumb, pacing nervously. He had revealed to Elizabeth Walsh more than he had intended. Everything, in fact. But he had realized he could no longer hide the reality of his plight from her.

And what Elizabeth had suggested about the portals made sense within the context of the absurd reality that Marvin found himself in.

It was beginning to dawn on Marvin Fischer that perhaps the chore ahead for him involved something bigger than bringing Rubi Valdez back to life.

Something a great deal bigger.

45

THROUGH AMSTERDAM

After three hours hard sleep, Marvin's phone alarm woke him. Instantly alert, Marvin rose from the low-lying bunk with its thin mattress, swung his legs over the edge, and rested his socked feet on the tile floor. He rubbed his face and sniffled, took in a breath to get the blood moving, stretched to the wall to throw the light switch, then got up and crossed to the other side of the room where he jostled Amina and Tony awake.

Marvin could already smell the coffee. While Amina and Tony took turns in the bathroom, Marvin followed his nose through the hallway to the main office, where Scott Middleton stood over a pot of brewing coffee.

"You're my hero," said Marvin as Middleton handed him a cup.

"That's three cases, sir," Middleton winked.

"Done."

Ten minutes later, the four of them piled into Middleton's car, and they were off to Newcastle.

~

Marvin hated coach seating, but the trip was getting more expensive than anticipated. His suitcase was stuck at the Balmoral with Tony's, and he'd have to get them shipped back to the states. He cringed to think that he'd also be charged a fee by the rental company for abandoning the Bentley. Then there was the payment he'd eventually have to cough up for Amina's services, which they still hadn't discussed. Despite the frown on his face, Marvin was glad to be traveling KLM with an on-time departure from Newcastle at 10:05 AM. He was pleased that Tony's head was feeling better, that Amina still looked like brand new, and that he was enjoying his fourth coffee of the morning. The KLM coffee wasn't bad, or maybe he was becoming less fussy.

Marvin stretched his legs into the aisle before being reprimanded by the flight attendant for creating a trip hazard. Marvin grimaced, took another pull of coffee, and reeled his long legs back in toward him.

"Marvin, are you paying attention?" Amina asked. She was seated in the middle of the row to Marvin's right, with Tony beside her at the window.

"I'm payin' attention."

"I am trying to present you boys more detail about Teotihuacán so that our journey will be successful."

Tony suddenly turned away from the window. "Hey, what if I see Abiku Madaki staring at me through the window?"

"Pull the shade," Marvin joked.

"Let us stay focused on the mission, gentlemen."

Tony had studied up in the car that morning on the way to the airport, while the adults chatted about morning traffic and airport security. Homework had gone by the wayside. "When I Googled Teotihuacán, I couldn't find anything about the clover," said Tony. "There's three pyramids—the Pyramid of the Moon, the Temple of the Feathered Serpent, and the Pyramid of the Sun, which is the biggest one and has the tunnel."

"Correct," affirmed Amina, "along what they call the Avenue of the Dead. Whoever built Teotihuacán worked to a master plan. It was probably the largest city of its time, thriving on an industry of obsidian tools. For unknown reasons, the city was abandoned and burned. When the Aztecs discovered it in AD 600, they likely used it as a site for spiritual rituals."

"What about the clover?" Marvin asked. "It's at the end of this tunnel, under the pyramid?"

"Yes," said Amina. "The tunnel has never been open to tourists. Scientists believe the tunnel was formed by lava flows. It is about 300 feet long, and at its termination, directly under the center of the Pyramid of the Sun, is the clover. It consists of four small alcoves, each oriented towards one of the four corners of the universe. Four alcoves, like four leaves, hence the reason why archaeologists call it *the clover*."

Reflecting now on Elizabeth Walsh's portal theory, Marvin probed, "Any factual basis for this thing actually being a gateway? A portal to the other side?"

"There is no historical record of anyone actually passing through a gateway. But perhaps in foregone millennia, the ancients did indeed pass to and from the After Worlds, giving birth to the myth."

"Assuming it's not a myth, is it possible the gateway might already be closed?"

"It is certainly possible that there has been a greater effort by evil forces to close off all gateways permanently, preventing anyone from ever passing through them again. Why? Is there something I should know?"

"The Pyramid was attacked, the opening to the tunnel blown away. My office has evidence that it was Madaki."

Amina's eyes narrowed. "Fascinating. As if Abiku Madaki is trying to control where and how spiritual travel takes place. Monitoring the portals."

"Sealing them off."

"Good deduction, Marvin," said Amina. "It is good to see your spiritual side awaken."

"Snap!" said Tony. "Then how are we going to get in the tunnel?"

"It does elevate the level of concern," said Amina. "Does this create an obstacle for us?"

"Shouldn't," said Marvin, "the tunnel isn't blocked, but it's smashed up pretty good, and it's gonna be barricaded, 'cause of the investigation."

"We will have to find a way to sneak in after hours."

"Way dope!" said Tony. "More night work!"

"Oh joy," Marvin pouted.

"Relinquish your complaints, Marvin." Amina patted Marvin's hand. "Positive energy."

Marvin drained the last of his coffee, then craned his neck in search of a flight attendant.

It was just before noon at Amsterdam Airport when Marvin meandered in line at the arrival gate behind Amina and Tony. With his peacoat slung over his arm, Marvin was a mess. He needed a shave, his shirt was stained with coffee from the spill on the TransPennine, his tie doubly so. Everyone was famished and needed to freshen up. Amsterdam Airport was a major travel hub, so they would take advantage of the 2-and-a-half hour layover and make purchases in the terminal where there were plenty of shopping opportunities. Marvin would be obligated to absorb all expenses. They would purchase essentials and even some new clothes, sleep on the flight to Mexico City, and take a taxi straight to the pyramids without missing a step.

Then Marvin remembered the Tindals. Tiffany, in particular. He was obligated to call her. With the time difference he hoped to catch voicemail. But Tiffany picked up on the second ring, going into mild hysterics when she learned of the trip to what she thought was a "dangerous" place. Again Tony assured her that everything was fine, and he had even completed some of the homework assignments.

"Don't mention the After Worlds," Marvin whispered into Tony's ear.

After a few more seconds Tony clicked off and handed Marvin back the phone.

"She okay with everything now?" asked Marvin.

"I told her I'll call when we're on the way home. Everything's dope."

After a quick tasty brunch of wrapped scrambled eggs with peppers and cheese, coffee, and orange juice, the trio stopped for toothbrushes, cleansing wipes, and shaving supplies. Amina also selected three mini flashlights and some batteries.

"For the tunnel," she said to Marvin at the checkout.

Next came undergarments for everyone, Levis and a new hoodie for Tony, and a sporty jumpsuit complete with a new set of walking shoes for Amina. She was unsuccessful in talking Marvin into transitioning to a companion outfit. "And look like a married couple?" said Marvin. "My suit is my home." They hopped across to Banana Republic, where Marvin selected a pure white shirt and a brand new suit in classic navy. He went right past the tie rack. Amina's face wrinkled. She wondered why he would not purchase a replacement.

They ducked into the restrooms to clean up and change, discarding their older garments. Marvin emerged from the men's room, clean-shaven and satisfied, and rejoined his company. Amina fiddled with the sports bra beneath the jumpsuit, then smoothed her open hands pleasantly against the new fabric. In the trendy outfit of pale blue, white and black stripes, Marvin thought she looked like the living flag of Botswana. He cracked something wise about it. Amina frowned, placed herself firmly in front of the man, and in the swarm of lively crowds she strained on tiptoes to get closer to his face. Without emotion she reached up and fixed the knot on his stained tie, which had gone crooked. "Better," she said. She patted his cheek and dropped to turn away.

Marvin looked coolly at nothing in particular and said, "Thanks."

They crossed to Nespresso where Marvin purchased tea for Amina, a luxury soda for Tony, and, since they were out of Tarrazu, a large dark *Gevalia Kaffe* for himself. Then they bee-lined to the departure gate for KLM/AeroMexico with four minutes to spare.

46
BIRTHPLACE OF THE GODS

Between the shifting colors of the tourist's sweaty clothing, the rippling heat waves found their way up from the hot pavement of the Avenue of the Dead and escaped into the azure sky. The hot sun meant everyone was in shorts and T-shirts, tanks and bikini tops, the smart ones in sneakers or loafers. The unprepared wore sandals or flip-flops, their feet aching now from all the sightseeing. Many would wake up with blisters in the morning. Most had traveled here by bus from Mexico City, as part of a tour group, and could not even pronounce *Teotihuacán*.

And as evening came and the crowds dispersed and the buses departed, the place quieted and the spirits of old emerged to reclaim their sacred grounds. The young boy who had once helped his father excavate volcanic glass for the eyes of the temple serpent facades; the farmers returning from the fields where they'd once tended the corn; the women who had once prepared the maize and the meats for the night's tamales. The ceremonial priests guarded the platforms surmounting the shrines, now in ruins after centuries of decay and trampling by the Aztecs, the Spaniards, and more recently, the daily barrage of vacationers from around the world who had trudged and traipsed absentmindedly, desecrating the once-holy site and wanting only to escape the heat and return to their comfortable hotels and air-conditioned restaurants.

But the Teotihuacáno spirits of old—the ancients and ancestors who had erected this place—beginning with the *Pirámide del Sol* over the subterranean tunnel and the hallowed clover, then adding shrines and temples and living quarters, and the great avenue where the gods were satisfied and the sacrifices were made and the work carried out to create the central and thriving metropolis of Teotihuacán, welcomed now the peace afforded by the coming of night, when they could swoop reverently over the place they once called home.

The numinous Avenue of the Dead was now eerily stoic, slipping into restful and quiet repose, the clatter of footsteps gone for the night. The rugged stone stairways rising up the pyramids could dismiss the day's human salvo, instead now welcoming visits from the ghosts who had cut the bricks and laid the stones, paved the avenue and tamed the foothills—the merchants and the potters, the architects and the plasterers, the artists and the sculptors, the painters and the teachers. The ghosts moved silently and invisibly and without haste, reflecting and recalling and venerating their formerly vibrant and arduous lives with ruminations of wistfulness.

And now high above in the cool firmament that had become sapphire blue with the night, the Boeing 787 blew past overhead, bursting the night sky with a blast of heat and noise, careening and hurtling toward Benito Juárez International Airport 32 miles southwest to Mexico City.

And the Teotihuacáno ghosts, sensing another human invasion—unexpected and unwelcome but soon forthcoming—skittered and darted and scattered in unsettled rustles back through the portal to the After Worlds and left the street dead and soundless.

THE TEMPEST IN GLASS

~

There was something murky about the air in Mexico City. Marvin Fischer twisted his nose and couldn't quite place it, and maybe that's because of all the places he'd traveled, he'd never been to Mexico City, and he had formed a rather unglamorous opinion of the place. To him it was a city in decay, its heyday over. He knew it was likely a false and unfair judgment, so at 9:52 PM, when Marvin Fischer had led his tiny group through the terminal at Benito Juárez and had been happy to bypass luggage claim, he'd passed through currency exchange where he'd secured 4,000 pesos and determined to set aside his bias.

Amina and Tony followed Marvin to the taxi desk, where he asked to purchase a taxi ride to Teotihuacán, an absurd request at such an odd hour.

"Pyramids closed now," said the clerk, trying to look busy.

"I know," said Marvin. "I'd like to make the purchase anyway."

The clerk nodded, made the sale, handed Marvin the slip, and pointed. Amina and Tony followed Marvin again as he approached the curb, signaled an attendant wearing a white shirt with broad black stripes, and showed the slip to the attendant, who looked at the slip, and when he saw *San Juan Teotihuacán*, repeated the clerk's message, saying "Is closed now, señor."

Marvin insisted on procuring the cab anyway—he'd paid for it. So the attendant turned and craned his neck and flagged a green classic VW Beetle with a white roof waiting sleepily on the curb 40 feet away. It was a slow time of night, and the cab drivers were accustomed to playing on their smartphones or catching a nap or two—or three.

But the Beetle fired awake as if always on alert, and circled and stopped by the guests, where the attendant stepped to Amina and opened the rear door for her, and then for Tony with his backpack opposite, and finally the front passenger door for Marvin Fischer. Marvin tipped the attendant generously, receiving a bow of thanks in return and the careful click of the door being closed.

DIRK EICHHORST

And then Marvin glanced to his left at the cab driver and knew why he had formed his opinion of Mexico City. The cab driver was living the stereotype, sporting a short-sleeved yellow collared shirt and loose pants that seemed his only pair, wrinkled and dullen with the drab stains of money and grease wiped from his meals. The man's hair was shiny black, the thick mustache completing the round and tanned face, the weary eyes appearing like they had just been awakened from some jaded dream. The license on the dash showed the picture and his name as *Julio Peña*. The cab smelled of old smoke and sweat. On the floors were wrinkled papers, a cigarette butt, and someone's sock.

Marvin handed the paper slip and Julio Peña looked it over through eyes at half-mast and the clicking of his awakening tongue on the roof of his mouth.

"Close!" Julio burst, the voice booming in antithesis to the bleary face and drooping frame. He said *closs* not *closed*, maybe realizing he'd bungled the word, but not caring. He'd gotten by with it all the time, anyway. The drivers who spoke the best English were saved for daytime hours, when it was busy, and there were more tourists and people to impress.

Marvin waved 100 pesos in front of Julio Peña's face and ordered him to make the drive to Teotihuacán anyway.

Julio wagged his head and insisted again that the place was now *closs*, as it was well past their *clossing* time of five PM. Marvin grew tired of Julio's lousy English and the two men launched into a verbal jousting war in Spanish in different dialects. Tony laughed and Amina smiled and after 30 more seconds of elevated tones and animated gestures, Julio finally relented, punched the gas, and violently turned the wheel deep toward the Mexican Valley. Marvin wondered how the guy kept his job.

The famed Moctezuma had met his fate here in the valley many centuries earlier, when Cortez had overtaken the Aztecs at a time when the valley was still lush with lakes at the height of classic Mesoamerican culture. Today the lakes were virtually extinct. The valley was an enclosed wasteland with no natural outlet for water flow, and at 7,200 feet above sea level, the mountains and volcanoes surrounding the valley reached elevations of over 16,000 feet, trapping the hot and sticky air even in the spring. Now past nightfall the temperature had dropped to the 60s.

Amina had rolled down the back window to escape the stench of Julio Peña's Beetle, the windy ride making her hair a tangled mess. But traffic was light, and Julio had sped most of the way along the MEX through the ancient Trans-Mexican volcanic belt to make the trip in just under an hour.

Now they got closer and the trees cleared to reveal some of the old stone residences at the perimeter of the empty city. As Julio turned right off the MEX 132, Marvin pointed saying, "Puerta Uno, por favor."

"Close. Close!"

"I know it's closed!" Marvin grunted.

Really? Again? The whole experience had become a tedious nuisance. And now Amina was suggesting they drive instead to *Puerta Two*, which would put them closer to the Pyramid of the Sun. Marvin could not convince Julio, so he settled on Puerta One just to get rid of the guy.

It was almost midnight when Julio finally pulled into the dark parking lot at the visitor entrance of Teotihuacán and rounded the taxi to Puerta One. Amina and Tony popped the doors in the back and happily slid out of the cab while Marvin dug into his breast pocket and produced a wad of bills. Marvin rifled through the stack and pulled a bunch. "1,000 pesos. Bueno?"

It was way too much, but Marvin wanted no more haggling. Julio's face was flat and peeved even as he snatched the gratuity from Marvin's outstretched hand and said, "Muchas gracias, señor."

Julio stuffed the money in his shirt pocket. Marvin said 'you're welcome', then slipped out of the car and slammed the door a little harder than he needed to. Marvin heard the engine squeal as Julio put the car back into drive, and the green classic VW Beetle with the white roof rolled swiftly away and back toward the highway.

It didn't occur to Marvin that Julio Peña had become intensely curious about the little entourage making such an excursion to the tourist site at this late hour.

But Marvin Fischer wasn't thinking about Julio Peña anymore.

His first sight of the grand Avenue of the Dead hit Marvin with a wallop. They'd come in from off the guest services area, Tony following Amina hurriedly across the pavement to get a look at the Temple of the Feathered Serpent before making their way north to the Pyramid of the Sun. But Marvin had stopped here cold in his tracks, something spooky about the avenue grabbing him, and he felt almost as if the ghosts of the past were watching him. It was a strange and edgy sensation, not something Marvin was used to, being more commonly caught up in the physical to-do with everyday priorities in the secular world of intelligence mostly free from spiritual lines of thought. But these last days had shaken Marvin's *chi* and he thought maybe that's why something had stopped him here so profoundly. What was it about this place? He hated this new acuity, and the uneasy sense that he was being watched and even mocked as he stumbled his way through this madcap adventure. For a moment Marvin was reminded of the mood at Castlerigg.

"Hey—!" came the half-whisper call from Amina, who was already many yards ahead and turning around to prompt the man onward.

"Yeah yeah coming…" said Marvin, taking a step and then stopping again. He heard the continuing *tap-tap* of Amina's and Tony's shoes skittering across the way toward the temple, but he just kept looking down the immense street where he now stood dead center, looking straight north to the Pyramid of the Moon beneath the sharp and piercing gleam of moonlight. Beyond the Moon Pyramid stretched the Sierra Madre Occidental, its mountainous crests formed millennia ago when the earth's mantel had folded under the violent force of igneous rock when it burst from the sedimentary layers. The Avenue of the Dead itself stretched long and perfectly straight and wide, flanked by hundreds of smaller pyramid-like buildings, with the two giant pyramids way down the stretch. Marvin could already see the Pyramid of the Sun off to the right—to the east—maybe a half-mile up the avenue, where he'd soon find himself. Marvin guessed the ancient street to be well over a mile long, straight as an arrow, wide as a ten-lane highway, lined with the stone buildings.

Marvin stood mesmerized. He had never seen anything like it, not even in books. The place was colossal, a powerhouse of urban advancement that had once been the major metropolis of Mesoamerica. Marvin recalled what Amina had explained to him on the flight from England, that the Aztecs had discovered Teotihuacán in 600 AD—burned and abandoned—believing all the little pyramids lining the sides of the avenue were tombs. It turned out they were not tombs, but the name *Avenue of the Dead* became the label by which the world would distinguish this street. Yes, Marvin could understand why the Aztecs might have thought the little pyramids were tombs. They were systematically spaced along the entire length of the avenue, past the Sun Pyramid, all the way down to the giant Moon Pyramid.

What innovative and religious cosmopolitans the Teotihuacános must have been.

Now the city was silent, dark, and abandoned.

Eerily dead.

"Mister Fischer! Come on!" Tony called, from even further away now. Marvin snapped back to the moment and reengaged. The boy was already at the foot of the Temple of the Feathered Serpent, what Marvin considered an unnecessary stop. He wanted to get to the Sun Pyramid and make their way down into the tunnel and get to the clover. But the boy wanted to see the temple, something Amina had said about carvings of Quetzalcoatl.

Marvin quickstepped across the avenue and caught up with the two, who had stopped at the face of the temple, a pyramid of weathered and fractured volcanic rock. Its stone steps led up high to its peak, its walls adorned with bas-reliefs of the ancient god.

Marvin approached beside Amina and behind Tony, the boy crouching with hands on knees, transfixed at the giant rock sculpture of the mythical creature Quetzalcoatl, the snake-like face with the fangs, the stone brows flowing over deep-set, concave eye cavities.

"That is where the obsidian stones would have been," Amina offered quietly. "In those cavities. The eyes."

"Wow," Tony gawked, then turning to Marvin, "It's Quetzalcoatl!"

"That's him, huh?" Marvin said with a frown, turning his gaze north through scattered trees, toward the Pyramid of the Sun.

"Look, Mister Fischer," said Tony with excitement, his flashlight winking on. "Those are the feathers. Remember?" Tony pointed to the wreath of leaf-like protrusions surrounding the head of the snake. "The quetzal feathers, like we saw when he came to try and rescue my mom, right before the accident!"

"Oh yeah…" Marvin stared at the stone likeness now, imagining it coming to life, the pool of light from Tony's little flashlight moving like a probe across the snarling nose and stone fangs, and Marvin recalled the vision of the reptile he had seen right before the fateful sound of the cars crunching into Rubi Valdez.

Amina said, "I wish I could have been there with you when you saw the creature, alive and moving, like you did."

"It was only for a second," said Marvin.

Tony reached out and touched the statue, enthralled.

"Hate to break up the party, but we gotta keep movin'," said Marvin. "Come on."

Standing immovable against the deep starry sky was the massive silhouette of the towering 215-foot Pyramid of the Sun. Its base was wide, a gradual ridged slope rising to its apex, with a 248-step rock stairway escalating straight up the center. Making it all the way to the top for a grand view of the city was a primary goal for tourists, but Marvin squashed Tony's request to make a quick jog to the top and down, Marvin insisting they needed to get inside the tunnel.

They passed between two low-lying structures and entered the plaza in front of the immense building, and now they could see the mass of stone rubble piled near the base, where Abiku Madaki had made his mark a week earlier with the blast that had intended to take out the entire structure but had failed to do so. The blast had, however, created a significant hole near the entrance of the tunnel. It was the exact opposite effect of what Marvin assumed had been Madaki's goal: to seal off the tunnel and render the clover inaccessible. But the evil spirit had failed in its materialistic attempt at destruction, and now the gaping hole was left at the entrance to the tunnel instead, providing an ironic welcome for the trio of religious travelers. The area had been closed off to the public with wooden barricades, metal stanchions and rusty slouching chains, as the Mexican authorities and archaeological team had not yet begun cleanup of the site. The investigation had finished, but the bombed ruins had been left in situ for a while longer in case the team needed another look. In the coming weeks the place would undergo cleanup and restoration. But for now, it was off limits to everyone.

Everyone except for Marvin Fischer and his little band.

The trio slipped easily beneath the chains and walked unhindered toward the tunnel. Marvin's heart rate increased and the apprehension grew as he took the lead now and walked with the boy and the woman between the first jagged rocks and pebbles left from the blast, until soon they were all stepping carefully over piles of rubble, taking care not to catch a toe or twist an ankle. And as they navigated carefully to the depression at the base of the pyramid complex, Marvin got his first glimpse down the dark and deep and foreboding pit that was the opening to the ancient tunnel, and Tony called in a disturbed tone, and Marvin turned around to spot three bright lights way down the avenue, bobbing up and down, seemingly coming toward them.

Shit—The Mexican Police.

Julio Peña had sold them out.

47

SUBTERRANEAN

"I knew that guy had it in for me!" Marvin grunted under his breath about the damn cab driver as the approaching lights—still several hundred feet behind them—appeared to pick up pace.

"You were not the most agreeable traveler, Mister Fischer," Amina scolded.

"I was nice! He was twitchy!"

"Click off your flashlight!" Amina commanded Tony.

But it was already too late. The distant lights danced and bounced faster as their owners again picked up speed, and now Marvin could hear the soles of heavy boots clattering on stone.

"Hurry!" said Marvin. "Get down in there!"

"Tell them who you are." Amina suggested. "You are part of the investigation."

"It won't fly. We gotta move. You been here before?"

"No."

"I thought you'd been here before."

"An incorrect assumption."

"But you know the tunnel. The route. You know the passage."

"I will get us through."

"Get movin'," Marvin ordered.

"Movin'."

Amina Karimova pushed ahead, Tony at her heels and Marvin taking sweep. And now through the darkness Marvin could see in the pit that there was a stairway leading down into the earth. And beyond the reach of the cutting moonlight the gaping hole plunged into pitch-blackness. Marvin watched Amina step over and across the stony debris, again taking care not to trip. She produced her little flashlight and clicked it on. Tony and Marvin followed suit, the tiny beams seeming extra bright in the black darkness. Amina took the first step onto the stairway that the ancients had cut out of the bedrock. She began the descent of almost twenty feet, kicking aside stray pebbles and rocks left over from last week's blast. Tony went next, his flashlight beam twittering across the red and gray stone.

Bringing up the rear, Marvin took his first step onto the stairway and, hearing the voices shouting in Spanish, looked over his shoulder at the approaching lights, the garbled commands echoing along the wide street and ricocheting off surrounding shrines.

Marvin turned back to his group and continued down. He watched Amina reach the second to last step and hop off, her feet crunching into the pebbles and stones on the ground at the beginning of the tunnel. Shining her light deep into the dark void before her, she stepped aside for Tony.

Marvin made it down and now they were all three below the earth's surface, the little beams of their tiny lights hardly enough to cut through the black air. The jagged tunnel led them immediately left. Their flashlight beams revealed a rich brown color to the dusty and rocky earthen walls of the cave, the mine-like shaft having an ovality of about seven feet. The walls and ceiling had been plastered centuries ago and lined with basalt slabs. Bits of debris from the blast still lay scattered across the floor and embedded into the walls. Within a few seconds, Marvin felt a temperature drop of several degrees, and sensed a gradual slope downward as they carefully traversed the trail.

"We're declining," Marvin observed.

"There is a gradual descent until the tunnel terminates at the clover," Amina answered, shining her light ahead. "About three hundred feet further."

After a few more paces, the effects of the explosion were no longer evident. The group rounded gradually to the right where the tunnel became impossibly narrow, and man-made modifications had flattened the walls. The cramped passageway now gave the impression of a small closet.

Amina stopped and turned to them. "It gets rather claustrophobic right here. We will have to squeeze through." She turned ahead and continued into the constricted passage, slipping her svelte body into the narrow shaft with ease. Tony followed, and then Marvin, twisting and grimacing as the buttons on his new suit scraped the dusty wall. Now Tony was speaking in excited phrases, as if this were some Disneyland ride. Marvin guessed the kid was having the time of his life, feeling like an adventurer, having never dreamed of being in such a compromising situation. The boy was eagerly following Amina through the tight jam, trusting her in this womb-like part of the tunnel, where he probably felt safe and secure between the grown woman before and the tall man behind. Marvin smiled. Oh to be a kid again.

After a few more yards no one spoke. The air became moist as they stooped to continue deeper into the earth along a third section of the tunnel, where the ceiling height slanted low. Marvin wondered why Abiku Madaki—if he'd wanted to destroy the clover—hadn't dug himself all the way in and planted his bomb right at the clover itself? Why blast the opening? Had something prevented him getting in? Maybe the good spirits—even Shada herself—had been part of an invisible resistance to Abiku Madaki's attack plans, taking place beyond the visible realm?

Or had someone else helped fight off Madaki?

Saint Peter maybe?

The tunnel suddenly opened into two pockets, one on either side of the main shaft. The group stopped, shining their lights into the grottos.

"Is this the clover?" Tony asked excitedly.

"No," said Amina, pausing. "The grottos were closed off at one time by the Teotihuacános for unknown reasons. See?" She pointed to broken sections of stone near the perimeter of the nooks. "You can still see where the block-off wall was, before archeologists broke through them in the 1970s."

Tony lifted his light and touched the fragmented remnants. "Wow!"

And now they began to hear voices echoing behind them.

Tony turned and said, "Those guys are in the tunnel!"

"GO!" Marvin barked, looking behind him.

"Maybe we could collapse the tunnel behind us!" said Tony. "Blast it and block them off!"

"Yeah? How? You got a firecracker?"

The group continued past the two mysterious chambers at a hurried pace and veered right, following the tunnel's path.

"So to ask the obvious," Marvin spoke up as his shoulder brushed the wall, "what exactly are we gonna do when we get to the clover?"

"I have no idea," answered Amina.

"That's what I thought," Marvin frowned.

"Is someone going to meet us there?" Tony asked. "Someone from the After Worlds?"

"I do not know, Antonio. All we know is that Dante Alighieri sent us here, and we trust him."

"Hey what's this?" Tony stopped and bent down to pick up a strange, round, metallic object the size of a ping-pong ball. He lifted it to his face, studied it, and brushed some of the dirt off to reveal a bright shiny yellow finish.

"It's gold!" Tony exclaimed.

"What are you stoppin' for? Keep movin'!" Marvin pushed.

But Tony picked up another one of the metallic objects and looked it over.

"It is not gold," said Amina. "It is pyrite. There are hundreds of those little balls in these caves. Most of them have been removed for study by archaeologists. Vibrations from the blast must have jarred some more of them loose."

"What are they for?" asked Tony.

"Nobody knows." Amina said as she wheeled around and twisted through a tight turn.

"Doesn't anybody know anything?" Marvin whined.

Tony threw the metallic rock against the cave wall, where on impact the ball burst into a powdery cloud. He picked up another one and threw it against the wall, watching it burst, then heard Amina calling from up ahead.

Tony picked up pace again. Lagging behind, Marvin bent over to pick up another of the metallic orbs, standing up and examining the silly treasure curiously. It seemed an innocent-looking ball of apparently no consequence. And yet, something deep within Marvin's spirit told him to hang on to it. What was this strange feeling of obligation to the orb that he felt? And from where had it come? After a moment's thought, Marvin stuffed the golf ball-sized orb into the front right pocket of his suit pants, then shot off again through the tunnel to catch up.

"So what are we gonna do when we get to the clover and the police show up? Ask them to wait a minute while we figure out how to cross over?"

"Don't ask questions Marvin. Just tread wisely!"

Marvin shook his head and turned around to keep tabs on their pursuers, shining his light behind him. He could hear the hustled chatter of their male voices but still could not see them, not even the beams of their lights. The voices went silent again. "Ya know we're basically cornering ourselves."

"How is it that a man in your position can speak in slang and contractions?" Amina blurted. "*Ya know* ... *we're gonna*. Surely you do not write your reports in such fashion for your superiors? How is it that you get by with such lazy speech?"

"I've got a proof reader. And I don't always talk like that, do I Tony?"

"Usually."

Marvin wrinkled his nose and turned to see light emerging behind them. He thumbed over his shoulder. "They're gettin' closer."

"*Gettin'...*" Amina pestered.

Finally the tunnel opened up into a wider space, and into a dead end. Amina stopped and Tony nearly ran into her.

"It's a dead end!" Marvin moped.

"Did you expect the tunnel to go on eternally?" Amina snapped. "I told you it terminates here. This is your clover, Mister Fischer."

Marvin fanned out beside Tony and they all looked at the underground end room before them. With a tapered ceiling rising like a cone, the center of the room was circular, with four pocket-like chambers cut into the brownish-orange walls, oriented toward a different direction.

"The *sancta sanctorum*, holy of holies." said Amina, "Each nook represents one corner of the universe."

Marvin looked around. There didn't seem to be anything particularly special about the place. It was just a dirty old cave. He said, "What are we gonna do? Stand here and chant? Throw orbs at the wall?" He looked again behind him down the tunnel, scanned for police, then turned back to Amina.

The woman bit her lip, and Marvin could see she really was vexed. "Didn't you figure this out on the airplane flight?!" Marvin scolded. "Those guys are comin' right at us!"

"Quiet!"

"We should call to him!" said Tony.

"What?"

"Dante! Dante!" Tony called.

Thinking it was worth a shot, Marvin called too. "Dante!" he called. "Dante!"

Amina stood silent, not watching the men, pondering, thinking.

"Saint Peter!" Tony called.

Nothing. They stopped calling.

And now the voices of the police became audible.

"In about 60 seconds we're all gonna be in handcuffs."

Amina glanced quickly around the tiny room. "Do you see anything in the nooks?"

The trio looked into each of the four mini chambers of the cloverleaf. Each nook appeared nearly identical, no unique feature jumping out from any one of them.

"Isn't this where we need a magic key or somethin'?" Marvin asked with bluster. "Somebody sticks a hand in a hole and loses an arm?"

Amina ignored the man.

"Wait a minute," said Marvin. "You said these guys believed this place was a gateway to the underworld. But we wanna go *up*," he pointed, "that way. Right?"

Marvin looked up and was joined by Amina and Tony.

"The Empyrean…" Amina said quietly, moving directly into the center of the cramped room and, stooping and craning her neck, she saw a pinprick of light directly above them.

"Doctor Karimova I see it!" Tony pointed to the cracking light above.

"How can this be?" Amina mulled.

Marvin pushed in and peered over her shoulder. "I think he's expecting us. He's waitin' for us. It could be Saint Peter!"

The mumbles and shouts from the police grew louder.

"They're almost here!" Tony pointed.

"Mister Fischer," Amina glowered, stepping up to face Marvin squarely, "there simply cannot be an opening at the top of the pyramid."

"Well there is now. It's gotta be Saint Peter signaling."

Now the cracking light above became a bright glowing beam that opened wide and spilled down into the chamber, growing with intensity, as if some otherworldly door were opening, ready to receive the travelers.

"But we cannot be certain it is Saint Peter!"

"Dante sent us here! You yourself said we trust him! Now get in the center!" Marvin ordered. "Hurry! Everybody in the center of the beam!"

Amina and Tony quickly obeyed, joining Marvin in the middle of the clover chamber. Marvin felt Amina press into him, close enough she could have kissed his tie, and he got a pleasant whiff of her perfume. Joining his upward gaze, Amina's eyes lifted toward the bright and unmistakable point of light directly above them and all their faces blazed yellow in the glow.

"Closer!" Marvin cried as he grabbed the fabric of Tony's jacket and pulled him in tight. Their arms went around each other—and as Marvin glanced over his shoulder and saw the first face of a policeman rounding with a determined smile with light and gun in hand—the glow above the trio expanded radiant in an instant, and Marvin felt the sensation of being yanked off his feet by a powerful invisible elevator.

And Marvin was hurled into the air and then he heard what sounded like an EXPLOSION.

48

AFTER WORLDS

The next thought entering Marvin's mind was that he had no idea how long he had been blacked out, but it couldn't have been long, because he felt himself groping helplessly through the air and spinning, falling, flying aimlessly like a toy hurled by an angry child. Marvin was surrounded by bright yellow light but he could see nothing else through the whirling color—no landscape, no cave, no people—his breath escaped him and he couldn't inhale as he remembered himself in a flash in Detroit as a police officer with Caroline, before she had died.

He saw Caroline's face and the jet black hair and the smile and the sweat and then the coffin and then...

CRASH! Marvin's body landed hard on something powdery but solid and heavy, and he felt his body tumbling down a decline, out of control, head over heels, and he could not stop himself from rolling and tumbling and cartwheeling down the slope, and his lungs expanded and he was coughing violently now, his eyes wide with fear and total helplessness as he rolled and rolled down, and finally the bright yellow light dimmed enough that he could see that it was sand—black sand—that he was tumbling down, a giant sand dune, and the slope diminished and he finally rolled to a stop on his back.

Marvin lay panting, arms fanned to his sides and legs spread wide, catching his breath, staring up into a bright white and yellow sky with no clouds and no sun.

And then came chunks of something falling from the sky and hitting the sand around him, chunks of what looked like rocks of varying sizes, some of them tiny like golf balls and some of them big as a car, falling from above and landing around him, and then he heard the remnants of rumbling shockwaves from whatever blast had caused the explosion he was certain he had heard.

As Marvin's head cleared it dawned on him that he was out in the open and exposed, and that he could at any moment be struck by falling debris. He'd better find cover. In a burst of adrenaline Marvin bolted up to a sitting position and pivoted on his hip and then he saw it.

The Pyramid of the Sun—it's top blown to pieces like the top of a spent volcano, smoke and dust and rock and ash billowing from its gaping mouth.

The entire top and most of the sidewalls of the pyramid were completely gone, leaving a smoldering shell of what had once been a symbol of grandeur in the Mexican Valley.

And what was most odd about it all was that the only thing sitting in this desert of black sand was what was left of the Pyramid of the Sun, and some rolling black dunes and distant mountains and rocks and boulders, but no trees and no grass or anything else, not even the other pyramids.

Nor any of the shrines.

Nor the Avenue of the Dead.

Nor the dark starry sky with its moon.

It was all gone.

Everything that was once the great city of Teotihuacán was gone except for what was left of the giant pyramid, smoking and withered like a shelled military compound, dropped in the middle of this sandy black valley of dunes and rocks and distant hills and mountains.

And where were Amina and Tony?

Marvin coughed, tipping to his hands and knees.

Terror gripped his heart.

Where was he?! …. What happened?!

With both hands flat on the powdery black surface and his knees pressed into the hot sand, he stared at the strange ground beneath him, totally helpless and powerless and clueless and defenseless, ready at any moment to be swept off his feet again and hurled through space at someone else's mercy.

He was a salmon caught in the jaws of a mighty bear.

Marvin dug his fingers into the scorching sand as his brain groped and his spirit whirled with no place to land, seeking answers, seeking solutions.

Seeking HELP.

Falling debris pounded into the sand. Gathering his wits, Marvin stood up, his face and his hair and his eyebrows and his suit and his tie covered in powdery black dust. He felt the searing sand pour into his shoes and under the arches of his feet. The pasty black soot was already beginning to crust around Marvin's watery eyes and he took his sleeve and wiped vigorously so he could see better. He blinked and coughed and looked around at the wasteland surrounding him and took a deep breath.

"Tony!" he called. "Amina!"

"Marvin!"

Marvin turned instantly in reaction to the woman's voice and scrambled to a pile of jagged boulders not far away. As he rounded the tall black rocks, he found Amina, covered in soot, getting to her feet and coughing. Marvin grabbed her arm and helped her up, pulling her into a sheltering nook in a giant rock, himself still coughing and catching his breath.

"Where's Tony?" Marvin asked desperately.

"I…" Amina coughed… "…I do not see him!"

Debris still rained down, from high in the sky and pelting the sand around them, smaller now, dissipating, sending the black powder flying in rings and creating small craters at point of impact. Marvin looked around in panic, searching for any sign of the boy. He looked again at Amina.

"You okay?" he asked.

Amina nodded and gulped and spit sand out of her mouth, clutching Marvin's arms with both hands as she regained her balance and breath.

And then a shape rounded another boulder not far away, the shape of a boy covered in soot and wobbling on his feet, reaching an arm out to one of the boulders to steady himself. "Mister Fischer!" Tony called. He'd apparently lost the backpack. So much for the homework.

"Tony!" Marvin helped Amina rest against a rock and then hurried to Tony, hopping over rubble and dodging the shifting sand and stones. Marvin reached Tony and took his hand, looking into the boy's face.

"Are you hurt?" Marvin asked.

"No," said Tony, blowing the dust from his lips. "Is Doctor Karimova okay?"

"Yeah she's over there," said Marvin, helping Tony step over jagged rocks.

They regrouped with Amina and gathered together inside the giant concave boulder, Amina bent over with both hands on her knees, her breath steadying. Marvin leaned against the rock and let his head tip back, closing his eyes, while Tony rustled his fingers through his hair and coughed.

"I am so thirsty," said Marvin.

"Yah," Amina concurred.

"What happened?" Marvin asked.

"We crossed over," Amina gasped and gulped.

"We did?"

"We crossed over," Amina repeated. "We must have. But that was no friendly invite."

"What do you mean?" Marvin turned to her and strained through crusty eyelashes.

"That explosion," Amina coughed. "It was indeed the gateway. Someone blew it up right as we were crossing through. Destroyed it."

"Destroyed…" Marvin pondered, and he felt his heart fall into his gut.

"If we are right," Amina continued, "about Abiku Madaki closing the portals, and the clover was the last gateway…" Amina gulped, "I think Abiku Madaki tricked us. He lured us to that light. And as soon as we crossed over, he blew the place to hades."

The three companions locked eyes and Amina said the unimaginable.

"Gentlemen, I am afraid we may be trapped in the After Worlds."

49

FEATHERED SERPENT

It was nearly vertigo that came to Marvin Fischer as he circled round on his feet, his shoes burning hot in the soft black sand beneath his soles. He visually absorbed his surroundings without any reference to make sense of them. The sandy dunes and rocky mountainous terrain had a familiarity to them, in the sense of distance and height and depth, of left and right, of breathable air and of gravity and of the sensation of daylight on his face. But there was no discernable point of origin for the light, no sign of life, nor sound, or any moving thing at all.

"I don't feel anything," said Tony fearfully.

Marvin felt it too—or rather—he *didn't* feel it.

The whole atmosphere of the place had the incoherent detachment of being part celestial and part terrestrial, somehow faltering between the two on some metaphysical seesaw. This, together with the peculiar lack of any living being, a place absent of the bioelectricity from animal or insect or plant, void of activity or movement, was ominously disquieting. The juxtaposing yellow sky with the black surface of the planet yawned with eerie lonesomeness. The smoke and ash from the nearby explosion hung sleepily in the sky, slowly descending and finding rest, while the surrounding air seemed clear and stagnant. Marvin felt as if he were standing in a three-dimensional photograph. The blank stare on Tony's face and the searching gaze in Amina's eyes told Marvin that they were experiencing the same oddity. Marvin, scanning the horizon, tipped toward Amina. "What do you make of it?"

"I sense no consciousness," Amina confessed. "It is like death."

The three adventurers stood side by side in equal bewilderment.

"This is the After Worlds?" asked Marvin, still gazing at the alien landscape.

"It can't be heaven." said Tony.

And for another moment the three travelers all stood staring, until Marvin spotted a dark shape appearing quietly from around a nearby low-rising dune. Marvin froze in place. His eyes locked hard on the image. He pressed his lips together and swallowed. The shape seemed of a man, the heavily clad feet shuffling across the gritty black sand and gravel, the only audible sound now to cut through the dead air.

Amina and Tony turned now and saw the man too. It looked to Marvin that the approaching figure was dressed in some kind of armor, but not the armor of a medieval knight. It looked more like a covering of one piece, overlapping panels of some unknown substance, a suit that moved with the man as he did, almost as if it were a part of his body. In his right hand, the man grasped the hilt of a gleaming orange sword with a blade longer than a samurai's.

As the man came closer, Marvin recognized the dark skin, the bald head, and the short goatee as the face of the Somali terrorist, Abiku Madaki.

"Marvin Fischer!" called Madaki, the face hard with arrogance and strength.

Glaring at Abiku Madaki, Marvin's crystal blue eyes seared with anger and defiance. They did not reveal fear. Marvin was beyond that now. But he did not know what to say, and he did not know how to confront this supernatural adversary. Now Marvin knew for certain, this Madaki was no human, no Somali terrorist. That had all been a ruse, a trick, a cover for whatever assignment Abiku Madaki had had on familiar earth.

Abiku Madaki ended his foreboding approach about 25 feet in front of Marvin Fischer. "Do you know where you are." Abiku Madaki said it as a statement rather than a question.

Marvin wanted to appear strong, but he was completely powerless and he knew it. As far as Marvin knew, he himself was still human, with the same frailties and limitations that he'd had when he was on earth.

And he had absolutely no idea where he was now.

"No I do not," Marvin confessed loudly across the still sands toward Madaki.

"You are in the After Worlds," confirmed Madaki. "It is a desolate and shadowy reflection of what your God intended for the afterlife. But, Marvin Fischer, that is of no consequence to you and your friends. For you have brought me what I need." Madaki's eyes shifted to young Antonio Valdez.

"That boy. I will take him now," said Madaki.

For a moment Marvin and his friends stood still and silent. Then Marvin took a step toward Antonio and rested his left hand on the boy's shoulder. Amina followed suit and crowded closer to shield the boy. She grasped Marvin's sleeve, and Marvin reached to clasp Amina's other quivering hand into his. The trio stood now unrelated by blood, but yet somehow merged into a formidable family unit, solely committed to each other and impenetrable.

Abiku Madaki took another step forward, irked by the delay in response to his command. "I said, I will take that boy."

Marvin scowled, firm and unmoving. "The hell you will."

"Mister Fischer," Madaki continued calmly, "it is for this purpose that I have allowed you to pass through. Let us dispense with the chasing and the hunts and the hiding."

THE TEMPEST IN GLASS

Marvin peered at Abiku Madaki knowingly now, as his thoughts knit together. "So it *was* you who destroyed the Cathedral, and the Mosque." said Marvin. "And the pyramid too."

Madaki nodded. "Erzok's plan will come to pass, Mister Fischer. And *The Great Nahmes* will be defeated."

The Great who…?

"Now," said Abiku Madaki, pointing his fiery sword at Tony, "I will take that boy."

Marvin expected a violent wind to suddenly stir up and overtake them. Instead, the sand surrounding Marvin and his friends began to ripple. Marvin's eyes darted from Madaki down to the sand. Now the sand seemed to be almost boiling. The sand bubbled and shifted and moved, until from within the center of each sand bubble formed a head, one head in each sand bubble, until the heads rose from the sand to reveal complete bodies made entirely of sand. The people of the sand rose up like pillars, human-like, their heads swaying and roiling on their necks as they constituted, black as charcoal with shades of gray, merged as one with this strange world, yet somehow each distinct and ominous in its own right. The people of the sand stood each exactly the same height—seven feet—and had exactly the same build—lean and sinewy—their faces featureless except for the approximate structure of a humanoid, expressionless and vacant, as they each seemed incapable of thought or of reason or of discernment of purpose, until they each finally stood straight and silent. Each creature from the sand held a bright orange sword like their apparent master Abiku Madaki, each of them looking around now through lifeless gray eyes at their surroundings, and in an instant as each of their gazes locked onto Marvin and his friends, the people of the sand seemed to understand why they were here, why they had been summoned, what their purpose in this moment was.

Yes, they were Abiku Madaki's minions, about 50 of them. They had Marvin and Tony and Amina surrounded within their circle of terror, orange swords flickering under the blazing sky light, and like a platoon of armed Frankensteins, they began to descend slowly towards their three human victims.

Tony pressed into a tighter huddle with his adult companions. Leaning into Amina, Marvin suggested, "Now might be a good time to get Shada involved."

"I cannot sense her. I feel no connection," said Amina as calmly as she could.

As the small army of sand bodies closed in, Marvin watched Madaki's expression change from one of confidence to one of concern, and even though Marvin didn't know what had caused the sudden shift in Madaki's countenance, the impending feeling of doom lifted from Marvin's heart. Marvin followed Madaki's gaze toward the surrounding sandy surface, which was again bubbling and boiling. Except this time, what emerged from the hot reflecting black sand were not humanoid heads and bodies, but long, slender ropes. First there were ten, then 20, then a hundred long and slithery rope-like creatures emanating from the ground and winding and gliding towards the people of the sand.

Marvin sensed a confrontation, a defense from some unknown source.

The next moments were a blur as Marvin realized the ropes were not ropes at all, but rather they were like white snakes, each 10 feet long, with black eyes and gaping mouths with fangs of long needles. And the tense, controlled confrontation of moments ago turned immediately into swirling bedlam. The white snakes attacked the black people of the sand, wrapping themselves around the bodies and squeezing mercilessly like boa constrictors. There came hissing and thrashing and awful screeching from within the chaotic mayhem as one of the people of the sand, with a white snake wrapped once around the neck and thrice around its waist, groped to free itself but exploded under pressure, the sandy body falling to the ground in an impotent heap. Another sand person whipped its sword with a blinding thrash, slicing a white snake in two.

And then, out from among the long white snakes and directly behind Abiku Madaki, the surface of the sand rippled and exploded 40 feet into the air in a shower of gravel and flying particles of sand, as another snake emerged from below, this one many times larger than the narrow and thin white 10-footers, this one a true giant and enormous reptile, thick and strong, rising and towering high over Abiku Madaki and his circle of minions. The giant snake had a huge head and a pointed snout, fangs like skewers, dark eyes black as obsidian. Iridescent blue-green feathers spewed from behind its head; the scales of its body glistened like turquoise. The reptilian dragon hissed and curled upward in terrifying grandeur, the eyebrows creasing with ferocity and the eyes of marble focusing now on its target.

"It's Quetzalcoatl!" Tony shouted.

Abiku Madaki's eyes widened in alarm. "You!!" Madaki shouted, looking up into the seething face of the giant snake. "How did you get...!?"

Before Madaki could finish the question, Quetzalcoatl lurched forward, the gaping jaws opening wide to snap down hard on Abiku Madaki. Jumping aside, Madaki hurled himself across the sand in a tuck-and-roll to avoid the crushing jaws of the beast. The snake whipped its tail as Madaki slashed his orange sword, while the white snakes attacked and fended off the people of the sand until Marvin cried —

"Run!!"

50
TOLTEC PRINCE

Marvin led Amina and Tony on foot across the soft sands toward a series of smaller hills, hoping they could make it and escape the battle. Marvin and his group reached the hills and took cover behind a wedge of sandstone and turned to watch the fight blazing a hundred feet away.

The giant Quetzalcoatl, still engaged in close combat with Madaki, took a hard hit from the sword, but swiped his tail in a whoosh, smacking Madaki hard across his side and sending him sailing toward a slab of stone. Madaki struck it hard and fell, rolling to the sand. He bounced immediately back to his feet, but could only watch as Quetzalcoatl, his massive scaly body gliding effortlessly across the sandy landscape, turned his efforts to Marvin and his companions.

With a swift swoop of his tail, Quetzalcoatl scooped up Marvin and his friends and carried them away from the chaos, sliding swiftly across the sand toward a towering and sprawling mesa not far away. Madaki shouted after them as his sand minions followed, but the snake was fast, and before long reached the mesa and when

Marvin thought they were on a collision course with the massive rock, Quetzalcoatl powered his way through it with a flash, and in the next instant was gone. Marvin found himself twisting and turning as he slid through a tube of polished stone slick as oil. Marvin slid down and around, through the long, seemingly endless tube and as he spun out of control he caught out of the corner of his eye Amina and Tony behind him, the echo of their crying voices bouncing into his ears. His eyes held wide with a mix of wonder and fear—and a hint of relief—because he no longer saw Madaki nor his minions. Marvin continued the ride through the long tube on his buttocks and back until he came flying out the other end.

For three full seconds Marvin Fischer hurtled through mid air until he landed with a smack into what felt like water.

Yes, it must have been water, and he was fully submerged in it, holding his breath and flailing, trying to gauge which way was up, if the direction of *up* even existed in this strange other world. Marvin paddled his feet and swished his hands through the refreshing liquid, cool and crystal clear, and his head finally broke the surface, where he let out an explosive cache of stored breath, drops of water spewing from his lips as he opened his eyes and tried to get his bearings. As he kicked his feet to stay afloat and flapped his left hand under water, Marvin lifted his right hand to his face and wiped his eyes and blinked and snorted, catching his breath.

"Mister Fischer!" Tony coughed. Marvin turned and saw the boy not ten feet away, flailing on the water's surface. Marvin swam to Tony and grasped his arm as Amina rocketed up close behind, her eyes wide and her mouth gaping as she drew in as much air as her lungs would allow. Marvin and Tony moved toward her and the three of them hung there treading water, finally gaining some sense of themselves as they recovered their breath. Amina coughed and Tony wiped his face as Marvin glanced about their surroundings.

They were in the center of a large circular pool, magnificent and almost perfectly round, a supernatural spring, lit forcefully from below by a bright and unseen light from some unseen power. Marvin's eyes followed the shaft of pool light up high towards a towering cavernous ceiling, where the light danced on a dome of black rock polished to a mirror. The luminescent pool was the centerpiece of this underground palace, which seemed to have been constructed out of what was originally an immense natural cave. The pool itself was surrounded by a deck of smooth turquoise. The cavern was wide and gaping, carved out of the natural walls of the black rock, echoing the circular shape of the central pool. Part of the illustrious surrounding wall was covered in sparkling jewels, another section decorated with seashells, another of deep red stone, and the final stretch was of hammered gold. Jagged sections of black rock protruded randomly from the walls, through the décor of its makers, creating a pleasing harmony of nature and of art harkening of earth.

What Marvin found most curious about this cavern were the dark openings along the entire perimeter of the cavern, at precise intervals, yawning like mouths ready to swallow them into the bowels of the mesa.

The whole place echoed of a grand vision of the clover at Teotihuacán. The entrances to these super-tunnels were beautifully and deliberately cut and adorned with elaborate designs that Marvin could not discern, because he was too far away and still struggling to stay afloat.

Marvin managed a gasp to his friends as he treaded, "Can you swim?"

Amina nodded, wiping her face. Tony coughed 'yeah'.

"Let's get to the edge," said Marvin.

They began the 50-foot swim to the turquoise deck at the edge of the mystical glowing pool. Marvin felt light in the water, even in his suit and tie and shoes, which he knew were ruined, but right now he didn't care. He reached the edge of the pool and rested his elbows on the side of the smooth polished blue-green surface, glancing behind him and lending a hand to Tony as he arrived to his left, and Amina on his right. Clasping the side of the pool, they began to catch their breath, looking around again at the space. They were alone, and it was quiet. The only light in the place beamed from the water of the bottomless pool beneath.

"What is this place?" asked Tony.

Marvin continued to look around, just as uncertain as Tony. Where were they?

Was Saint Peter here?

Rubi Valdez?

Marvin lifted his right arm and spread his palm flat on the surface of the blue stone, then sloshed his left hand up and with a single pushup lifted himself up. He swung a leg onto the deck and came up out of the water. Tony followed Marvin's lead and pulled himself up as Marvin stretched to offer his hands to Amina, hoisting her easily up out of the clear liquid until all three of them now sat at the edge of the pool like lost prisoners of war. Dripping and soaking wet, the three of them stood up and rotated slowly around, looking for signs of life or death or anything—or anyone.

"The tunnels," Amina observed. "Those tunnels in the wall."

"Yeah," Marvin frowned. "What are they?"

Tony was already counting them. "There's 37 of them," he finished.

"Thirty-seven tunnels, all in a perfect circle..." Amina pondered.

Marvin's eyes lifted to gaze above the pool to the towering 100-foot ceiling, and his eyes landed on a small opening 30 feet above the pool, where he and his companions had been jettisoned from wherever they had come until they had landed in this pool. "Thirty-eight," said Marvin, pointing up toward the hole that had been their salvation from Madaki.

Amina and Tony joined his gaze to look at tunnel number 38.

"Thirty-eight tunnels..." Amina repeated.

"Like Castlerigg!" Tony exclaimed. "There were 38 stones at Castlerigg Stone Circle!"

Marvin's jaw dropped and Amina gasped as they realized the coincidental numbers.

"My God, you are right, Antonio," Amina affirmed.

"It's still not makin' sense," Marvin quizzed.

But somehow it did.

There was a commonality—a resemblance—some connectivity from the earthen world from which they'd come, to this new and unfamiliar and strange place.

And that familiarity offered hope.

"Wait!" Tony put up a hand. "Do you hear that?"

Marvin's wet heel squeaked as he rotated on the deck. "What?"

From somewhere came an echo of breathing, as if from some giant mass, a brushing against stone, getting louder.

Getting closer.

Marvin, remaining calm, pitched his ear and hoisted a finger, rotating again on his heel. "It's comin' from one of the tunnels."

And as they waited helplessly there was nothing they could do, no place to hide.

All they could do was wait for whatever was coming their way.

And as the sound approached it became clear to them which tunnel emanated with the sound. They all turned to their left to face squarely into the dark mouth of a tunnel 40 feet away.

And from the mouth of the tunnel emerged the giant snake Quetzalcoatl, his massive body and long scaly self, pulling out of the hole and his black eyes and feathery head gazing upon his visitors.

And as the giant heroic snake approached, he transformed into a mist of twisting blue-green flames and bursting flashes of white, and within seconds the snake was gone, and appearing in its place its avatar—the form of a man—sculpted of pure lean muscle. The human avatar wore a mask adorned in a shiny mosaic of tiny polished turquoise stones and seashells, with large oval eyes in lenses of what looked like transparent green obsidian. The nose of the mask was wide, the nostrils large, the mouth a wide slit with heavy lips. The ears were thick and stretched and pierced. Lustrous blue-green feathers shined along the outer edge of the mask. The warrior's skin was a deep yellow-brown, the waist wrapped in dyed cotton with interwoven jewels and crystals. On the forearms were wristbands of gold. The man wore a necklace of pale white seashells and carried the black spear of a warrior, and a round shield painted in mazes of blacks and reds.

This was Topiltzin, once the mighty leader of the Toltecs many centuries before on ancient earth, the man deified by myth as the legendary Quetzalcoatl, god of wind and rain.

And of peace.

Emanating now from the darkness of the adjacent caves were the white snakes, in coiled groups, gliding into the cavern until they separated out behind and beside the legendary Topiltzin. The white snakes became wisps of white flame and merged into the forms of people, the Toltec warriors faithful to their priest-ruler Topiltzin. They materialized silent and dutiful in a grand display of welcome with their spears and shields, wearing blacks and reds and the cylindrical hats and feathers of Mesoamerican fighters. Some had body paint and tattoos and nose plugs of obsidian. The earlobes were pearlescent discs. Then came another crowd, all women, emerging a few at a time from various of the other tunnel openings, all dressed in woven cotton petticoats of bright primary colors, necklaces and bracelets of copper and jade, their black hair tumbling luxuriantly across their shoulders and down their backs. The women stopped and stood along the wall behind the men, gazing curiously at the three new visitors. There was not an imperfect face or body among any of the men or the women.

After the quiet assembly of exotic Toltec troops and the women, Topiltzin the priestly prince advanced toward Marvin and Amina and Tony, stopping and standing before them directly.

Tony lunged forward and hugged Topiltzin Quetzalcoatl tightly. "Thank you!" Tony said through wet eyes. "Thank you for trying to save my mother!"

Topiltzin put a hand on the boy's shoulder, tilting his gleaming mask down toward him in a gesture of comfort, the bright green feathers of his mask rippling gently in some faint otherworldly breeze.

Marvin and Amina shared a look.

Amina had been right!

It had been Quetzalcoatl who had appeared in Phoenix on the morning of Rubi Valdez' accident, trying to save her from Abiku Madaki's attack.

And now, for some reason, Abiku Madaki wanted Antonio Valdez too.

Topiltzin Quetzalcoatl mumbled something in a calm, even voice, speaking as if in some sort of response to Tony's embrace and tears.

To Marvin, the man's words sounded like gibberish.

But Amina woke to them. "It seems he is speaking some version of Nahuatl."

Marvin looked at Amina like she was from Mars, until he heard Tony respond to Topiltzin in his own language. Tony turned excitedly toward Marvin and Amina.

"I can understand him!" said Tony.

Marvin's face glowed with curiosity as he rocked his head toward Amina. "What's goin' on?" He watched the thoughts roll amidst the golden flecks of Amina's sparkling eyes and she smiled.

"Someone has enabled Tony..." said Amina. "I do not know who, or how… but a gift of language must have been given to Antonio during our transport. We are fortunate that Antonio can translate. I have a thousand questions."

51

FLICKERING POOL

Marvin peeled his wet coat off of his arms with great difficulty. He may as well have been confined to a straight jacket. He had been directed by Topiltzin through one of the tunnels and into this private chamber, in order to strip out of his wet garments, and had been given a long turquoise-colored robe to change into. Finally Marvin pulled free of the suit jacket. He was about to fling the jacket onto a stone bench when he remembered his smartphone. He found it in the damp breast pocket and removed it. The phone was covered with wet droplets, and the crack it had suffered on the rail carriage had worsened.

Certainly the phone was fried.

There would be no more calls to or from Elizabeth Walsh.

And no more guiding texts from Saint Peter.

He tossed the useless gadget aside and began to tug out of his suit pants. As he yanked the pant leg over his foot, he remembered the metallic orb he had stuffed into the pocket. He reached into the pocket and was pleased to find that the orb was still there. He pulled the sphere out, set it carefully on the bench, and reached for the turquoise robe. The robe was sleeveless and long, extending down to his ankles. It was soft, dry, and comfortable. Marvin retrieved the orb from the bench and dropped it into one of the robe's generously sized pockets. He exited the chamber and followed a page back out into the pool cavern.

The cavern was empty of all activity. The page veered off into another tunnel, leaving Marvin to himself in the strange and lapping glow of the pool cavern. He stepped toward the wall, this one covered in jewels, and ran his hand over the carefully inlaid gems. Jutting from behind the jewels was a part of the foundational wall—of the same black material as the rocks and sand where they had first crossed from the other side. Although they had traveled from there at high speed through some sort of tube, Marvin guessed they were still on the same plane or space—wherever that may be—which meant that Abiku Madaki may still be hot on their scent. Marvin inhaled with thoughts of being captured, then walked across the turquoise platform and stopped at the pool's edge. He hoped this place would be safe and secret enough to keep Madaki and his army out, long enough for Marvin and his team to come up with another plan.

Marvin's thoughts evaporated when he saw Amina emerge from one of the tunnels, wrapped in a sari-like turquoise silken robe, hers more refined than Marvin's. It was the first time Marvin experienced Amina with her hair down. Someone had done a magnificent job untangling it from its watery mop into a finely brushed, shoulder-length cascade of golden-brown elegance. Amina floated across the platform with her easy grace. Marvin was surprised to find himself fully engaged by her beauty. As the distance closed between them, he observed she had retained the gold hoop earrings in her ears. Man and woman were momentarily alone, the light from the pool flickering serenely in a bid to relax, and there was something fantastically romantic about it. Marvin's mind succumbed as he considered where this situation might lead in another context. Although the familiar scent of Amina's perfume had gone, Marvin's memory of it was piquant enough. He did not know what to do with these unexpected sensations of amorousness, beholding Amina not only as an intelligent university scholar, but suddenly as a desirable woman of the flesh. He felt suddenly like a panther ready to pounce on its prey.

As if reading his mind, Amina gifted Marvin with a hypnotic smile as she arrived at his side. Her makeup had washed away, but she appeared refreshingly attractive. Marvin considered blurting some wise crack but thought better of it.

Amina opened her mouth to form a word, her eyes trained on the gentle ripples of the crystal pool before them. "The setting feels Arabian, yet we are in Mexico—sort of—but the robe strikes me as rather Indian."

"Got lipstick? I'll paint you the Bindi."

Amina tilted her head. "You know the term."

"I vacationed on the Malabar Coast once. With Caroline."

"Caroline... your wife."

"Yeah."

"Of course."

"What do you think happened to our clothes?" asked Marvin.

"I should think they are being repurposed at market."

Marvin chuckled and lifted his right index finger to poke Amina's shoulder.

"What are you doing?" she asked.

"Seeing if your body was actually there. We're still flesh and blood. Not spirits."

"Our bodies did not convert."

"Convert?"

"The passage from familiar earth to this place has not resulted in the transition of our base corporeal bodies into the sublime and ethereal."

"What about Topaz, or whatever his name is?"

"Topiltzin Quetzalcoatl seems rather solid as well."

"Doesn't that strike you as odd? Aren't we in the spiritual realm?"

"That we are physically present in another realm I can affirm with a degree of certainty. As to the spiritual dynamics of this realm, and where it falls in the hierarchy of the After Worlds, I have much to observe and learn. Wherever we are, it is not representative of what we have come to expect, is it Mister Fischer?"

Leaning toward Amina, Marvin asked, "So can't our new friend just turn himself into a snake again? And get us out of here?"

"Don't ask questions Marvin," Amina said brusquely. "Just wait."

The sudden cold turn was somewhat startling. Marvin guessed the woman was growing tired of being challenged while she was still processing. In his own defense, Marvin told himself that Quetzalcoatl had been renowned in Mesoamerican myth for being a god. Why couldn't he continue to use those powers? Well, Marvin reasoned, they were not in Mesoamerica, they were not even on the earth anymore as far as he could tell, and whatever powers Quetzalcoatl had on the other side may not come to full manifestation in the other realms. Whatever the case, Topiltzin Quetzalcoatl was clearly a force of power and reckoning, yet he was hiding down here away from Abiku Madaki.

"I guess you're right," Marvin relented. "We don't exactly know what's goin' on yet."

Amina nodded a level of understanding. "This is not heaven," she said pensively. "We are in limbo."

52
MYSTICAL ORB

At that moment Marvin observed a single page, one he hadn't seen before, enter from one of the tunnels across the cavern. The page was shirtless, dressed in a red skirt with white strips of cloth wrapped around wrists and ankles. The top of his head was shaved, the hair at the sides long and plaited, winding around the head, its end dangling down like a whip along one shoulder. The fancy page carried a tray with several small cacti, and a single cylindrical black vase covered in painted symbols of white and orange. Marvin gently elbowed Amina and gestured toward the page across the cavern. Together they watched the page orbit the deck until he stopped at a round cobalt table next to the pool's edge. The page set the tray down onto the table. He picked up one of the cacti and, with one skilled motion, stripped it of its needles. Then, between two flat stones, he squeezed the body of the naked cactus over the painted vase. Translucent liquid dripped from the cactus and into the vase.

"Wonder what that guy's doin'?" Marvin quizzed.

Suddenly Tony burst from another of the tunnels, racing around the deck of the pool, dressed in his own turquoise robe, hands waving in the air.

"I was right! I was right! I was right!" Tony shouted.

Marvin and Amina's eyes swung quickly to watch the boy race around like a six-year-old at a birthday party.

"Mister Fischer! Doctor Karimova!" Tony's energetic voice echoed across the huge pool chamber as he ran to meet them. "There's life on other planets!"

"How do you mean?" asked Amina.

"Topiltzin just explained it to me!" Tony said. "This thing we're on—it's a planet! It's that yellow planet I saw in my dream! And on the road to Castlerigg! Remember? The yellow planet is like earth! Except it's way beyond our solar system, way, way, way beyond anything our telescopes on earth have ever been able to see!"

"How do you know?"

"Because this planet is supposed to be heaven!" Tony exclaimed.

"Supposed to be?" asked Marvin.

"Or—part of it…" Tony tussled his brown hair to aid its drying. The wound on his forehead had been lightly redressed and was hardly even in need of a bandage. "I told Topiltzin everything that happened to us!" Tony continued. "Why we're here, and how we got here. And that we're looking for Saint Peter. Maybe my mom is here!! Oh—And Topiltzin wants to show us the Jalisco Inscription!"

"Alright buddy slow down," Marvin squinted, "What's this *jello inscription* thing Topaz is supposed to show us?"

"The Jalisco Inscription. I'm not sure. But Topiltzin says we have to see it!"

Marvin pulled the metallic orb from his pocket and turned quietly to Amina and Tony. "I'm gonna show this thing to Topaz."

"Topiltzin," Amina corrected.

"Yeah whatever."

Tony's eyes lit up at the orb in Marvin's hand. "You kept one?"

Marvin palmed the ball as three of Topiltzin's pages, each with a shiny blackstone cup in hand, approached the edge of the luminescent pool. The pages scooped some of the clear water into the blackstone cups. They stood, approached Marvin, Tony, and Amina, and handed each of them one of the blackstone cups. The blackstone cups were beautifully engraved and painted with symbolic markings of white and orange circles, triangles, squares, and abstract faces.

Marvin peeked at the clear liquid in the cup. "There's no coffee?"

Tony slurped the water without question. Marvin looked to Amina for an approving nod, then took a draw. The water was excellent, better than any filtered water he had experienced back on earth.

Finally Topiltzin Quetzalcoatl himself appeared from yet another of the tunnels, one slightly larger than the others, and with different, ornate carvings around its entrance. The prince's personal chamber, Marvin guessed. Topiltzin approached his visitors and bowed a greeting. Marvin could not see Topiltzin Quetzalcoatl's face due to the mask of turquoise and shells, and he wondered why the guy would wear it all the time.

As Marvin prepared to sip again, Topiltzin poised himself directly in front of Marvin, extended an arm straight forward, and opened his palm. Marvin paused mid-sip, looking into Topiltzin's outstretched palm—clean, cocoa brown, and empty.

Marvin watched Topiltzin's eyes, steady and expressionless, peering at him from behind the obsidian lenses of the turquoise mask. "What?" asked Marvin.

Topiltzin blurted something in clear Nahuatl.

Tony tilted his head. "He said you're supposed to give him the thing in your pocket."

With somewhat guilty amazement, Marvin turned to Tony. "I was gonna."

Marvin dipped his left hand into the pocket of his robe. Grasping the orb, he removed the metallic ball and extended it towards Topiltzin. "This?" He dropped the orb into Topiltzin's open palm. The Toltec prince wrapped his fingers around the orb and gently rotated the bright shiny object in his fingertips, examining it delicately, as if he had not seen one in centuries. Then he grasped it firmly and squeezed, and again opened his palm. Topiltzin studied the object intensely, as if obsessed, holding it up toward the tall ceiling, then against his chest, and up to his ear.

Then Topiltzin pointed at Marvin's drinking cup. After a pause, Marvin suspiciously handed the cup to Topiltzin. The prince took the cup abruptly and with a quick and deliberate sweep of his arm, scattered the water onto the floor.

Then Topiltzin stepped toward the luminescent pool, squatted down, dipped the cup into the pool, lifted it, dumped half the water back into the pool, and stood up. Walking toward the cobalt table where his fancy page worked the cacti, Topiltzin waved for Marvin to follow.

Marvin glanced at Amina, then followed Topiltzin. Amina and Tony went after them. Topiltzin stopped at the cobalt table and extended Marvin's drinking cup toward the fancy page, who, apparently clear about what was to be done in this mini-ritual, took it, and then like a chemist in a lab, mixed it with the juice he'd squeezed from the cacti. Topiltzin tossed the metallic orb three feet into the air above the table, where it landed with a sharp tap, and then rolled slowly toward the table's edge. Topiltzin raised his spear and swung it down hard, smashing the orb into powder on the polished edge of the cobalt table.

Topiltzin took Marvin's drinking cup from the fancy page, held the opening below the edge of the table and, using his spear, swept a generous amount of the powder into the juicy blend of Marvin's drinking cup. Topiltzin swished the solution, held it to his nose, and extended the vessel back to Marvin.

Marvin frowned, took the cup, glared into it, then stared at the prince. "You want me to drink this?"

Topiltzin gestured and nodded.

Marvin turned warily to Amina. She peeked into the cup. "I would listen to the man," she said with a twinkle.

Marvin turned back to Topiltzin just to make sure there was no misunderstanding. Topiltzin stood firm. Marvin sniffed the concoction, grimaced, took a breath, and held the cup to his lips. He slurped, then gulped, then tipped the cup back and drained the vessel of its repugnant pulque. Marvin coughed, leaning forward, and dropped the blackstone cup to the floor. He coughed again and heaved, clutching his chest.

"Did it taste good?" asked Tony.

"Are you kidding?" Marvin hacked. "It's dirt!"

Amina stepped behind Marvin and rested a hand on his back. "There, there now."

Marvin tilted his head to Amina's smirking face, glowering at her for teasing him like a child. He wrenched his jaw and shifted an accusing glare toward Topiltzin. The warrior stood, hands folded in front, observing Marvin's reaction and behavior.

Marvin's hard stare fell away as he felt something tingle below his breastbone. Struck with nervousness, his eyes darted back and forth. "Is something supposed to happen?"

Topiltzin, apparently realizing that Marvin had recovered enough from ingesting the drink, gestured for his guests to follow. Marvin rattled his head as his eyes cleared and he followed, wondering how much more of this ritual his body could manage.

53

HIDDEN BELOW

In the underground city that Topiltzin referred to as *New Tollán*, the tunnel was of black stone, flint-like and glossy, finely chiseled to an almost perfectly hewn cylindrical corridor. The air was dry and cool and refreshing. Instead of the cutting beams of flashlights, glowing yellow orbs along the tunnel's ceiling cast their golden ambience upon visitors as they walked along the perfectly smooth walkway.

This was tunnel number 38, the most central and largest of the elaborate and ornately decorated holes dotting the walls around the luminescent pool cavern. The entrance jamb of tunnel number 38 had been ornately carved with complex symbols and glyphs, densely packed images sacred to the ancient religious customs of the Toltecs during their prime in the city of Tollán on familiar earth. Upon passing through the tunnel's entrance, Marvin Fischer had observed images on the jamb that made no sense to him. Somewhere amidst the dazzling carvings of zigzags, squiggly lines and squares—all brightly painted in reds, yellows, greens, and blues—he thought he'd seen a conch shell with a head coming out of it, a star, a coyote, a man wearing an eagle's beak helmet, and a four-petalled flower with a human face at the center.

Oh yes, Topiltzin had believed in the dizzying pantheon of gods common to the Mesoamerican custom, the gods who governed the systems of duality, providing rain and fire, light and darkness, bringing war and peace, creating male and female, guiding life and death, and moving time through astronomical cycles. But one day during his time as ruler of the Toltecs, atop a rocky outcrop beneath a sky cracking with the pink of sunrise, Topiltzin had meditated amidst the morning breeze and sensed that something was not right. It had been then, during solitude, that he had felt an intense connection with the divine, and had then come to his own understanding of a single master, one god behind them all, a supreme being whom he had known then and still today only as *Hunab Ku*, a name whose origin had been shrouded in mystery, passed down by oral tradition in various forms among the Mesoamerican cultures as they had migrated and settled across the mountains and valleys since 6,000 BC. It had been in that single moment, within the span of an instant, that Topiltzin had come to believe that Hunab Ku was the single source. And although highly unusual within the worship rituals of the Mesoamericans, Topiltzin believed that for true peace to be obtained, the one true god, Hunab Ku, must be discovered and known and satisfied through peaceful means.

Now, as Topiltzin Quetzalcoatl led Marvin and his friends through the winding tunnel below the black planet's surface, a place so far unknown to Abiku Madaki, Topiltzin explained, with Tony translating, the state of the planet, and the situation in which the prince and his Toltec people now found themselves.

Everyone here had died their earthly deaths and had been supernaturally transmuted into new bodies. Their bodies were no longer destroyable in the earthly sense, but under duress they could be excised and cast off—even trapped—in other parts of the After Worlds. Topiltzin himself could transform and travel spiritually in an instant as long as there was no interference. That is: no resistance from an opposing force, which could come in the form of a spiritual blockade erected by Abiku Madaki. Topiltzin confirmed what Dante Alighieri had alluded to, that the After Worlds is vast with no levels per sé, further explaining that each of the 38 tunnels in the pool cavern, and each of the 38 monoliths at Castlerigg Stone Circle, represent one of the 38 heavenly planets of the After Worlds intended by the supreme god, Hunab Ku, as the final paradise. Re-born souls, in their new perfect bodies, were to be released from grief and opposition and harm, free to roam and explore the vast beauty of the After Worlds, enjoying all the gifts of harmonic life, in eternal peace with Hunab Ku, who dwelled forever in the definitive, highest Paradise, what Dante had referred to as *The Empyrean*.

"What went wrong?" asked Marvin.

Topiltzin explained through Tony that he does not know exactly what went wrong. They believed that the conflict—the excising of spirits and the occurring blockades—were not part of the original design for the After Worlds. The opposition was to have been subdued, controlled, and crushed by Hunab Ku. Somehow, Abiku Madaki persisted, creating havoc and unrest in the After Worlds. Topiltzin and his people now prayed for deliverance, for true peace, and for the final completion of the heavenly After Worlds, as they believe Hunab Ku intended. Hunab Ku desired only goodness and love for all humanity. But Topiltzin and his people had confined themselves to these caverns because of the interference, afraid to go out, for fear of being captured by Erzok.

"Erzok?" asked Marvin, looking to Amina for recognition. "He knows Erzok."

"It is my contention, Marvin, that Erzok is the primary conductor here, not Abiku Madaki."

Marvin shifted his jaw. All this spiritual muck was continuing to thicken against his liking. He dreaded the thought of what the forthcoming 'inscription' would tell them.

Now Tony stepped to Marvin and walked alongside him. "I asked Topiltzin if this planet has a name," said Tony. "He said not really. I'm going to call it exoplanet 'RMV-b'."

"What's that mean?"

"'RMV' is an abbreviation of my mom's full name, *Rubi Maria Valdez*," said Tony. "And then the letter 'b' because I bet this exoplanet orbits beyond our Solar System, in a new system, probably the first in the catalogue of this newly discovered system. When we get back home, I'm going to give my suggestion to the International Astronomical Union."

Marvin smiled at Tony's dream of contributing to astronomical progress as they kept pace behind Topiltzin. Presently, the group came to an opening in the floor, a wide circle with a narrow stone spiral staircase leading downward. Topiltzin began the descent. Marvin and his friends followed silently. Down and down they went, winding their way deeper into the bowels of the planet. Suddenly Marvin stopped, lowered his head, and pressed his palms against his temples.

Amina grasped Marvin's elbow. "You okay?"

Topiltzin stopped and turned, observing Marvin carefully.

Marvin put a hand to his stomach. "I feel weird."

Amina examined Marvin's troubled face, gauging his eyes. His pupils were dilated. She put a hand to his forehead. It was dry and clear of sweat.

"That solution you drank?"

Marvin nodded. "I need coffee."

Amina flashed him a benevolent smirk. "Come on," she urged.

Marvin took a breath and they continued down the steps.

Finally, the stairway ended, spilling its descenders onto the sprawling floor of a large, wide, and tall cave-like corridor, sparkling black like the tunnel above and the staircase from which they'd just stepped, and the four adventurers paused here at the foot of the stairs.

Along the walls of the corridor, two hundred of Topiltzin's warriors stood posted shoulder to shoulder, a hundred to a side, spears in hand, motionless and with the discipline of soldiers at attention. Topiltzin explained that the Jalisco Inscription's location was so secret, that the guardians of the ancient engraving were never to leave their posts.

Marvin gazed with volatile eyes at the massive object occupying the length of the corridor's center, the object that certainly must be the Jalisco Inscription. Like a giant deep green table, it was a block of solid green rock, like a single brick, standing heavily on the floor of the cave. It stood glistening, three feet wide along its length, rectangular with sharp corners, its walls mirror-like, a commanding slab of rock with writing etched meticulously on its surface. The table was so long that, even with the orbs above showering their beams of golden light, Marvin could barely make out the table's end further down the corridor.

Topiltzin led his visitors closer to the table, opening his arms out reverently in a wide gesture towards the glistening slab. He mouthed words to Tony.

"This is the Jalisco Inscription," Tony marveled at the gleaming piece of polished rock. "He says it's the only one. There aren't any copies."

Mesmerized by its iridescent glow and substantial mass, Marvin wondered how in hell they got the thing down here. Were he an intelligence-gathering agent, this would be the jackpot. And indeed it was. In a rush of clarity, Marvin knew that for his present quest, this was the mother load of information, a giant piece of the eternal puzzle, a missing link of seismic consequence.

Marvin set his eyes to the inscribed characters. The writing was arranged in neatly set vertical columns, with a single line separating each column, like a Hebrew scroll, except carved into stone rather than written with ink on vellum. Strangely, there was no dust or dirt or debris on the glossy surface, nothing to detract from the beauty of the green stone.

"It's obsidian," Amina stared with awe. "Rare green obsidian." The connection seemed to click in her mind. "Of course—there are large deposits of green obsidian in Mexico. Was this transported through a gateway from earth? Old earth, from where we've come?"

Topiltzin waved off the question and babbled to Tony in Nahuatl. Tony stood silent, his jaw dropping. Marvin and Amina waited with baited breath for words to proceed from the boy's mouth.

"Well?" Marvin prompted. "What'd he say?"

"He said God wrote it. Hunab Ku. After he got mad at the wooden people," Tony's eyes turned fearful. "And Hunab Ku brought a curse down on them."

Marvin glanced worriedly to Amina. "The wooden people?"

Amina's eyes narrowed. "The wooden people... of course, from the Mesoamerican creation myths, after the influence of the Spanish invaders who brought Catholicism. As you and I might see it, Marvin, the divine curse against the wooden people might be likened to the fall of Adam and Eve. The fall from Eden."

Marvin and Amina locked eyes.

"So why would God write this thing, after that curse?" Marvin asked. As he pondered, Topiltzin kept babbling to Tony.

"It's a record," Tony continued. "A record of events in the After Worlds. After the curse. The inscription was in danger of being destroyed by Abiku Madaki, so Topiltzin and his men moved it into this cave to hide it."

To Marvin the slab looked like an artifact, like something that belonged in The Smithsonian on earth. Except that this was nothing like anything that could ever be discovered on that old and corrupt planet.

It was becoming apparent that this magnificent treasure had gone unseen by any human before them.

DIRK EICHHORST

Written by God in another realm, not intended for human eyes.

54

THE JALISCO INSCRIPTION

Amina Karimova was the first to slowly and gently reach out a hand to touch the stone delicately with her fingertips. It was smooth as glass. There came no zap, no electrical sizzle, no scolding lightning bolt from above. "It's absolutely magnificent," Amina beamed, engrossed by the etching in the stone.

"Looks like cuneiform," suggested Marvin.

Amina's eyebrows lifted as the corners of her mouth bent. "Impressive suggestion, Marvin. But it is not cuneiform. These are not figures formed by a stylus."

Marvin leaned in alongside Amina and examined the text further. The characters were complex, sharp, and crisp, as if etched by a laser.

"Nor are they Mesoamerican glyphs," Amina observed. "This is a language, reminiscent of Aramaic, hints of Syriac, even Chaldean, but yet it is none of those. This form of writing is alien to me. I am not a cryptologist or a textual critic Marvin, but I have been around enough scholars and ancient texts to know that this artifact is unique to everything. Most intricate and highly advanced."

Marvin could no longer take the suspense. "What exactly does it mean?"

Topiltzin stepped up now and took Tony's arm and spoke into his ear, pointing at Marvin. Topiltzin spoke quickly and with energy, gesturing with his hands and pointing along the stretch of the slab and embellishing his words.

"Mister Fischer?" Tony looked puzzled.

"What?"

Topiltzin stepped urgently to Marvin and shoved his shoulder.

"Hey, cool it," Marvin said defensively.

Topiltzin continued to jabber, pointing wildly to the inscription. Then he set one hand on Marvin's shoulder and the other flat against Marvin's stomach, and rubbed. Marvin backed away. "Okay this is gettin' weird."

Topiltzin tossed up his hands, apparently frustrated, and gestured for the trio to follow him. Topiltzin led the group further down the corridor, past the line of dutiful guards, along the side of the slab that continued for some one hundred feet, until finally they came to the end of the slab. Topiltzin stopped, turned, and pointed.

Here the slab was not clean and smooth and polished. Here, the last section of the stone was roughly hewn and bare and blank, with the end of the obsidian slab rugged, chipped, and broken.

"Is part of it missing?" Marvin asked.

"No," Amina concluded. "It has not been finished yet."

Topiltzin again began to speak with Tony as Marvin and Amina examined the spot where the writing ended and the smooth reflective surface gave way to the natural unpolished stone.

"You see?" Amina pointed, leaning her head closer to Marvin's. "This seems to be the last fragment of a sentence, the last piece of a thought, and then it just ends." Amina was amazed. "Marvin, this is an incredible find. Whatever this is, Topiltzin and his people are guarding one of the most important written chronicles in universal history."

"It's like—a part of the mind of God."

"Exactly! Something happened here in the After Worlds, that God felt was of significant importance. So much so, that he wrote it down, documented it, and is now protecting it."

"Like a Bible."

"Like a Bible *part two*." She turned to face him. "The Bible we know is a record of Jewish and Christian history and religion as it unfolded on physical earth. This Jalisco Inscription must be the record of events that unfolded in the After Worlds."

"Or is it just a continuation?"

Amina turned pensively and set her palms flat on the stone's surface and leaned on it heavily. "Or, it is concurrent to our own Bible, a record of events that happened *here*, in the spiritual realms, while at the same time, earth history was happening *there*." She paused again. "If only we could read it."

"Whose language is it?"

Amina sighed resignedly. "I believe it may be the language of God alone. It seems even Topiltzin is unable to decode it."

"And why is the thing broken off? Why is the ending not written?"

"Perhaps because the ending is in question."

Topiltzin stopped his side conversation with Tony now and approached Marvin. Leaning over, Topiltzin again began to rub Marvin's stomach. Marvin yanked himself away. "Will you cut that out?"

"He says you have to read it!" said Tony to Marvin.

"What? I can't—"

"Marvin!" Amina snapped. "Be obedient. This is important."

Marvin paused, scowling, then allowed his gaze to drift upward. He spread his arms out in offering to Topiltzin, who began poking at Marvin's stomach. Marvin clenched his lips tight at the awkwardness of the exercise. Topiltzin stood up, pinched Marvin's cheeks, then turned Marvin's head side to side. With the fingertips of one hand, Topiltzin propped open Marvin's eyelids, first the left, then the right. Topiltzin stood back apparently baffled. Instantly then, as if in desperation, Topiltzin slapped Marvin hard on the cheek and then backhanded him on the other with a smack.

"Ah..! that's it Topaz!" Marvin hunched away. "I am not your voodoo doll."

Topiltzin frantically pointed at the obsidian slab, looking at Marvin. Amina, squinting now, stepped to Marvin's side and took his elbow. "Marvin, walk with me." She led him back a few steps along the slab, to where the writing was especially heavy, and released his elbow. Marvin stopped, looking dejectedly at the stubborn writing in front of him. Amina leaned into him and whispered, "I think what Topiltzin is trying to say, as Antonio indicated, is that *only you* are going to be able to read the inscription."

Marvin looked at her, incredulous. "Me? How—?"

"He keeps prompting you. Perhaps the solution you drank will give you some insight."

"I haven't been able to read a single damn syllable of this thing. What do you think is gonna happen?"

"Don't ask questions Marvin! Just give it a shot! What else are we going to do? Now lean over. Inspect. Search. Scrutinize. Investigate. Discover! You are an analyst of intelligence, are you not? A puzzle solver. Do your thing!"

Marvin's sizzling stare seemed enough to fry her hair off. Amina eased away to give him space. Marvin glanced at Tony, then at Topiltzin. Marvin took a breath, decidedly shaking off the attitude. He obediently clasped his hands behind his back and leaned over the inscription. Looking now in earnest at the writing, Marvin wished he'd had his reading glasses. He wracked his brain, trying to recall anything at all from the ACTIC where codes were deciphered, secret messages cracked, hidden clues uncovered. He wished intensely that Elizabeth Walsh and Lyle Stratton were here to help him.

But they were not, Topiltzin did not know the language, nor did Amina.

So it was apparently all up to him.

Placing his right hand on the slab's surface, Marvin knelt down to one knee and, for what it was worth, carefully began to examine the walls of the slab.

For a moment, he put his ear to the mirrored wall of the table and just listened.

Nothing.

Marvin stood up. He jostled his shoulders and wagged his head. Determined now to cast aside his doubts, he refocused, leaned in again to the slab, and rested both hands flat on its surface. He took in a breath and released slowly. He tilted his head slightly to see Tony and Amina standing close by, silent, expectant, hopeful. Marvin turned his eyes back to the writing. He studied it again, intently, squinting, tilting his head, then moving around the end, he worked himself to the other side of the table, keeping his eyes always on the writing.

The writing. The writing. The writing.

Marvin crouched down, bent, leaned, tried to look at the thing upside down.

He probed.

He scanned. Surveyed. Contemplated. Studied.

He listened again.

Still nothing.

It was senseless. What could he possibly glean? He had no knowledge of the thing, no background in religious writing whatsoever. He had absolutely no idea what he was doing. He felt like an idiot.

After two more minutes of total silence and intense appraisal, Marvin stood up, put a fist to his waist, and stared at the puzzle, ready to give. That is when Marvin's eyes became suddenly washed in a white glare, and he felt his head go faint. His fist dropped from his waist and his left knee gave out. He reached for the stone and caught his balance.

Amina stepped forward, perhaps in a bid to aid him, but Topiltzin grabbed hold of the folds in her robe and quickly restrained her.

Marvin regained his stance and released his grip from the stone. He felt woozy. He put one hand to his face as if that might help clear the glare from his eyes. Was he dehydrated? He pulled his hand away and blinked, opening his mouth wide, shaking his head, and the blaring glare cleared. He shook his head again. The feeling came back. Stronger. A dreaminess. A sense of disembodiment from physical reality. His mind was drifting off. But where to?

Of course—he now realized through groggy reasoning that he must have ingested a psychotropic substance by drinking that concoction given to him by that damn Topaz. He was a slave now to a transformation, something was happening to his senses. He took a deep breath and felt himself losing control of consciousness. Instinctively he grasped the blunt edges of the slab again between his fingers, standing stiff and solid, the unfamiliar glare returning to his eyes, as if plunging into a trance.

"Topiltzin," Tony turned to his new friend. "What's happening?"

Topiltzin held up his hand, an indication to pause and watch.

"Marvin?" Amina held still. "Are you okay?"

"Don't ask questions Amina," Marvin said in a soft low monotone. "Just shut up."

Amina's face contorted in protest as she lifted abruptly to her toes, then, in an apparent effort of self-restraint, lowered herself and curled her lips inward.

The glare in Marvin's eyes intensified. There was a total lack of movement and a complete cessation of engagement with his companions. Marvin Fischer was somewhere else.

~

Marvin felt no fear. The cave was gone and he was alone. All he could see was the text in front of his eyes, waving like lapping water against a mystic shore. Marvin Fischer stood motionless and quiet, his posture frozen. His breathing slowed. His lower lip quivered, but no sound emerged. He could no longer feel his legs or his arms. His ears absorbed the familiar tones of voices nearby, but the words were fog.

Marvin's chin dipped and his eyes fixed again upon the text before him, following the lines of etched figures and emblems and characters in their neat rows of crosshatched patterns, like a complex computer code. He was not sure what had happened to him, but he let it control him, a power that held him locked and tied into the spiritual energy between his body and his brain to this mysterious piece of rock before him. Rapidly Marvin's eyes traversed the lines of text, across the dots and slashes and curves, until suddenly his mind opened up to a level of consciousness he had never before known or experienced.

Then came white-hot terror.

At first Marvin's mouth opened innocently. The soft puff of air hissed from his throat. His eyes blazed yellow when the first scream shot wretchedly from his abdomen. The scream came from the deep, tearing into his throat, his insides ripping to shreds beneath the turquoise robe. His body lurched forward and pounced on the text of the inscription. The scream stopped. Marvin heaved emptily, his breathing rate skyrocketed, his face beaded with sweat. His arms reached out, fingers on his hands spanning wide. The fingers clawed and the fingernails grated painfully into the tiny grooves of the writing. His head tipped and turned and his right ear slammed down hard to the slab's surface. The burning heat seared through his cheek. His head began to shake. His lips pinched. A defiant crease chiseled his face. His arms trembled. His buttocks clenched and the calves of his legs contracted and his toes crunched into the sandals on his feet.

The beading sweat on Marvin's face began to pour down in streams. Again he screamed. His fingers screeched across the letters, the words, the message.

The record.

The strange and terrible and unspeakable history surged into Marvin's sub-conscious in a millisecond, exploding all reason and understanding—

> A blazing white comet crackling down across a black heaven.
> A formidable clash of great power.
> Silver-winged beings fighting in mangled terror.
> Millions of voices screaming and crying out in death.
>
> A figure in a gleaming white robe…
> And a Sumerian…
> The Third Dynasty of Ur…

Marvin's body slackened and his body became mush. His hands slid off the green obsidian and his body crumpled heavily and crashed to the black floor.

"Marvin!" Amina rushed to Marvin's side and this time Topiltzin let her go to him. Amina's golden-brown eyes were saucers of shock as she feared Marvin might have expired. Panicked, she knelt beside him and put a hand to his face. She leaned in and listened for breath. Frantically, Amina turned to the prince for an explanation.

Topiltzin remained calm, producing a small jade vial from his waistband. He handed the vial to Tony, and after a moment's pause Tony understood. He rushed to Amina's side with the jade vial and popped the stone plug and saw the liquid inside.

Amina tugged at Marvin's shoulders and scooted her bent knees closer and, taking him into herself, she rested his head gently on her thighs and cradled his temples between her hands.

"Marvin..." she said softly.

Marvin was unresponsive. Amina reached for the open vial from Tony and poured the revitalizing water across Marvin's dry lips. He swallowed reflexively.

"Marvin..." Amina said again, her face a desperate mix of concern and affection. She pressed her palm against Marvin's forehead and felt the pumping of blood through the arteries in his neck. The color returned to Marvin's face. He groaned.

Breath gushed into Amina's lungs as relief spread through her. She wiggled from beneath his head and swung around on her toes, squatting to face him. She grasped his robe with both hands and raised his limp form. "Hey," she said gently. "Hey," she said again. She blew into his face. And when it looked like Marvin was about to drift to sleep, Amina said with force, "Hey!" She shook him. "Marvin!" Her face went cold and she slapped him across the face. "Wake up!"

Marvin's head jerked and his body twitched and his eyes sprung open. He lifted his head sharply within inches of Amina's smooth, probing face, the full lips licked now by her tongue. Marvin blinked and inhaled deeply. His eyes focused on Amina and he smiled smally.

Amina released a deep sigh and leaned privately to Marvin, nose to nose, and whispered, "Don't you ever scare me like that again."

"Right," Marvin said cloudily.

Tony leaned in. "Mister Fischer what happened?"

Marvin swallowed hard. Amina shifted and put her arms behind Marvin's shoulders. With Tony, she helped Marvin sit up against the wall of the obsidian table.

"Coffee..." Marvin said droopily.

"Marvin!" Amina frowned impatiently. "What was it?" she demanded. "What did you see? What did the inscription say?"

"It was..." Marvin balked, seemingly trying to focus his mind.

"It was what?"

Marvin lifted his head and locked on Topiltzin, who remained the silent and calm observer. Marvin focused on the warrior's turquoise mask.

"Topaz… I need you to take us to see Gilgamesh the Wise."

55
THE CENSER

Her small soft face had begun to hone into focus as the effects of the drink had worn off. But the bright, child-like glee in Amina's eyes had quickly become Marvin's most immediate cause for annoyance. The woman's usual adult charm had given way to a hyperactive inquiry that Marvin wished away. She had sprayed him with questions while he was still trying to figure out if he had two arms or four.

After a quick physical, Topiltzin had determined that Marvin had suffered no permanent damage from his analysis of the Jalisco Inscription. The inebriating effects of the orb pulque had had the desired effect in opening the channels of Marvin's unsuspecting mind, launching him dangerously into the stratosphere of psychedelic hell while giving him the buzz of a lifetime. The ritual had been a necessary step in the translation of the inscription, and, as Topiltzin had explained, would not have been possible without the Teotihuacáno orb from earth as presented by Marvin Fischer. The ingestion would certainly have been against the recommendation of any licensed physician, and could very well have killed him. The event had taken its mental and emotional toll and had brought Marvin to the point of weariness, and Amina's constant beckoning was not aiding his recovery. Nevertheless with her help and that of Tony's, Marvin had managed to get back to his feet and shake off some of the lingering wooziness. Propped at the elbows by his friends, Marvin slowly wobbled his way out of the heavily guarded cave and through the long tunnel on the return trip to the cavern.

Topiltzin had begun to express familiarity with the legendary Gilgamesh, and Amina was dying to know what else Marvin had gleaned from his reading of the Jalisco Inscription. Marvin had mumbled an answer that he had more *felt* the inscription than *read* it, that surges of imagery had exploded through his mind like Raytheon Sidewinders, beholding some level of meaning, most of which was completely lost on him. But the name *Gilgamesh* had recurred prominently throughout the interpretation, especially toward the end of the writing, which had piqued Marvin's sense of the man's importance and the need to locate him.

Other than the critical lead on Gilgamesh, the only thing Marvin could share with any degree of confidence was that the Jalisco Inscription did indeed seem to record tales of immensely significant spiritual events that had unfolded since the creation, supercharged with divine meaning, hitherto undisclosed to humankind. Marvin was unable to pinpoint specifics, but the images had not been good, and Marvin now felt an increased sense of urgency in the matter of pursuing Gilgamesh. The summation of Marvin's analysis was that there was a high likelihood that the story in the inscription was incomplete, that events leading to its conclusion were in constant flux, and that the outcome of those events would inevitably contribute toward the ecstasy or the agony of all involved.

~

It was un-pressed and stiff, but it was clean and it would have to do. Marvin stood alone in the same private chamber where he had originally donned the turquoise robe, which now lay draped over the stone bench. Marvin was back in his own dry shirt and navy suit, bending his knees and elbows to work the rigidity out of the fabric. He checked the pockets and put a finger through a hole in the pants. Damn. He flipped the ends of the old tie from Caroline around his neck and tied an easy half-Windsor, keeping the knot loose. The double-stains of coffee had faded only slightly since the rinse in the luminescent pool; the original oblong coffee stain having been joined now by the other glob and dabble which Marvin lied to himself gave the thing a sort of urban, modern-art edge to it. After tightening the laces on his Johnston & Murphy's, Marvin stepped back out into tunnel number 17, nodded to the posted page, and meandered lazily through the tunnel back toward the pool cavern that he had come to learn was the center of Topiltzin's New Tollán.

Marvin's vision had cleared and he felt balanced. As he strolled centrally through the flinty hall, he experienced a few brief seconds of contentedness. The wearing of his own clothes evoked feelings of normalcy. His heart lifted. Then as he looked ahead to the glints of reflecting water dabbling on the painted glyphs in the black cavern, he remembered that he was despairingly stuck here in the After Worlds, with as yet no way to get home. Did he dare console himself in the promise of Gilgamesh? What if it was more bad news? More conflict? Marvin felt a hazy cloud drop from his throat to his stomach. The brief gift of hopeful feeling had irretrievably escaped him. He sighed. He wished he could lose himself in a cup of Costa Rican Tarrazu on the patio back home at The Bean Sack. Suddenly he felt hungry for salted nuts.

As he neared the mouth of the tunnel, the sound of shaking or rolling gravel came to him. Not aggressively, but almost soothingly. Marvin reached the mouth of the tunnel, entered the pool cavern, and paused. The gravelly sound persisted, louder now. Glancing to his left, Marvin counted ten of Topiltzin's warriors standing in a circle about twenty yards away, dressed in colorful headdresses bejeweled with precious stones and feathers, with fringed white skirts striped in red, waist-length cloaks with hems of seashells and gold. Each man also wore an unpainted ceremonial mask of baked clay, expressing varying degrees of disenchantment. As beautifully as the ten warriors were dressed, they were not dancing, nor performing, nor engaged in combat exercises. They were standing around a miniature pyramid, with a small platform on top of it. On top of the platform was a large oval basalt bowl with smoke rising from it. Marvin could not see inside of the bowl, but he imagined it must be filled with burning coals or some such thing. He took two steps closer and began to smell the smoke, a pleasing sweet aroma that he found unfamiliar.

The ten men around the basin of coals were humming quietly and evenly in long, drawn out tones of deep, monotonous guttural notes. To Marvin it seemed almost as if the men were groaning. Was it some sort of song? The men stood poised and motionless around the smoldering temple of coals, seemingly in deep concentration around the basalt basin.

Behind the ten fancy warriors sat twenty women, adorned in jade-bead necklaces, their faces painted in paste of shimmering crystals, their bodies draped in bright green, shift-like dresses with embroidered hems of geometric designs in gold and blue. Each woman had long dark hair, brushed straight down their backs, with long pins decorated with jewels and fine shells, tucked through bundles of hair on top of their heads. Each woman sat on a polished square bench of jade behind the standing men. It was the women who were quietly and rhythmically shaking seashell rattles that produced the gravelly sounds that had echoed into Marvin's ears as he'd passed through the tunnel.

From this distance it was difficult to tell for certain, but it looked to Marvin that the eyes of the ten warriors were closed behind the openings in their masks. Their hands were clasped behind their backs, as the smoke from the coals drifted up slowly toward a natural opening in the cavern and out into the yellow sky. Was this breakfast? Or lunch? Marvin had lost all sense of time.

"It's a prayer censer."

Marvin snapped his gaze to the right. He hadn't even noticed Tony step beside him. Tony had emerged from his private changing chamber also, back now in his familiar Levis and new orange hoodie. He looked refreshed and clean, and, Marvin thought, maybe even a bit happy. Marvin smiled inside as he privately admired the positive outlook that the boy always seemed to display. Marvin took it as a personal inspiration, a fitting counterpart to his own pessimistic, even cynical views.

Watching the basalt bowl of burning coals, Tony said, "They're praying for the deliverance. For the completion of the After Worlds." Marvin turned back to the scene before them. Of course. The meditation. The rising smoke. The humming men. Prayer. Hhmm. Marvin gestured his chin in their direction. "I hope they don't give away our location with that fire."

Tony lifted his gaze and watched the smoke tumble up and out through the hole in the cavern. "I'm sure they know what they're doing, Mister Fischer."

A response formed on Marvin's lips but did not come forth.

Tony continued, "I'm going to find Topiltzin. He's meeting with some of his men about Gilgamesh. Down tunnel number 23. And there's food!"

"Okay buddy, 23. I'll catch up to you. You seen the professor?"

"She's still changing." Tony dashed off.

Marvin was pleased with news of the forthcoming meal. He was famished. He returned his attention to the unusual 'prayer' event. The men and women around the prayer basin were solemn, focused, serious. *Committed.* Marvin's thoughts rewound to his conversation about prayer with Pastor Deckland. Back home. Marvin still had no idea how prayers reached God, or how God heard them, or how God sorted through them, or what he did with them, or where he kept them or how he decided to respond to them and when. Gazing casually around, Marvin noticed a series of vertical glyphs of wavy lines on the surrounding walls and guessed they might depict the rising prayers. He turned and watched again the smoke lifting from the center of the basin. Maybe prayer was nothing more than the damn smoke itself. No, that couldn't be. What about when Marvin had prayed for Rubi Valdez? There had been no smoke. Maybe there *should* have been smoke. But there had been only unrehearsed, verbalized thoughts. His prayer had been mere words uttered into thin air, launched out into the clear sky until they dissipated into nothing. How far could those thoughts go? How would God hear them? Or know them?

Maybe there was some science behind it. Maybe the prayers traveled at the speed of light, or at many times that of light. But certainly the prayers were not physical. The prayers must be immaterial, bodiless, incorporeal. Maybe the prayers were metaphysical, able to intersect with the physical creation, integrating into the spiritual through some transformative mutation, an elaborate telegraph put in place by God when the whole idea of life on earth had been designed. Maybe prayer traveled through invisible lines, spiritual cables that transported human thought like electrical pulses through a telephone wire, until it reached God, where the prayer was converted into God's language, and he would then decide to act, file away, or discard.

Or maybe the prayers traveled through the electromagnetic spectrums of spiritual cell phone towers, bouncing from one transcendent antenna to another, all the way up to the base station of God. Did some of the prayers get lost on their way up? What if there had been a spiritual short circuit of some kind? What about those poor people who had prayed, whose pleadings and beggings and praises had been doused or extinguished before they'd ever had a chance of making it to the top of God's list? And what of Marvin's own prayer for Rubi Valdez? What had really become of it? How did little, insignificant Marvin fit into all of this? Who cared?

Maybe extraterrestrials were involved…

Now it was getting ridiculous. Marvin would never solve it. It was a useless train of thought and he was beginning to become embarrassed with himself. The pursuit of resolution was a shameful waste of his time. The truth or belief or myth or science of prayer—whatever it was—remained a mystery that would never be understood, yet was a practice that had endured since the beginning of time, and now carried on even here in the After Worlds.

Marvin resolved he would give up on the issue and focus on the task at hand. And the task at hand was to get the hell out of here, find Gilgamesh—if he even existed—and hopefully, finally, somehow—get to that Saint Peter and learn the whereabouts of Rubi Valdez. He reminded himself that the success of his mission rode entirely on finding that saint. With the saint this fiasco had begun, and with the saint the whole mystery would be solved, bringing resolution to this entire ordeal. He must find Saint Peter! When Marvin thought about all that remained in his quest, it seemed he was still at the very beginning of the exhausting trail.

And yet he had already come so far.

How much further?

56
THE OLDEST STORY IN THE WORLD

Amina emerged from tunnel number 32, the women's side, after having changed back into her dry jumpsuit. She had tied her hair back up, retained the winged golden hoop earrings that were her constant companions, and had applied a conservative amount of the women's unusual makeup to make her eyes bloom and her cheeks shine. The elegance of her blouses and slacks were missed, but Amina was grateful to get out of the turquoise sari and return to the practicality of the sporty jumpsuit. She presumed there would be more walking and trekking ahead as they would soon depart for their journey to connect with Gilgamesh the Wise.

As Amina strolled into the pool cavern, she noticed Marvin across the way goggling at the group around the prayer censer. Amina smiled to herself. There he was again, back in his suit, deep in thought, probably trying to figure out what was going on. Amina found herself swept with pleasant feelings of fondness for the man. While her heart lifted at the prospect of bonding, she feared landing in a position once again of wanting, only to fail in the end. She'd grown tired of losing. But she determined this time not to let her apprehension deter her. She would at least practice on Marvin and see where it went. If he was receptive, perhaps something magical would happen, and a romance would finally sparkle to life in her lovesick world. She pretended not to care as she sauntered in his direction.

Marvin, hands behind his back, turned from the scene at the prayer censer to face Amina as she approached. "How are the sports duds?" he asked.

"Clean and dry," Amina smiled, brushing aside the bangs from her face. "The suit?"

"Stiff," Marvin grumbled. "I think it shrunk a little."

"Well," Amina tried for a compliment, "Your handsome look remains fully intact."

Marvin smiled. "Thank you young lady. So hey, we're supposed to meet up with Topaz and his guys in tunnel 23. Tony's already there. I guess there's food."

"Splendid," said Amina. "My body is in need of sustenance." She was disappointed how quickly he had dropped her attempt at flirtation. No comment on the fresh makeup. Not even a wise crack. She was already failing.

"We're also gonna plan for the trip to Gilgamesh," Marvin continued. "What can you tell me about this guy? He any good?"

Amina's eyes flickered to the necktie around Marvin's neck. The tie was still dreadfully stained. It had been ruined further by the water. It was a shriveled silken mess that Marvin refused to let go. He no longer needed it and he was being inanely stubborn about it. Why? Amina was aching to know the story behind the tie, if there was a woman involved, and if there was anything of substance behind the relationship. She pushed aside her thoughts to answer his question. "Why don't I tell you about Gilgamesh while we walk through tunnel 23?"

"Splendid. Shall we go?" Marvin said playfully, imitating Amina's vocabulary and polished demeanor. He held his elbow out for her.

She took it and smiled. "Why thank you, sir."

Perhaps the man was fond of her after all.

It was a pleasant walk through tunnel 23 to the dining area. In that time, Marvin listened attentively as Amina relayed a short overview of the fabled Gilgamesh.

Gilgamesh had been a renowned king of ancient Uruk of Mesopotamia, in the Fertile Crescent, what is now modern day Iraq, along the banks of the Euphrates River. Historians had widely accepted Gilgamesh as the historical fifth king of Uruk, who had reigned in the 26th century BC. The Sumerian list of kings recorded his reign as having lasted 126 years. Sumer had become the center of study for archaeologists for its innovations in writing, irrigation, governance, and architecture, thus ranking the Sumerians as the creators of civilization. As king of Uruk on the banks of the Euphrates, Gilgamesh had built and ruled over a large city of burnt brick and copper, a city that had been a great center of culture and economic success in ancient Sumer.

In his time, Gilgamesh had risen to such fame that, in subsequent years, he had been mythologized by the culture as an epic hero. Amina recalled that his profound influence led to the myths of his divine status, culminating in the celebrated tales first discovered at Ninevah in 1845 AD. The stories had first been written on various stone tablets in Assyrian cuneiform, then finally assembled with a common theme by a Sumerian priest, becoming known ultimately as *The Epic of Gilgamesh*.

The story told that Gilgamesh had begun as a selfish man of pride and arrogance, but that the gods had taught him humility through forcing him to endure tasks, adventures, and hardships. Gilgamesh conquered enemies, built great monuments and sought great knowledge, tamed wild animals, and killed Humbaba the giant and Ishtar's Bull. Gilgamesh became a powerful figure of courage and honor, and as the returning king, desired the improvement of people's lives in his city.

But the greatest quest of Gilgamesh—the undercurrent and reason behind all of his mighty adventures—was the attainment of everlasting life. As the myth went, to learn how he could live forever, Gilgamesh had crossed a great sea by boat in search of the only survivor of a great flood, when waters had covered the earth and destroyed every living thing. The earthly account recorded that Gilgamesh had left his city of Uruk to learn how to avoid death, met with this flood survivor, and had returned with knowledge and wisdom for how to live.

But Gilgamesh had never been able to attain immortality.

"So if he couldn't attain immortality," Marvin questioned, "how are we gonna find him here in the After Worlds? Isn't he dead? ... Like... *dead dead?*"

"As we are learning, Marvin, there is both truth and misinformation in all myth. We must continue forward so that we may discover. I believe that at this juncture, we must take the Jalisco Inscription at its word, and proceed with finding the great king of Uruk."

Marvin nodded in agreement as Amina continued, saying that the myth of Gilgamesh had become so unlikely and exaggerated, that some had begun to question whether the man had ever existed. Amina explained that after the discovery of the Assyrian tablets, European archaeologists had intensified their expeditions in search of physical evidence of the ancient king. The expeditions had proven fruitful, as evidence uncovered in ancient Uruk had even corroborated biblical events, and both tales were similar in some of their stories, such as that of the global deluge. It had become widely accepted that Gilgamesh had been an actual person, and as such, his life force must still exist somewhere, hopefully here in the After Worlds, as the Jalisco Inscription seemed to indicate.

Marvin's blue eyes squeezed with intense concentration as Amina shared that most archaeologists concurred that the original epic of Gilgamesh had been written around the year 2100 BC, predating Homer's Odyssey by 1,300 years, and predating the books of Moses of the Bible by seven centuries.

That made The Epic of Gilgamesh the eldest written account ever discovered on planet earth—the earliest major work of literature.

The historic Gilgamesh was the hero of the oldest story in the world.

57

MESABENDERS

The tamales were delicious. Made of a corn wrap stuffed with cheeses, chili, and meat, tamales had been a staple for the Mesoamericans back on familiar earth, and even though the Toltecs no longer required food in the After Worlds, tamales were a pleasure to enjoy as part of heavenly bliss. At least *that* part of the After Worlds seemed to be functioning as intended, and as Marvin took another bite, he watched Tony load up his platter with seven more of the handy snacks. Together with a side of guacamole and rice, it made for a hearty meal. Apparently one of the tunnels led to a garden, where some of the Toltecs maintained the growing of vegetables and plants, and where they prepared the tasty dishes as a means of entertainment.

As they reclined on thick woven cotton mats in a lazy circle around the floor eating their meal, Marvin watched Amina engage energetically with Tony in a frenzied back and forth with Topiltzin, confirming that her understanding of Gilgamesh jibed with what Topiltzin knew of the former king of Uruk. Amina expressed that it was imperative to separate the mythical Gilgamesh from the historical one, and Topiltzin was an encyclopedia of knowledge on the subject. Although Topiltzin had never actually met the famed Gilgamesh, it had been affirmed through multiple eye witnesses that Gilgamesh did indeed reside on the far side of this black planet, in the city of *Temple Mansion*, and that Gilgamesh's encounters with the evil Erzok had become just as legendary as his killing of Humbaba the giant in the mythical tales from ancient earth.

But Topiltzin was desperate to explain—as it was now, here in the After Worlds—that Gilgamesh's role in the spiritual war had been a direct threat to Erzok's goal of domination, making Gilgamesh one of Erzok's prime targets. Almost 2,000 years ago, in earth terms, an epic battle had taken place in the After Worlds between Gilgamesh and Erzok, but Gilgamesh had failed in killing Erzok, the ultimate evil, and had been defeated and rendered powerless by Erzok. Gone now was the rank and status of Gilgamesh. The once powerful king was now limp, lame, and entranced in an eternal state of frozen stagnation. For those reasons, Topiltzin wondered what could possibly be gained by going to see Gilgamesh the Wise.

"There has to be a reason," said Marvin, receiving a confirming nod from Amina.

Topiltzin agreed, promising to travel to the city of Temple Mansion across the black planet and take them to the banks of the Euphrates River, the final resting site of Gilgamesh on earth, and where Erzok had returned Gilgamesh's body in a show of conceit. It would now be up to Topiltzin, Marvin, Amina, and Tony to figure out a way to bring Gilgamesh back from his confining trance.

To avoid detection by Erzok and Abiku Madaki, Topiltzin Quetzalcoatl and the Toltec people had kept their activities clandestine, beneath the surface of the desert, operating strictly within the bounds of the caverns and the miles of tunnels they had maintained. But traveling to Temple Mansion with three humans would present its own set of challenges. Topiltzin mused that Marvin's group would have to endure a certain amount of exposure outside, in the open desert and beneath the sky, since the network of tunnels did not extend the full distance between New Tollán and Temple Mansion. Since Marvin, Amina, and Tony were still in their corporeal states, it would not be possible for them to travel spiritually and instantaneously with Topiltzin and his warriors. Even if they could, the interference could stop all of them at any moment. There were no open gateways that could get them there in the blink of an eye. Given the intensity for which Madaki wanted to capture Tony, they would be vulnerable to ambush along their journey.

In lieu of these complications, Topiltzin suggested a plan for their trek to Temple Mansion. Topiltzin explained that although RMV-b reflected familiar earth in certain ways geographically and topographically—which agreed with Dante's descriptions—there were vast differences. RMV-b was a Pangaea-like planet, formed essentially of one large landmass with its tectonic plates, with some lakes and rivers and a few scattered islands, atop the gigantic deep sea that covered most of the planet.

And they had an advantage. To protect the righteous inhabitants of RMV-b from Madaki and Erzok, Hunab Ku had created a series of shifting panels amidst the dunes and mountains and mesas and rivers of the planet, panels that shifted at varying intervals, giving cover to travelers. The panels were invisible—some flat, some concave or convex—and placed at thousands of locations across the planet. The shifting panels, which Topiltzin called *mesabenders*, were likened to looking into a mirror, except that instead of seeing a reflection of oneself, one would see a likeness of topography far off in the distance, from an angle between 15 and 65 degrees.

"A bending of the landscape," Amina nodded in acceptance. "Very clever."

"It's gonna make navigating by sightline a jumbled mess," Marvin frowned.

"But it'll be harder for Abiku Madaki to follow us," observed Tony.

"That is right young man." Amina winked at Marvin. "That is positive thinking."

And it so happened that Topiltzin and his Toltec scouts had become masters of the planet, having traveled extensively doing reconnaissance and searching out supplies, and had become skilled at anticipating the shifts in the mesabenders and at using them for cover. The mesabenders were not a secret to Madaki, but the panels were unpredictable to him and provided a significant advantage to anyone desirous of keeping out of Madaki's vision. This, then, is how Marvin and his team would travel to Temple Mansion, guided by Topiltzin, by way of the tunnels first, until the tunnels emptied onto the surface of the planet and exposed the convoy to the elements. And positively Gilgamesh—now that he was no longer deemed a threat—had fallen beneath Erzok's radar. This also would work to their advantage and give them an edge.

The plan sounded reasonable to Marvin Fischer. What other choice did they have? Topiltzin had already sent out a dozen scouts as preparation for the upcoming journey.

And another group of Toltecs were already preparing the Mushussus.

Marvin's face wrinkled in confusion. "The Mush-*whats?*"

It was a barn-like cave, and when Marvin Fischer first laid eyes on the Mushussus, he wished silently for his ultra-blue Jaguar. Tony beamed and immediately began to pet one of creatures on its scaly flank. The animal turned its head to stare at the boy. It seemed a gentle animal, but with the look of power in its eyes. Amina mooched up beside Marvin. "I presume, Mister Fischer, it may be much like riding a horse."

"I've never been on a horse."

"Or perhaps a camel."

The Mushussu did in fact resemble the camel, with notable differences. The Mushussus were other-worldly at first sight, made famous by Babylonian legend, depicted on the palace of Ishtar as having four legs, a long neck and a large dragon-like face, a pair of small horns on its head, and a thick tail. Like the reptilian creature Quetzalcoatl from Mesoamerican myth, the Babylonian Mushussu was proving to be based in reality. A reality far-removed from daily life on familiar earth.

Topiltzin approached the human trio hurriedly, meeting Marvin's eyes and then babbling something to Tony.

"They're ready to go," said Tony. "This one's mine! I'm naming him Mushroom!" Tony smiled as he put a foot into a stirrup. A Toltec warrior helped Tony hoist onto the saddle. "This is awesome!" Tony tugged the reins and steered the animal around. "My mom would say this is dangerous."

Tony and his beast followed obediently between Topiltzin's warriors, solid and steady, already heading down the tunnel.

"They seem well trained enough," Marvin observed, turning towards the Mushussu in front of him, shaking his head at the thought of walking the distance on these mysterious creatures. Marvin returned the curious stare of the beast with a solid look of his own. "You behave yourself," Marvin told the animal.

With the assistance of two warriors, Marvin and Amina mounted their beasts and were quickly trotting off, following Topiltzin down the huge passageway, accompanied by a protective squad of the very best of Topiltzin's warriors. Marvin's beast snorted and wagged its head, falling in line with the rest of the group, and within moments, the small convoy of two dozen Mushussus and their riders began the first leg of the journey through the tunnel beneath the vast black desert.

58
TEMPLE MANSION

The last thing Marvin Fischer expected to see after exiting the black tunnel was the endless rolling fields of bright wildflowers teeming with jumbo butterflies under the yellow-white sky. The convoy of Mushussu travelers, taking full advantage of the mesabenders to avoid detection by Abiku Madaki, had been greeted with bursting colors of vibrant fauna for the last while. The black barren desert, which Marvin had assumed covered the entire planet, was far behind them. They had traversed into a new ecosphere, something much more pleasing. Even beneath the odd sky, Marvin felt a sense of familiarity and peace as the feet of his Mushussu brushed through the stems of grasses and florets.

Now Amina expressed a temptation to dismount and explore the butterflies, particularly the purple ones, being her favorite color. Tony swiftly dismounted and chased the conspicuous flapping creatures through the fields, hopping and leaping trying to catch them, all to Topiltzin's immediate disapproval. The Toltec leader seemed much annoyed by the distracting flowers and butterflies, and, with some embarrassment, Marvin scratched his temple with his forefinger as Topiltzin demanded that Marvin get control of his 'son'. Tony endured the scolding for a few more minutes until finally snatching one of the purple-winged insects and delivering it to the hands of the child-like Amina atop her Mushussu.

Like an oversize purple monarch, the butterfly rested peacefully on Amina's finger before quivering in jagged lines back to the fields to join its counterparts. Marvin could almost see the peeved expression of the Toltec prince behind the turquoise mask as he waved Tony back on to his Mushussu.

Topiltzin had sent his best scouts ahead, behind, and above, to keep abreast of any threats. Marvin had been silently impressed by Topiltzin Quetzalcoatl's clear command of his warriors, and by his tactical maneuvers between the mountains and canyons. The peaceful prince had managed to successfully lead his visitors across a large portion of the Pangaean continent, and when Tony finally gave his attention back to the Toltec leader, he listened to the babbling Nahuatl, and chuckled that Topiltzin was demanding there be no more 'rowdy disobedience' from the group.

Marvin didn't even have to concentrate on riding the Mushussu. The creature's gait had long settled into a lazy rhythm with the others in the promenade. They spent what Marvin guessed was at least an hour winding through a twisting stretch of tight trails between towering walls of stone. Topiltzin and his Mushussu broke form and wandered off the trail, approaching a solid wall of rock. When Marvin thought Topiltzin was about to smack into the wall, he passed right through the wall as if it were a sheet of colored air. Marvin himself had been fooled by the mesabender. The rest of the convoy followed Topiltzin through the mirage and, not far in the distance, over a few more jagged hillocks, the mighty Euphrates River peeked from beyond the stands of palm trees. Marvin's heart lifted at the first glimpse of the mighty river. In ten more minutes the convoy was nearly fifty feet from the water's edge, where

Topiltzin steered the party sharp left to follow the bank. Looking across the lazy flow of shimmering emerald green, Marvin guessed the river to be a half mile wide, its subdued power creeping between shores of fertile green on the convoy side, and rugged moguls on the other.

Marvin had no idea how closely the geography of RMV-b mirrored that of familiar earth. But if his memory served, the Euphrates River originated from the union of the Kara Su and the Murat Su many hundreds of miles north, traveling through Turkey, Syria, and Iraq, the land that was once ancient Mesopotamia. The Euphrates would eventually merge with the Tigris to the south, until they both emptied into the Persian Gulf, if the gulf even existed in this Pangaean world. As the geographical slide show played in Marvin's mind, a butterfly passing his face snapped him back to focus.

To the convoy's right, spanning the width of the crawling sheet of water, was a strange-looking, pearly and iridescent bridge. The bridge's sidewalls of opaline spindles were bolstered by intervals of gleaming columns reaching fifty feet toward the sky. Topiltzin turned onto the bridge and began leading the convoy across. Perched atop his Mushussu and swaying gently with the creature's gait, Marvin looked over the sidewalls of the bridge and down into the river as they marched across the connector. He got the sense they were passing from one ecosphere into something new. They came to the other end, where rows of giant Sakura trees flanked the mouth of the bridge, their long, blooming branches fanning millions of soft petals over lush grasses. Amina and Tony followed Marvin beneath the soothing canopy of gentle pink with the delicate smell of cherry, and onto the grassy pasture. With the river moaning behind them and Topiltzin still in the lead, the Mushussus spilled up the side of the moderately rising knoll and, after cresting its peak, Marvin's jaw fell to his saddle.

Stretched out before them, for as far as the eye could see, was a sprawling city, sparkling with gold and emerald and white and crystal clear glass.

The city of Temple Mansion.

It was immediately clear to Marvin that this was not a city built by man, or by woman, or by child, or by beast.

This was a city built by God.

There were no watchtowers. No fortification walls. No soldiers guarding.

Beaming with excitement, Tony trotted up beside Marvin. "Mister Fischer, look at this! It's way dope!" The boy's fervor brought a smile to Marvin's face. Amina was equally enthralled.

Topiltzin led the convoy into the city, straight down the center of a wide smooth street of golden transparent glass, with streams of clear water on either side bubbling gently. The street was unmarked. No traffic lights, no pedestrian crossings, no sewers or trash or messy storefronts, no wires or mailboxes or electrical posts.

It was the picture of perfect beauty and harmony and bliss.

Marvin shifted his gaze off the street side and looked ahead, into the city itself. It was a checkerboard of expansive, generously portioned lush properties bordering the glistening main street. The convoy meandered past the gorgeous homes, marveling at the beauty. Marvin watched Amina's eyes become slits as desire played across her face. She was eyeing one of the mansions that she seemed to want as her own. Tony gazed up high toward the balconies adorning the second and third stories of another mansion. Marvin gawked at the perfectly manicured trees and shrubs with well-kept gardens decorating the perimeter of another enormous house. Its first floor footprint seemed larger than the parking lot of his condo community. The second level split into elevated bridges, connecting multi-level balconies adorned with lush tumbling vines bursting with colorful flowers and miniature waterfalls.

Each house was different in stature, structure, and color from the next, all of them equally exquisite and unique, each a feat of geometric excellence. Marvin wondered if Frank Lloyd Wright himself had a say in their magnificent design.

The convoy came to an intersection and proceeded through. Marvin looked down the cross street to see it was just as impressive as the main street.

Marvin shook his head in astonished wonder.

Everything was clean, quiet, and undisturbed.

The city was a paradise of the grandest form, bigger than anything Marvin had ever seen or known or dreamed of. Mountains lay beyond the great houses, their crests scraping the cloudless, yellow-white sky above.

Then the convoy passed an empty parcel. No home, no landscaping, just flat dusty ground. Marvin noticed now that many parcels remained empty, maybe waiting for the construction of the next grand abode. Still other plots appeared to have been cleared for construction, then halted and abandoned. Partial walls stood erect, with incomplete floors lacking in luster or color or solid form or beauty.

Marvin, nudging the reins of the Mushussu, guided the gentle beast alongside Amina. "What do you make of this?"

"Incomplete, like the Jalisco Inscription. And there is no one here."

Marvin's saddle squeaked as he turned to look back over his shoulder, and it came to him. Amina was right. The absolute most bizarre and peculiar aspect of this great city of colossal mansions was that it was a ghost town.

Marvin observed not a single individual anywhere.

No voices. No activity.

No person, no animals, no movement.

A fabulous heavenly city without a single citizen.

Marvin estimated they'd passed two dozen intersections and almost 100 mansions before the convoy rounded a circular road ending at four rows of long, rectangular reflecting pools. Here Topiltzin stopped, and the line of Mushussus behind him came to a gradual halt.

They were paused at what looked to be city center, on a wide driveway of white gravel leading up some 200 feet to the front entrance of a particularly enormous residence, the tallest of any. The reflecting pools, edged by low-lying flowers of fuchsia and white, extended the entire length of the driveway, echoed by lines of date palms spaced one every twenty feet. There was no gate or tall fence. The surrounding landscape was dotted with ornamental trees and carved greenery, with more flowers lining a four-foot landscaping wall of deep brown brick that surrounded the property in the shape of a decagon.

The mansion itself was a majestic ivory-white, its walls forming a large central structure as the main residence, with two smaller box-like wings joining at its center. Could the convoy have viewed the residence from above, it would have looked like three rhombus diamonds joining at their points. Narrow crystal windows climbed the walls of the large central building. From direct center of the large building, and from each of its wings, three tapered towers launched into the sky, their spires disappearing into the expanse. An ornate portico greeted guests before the yawning front yard, where two serenity gardens, each with a centered flame tree flashing red-orange, skirted the main driveway.

It was an open and inviting property, like that of a billionaire, where Marvin could easily picture friends and family gathering merrily for extravagant garden parties, weddings, and outdoor social and musical events.

But none of those merry events were going on. Like the rest of the city, the place was quiet and vacant.

Without a word, Topiltzin took an evaluating look around the property until he spotted one of his scouts emerging from behind a tall green hedge. Topiltzin spoke with the scout briefly, then continued up the driveway. The scout fell in line and the trailing Mushussus began to follow obediently as the line approached the residence ahead.

The convoy came to a stop near a stairway leading up to the center of the portico. The seven steps of the stairway peaked at a welcoming deck around what must have been the main front door. The enormous double doors of white reminded Marvin of the grand entrance to the University of Edinburgh back in Scotland.

Presently, one of the massive front doors yawned open, and two tall and decorated sentries emerged, the first sign of any need for protection, dressed in long robes of fine flowing gold and shiny golden helmets. They carried no weapons. Marvin, Amina and Tony glanced at each other as Topiltzin dismounted his Mushussu, stepped across the drive, and onto a narrower cobbled walkway of light stone. The two dignified sentries descended from the portico and met Topiltzin on the walkway. The way they greeted one another made Marvin think they knew each other.

Leaning to Amina, Marvin whispered, "The palace of Gilgamesh?"

"I presume Topiltzin is seeking permission to speak with the primary resident."

Though he could not understand the words, Marvin watched and strained to listen as Topiltzin spoke with the sentries. The two sentries turned, marched back up the steps to the portico and re-entered the residence. Topiltzin put his hands behind his back and waited patiently.

One minute later, the two sentries reappeared shoulder to shoulder and then parted to make way for an aged and beautiful dark-skinned woman with short white hair, dressed in a burgundy robe, her hands folded neatly together in front of her. The woman in the burgundy robe cued and Topiltzin approached now up the seven steps. Marvin watched as the woman in the burgundy robe met Topiltzin on the portico. There was a brief exchange of greeting. As he spoke, Topiltzin motioned to Marvin, pointing then to Amina, and finally Tony. Topiltzin turned back to the woman in burgundy and there came a quiet but focused discourse.

"He is explaining our situation," Amina observed.

"I gotta say, the guy is good," Marvin said of Topiltzin.

"We are fortunate to have his assistance."

Now the meeting broke. Topiltzin stepped away and descended the seven steps to the cobbled walkway, waving toward Marvin and his friends. The woman in burgundy remained on the portico, watching. Several of Topiltzin's warriors approached Marvin, Tony, and Amina and assisted them in dismounting from their creatures.

Topiltzin gestured for Tony, who ran up the walkway to Topiltzin. Marvin and Amina watched as Topiltzin spoke with the boy. After a minute of conversation, Tony turned and ran back to Marvin and Amina. Eyes bright with excitement, Tony said "That lady in the red—her name is Siduri. She's been taking care of Gilgamesh ever since Erzok put him in the trance."

"Does Siduri understand our intent?" asked Amina.

"Yeah," Tony took a breath, eyes darting from Marvin to Amina. "Doctor Karimova, Siduri wants you to go in and wake up Gilgamesh."

59
AWAKENING THE TITAN

Amina's eyelids fluttered like erratic window shades. She stared at Tony as if paralyzed. She shot a look to Marvin and said, "I had presumed Topiltzin would conduct the awakening. I do not know how to do this."

"Whad'ya mean you don't know? You gotta!" said Marvin.

Amina turned to the enormous mansion, which suddenly looked imposing and intimidating. Her eyes landed on Siduri, standing by the rail on the portico. Even from the distance, Amina could feel the woman's expectant stare.

"You can do it Amina!" said Tony. "You have to!"

Bewildered, Amina breathed and turned to her friends. "Walk with me. I must speak with Topiltzin."

They stepped across the walkway to where Topiltzin stood waiting.

"Antonio," said Amina, "please ask Topiltzin if you and Mister Fischer may accompany me inside."

Topiltzin explained that only Amina would be permitted.

Amina turned away, pinched her bottom lip with her fingers, eyes searching blankly into the stone patterns of the walkway. The fingers of her left hand fidgeted. She looked up to Marvin, her head shaking mildly, the stormy clouds of panic rolling over her.

Marvin took a step toward her and rested his palms on her shoulders.

"Hey," Marvin coaxed her eyes with his until they connected.

They shared a long look until Amina said with impossibility, "I still do not sense Shada."

Marvin's chin tipped down as his eyes found a deeper part of her. "Siduri senses that you have the gift." He leaned in close to her ear and whispered, "I know you do. Go." His voice was gentle but strong. It was a confident assurance of her abilities.

"Thank you…" she whispered. Amina felt the ripple of nerves speeding through her. Her mind whirled deep into her being as her feelings activated, searching all of her experience, all of her knowledge of connecting with spirit.

Amina nodded, turned slowly, looked to Tony, moved toward the steps, and made a slow ascent onto the portico to join Siduri. Amina turned back to look once again at Marvin, then followed Siduri as she led her and the two sentries back inside the mansion, and the massive white door drifted quietly shut behind them.

The two sentries walked erect and dutiful behind Amina, who followed Siduri quietly into the entrance hall of the mansion. Siduri's bare feet clapped softly on the tile floor. The ivory theme of the building's exterior continued inside, and Amina wondered if the entire building were constructed of polished marble. The hall was like a spacious indoor courtyard. A large water fountain overwhelmed the center and trickled its echo through the large space. On either side of the foyer were two ornate sofas with large fluffy pillows, and two wide stairways twisting their way up to second and third levels.

They passed through the entrance hall into a corridor, which Amina sensed would take them to the center of the house. After a few moments they entered a vast, enormous hall, with walls of intricately patterned stone and a ninety-foot ceiling of complex arched rafters of ivory, red diamond, and gold. Soft diffused light spilled in from the tall crystal windows that had been visible from outside. Twelve marble-like columns stretched ninety feet where their capitols met the lavish ceiling. The floor tiles dazzled of shiny black jasper. It reminded Amina of the feeling she had when she'd visited City Chambers at Glasgow, only this hall was twice as big and ten times as breathtaking. There was so much color and pattern and beauty that Amina's eyes could not rest on any one detail. She sensed it was a place for dignitaries and people of power.

Or perhaps more accurately, *spirits* of power.

And now Amina's attention was drawn to the middle of the ceiling, where the central hollow tower reached all the way up to the tip of the spire, and concentrated light beamed down through a large diamond-like prism. Amina followed the beam down, it's primary colors swirling, to where the lively beam spilled and focused onto the prize: a large, throne-like, four-legged marble stool in the very center of the giant quad.

And there, on the marble stool, sitting quietly and still, was a single lone and bald and bearded and protuberantly muscular figure.

Amina's jaw dropped in stunned awe as she first spied the man from a distance, perhaps expecting him to say something, but in the very same moment realizing that it was impossible for the man to speak, because this was the mighty Gilgamesh, once king of Uruk, rendered mute and powerless and unaware and useless by the evil and terrible Erzok.

Siduri extended a hand toward the mighty sight, gesturing for Amina to proceed closer to Gilgamesh. After some hesitation, Amina turned her chin toward the man in the throne, wiped her forehead absently and swallowed, then walked cautiously across the fifty feet of smooth dark jasper until she became enveloped by the same colorful glowing beam that projected from above and splashed down and she came to within six feet of the historic legend.

And there she paused.

The immensity of the man flooded Amina's senses, an awareness of not just his physical stature, but of flashing reflections upon his unsurpassed accomplishments first as a tyrant, and then as the renowned king, the wise seer, the adroit traveler, the mighty killer of beasts, the passionate lover of women.

Gilgamesh's intense, enrapturing eyes were open comfortably, gleaming crystal brown, gazing straight ahead, but registering nothing. His bald head was the size of a basketball. His tan and rugged face was brutally handsome, his skin glistening with health. Both earlobes were pierced and adorned with polished black marbles. He wore no shirt. His jet black, tightly curled beard stretched like a cone, coming to a point in front of his wide and massive chest. A fringed purple satin cape lay on his shoulders, cascading to the floor behind him. The veins in his round shoulders and bulging arms pulsed as if he had just completed a workout circuit, the blood racing through his body in nourishment. A thick belt around his waist bore a sheathed dagger with a golden hilt. His waist and legs were covered in a tightly-fitting black garment that perfectly followed the contours of every rippling muscle in his thighs, his hips, and—Amina imagined—a perfectly formed buttocks.

Amina felt all of her defenses melting away. Gilgamesh reminded her of an Olympic wrestler, a barbarian of a man who could crush her tiny-framed figure like a beetle.

The great man was completely dead to his surroundings, but incredibly alive.

Air pushed into Amina's lungs as her breathing rate skyrocketed. She felt the blood pulsate through the arteries in her neck, became aware of her rapidly rising body heat. Her palms began to sweat. And as all of this had come wholly unexpected,

Amina clenched her teeth and froze the muscles in her jaw as she forgot all about her growing fondness for Marvin Fischer, and tried urgently to tame the wild animal inside of her and chase away the burning that rushed to the points of her breasts and seared her moistening pudendum, and she wanted him to take her.

She put a hand to her chest as if to gain control of her breathing.

Amina swallowed hard, burying the physical sensations, then breathed heavily and stepped bravely forward until she came within two feet of the giant perfect man, close enough to touch him.

Amina placed her palms together in front of her chest. She closed her eyes and allowed her training and instinct to guide her.

She must try again to summon Shada.

Shada could help her.

Amina stood straight and still in front of the venerable legend, her hands together in quiet meditation. She took three deep breaths, and exhaled each breath completely and with the controlled perfection of a master.

Amina stood, and she summoned, and she called.

But she could not sense Shada.

And she had no candles.

She had no incense.

She had no control over the light.

Or over the room.

Or over Siduri and the sentries watching her.

The only thing Amina could control was *herself*.

Softly, Amina began to pray, "Thank you Lord and Creator and Master, for watching over us. Thank you for helping us to find and act upon our divine life purpose…"

Amina trained her mind on her spirit and summoned her inner self to the surface, seeking holy entrance into this alien world and into this moment in a way that even she had never experienced. She had no idea how the spirit and mind flowed and connected with all the unfamiliar energy of this kingdom. Nevertheless, Amina would have to accomplish this feat by herself, on her own, from within herself. A process came to her mind which she had never done before, and, as far as Amina knew, which no other medium or spiritist had ever attempted. She prayed to the Supreme Being that she could attain permission from Gilgamesh's higher self for what she was about to do, that she could hear Gilgamesh and communicate with him telepathically.

She would send him energy, strength, and revival from within her own spirit.

"Help me now, oh God," Amina prayed, "to awaken this man for the completion of his purpose, toward the goodness and the reunion and the safety of us all."

Nervous sweat dripped from Amina's armpits and down her sides and down the small of her back. She hoped and prayed again that Gilgamesh's internal converter would accept her and translate her noble and genuine intentions for the good, and that he would not reach out in fury and tear her to pieces.

Amina opened her eyes.

She separated her hands and placed her left palm over the center of her sternum. Her heart pounded madly. She extended her right arm toward Gilgamesh's face. She allowed her open palm to hover over his face for several seconds, and as her hand drifted slowly and minutely closer, she felt a field of energy, a barrier, then a vibration, like the electric current she had felt when, as a little girl, she had accidentally touched the prong of an extension cord as she plugged into a wall outlet. But the electrical pulse she felt now traveled through her, and did not hurt her, did not burn her. Still, Amina was afraid. Drops of sweat dripped down from beneath the golden brown hair on the crown of her head and into her eyebrows. Pressing on boldly, she lifted her right hand another inch and placed her open palm on the center of Gilgamesh's forehead, and said, "I step forward to connect in truth and in love…"

Her palm made contact with the rough, porous, and warm skin of the forehead.

Warm with a life that was not from the earth, but, Amina sensed, from a life that was sustained by a force far away, a life force far greater than any energy she had ever felt before.

From whom was this power coming!?!

The depth of Amina's breathing intensified. She kept her palm flat against Gilgamesh's forehead as she felt the heat from his body glow into her. And although she wanted to remove her hand from his forehead she did not, and she could not. And she felt a power flowing through her and into him and between them, and from where it came she still did not know.

The heat in Amina's palm seared. She felt the energy, the surge, the waves of power pounding through her and she knew her body and her spirit were being used as the conduit. She began to feel lightheaded. Her eyebrows pinched and her nose peeled back with a snarl and her eyes blazed with gold. Then she snorted like a bull and the sound of her beastly puffs sprang around the resonant great hall. Her knees buckled and her muscles went to slush. But somehow, she managed to stand. Her blue and white and black jumpsuit was now completely soaked in sweat and the fabric was sticking to her legs, to her stomach, to her arms. Sweat dripped down her face and found the corners of her mouth. She tasted the salt and instinctively licked her lips.

Then Gilgamesh's right index finger twitched.

His eyelids fluttered and his brown eyes flashed.

The lips trembled and his shoulders lifted.

Wind surged into his lungs.

The two-thousand-year-old trance was cracked and broken.

When Gilgamesh saw Amina Karimova in front of his eyes, he gasped—and his mouth fired open—and his eyes burst wide and he shouted and yelled and shrieked in thundering bloodcurdling terror, and every single crystal window in the hall shattered with a boom, and shards burst and spewed clouds of clear sparkling splinters and powdery dust into the outside air.

Amina shirked backward in horror, sure to be pulverized at any moment by the monstrous man, and she thought she already felt her life ending as she tripped backward and smacked to the floor.

And finally the terrible scream ended, and Gilgamesh too fell, backward off of his marble stool, rolling to his side until he fell completely off the stool and landed with a crash onto the shiny floor.

Amina wobbled clumsily to her feet, backing off in fear, as Siduri and the two decorated sentries rushed in and past her.

"Get out!" Siduri shouted to Amina, pointing toward the corridor. "Out!"

Siduri and the sentries arrived at Gilgamesh's side and stooped over him.

Amina turned as the emotions tore over the storm that had passed through her, the fear and inconsolable sadness and dread that she could not understand, and she felt as if her heart would blow out of her chest and then her eyes exploded with tears. Amina gulped, trying to swallow the feelings and, lifting the back of her hand to wipe an eye, she bolted out of the hall and down the corridor, her cries calling back to her from the cold inanimate stone.

60
WHAT NO MORTAL IS PERMITTED TO SPEAK

When the windows erupted and the glass showered into the yard, the first thought Marvin had after the initial shock was that Abiku Madaki had found them, and that he had just bombed the hell out of Gilgamesh the Wise, taking Amina with him. But moments later when Marvin saw Amina race out the front door like a marathon runner, he thought there must be another explanation.

Amina dashed across the portico, unzipping the front of her jumpsuit and tearing at her skin as she ran down the steps. Marvin met her on the cobbled walkway, where Amina stopped and bent over. Resting one hand on a knee, she breathed heavily, and with the fingers of her other hand she grasped Marvin's hand tightly. Tony arrived beside them with Topiltzin.

In bewildered amazement, Marvin asked, "What happened? Did he wake up?"

The woman's eyes were on fire, her body soaking. She gulped and released her grip from Marvin, putting both hands to her cheeks. "Yes," she blurted.

Marvin put a palm to her forehead. "You're burning up."

Amina fell to her buttocks and began to strip off her shoes. Marvin heard a shout from the portico and turned. It was Siduri, who had emerged from the mansion. Siduri shouted something to Topiltzin, who turned to Tony and the two of them skipped up the steps to meet the woman in red on the portico.

Marvin turned his attention back to Amina, who had pushed the jumpsuit to her ankles. Marvin yanked it away and tossed the wet mess aside. He scooped up the nearly naked woman and ran onto the lawn, to the fountain at the serenity garden, and then leaned and dunked Amina's body deeply into the clear water. The woman let herself plunge completely before surfacing and wiping her face. It was the first sign of relief Marvin saw in her eyes. "You okay? What happened?"

"Some energy used me as a conduit," Amina gasped.

A small group of the nobles who had been congregating outside with Marvin rushed to the fountain. One of the noblemen carried a goblet, another a red robe. The first nobleman handed the goblet to Amina as she sat in the water fountain. She quickly drank down the refreshment. Marvin took the empty goblet from her and held it to the nobleman. "Thank you, more please."

Out of the corner of his eye, Marvin saw Siduri on the portico, in the midst of frenetic conversation with Topiltzin. Siduri's eyes met Marvin's and she was pointing at him. A foreboding wave invaded Marvin, but he turned back to Amina, putting a hand again to her forehead. She felt cooler. Thank God.

Amina sniffled and looked frumpily up to Marvin's face. And as Marvin looked at the woman, her face now almost like that of a little hurt child, her humanness struck him deeply, and for the first time he felt gratitude. The woman had taken great risks for him, for the boy, and she had made great sacrifices. Marvin suddenly felt a sense of moral debt as he looked into the woman's golden brown eyes. "Amina, thank you," was all he could say.

Amina swished an arm out of the water and grasped Marvin's hand. "Be careful."

"What do you mean?"

"I had an inexplicable connection with that man," she said. She looked away and pressed her breast under the sports bra.

Marvin squinted curiously. "Somethin' else I should know?"

"I feel danger. Darkness ahead, Marvin. And I still did not sense Shada."

"Okay. What else?"

He watched the storm roiling in her eyes. It seemed to him that she wanted to say something but it wasn't coming. She reached and grabbed hold of his tie. "Just be careful."

And then Topiltzin called from the portico. Tony bolted down the steps and ran to the fountain. Squatting next to Marvin, he said, "Mister Fischer, Siduri said you have to go in!"

Marvin's eyes went to the portico. Siduri was looking at him with fixed presumption. Marvin turned back to Amina and knew she would be protected by Topiltzin, and seemed in good hands with Gilgamesh's attentive nobles. Turning to Tony, Marvin said, "What about you? Comin' in?"

"Siduri said you have to go in alone. That's what Gilgamesh wants."

Uh oh. By order of the king.

Marvin's stomach plunged with angst. What fate awaited him inside?

Marvin swallowed and locked eyes again with Amina.

Her breathing calmer now, she said, "Go."

Tony put a reassuring hand on Marvin's back. "You got this, Mister Fischer."

A nervous chuckle escaped Marvin's lips. "Thanks, buddy."

Marvin stood up, locked eyes with Siduri on the portico, and stepped toward the mansion.

Marvin felt as if he were having an out of body experience. He'd witnessed the majesty of the European cathedrals and the ghostly hill of Glastonbury Tor. He'd walked the streets of Rome and had been entertained by dignitaries in elaborate palaces of Saudi Arabia. He'd been in the heart of the Capitol Building in Washington D.C., been a guest at the White House, and had overnighted in the expansive beach homes of millionaires.

But never before on earth had Marvin been overtaken with the grand sense of awe and wonder that was this place. As Siduri led Marvin through the long and wide and enthralling corridor to his destination, he could only guess at what mind and power had constructed such a marvelous place as this.

They reached the end of the corridor and stopped at the entry to the same great hall where Gilgamesh had just been awakened, where Amina had performed her marvel. All of the windows had shattered, leaving piles of white shards heaping on the black jasper floor.

Siduri motioned for Marvin to enter. He did so. Siduri and the sentries left, leaving Marvin suddenly to himself, alone in the splendorous hall.

The sting of anxiety seared Marvin's stomach. He was about to undergo the interview of his life.

And then he realized he wasn't alone.

Standing with his back to Marvin, hands clasped behind his waist and gazing through one of the towering holes that had once been a window, stood Gilgamesh, regally dressed in a flowing red cloak. Sensing that Marvin had entered, and that they had been left alone, Gilgamesh turned his head, his stern and solid eyes meeting Marvin's tentative stare. Gilgamesh held that stare for a moment, then swiveled fully to face Marvin, who remained near the entry twenty yards away. Gilgamesh strode from the window, passed the marble columns, his monstrous and imposing figure governing the entire hall. As Gilgamesh walked commandingly to the center of the room, it seemed to Marvin that the air itself parted to give way to the man. Gilgamesh reached the marble stool, stopped, and stood. Leaning against the stool was a long staff of carved sassafras adorned with jewels. Not far from Gilgamesh's stool had been placed a second stool, equal in size and design to the first.

"Come," Gilgamesh offered, his deep-toned voice resonating like the strings of a double bass in the New York Philharmonic.

Marvin, suddenly embarrassed at his dusty suit and tie, stepped across the shiny floor, the soles of his tattered shoes emitting an awkward *clop-clop-clop* as he strode to within ten feet of the titan.

"What is your name?" Gilgamesh boomed.

"I'm Marvin Fischer," he said with bravery.

"And what is it that you do, Mister Fischer?"

"I'm an intelligence commander. In Phoenix Arizona. On earth."

Gilgamesh looked at the floor, took one easy step forward and stopped, his long and full cloak flowing behind him until its hem caught up with his heels. He looked again to Marvin. "And who is the angel who awakened me from my trance?"

"That's Doctor Amina Karimova. Professor of Religion at the University of Edinburgh. Scotland."

Marvin decided to refrain from detail, not sure if Gilgamesh cared that much, or if Edinburgh, or Scotland, even meant anything to him. Gilgamesh took another step, released his clasped hands from behind his back and brought them forward, clasping them now comfortably in front of him. He remained silent, looking at Marvin, and Marvin felt like Gilgamesh was waiting for him to say something else.

So Marvin said, "I also came with a boy. Antonio Valdez. His mother Rubi died, after I prayed for her, and…" Marvin hesitated again, but when he saw that he had Gilgamesh's rapt attention, continued. "And Rubi Valdez believed that a departed saint had sent her to me, to pray for her safety. But then, Rubi Valdez died. We were hoping—that is, Antonio Valdez and I, and Amina Karimova—were hoping to find this departed saint, and we were hoping that you, sir, would be able to help us find him."

"And what is the name of the departed saint to whom you refer?"

Marvin swallowed. "Saint Peter, sir, from the inner circle of Jesus, the Christ. Saint Peter lived… many centuries after you lived on earth. Sir."

Gilgamesh drew a breath. Familiarity swept his face. He raised an eyebrow. "Saint Peter."

"Yes sir," said Marvin.

"Simon Bar-Jonah."

A rush of adrenaline burned Marvin's sinews. He tried in vain to conceal it, gulping and inhaling deeply. He barely got out—"Yes."

Gilgamesh too drew in a deep breath, gazed up into the air of the room and up toward the tall ceiling and its bright and large prismic window in the spire. Then, decidedly, Gilgamesh released his clasped hands, stepped to his marble stool, and sat down, his face hard with contemplation.

"I know this Saint Peter," Gilgamesh pondered.

Marvin watched the giant, whose mind seemed to be spinning at a thousand miles an hour.

Gilgamesh continued, "And I believe I may know this Jesus, the Christ, of whom you speak. Perhaps by another name. He is a god, yes?"

"I do believe so, yes. Most certainly. The Creator." Marvin was trying to talk like Amina.

Gilgamesh sat perfectly still for several seconds. His eyes blinked. Marvin guessed the man was processing centuries of knowledge, mountains of information every second, assembling it into some sort of order. At least—Marvin hoped so.

Then something plunged inside Marvin's lower abdomen. He squeezed his buttocks and pelvic floor muscles. Then he bobbed on his knees, glancing around the hall with flicking eyes.

Gilgamesh squinted. "Mister Fischer, you are troubled."

"I…" Marvin started to say. He tried again to speak, looking at Gilgamesh, whose eyes remained fixed and strong and demanding.

Finally Marvin admitted with embarrassment, "Sir—I have to go to the bathroom. I drank something. And it just hit bottom."

Gilgamesh raised his eyebrows. His mouth produced a small sideways grin, in the first sign of amusement and humanity. "You must not urinate," said Gilgamesh.

"Say again?"

The grin fell away. "Tell me, Mister Fischer. Have you urinated since you left the pool cavern?"

"No. I don't think so."

"And how is it that you were able to decipher the message on the Jalisco Inscription, so that you knew to come find me?"

Marvin's jaw dropped.

Gilgamesh knew about the Jalisco Inscription?

"I drank something," Marvin revealed.

"Yes. You drank the power of the orb."

"How did you know that?"

"You have been given a great power, Mister Fischer. You must not urinate, or you will lose this power."

"You've got be kidding. How long do I have to wait?"

"Until you have completed the mission."

"But I already read the inscription. And I found you."

"You will need this power again."

"When?"

"This I do not know. But you will find out. There is something ahead for you. Something that will require great strength and courage."

Marvin tried to forget that he had to go pee, and latched onto the thought prompted by Gilgamesh's comment. "Okay, so, let me ask you something, sir," said Marvin. "Why was the Jalisco Inscription not finished? Why is this new earth, or whatever it is, not complete? And why are you here?"

Gilgamesh winced an eye. Marvin felt he was about to be reprimanded by some ruthless dean.

"Mister Fischer, what is your understanding of what is to come for all eternity?"

Marvin's mind and heart were challenged again by the question. He thought back to his time at church with Caroline, and what he had always been told and taught there. "God will…" Marvin began, "God will bring us all to heaven. Well, those of us who believe, anyway."

"And you are familiar with the passage in the sacred texts, which speaks of the third heaven?"

Marvin's face winced, as if uncertain of an answer on the final exam. "Sort of."

"And Saint Peter sent for you."

"I think so."

Gilgamesh crossed his arms and tilted his head, glancing away for a moment as another knowing look swept his face. He leaned his head back toward Marvin. "Mister Fischer, I believe there is something that you must do."

"And what is that?"

"It may have something to do with what was overheard in the third heaven."

Marvin did a double take.

Gilgamesh cocked his eyebrow, leaned forward, his eyes blazing into Marvin's, and said in a husky whisper, "It may have something to do with *what no mortal is permitted to speak*."

The blood drained out of Marvin's head and he almost fell over.

That statement sounded awfully, horribly, and disparagingly familiar. Marvin's mind whirled back to what Amina had said over their breakfast of Viennoiseries in Edinburgh. His heart began to pound in his chest. Marvin's mind scrambled to recall what Amina had mentioned, something about somebody being *caught away* to the third heaven—and yes—overhearing something, *something that no mortal is permitted to speak*. Something of a most secret nature that had presumably been discussed in the third heaven. Marvin looked back to Gilgamesh. "What did you say?"

Gilgamesh uncrossed his arms and held out a hand towards the other stool. "Sit down, Mister Fischer. Let me tell you my story. I believe it will be of great interest to you."

After a moment's hesitation, Marvin installed himself on the luxurious stool and felt the cold stone through the seat of his pants, immediately aware that this eased his desire to micturate.

Gilgamesh swiveled toward Marvin, faced him squarely, and put his hands on his knees. "When I lived as a king on earth, many thousands of years ago, I prayed to my god, *Shamash*, who helped me achieve many things. But I lost a dear friend to death, and I became afraid of death. The fear of death tore at my stomach. I longed for immortality. I traveled across the grassy plains and the scorching desert to find eternal life. I traveled across the mountains and the Great Sea to visit a very wise man, who taught me many great things. I thought this man could teach me how to live for days without end. I was given a chance to accomplish this thing, my quest for eternal life, by myself. But, no matter how tall he is, no mortal can reach up to heaven. No matter how wide he is, no mortal can stretch across the earth. So, I failed, and so, I died. For many centuries I lay my head in the earth, where the stars do not shine, and where there is no sunlight.

"And then, many centuries later, and much to my surprise, I learned that it is possible for a mortal to gain eternal life. As I lay there in the grave, here by the Euphrates, a god much greater than Shamash came to awaken me. And this god, The Ancient of Days, *The Great Nahmes*, took me up out of the grave and brought me to the third heaven. The Great Nahmes told me that he would call me to a great and mighty deed, one greater than anything I had accomplished as the King of Uruk many thousands of years earlier. The Great Nahmes told me that my task was forthcoming in the centuries ahead. When I asked The Great Nahmes what this task was, he said that he could not tell me. But what he did tell me, Mister Fischer, shook me to my bones."

The chill shot through every nerve in Marvin's body as he listened. "Go on… please."

Gilgamesh continued, "The evil one—Erzok, the Prince of the Power of the Air, the arch enemy of The Great Nahmes since before the creation—had gained great power. Much more power than even The Great Nahmes had ever intended to allow him. You understand, Mister Fischer, that Erzok has been trying to destroy The Great Nahmes, ever since the day Erzok was cast out of heaven as a blazing white comet across the black skies."

Again Marvin's mind raced, recalling his visits to the church. Cast out of heaven? Surely Gilgamesh must be referring to—

"Erzok wanted only death and war and struggle," Gilgamesh went on. "The Great Nahmes did not want death and war and struggle. He did not want sickness and suffering. The Great Nahmes wanted only peace, harmony, and goodness for his creation, for both the human and the beast. But then, Erzok came to destroy. You see, Mister Fischer, the unfortunate fall of the man and the woman, in the Garden of Eden, was never supposed to be. Already before that time, Erzok had gained in strength, beyond what even The Great Nahmes had foreseen.

"So The Great Nahmes decided to rescue his creation from this evil Erzok, and he began the greatest part of his creation, the creation of a Super-Earth, 100 times larger and more beautiful than the earth from which you and I have come. This planet, Mister Fischer—the one on which our feet now rest—is that Super-Earth. But it has not been finished. It is not finished! It has been interrupted because of the interference and the evil power of Erzok. It is but the beginning of God's grand plan, the plan to complete 37 other such worlds, where the souls of the righteous may dwell, to be part of the ultimate heaven that has been the plan ever since that terrible day in Eden. The Super-Universe, Mister Fischer. *Paradiso*. One never-ending existence, free from all evil, an un-ending expanse of stars, planets, galaxies—there is no edge of space—no final destination of Paradise at the outskirts of creation. It is to be everywhere and unending! The Great Nahmes has been preparing these places for all those who have been called by him."

"What are you saying?"

"Mister Fischer, *I am the one* who was told these unspeakable things."

Marvin sat silent and dazed, not sure he was hearing correctly. "Say again?"

"I am the one who was caught up to the third heaven. To the Empyrean, to God himself. It is I, Mister Fischer, who heard what no mortal is permitted to repeat."

"I don't understand—"

"You see Mister Fischer, The Great Nahmes, the greatest among the gods, has lost his grip on the control of the universe that he himself created. He did not want for any man to know this. He did not want Erzok to discover how much evil power he had gained. The plan for The Great Nahmes' creation has been overtaken by one who has risen in power and become a true threat to The Great Nahmes. Erzok has become, I am afraid, a power that can overthrow and defeat The Great Nahmes, and to have his way with all creation. Erzok is a worthy and powerful enemy, Mister Fischer. The battle is not a certain victory. The good can still lose to the bad. Light can still lose to the dark. If Erzok is successful in this way, he will win the ultimate victory over history. Over humankind. Over The Great Nahmes. And the great and wonderful plans that God has for his people will not come forth.

"This is the great secret, Mister Fischer, that no mortal is permitted to repeat. But I am no longer mortal. The Great Nahmes has granted me my wish of immortality, because my eyes were opened and I came to believe in him as the one and only God for all. And I believe it was for this moment—for this mission—that The Great Nahmes called me to many years ago, when he raised me from the grave and brought me to the Empyrean and told me these great things. The ban of impermission has been lifted from upon me, awaiting this very time, where you and I now sit, and where you and I now speak as friends."

Gilgamesh leaned back and sat up straight. "And so I have just told you." He sat silent and watched Marvin for a reaction.

A full minute passed before Marvin realized that Gilgamesh had finished his overwhelming sermon. Marvin sat dumbfounded, silent and cold and hard and jaded. The search for Saint Peter and the mission to bring Rubi Valdez back to life seemed suddenly like a paltry and meaningless request compared to what Gilgamesh had just described.

"So now what?" asked Marvin. "What am I supposed to do?"

"We must do what we think is best, Mister Fischer. I believe that it is *you* that I am meant to help. You are my great deed, foretold to me long ago by The Great Nahmes. From what you have shared with me, the wonderful Saint Peter has led you on this journey, and has guided you to me. So now, together, we must discover what it is that the great saint—and the God of gods, The Great Nahmes—has determined next for how to defeat this evil enemy Erzok. The time has come."

Gilgamesh reached for his bejeweled staff that leaned against the marble stool, grasped it, and rose from the stone seat. "And that is why I am going to take you across the Great Sea."

61

METAL AND AXE

Marvin and Gilgamesh reacted in unison when they heard the first sling of metal against stone, and the shouts of attack ricocheted through the long corridor into their ears. Hurriedly, Marvin followed Gilgamesh through the corridor and the entrance hall and out onto the portico.

The eruption of ferocious battle mounted as the Toltec brigade fully engaged Madaki's militia—the seven-foot soldiers of black sand with their flaming orange swords. Topiltzin had already transformed into the mighty Quetzalcoatl, confronting Abiku Madaki head to head, the giant snake's long red scaly body writhing against the onslaught of spears and blazing swords.

On the portico, Marvin helplessly watched the mayhem, the mess of tangled bodies, the clashing of sword and axe and spear. He hadn't a clue where to focus or how to engage. Amidst raging blurs of violence, he watched a Toltec smash with a sand soldier and topple together into the water fountain. There was the flying of spears and the hurling of axes through clouds of dust, the flashes of teeth and cutting eyes, but no blood—only the spray of sand

and the burst of energy vaporizing into oblivion as the battle between spirits ensued.

Then Marvin's eyes bulged when he spotted Tony, frightened and surrounded and encircled by a tight huddle of Madaki's evil sand soldiers.

"Tony!!" shouted Marvin. Gilgamesh's face flared crimson as he removed his cloak and hurled it aside. Like a hulking dinosaur on the hunt, Gilgamesh leapt off the portico with a thud. Marvin followed down the steps and into the beautiful front yard, which had been transformed into a war zone.

Gilgamesh reached to catch an axe tossed from a fellow warrior, and without missing a step and with a resounding call of rage, Gilgamesh the Wise and the King and the Warrior approached the attackers as straight as the flight of an arrow, swung his axe, and annihilated three of Madaki's sand soldiers with a single cyclical blow.

Marvin's eyes darted, eyelids flickering with confusion. He ducked a flying spear, completely out of his element and totally ill-prepared to take on such an event.

But he couldn't just stand there.

"Mister Fisher!!" Tony called from within the group of sand soldiers.

Marvin's eyes met with Tony's for a split second as Marvin made his move and ran straightaway into the chaos. Dodging the swing of a flaming sword, Marvin volleyed a bed of trampled flowers to grab a felled spear, then zigzagged his way toward the band of sand soldiers surrounding Tony. And as he ran, Marvin felt the burst of a powerful surge rushing from his abdomen through to his extremities. In a nanosecond he realized what it was—

The power of the orb!

His muscles ignited with a strength he had never known or felt. Fire in his eyes, Marvin hurdled a row of bushes and blitzed a sand soldier. The sword came across but Marvin evaded in a spin fast as a thunderbolt, then stepped and put all his weight into the spear and plunged it into the soldier. The sandman crumpled to the ground, its body dispersing into the dust.

"Mister Fischer!" Tony called again.

Marvin dashed forward, closing the gap, then fell backward as the giant Quetzalcoatl's tail smacked two soldiers and sent them spinning like frisbees. Quetzalcoatl clamped his teeth down on another sand soldier, popping it into a misty cloud that showered to the ground. But the distraction gave Abiku Madaki the chance to wield his sword, striking Quetzalcoatl in the head with a solid blow. The snake reeled and turned once again to engage.

As Marvin watched the encounter unfold, he suddenly thought of Amina.

Where was she?!

But he couldn't take his focus off Tony.

He had to get to Tony!

Calls and shouts echoed as Marvin looked for Gilgamesh but could not see through the blur of battle. Desperately, Marvin thought about what he might possibly do to overcome Madaki. Before he could take another step, there came a sharp blast of wind. Marvin closed his eyes and turned away as debris flew into his face and pelted his body. The mighty wind formed a vacuum, whipping around Tony and the sand soldiers, and Marvin knew it was too late.

The roar was deafening and the ground shook. Marvin dropped to his knees and fell headlong, face down in the grass, clawing on his stomach toward the garden wall for cover. Helpless now, he lifted his head and watched as Madaki, Quetzalcoatl, Tony, and the surrounding sand soldiers were swept together up into the cloudy gray wind tunnel, just as Dante Alighieri had been stolen from them at Castlerigg.

Marvin watched in horror as Tony's body twisted and flailed, rising higher and higher until Marvin could no longer hear the boy's cries.

Marvin lay frozen, eyes wide and mouth agape in amazed abandon, and the wind died as quickly as it rose and the air cleared.

The sounds of battle faded to distant shouts. Marvin felt the power of the orb dissipate as he stopped fighting, and fixed on the spot where Tony had stood only moments before.

And now the boy was gone.

The remaining sand soldiers dispersed as Topiltzin's warriors chased them toward the river, until one by one they melted back down into the sand and disappeared.

Marvin heard only his own labored breath. The sounds of battle had died. Abiku Madaki had gotten what he came for. Marvin swallowed hard, grabbing the ledge on the garden wall and working himself to his knees. Waiting for strength, he finally stood up. Straightening, Marvin walked slowly forward toward the point where Tony had vanished. The yard was in shambles. Marvin tottered along the side of the four-foot garden wall, bewildered, stunned, and dazed. His eyes meandered without aim until his gaze landed on the ground.

Marvin stopped.

Next to the four-foot wall among a group of crushed white flowers, Marvin found the boy's binoculars lying alone. In denial, Marvin staggered to the specs but could not bring himself to pick them up. The dusty frame and lenses looked up at him pleadingly. Marvin's head drooped and his chin sank to his chest. He closed his eyes and felt the anger burn through his veins. His hands found the back of his neck as he bent forward and faced the trampled ground. For a long time he held the defeated pose.

Marvin had lost Tony.

Now what?

How would he ever get the boy back?

Where had he been taken?

Rising again, Marvin tilted his gaze to the bright sky, releasing his hands from behind his head. Panting, he began to circle and pace. His face hardened as the loss overwhelmed him with dread. He vowed that he would get Tony back. No matter what.

"Mister Fischer!" Gilgamesh lumbered around the wall with Amina.

Marvin groaned in relief when he saw Amina, disheveled and dripping wet, dressed still only in undergarments, but safe, unbroken, and on her feet. Their eyes met. The relief reflected in her told Marvin she had been worried about him too.

"Mister Fischer," Gilgamesh said again, dusty and wet and tossing his axe to the ground, "If there is any hope of saving the boy, we must go immediately!"

Amina stepped to Marvin, grasped his arm, and searched his eyes.

"Marvin, let's go."

Marvin breathed and kept one hand on his hip, rubbing his face vigorously with the other. He sighed deeply, then leaned down to the crushed flowerbed and picked up Tony's binoculars. He brushed them off carefully with his fingers and draped the blue cord around his neck, where the binoculars dangled on his chest in front of the shriveled and stained tie with its jagged ebbs of navy and white.

"Yeah," said Marvin. "Let's go."

62

WHY DO YOU DOUBT?

They would have to walk a mile and a half to the bridge, cross the Euphrates, and then walk another four miles along the river where Gilgamesh hoped to find the boat. The nobles at the palace had said that the regular scouts reported that the boat had not been touched in eons—per the king's order—before Erzok had stricken him mute and powerless long ago. As far as was known, the boat remained as it had been left.

Once across the bridge, Gilgamesh led the way along a dense and marshy trail beside the Euphrates. Only Marvin and Amina traveled with him, on foot, under cover of the sloping knolls and palms, and finally through the foliage and thick reeds of the bank. No soldiers or nobles or scouts or Mushussus came with them. The silver metal blade of the machete glinted under the bright skylight as Gilgamesh clobbered the tall reeds and pushed through the remnants. There was the ting of the blade as it cut, the soft wind coming off the river, and the rustling reeds as they bent and broke and gave way to the three adventurers.

Along the path of muck, gravel and grass, Marvin and Amina walked shoulder to shoulder, several paces behind the powerful friend who cleared their way. Amina spoke quietly and reservedly about the experience of awakening Gilgamesh and Marvin did not ask any questions about it. Their conversation turned lighter with talk of the clothing. Marvin's suit and tie showed deep wear, but Amina had traded in her soaked jumpsuit for an ankle-length tunic of finely woven cotton, a wide belt, a colorful embroidered shawl, and a hearty pair of walking boots—all gifts from the lovely Siduri. Amina relished the comfort and fresh style, apparently feeling quite special, and now she made a show of it. By Marvin's assessment, it looked as if she were strutting her stuff at Heidi Klum's *Project Runway*. He teased her, this time with a welcome lightness in place of his usual brooding, and she seemed to enjoy the amusing flattery.

Marvin made reference now of having to urinate, and the strict recommendation from Gilgamesh not to do so. His mood turned and he anguished over Tony. Then he shared with Amina in detail what Gilgamesh had told him in their mind-bending conference at the mansion hall. It was a spaghetti mess of theology that Marvin could not clean up. He wrangled to solve the impossible puzzle, to find escape from the jungle of questions. His attitude became rude and he converted to squabbling with Amina about it.

"Sorry," said Marvin. "I have to go pee, and I haven't had coffee since… when was it? The train?"

"You had coffee at the Constabulary."

"Oh yeah."

"In Penrith. Then you had it again upon arrival at Newcastle, and again in Amsterdam. A large and then a refill if I recall, before boarding."

A flustered sigh flew. "Yeah well, I've got a splitting headache and I'm gettin' irritable. I can't think straight."

"Perhaps the weaning from caffeine holds promise. Substance dependence can be problematic."

"They probably don't even know what coffee is around here," Marvin gusted. And then, "Why couldn't God have just locked up Erzok before he gained so much power? Why all the drama? It's not logical."

"Marvin Fischer, if you are to have any hope of understanding the supreme power, you must dispense with your desire to find logic in it. God directs his universe in accordance with passion and feeling—not logic. If it is logic you seek, you shall never understand."

Marvin tried to think happy thoughts, but could only scowl at the clinging unsettled mood, and the mud on his shoes. Finally the trek was behind them. The reeds parted, and they arrived at a small cottage by the shore, where the river gave up and spilled into a vast and deep aqua-blue ocean. The cottage was a single box, pale white with a pitched roof, a weathered door locked by a crossbar, and simple square windows. Gilgamesh stopped and stood. He gaped ineffectually at the cottage and the encompassing yard. It seemed abandoned and ill preserved. Marvin and Amina stopped at his side and looked around.

"What's this?" asked Marvin.

"The boat house," said Gilgamesh.

Gilgamesh lumbered forward across the yard and approached the front of the cottage. He passed the door and stopped to peek through a dirty window. He moved away and walked around to the back, to the ocean side of the building. Marvin and Amina followed Gilgamesh to the shoreline, their feet crunching onto the narrow beach of seashells. Tethered to a single post at the water's edge lay a small sea canoe, dark brown and weathered, beached among the tall reeds and draped in dried seaweed.

Marvin looked at the small craft with uncertainty. "We're gonna cross the ocean in that thing?"

"Wait here," said Gilgamesh, crunching away to the cottage. Marvin watched him doubtingly. Then, pushing through the tall reeds, he took another step toward the rickety craft and looked inside at the splitting boards and rotting peg nails. "You've got to be kidding." The sea canoe was shallow with a square stern and a long pointed bow. Marvin guessed the boat to be no more than 25 feet long, with a beam of about six feet, with short sides, narrow gunwales, and no cover.

It was suicide.

Amina adjusted the shawl, joined Marvin in examining the boat, crossed her arm in front of her waist and with the other touched her face with her fingers. It was the pose Marvin had come to expect would be followed by some sort of observation or profound comment. But she said nothing. Instead, Amina turned and walked slowly along the shoreline a few yards down, looking into the shallow waters of the shore and out across the sea. Marvin wondered what she might be thinking, but turned his attention back to the questionable boat. He began to wish himself away from all of this. Doubt returned. He thought of Mother Theresa. How had she done it? How had she pushed through?

Marvin was stuck in his thoughts when he realized Amina was moseying back toward him, arms crossed in front of her, guarded. She stopped and looked down, and with the toe of her boot pressed meaninglessly into the damp sand and tiny seashells.

"So," said Amina. "I was thinking about those Viennoiseries."

"Yeah?"

"They were quite delicious."

"Yeah. Coffee was good too."

"I'd like to try one with jam next time."

"I'm not much of a jam person. But that glaze was stupid good."

Amina smiled in amusement.

"Tony talk." said Marvin.

"Perhaps just the two of us next time. And there's a silly game at the park we could play."

"Pastries and games. Sounds like fun."

"So do we have an agreement?"

She was being light, playful, going somewhere with it. Marvin looked at her. The arms were still crossed. But the golden hazel eyes were glowing up at him now, capturing his face in a way he hadn't quite seen before. Something had dropped away. Some veil, some inhibition. "Are you askin' me out?" said Marvin.

"I suppose I am."

"Well as long as you're buyin' this time."

Amina chuckled.

Then Marvin nodded and smiled. "Sure," he said. "You're on."

"Okay." Amina smiled with reserved merriness in her hazel eyes. She took in a deep breath, as if a weight had lifted. She looked across the sea and let her arms down.

Marvin felt a primal shift within his spirit. He had just accepted the offer of a date from the woman. Having been single for so long after Caroline's death, it was an unexpected and totally unplanned event. His life was now about to turn on its heels. What had he done? Suddenly he felt fear and reservation, mixed with the promise of excitement and renewal. He tried to put off the new jitters and not begin yet another internal stream of analysis that would lead him in circles. He told himself to just go with the flow. Besides, the chances of ever making it back home seemed an impossibility anyway.

Amina swayed to the cottage. "What might be taking the man?"

"Let's go see."

Amina followed Marvin toward the cottage. They reached the door, which was open, and they stepped inside the small house. It was dank and dreary, with the smell of rotting wood and mildew. It was a single large room for one person, with a stove and kitchen utensils, some cupboards, a rusty sink and warped floorboards.

Crouched in the middle of the room, on one knee, was Gilgamesh, with head bowed, in a posture of prayer. Next to him was a small table, on which was a pile of small dusty stone statues lying as if dead from battle. The machete lay on the floor. Gilgamesh held his bejeweled staff erect in front of him, hands on its handle, on which his forehead rested. For another half a minute he did not move. Then Gilgamesh stirred and grunted and rose from his lowly posture, scuffing his feet on the dusty floor planks as he stood.

"Were you just praying?" asked Marvin.

Gilgamesh stood silent, his jaw hardening. He turned sharply to Marvin. "The Great Nahmes has called us to this. It is too late to doubt!"

Marvin sulked, avoiding the scratchy gaze from Amina.

Gilgamesh stepped to within an inch of Marvin's face. "Fischer, why do you doubt?"

Marvin felt he was about to be torn to pieces. Scowling, Gilgamesh moved with purpose to exit the cottage. Amina touched Marvin softly on his arm and followed.

Marvin exhaled, and went out.

63

THE STILL PEOPLE

Gilgamesh rounded again to the ocean side of the cottage where, on the old warping wall, a single weathered oar rested on two hooks. Marvin turned the corner with Amina. Gilgamesh leaned his staff against the cottage and reached and took the oar from the hooks and examined it. The oar was long as a vaulting pole, about 20 feet. Gilgamesh grasped it confidently as if it weighed nothing, and moved toward the boat. "Come," he said.

The trio moved to the boat. Gilgamesh set the oar inside of the boat, near the front. He yanked his golden dagger from its sheath and sliced through the dirty rope anchoring the boat to the post. Gilgamesh returned the dagger to its sheath, leaned over and pushed the boat partly into the water, holding the craft to stabilize it. "Get in the back," he said.

"Can't we put a motor on this thing?" waved Marvin.

"We must travel in silence," Gilgamesh warned.

Marvin skewed his jaw, standing over the boat. Gilgamesh, noticing Marvin's uneasy expression, said, "By the name of my father, Lugalbanda, and my mother, Ninsun, I will not return to the land until I have brought you to the good saint across the sea. Even if we encounter terror, we will conquer our terror. We must hope, and believe." Gilgamesh looked up to the bright yellow sky, then gestured to the stern. "Now come. Sit. We lose time."

Resigning to the inevitable, Marvin stepped into the boat. The craft wobbled. Gilgamesh steadied it firmly. Marvin turned and held out both hands for Amina. She took them, lifted a leg over and stepped onto the creaky planks of the boat. Together they settled onto the bench that spanned the width near the stern.

As Gilgamesh stepped into the water and waded to the front of the boat, Marvin wondered if this Euphrates River here on the Super-Earth was similar to the one on familiar earth. Was this ocean before them a reflection of earth's Persian Gulf? Would it open into the Gulf of Oman, and then the Arabian Sea and the Indian Ocean? Were they headed for Madagascar? Australia?

Gilgamesh lifted one leg up and over and into the boat, then leapt over the side and in. The boat swayed with his weight. Amina gripped the gunwale as Gilgamesh reached for the oar and the boat steadied. Standing near the bow with soaked feet set wide, Gilgamesh dipped the oar into the water. The paddle sunk into the sandy bottom and the big man pushed the boat off the shore. The craft drifted into the gentle roll of small waves and turned slowly until Gilgamesh pushed again and aimed the boat directly out to sea. Gilgamesh swung the oar starboard and plunged it again into the water and pushed, propelling the boat faster and straighter into the course of its destiny.

Gilgamesh spoke not a word, as with each sinking of the oar into the sandy seabed, he had to lean farther and farther as the water deepened until he could only skim the sand with the oar. When they were 500 feet from the shore, Gilgamesh could no longer touch the seabed with the oar.

And so Gilgamesh began to row. The water gurgled quietly as the boat cut through. Marvin watched the muscular giant alternate the oar, starboard to port and back, rhythmically and skillfully.

Marvin leaned to Amina's ear. "You know, my ass is tighter than his."

Amina failed to contain herself and hiccupped a chuckle.

"I've been workin' on it," said Marvin.

"Your ass is just fine, Mister Fischer," Amina smiled, keeping her gaze fixed before her. She shivered and pulled the shawl closed. Noticing, Marvin removed his suit coat, which was showing its wear, held it out over the water and shook the dust off. He draped it over Amina's shoulders. Marvin brushed his hands together, leaned forward, and set his elbows to his knees and tucked his hands in front of him.

"Thank you good sir," whispered Amina.

"Of course, milady." Marvin smiled contentedly and watched as the historic and mythical king rowed, and rowed, and rowed farther and deeper into the yawning Great Sea, toward the unknown horizon.

Marvin awoke to pitch black skies and water dark as onyx. He stirred and sniffled, blinked and yawned. The surface of the deep was placid and the air was cool but calm. Gone was the bright white and yellow sky. All around him was darkness. There was no moon. There were no stars. Marvin wondered how he was able to see anything at all. There was no color. Everything looked steely and ashen and dull. Gilgamesh remained at the bow, rhythmically rowing steadily without word or sound. Marvin looked down at Amina, the woman asleep leaning into him, her head on his shoulder. Through the cover of the warm suit coat he watched her chest move through the stable cadence of respiration. Marvin rested a hand softly on her hair and suddenly experienced a deep pang below his abdomen.

He winced. It was dreadfully painful.

He had to urinate badly. He was about to burst.

Marvin sat chiding himself for not taking more of the orbs with him when he'd had the chance at Teotihuacán. There were hundreds of them in that tunnel.

He could have filled his pockets!

Then Marvin began to rationalize the situation. The battle at the Euphrates was behind them. Somehow the power had come to him again and he had been able to slay that soldier with one blow. He was on his way to Saint Peter now, whose power surely exceeded anything Marvin could bring to the game.

And Gilgamesh was with them—the mighty king.

Power incarnate!

Marvin wouldn't need the power of the orb again.

He had to go!

Marvin gently slipped from beneath Amina and lowered her torso onto the bench that had been warmed by their bodies. She sniffled, but the eyes remained closed.

"Stop being cantankerous Marvin," she murmured.

She must have been dreaming. Satisfied that she was undisturbed, Marvin turned slowly, carefully, toward the side of the boat.

The boat bobbed slightly. Gilgamesh, sensing the movement, stopped rowing and turned to Marvin. "What are you doing?"

"I have to go pee," said Marvin with conviction.

"Your decision will have consequences."

"Yeah well, I'm dyin' here."

Gilgamesh shook his head, then turned back to the front and resumed rowing.

Marvin unzipped and loosened the boxers.

The light yellow liquid burst from him like water from a firehouse.

Marvin looked up into the black and starless sky and smiled as the urine gushed and the pressure disbursed. The stream of waste plunged heavily into the sea, wet and loud and strong.

The pain subsided as he emptied.

The stream finally died to a dribble. Marvin closed up.

And as he was about to turn around to sit, something in the water caught his eye. He squinted, looking heavily into the dark and deep and black water. Just below the surface, about four feet beneath the perfectly flat waters, was a small white light.

A pinprick, bright and clear.

Like an underwater flashlight aiming right at him.

Marvin blinked and rubbed his eyes. Was he seeing things?

Then there were two lights.

Then four. And ten. And twenty.

Within seconds there were dozens more.

The white lights popped and flickered and held their positions until in a matter of moments there were hundreds of them. The boat continued to move past, cutting silently through the quiet waters. The lights did not move to follow. But they were everywhere.

Some sort of sea creatures?

"Hey," Marvin whispered ahead to Gilgamesh. "I see lights. White lights, under the water."

Gilgamesh stopped rowing. He leaned carefully forward. The water dripped from his oar as he glanced left and right into the water. Gilgamesh straightened again, then dipped the oar back into the water and continued to row. "You do not need to know about them," he said.

"Hit me."

Gilgamesh stopped rowing and turned his ear toward Marvin. "What?"

"Just tell me. Please."

Gilgamesh resumed rowing. "Sit down Mister Fischer. And keep your hands in the boat."

"Come on. You're killin' me here."

Gilgamesh sighed. He had no patience for the game. "They are eyes," he said.

"Say again?"

Gilgamesh did not answer. Marvin looked again over the side and peeked through the dark. Sure enough—now he could see—

the pinpricks of light were set close together, two by two, as if belonging to a face.

Many faces.

My God, the man was right.

The little white lights were eyes.

"They are the *Still People*," said Gilgamesh. "If we do not rock the boat—you must forgive the pun—they will leave us alone."

Marvin looked again into the deep dark water. There must have been a thousand of them, peering at him from below the glassy water's surface, watching silently and unmoving. It seemed the faces and the bodies of the Still People were transparent or invisible, because Marvin could not see the bodies. Only the eyes.

Watching.

Waiting?

An uneasy fear rifled through Marvin's backbone. Tilting his head toward Gilgamesh, he asked, "What do they want?"

Gilgamesh pulled the oar from port to starboard. "They want souls."

64

DON'T ASK QUESTIONS

It seemed another hour had passed. But since Marvin's Rolex had stopped, he had no way of knowing for certain. It appeared they were floating aimlessly in the middle of the Great Sea with no sign of land. Standing firmly in the center of the boat, Marvin lifted Tony's binoculars to his brow for the hundredth time, hoping to finally see some destination pop on the dark horizon. A shoreline. A small island. Surely they must be close.

Still nothing.

Gilgamesh had continued to paddle along without complaint, and Marvin wondered if the man ever tired. Marvin guessed the temperature had dropped into the 40s. There was still no wind.

Amina, wrapped in the coat, stirred awake with a yawn. She rolled her fist to warm the tip of her nose. Marvin settled back down on the bench beside her and she snuggled up to his chest. He was getting a chill, but he kept his misery to himself. The eyes of the Still People had faded and vanished, which was comforting. He would not mention anything about them to Amina, fearing it would only launch her into disarray.

Marvin turned to the lady. Curled in the suit coat, she seemed even smaller to him now, like a kitten burrowed with its loving caretaker. "I'm sure Gilgamesh knows where he's going," said Marvin. "You think?"

"Don't ask questions Marvin." Amina yawned. "Just hold me." She nuzzled closer to him. Marvin put an arm around her shoulders. For a few moments they enjoyed the closeness in silence. Then Amina slipped one hand out from beneath the coat. She grasped hold of Marvin's tie as if it were a climbing rope, letting the weight of her arm hang from it. Examining the tie sleepily, she rubbed its smooth silk between her fingers. "Who gave this to you?"

Marvin dithered, then said, "It was a gift."

"From your wife."

"Mm hmm."

"That is nice."

He wouldn't tell her any more. Marvin's eyes scanned Amina's hand, followed her arm, then her face, and her soft brown hair. Her beauty was growing on him. He wondered if in time he would begin to feel romantically about her. "Hey, you lost an earring," he said.

Amina let go of the tie and felt her ears. Her right lobe was bare.

"Oh..." she said faintly and without concern.

There was a long silence. Marvin thought for the first time of taking the necktie finally off, and tossing it overboard. But the tie kept his collar closed and the chill out. So he left it. The watery craft cut through the placid ocean as the big man in front continued to paddle. Amina rested her hand on Marvin's chest and said, "Marvin, wouldn't you like to know what your name means?"

Marvin raised his eyebrows and blinked. "Oh yeah. I kinda forgot about that."

"Well?"

Marvin shrugged. "I know what it means."

"Really. Okay ...?"

"It means *awesome*."

Amina chuckled heartily. "Marvin do not be such a kook."

"Alright professor... what does it mean?"

"You really do not know?"

"No."

Amina's eyes shined. "It is of Welsh origin. It means *great lord who lives by the sea*."

"Hhm." Marvin paused. "I can live with that."

"So can I."

"Don't get any funny ideas. It's just gonna be a date."

Amina smirked thinly. She slipped her arm back underneath the coat, rested her head on Marvin's chest, and watched the canted sea. "Fair enough," she said. "But I believe in a great realm of possibility."

The loud and unexpected thrash and heavy gurgle from the bow of the boat sent Marvin and Amina jerking to attention. Together they looked forward, in time to see droplets of water falling from the air above Gilgamesh as he rested his palms on the bow of the boat, looking into the water. Most of the flying drops of ocean rejoined the sea; the rest of them pelted the inside of the boat with an agitating splatter.

"What happened?" asked Marvin.

"The Still People," said Gilgamesh. "They have stolen the oar."

Marvin's jaw dropped. He did not see the oar in Gilgamesh's hands, or anywhere else in the boat. He looked over the gunwale.

They were back. The Still People. Hundreds of white lights cutting through the blackness.

Still and unmoving.

"Who are the Still People?" asked Amina, looking over the side and into the water.

"Bad guys," Marvin spoke with dread.

"Oh God..." Amina pulled away as she saw the glow and pressed back into Marvin. He gave her a squeeze and then stood up and took a step toward the bow.

"Wait!" said Gilgamesh, holding out a hand as he continued to stare into the waters.

Marvin stopped cold. Amina rose now also, pulling the coat closed tightly in front of her. "Marvin what is happening?"

"Do not move!" Gilgamesh ordered.

Amina pushed herself into Marvin's side in an act of self-reassurance. Marvin put an arm around her waist. "Gilgamesh...?" Marvin prompted.

Gilgamesh turned slowly and faced them. "The boat is turning."

"What?" said Marvin.

"There is no wind. Why is it turning?" asked Amina with fright.

"The Still People. They are pushing the boat," answered Gilgamesh.

"Why would they push the boat?" asked Amina.

Marvin looked out onto the distant water ahead, over Gilgamesh's shoulder.

Something out there looked odd. Not right.

Different.

Marvin snatched Tony's binoculars that hung from his neck. He rubbed the lenses quickly and lifted them to his eyes and looked ahead.

He watched the water's surface in the distance, to starboard.

Was the placid surface of the sea moving?

He focused.

Yes—The water was rippling, waving, and swelling.

Not placid.

"Holy shit," said Marvin.

"What is it?" asked Gilgamesh.

Marvin slipped the binoculars from his neck, handed them to Gilgamesh, and pointed starboard. Gilgamesh raised the lenses to look, and he saw it too.

Gilgamesh lowered the lenses. "This is not a good sign," he said flatly.

"Marvin?" said Amina. "What is wrong?"

"The sea is swelling. Over there," Marvin pointed.

"The boat is being pulled," said Gilgamesh. "We are being pulled!"

"What does that mean?" asked Amina. "Can we turn around?"

"He lost the oar!" Marvin exclaimed.

"The Still People yanked the oar from my hands!" Gilgamesh defended, holding his hands open in front of him.

"Well can we paddle? With our hands? And turn around?" asked Amina again, her voice quivering. Marvin rolled up a sleeve, sat quickly down on the bench, and leaned over the gunwale with an open palm.

"NO!" shouted Gilgamesh.

Marvin fired him a look. "We're headed for those turbulent waters! We have to turn around!"

"Do not put your hand in the water!" Gilgamesh warned. "They will pull you in!"

Marvin retreated, looking again and watching as hundreds of white eyes stared at him, gathering around the sides of the boat and surrounding it. It was the first time he ever saw the eyes move. There were so many of them now that the water glowed like an illuminated swimming pool in Scottsdale. The air surrounding the boat bloomed white.

Marvin turned to Gilgamesh and begged, "What are we gonna do?"

Gilgamesh shook his head as Amina looked again toward the tossing waters. "It feels like we are moving faster!" she said, as the bow of the boat turned and headed straight for the rising waves. A moment later the boat reached the first large swell, sleepy and innocent, and rode the hump.

The boat swayed.

"We're gettin' closer!" said Marvin.

"I cannot stop the boat!" Gilgamesh insisted.

"We have to stop the boat!" Amina shouted.

"It is impossible!" said Gilgamesh. "We are at the mercy of the sea!"

"Wait!" said Marvin, holding up a hand. "Stop talkin'!"

The three of them stood perfectly still in the boat.

The boat met the next swell. The passing wave sloshed and slapped the bow and rolled under the keel.

Then, a low and deep and ominous drone sounded, coming from somewhere not far off.

"You hear that?" asked Marvin.

Gilgamesh listened, and turned. "Yes."

"What is that?" asked Amina.

The drone grew louder as the boat drew nearer to the waves and began to sway continuously side to side. It was so dark they could hardly see anything, and the bright eyes of the Still People creating the eerie wall of light around the boat made it almost impossible to see anything in the distance. Marvin took the binoculars from Gilgamesh and lifted them again to his face and focused on the turbulent sea that got nearer with each passing second. "Ahhh!" Marvin shouted in frustration. "I can't see!" He lowered the binoculars from his face and rubbed his eyes. The scary and ominous drone grew louder and the boat began to turn again, swaying and dipping. Marvin gulped and raised the lenses once again to his straining eyes, and a wave of terror washed through his fibers.

"Oh my God… This can't be." Marvin cried.

"What is it?!" Amina shouted.

Marvin lowered the lenses and pointed.

"I think it's a whirlpool!!"

Gilgamesh snatched the binoculars back from Marvin and looked through them.

And he saw it.

There it was—a gargantuan maelstrom, an immense circular vortex, daunting and menacing, one hundred yards away, swirling and roaring and pulling.

Horrendous.

The chimney had to be a quarter mile at its widest.

And they were headed straight for it.

"Holy SHIT!!" Marvin shouted.

The steady drone of one hundred zillion gallons of sucking power reeled before them as their tiny little boat was tractored closer and closer toward certain death.

There was no way to navigate around it.

"Gilgamesh!" shouted Marvin. "We gotta do *something*!!"

"There is nothing we can do!!" shouted Gilgamesh, dropping to his knees and clutching the gunwale. "We are going to go down!!"

The air was cold and Marvin was certain the water was going to be icy and cruel, but that didn't matter, because in mere moments they were all going to be slurped in and plunge deep into the dark and evil waters and that would be that.

As if drawn by static electricity, the little boat was predestined for the inescapable grip of the rotating monster, doomed to desolation.

They were all going to die.

The boat hit the chimney and tipped and swirled at the outer edge of the giant maelstrom and Amina screamed. Spinning out of control, the boat picked up speed around the perimeter of the raging waters and was drawn deeper and faster into the funnel, until Marvin had to look up to see the edge of the outer ring of the pool.

The watery vortex would prevail.

Marvin felt the little boat crack and he knew it was over.

In a matter of seconds they would be under.

In a futile attempt to survive, Marvin clung with Amina and Gilgamesh to the gunwales of the boat. Gilgamesh shouted something, but the vulgar rumble of the vortex was too loud for words to be heard. And as the frigid water swished and sloshed and violently tumbled up and into the boat, and she knew the end was nigh, Amina grasped Marvin's hands tightly and looked into his eyes—frantic—and he met her. Decidedly, Amina pulled one hand from Marvin's grip and she reached behind his head and pushed forward and met his lips with an impassioned kiss. Without hesitation, Marvin grabbed hold of her face and their lips pressed deeper into amorous union. Sodden and numb with cold, they looked into each other's eyes in stoic agony as the icy and angry waters beat against their faces and bodies. The boat whirled swiftly and speedily and horribly down into the center of the pool of death until the stern kicked and tipped up and the boat split in two, splintering and shattering as the bodies hurled and the mighty waters swallowed them mercilessly, and they went down shouting, yelling, screaming…

And dying.

PART IV

65
THEATER OF KISMET

The torrent of rushing water rolled steady and constant as the first sense of consciousness returned to Marvin Fischer. Awareness of perception came from his own shallow breathing as the warm and moist air passed heavily through his clogged nostrils. Marvin's eyelids were closed and thick, his muscles loose, his mind lazy. He twitched his fingers and felt his toes move inside his stiff shoes. In his semi-comatose state, Marvin's foggy mind explored the components of the rest of his anatomy one by one. It seemed to Marvin that all of his limbs were fastened and accounted for. He did not feel numb.

He felt no pain.

After accepting with bleary confidence that his body was fully present, he found himself sitting on a solid surface, leaning wilted against a rigid wall. Marvin sat woozily for several minutes without moving or testing his vision. He allowed breath to fill his lungs, slowly increasing the volume as his body fought to nourish the extremities with oxygenated blood.

Marvin's mind turned again to his surroundings. There was the steady rush of water and the pounding crash into what sounded like a deep basin. Marvin sensed light in his face as a shadow lifted. When he heard the first tweedle of a bird he stirred in confusion through closed eyes.

There came the peep of another bird.

Marvin weakly licked his brittle lips and swallowed dryly, and then began the laborious process of opening his eyes. With great effort his eyelashes ripped through their crusty trap and Marvin managed to narrowly peer through them.

Thirty yards directly before him, he thought he saw a sparkling waterfall. It poured down from a brown stony cliff from a hundred feet above, surrounded by palms and trees and vines with cheerful violet flowers. Colorfully exotic dwarf finches darted and swooped and hopped between the trees, across the sky, from twig to rock, their chirps weaving a restful tapestry of song.

Marvin blinked and sniffled. His tired mind wound up and his weary body creaked and woke slowly like a bear after the winter slumber. He rubbed the bottom of his nose with the back of his hand, then set one palm flat on the hard surface beneath him. He pushed himself up and sat, his back curved and his shoulders limp. When another minute had passed, Marvin found the strength to bend his knees and pull them to his chest. He wrapped his shins in his arms and clasped his hands and sat with eyelids at half-mast, groggy, slowly blinking and absorbing the environment.

When Marvin saw the twinkling waterfall again, and the flowers and the birds and the trees, he drew in a deep breath and released his legs and sprawled to his stomach. He crawled across the bright white marble floor toward the waterfall, so close, yet so far away. In a burst of desperation Marvin forced his body to bend and break and move. He twisted across the floor like a lizard and up to the edge of the basin where he found the glittering water. He reached with his right hand and scooped the cool water to his lips and drank. With both hands now he reached and scooped and drank until he could not drink anymore. His thirst finally quenched,

Marvin rolled over onto his back and stared up into the clear blue sky and watched the birds crisscross above him.

Was he dead? … Was this heaven?

Dante's Empyrean?

Marvin lay there for a long time and thought about where he had come from.

Oh yes… Gilgamesh.

Amina.

The sea.

The maelstrom.

Where was Tony?

Marvin rolled onto his side and felt strength and balance call to him. He sat upright and then swiveled to one knee, balancing himself with his knuckles on the white stone floor. He took another deep breath and forced himself to his feet. He rose like a blooming flower and lifted his hands to his head and rubbed his short hair. He felt his chin and the three days of stubble that was beginning to itch. He looked down and saw his clothes.

He was dry.

Dressed in the same clothes he'd worn on the boat.

Marvin looked slowly at his arms and held his palms open. He pressed his index finger into his bicep and pinched the flesh of his forearm through his tattered white shirt. He was still in his corporeal state. He rubbed his palms on his ripped and filthy suit pants, fingered the holes of his shirt, patted the length of the ratty silk tie he still wore loosely and stubbornly around his neck. He looked at his fingernails. His cuticles were dirty, his dry skin cracking.

This couldn't be heaven.

Where was he?

His senses heightening, Marvin's eyes darted around the small lagoon by the waterfall, looking for clues. Amidst the flowers and greenery and darting finches, Marvin caught sight of a strange animal sitting under the cover of a low hanging palm branch. Marvin's eyes narrowed, seeking to identify the creature.

It was a cat. Gray and ghoulish, with horribly wrinkled skin and no fur coat, the radar of its oversized, bat-like ears honed precisely on Marvin's form. The ugly gray cat had no interest in the chirping finches. Its sole devotion was to the unwelcome stranger—the intruder—the new potential quarry. The feline sat comfortable and unholy, poised on its rear, its two front legs straight and solid, its tail curled around its front paws. The feline's mouth and nose were expressionless. The long whiskers twitched. The cat was staring straight at Marvin with penetrating curiosity, through eyes smoky and dead. It was undoubtedly the ugliest, most foreboding cat Marvin had ever seen.

Marvin held perfectly still as the cat's cryptic and hollow eyes dug into him. Marvin was much bigger than this average sized cat, but found it most unsettling playing target to the diabolic tom's attention.

Marvin broke stares with the cat and looked behind him now, at the hard and glossy white wall where he had first awakened. The wall stretched up into the blue sky and into infinity. He swiveled on his toes and reeled in more information as his eyes messaged his brain.

The waterfall was set behind him, real as life, but it was inside of a giant white octagonal room, part of what looked like a giant terrarium, a glass house, a super-sized aviary. Marvin found himself at the center of it all, standing on a huge white platform spanning 100 yards. The wall where he had awoken continued along the entire perimeter. His eyes followed the wall around until they landed on a small opening to his left, ninety degrees offset from the waterfall.

It was the only visible entry or exit to the space.

Marvin took one more look at the ominous cat, still sitting with eyes locked on him. Marvin turned and moved his feet and made for the opening. Whatever uplift that had begun to renew his spirit now washed completely away as his pace increased, the blood flowed, his lungs filled and anxiety returned. When Marvin was only a few steps from the opening, a cold and bitter wall of air hit him in the face like a brutal arctic hand.

Marvin stopped dead. He knew he had to go through the opening. He had nothing to lose, and he was going to face his destiny and whatever laid in wait for him inside this nonsensical merry-go-round. He turned to look one more time at the beautiful waterfall and the warm air and said goodbye to the calming birds. Ignoring the cold and cruel air, he turned and faced the opening again and moved boldly into it.

When he'd passed through the opening he found himself in a boxy white hallway that stretched in one direction, and one direction only—to his left.

Marvin followed the hall.

The hall was six feet wide with towering walls, clean and bright and spotless, like pure glossy white opal, like the atrium from which he had just come.

Marvin could not discern a light source.

The cold air persisted, frosty and harsh.

Marvin wound his way through the corridor until it turned, and turned again, and then again. Marvin turned left, then followed to the right, zigzagging this way and that, into what Marvin began to realize was a series of connected passages that led seemingly nowhere. The light gray shadows in the blocky corners and sharp edges of the white walls and floors began to play tricks with Marvin's eyes. He turned around and his mind whirled. The place seemed to rearrange its layout with each turn he made. Blocks of architectural absurdity protruded and jutted arbitrarily from above and from the walls, each white and clean and pure and innocent and silent. Marvin took another few steps and rounded another bend that opened into a maze of choices.

Marvin felt like a lab rat.

Which way was he supposed to go?

Who was the mad scientist?

It dawned on him that he could no longer hear the rush of the waterfall. In fact he could hear nothing now except his own anxious breathing. Marvin turned around again. He chose an opening and continued down the corridor. After a few more steps he stopped and stood still, tilting his ear.

There was something about the floor that disturbed him.

The bottoms of his feet quivered through the soles of his tattered shoes.

It seemed the floor was vibrating.

And Marvin thought he heard a faint humming sound, coming from a location he could not specify within this surreal, geographically shifting labyrinth.

Marvin put his palm to the wall.

Same thing. A faint vibration, and he was certain he heard that deep, low hum.

The waterfall? Had he come full circle?

66

CYCLONE

Marvin continued down the corridor, following it left, then right, having no sense of direction or intention other than possibly—maybe—finding some way out, some other entrance to somewhere, or exit to some other place.
    But then Marvin stopped again. The vibration was increasing. He strained his ears.
    What was that?
    The rumbling?
    Marvin put his hand to the throbbing wall again.
    Yes, something very big was close by.
    But what was it?
    Was it mechanical? Hydraulic? Electrical?
    Supernatural?
    Marvin moved on, frantic, around the next bend and into another corridor. He ducked underneath an obstructing rectangle and spun to his right.
    Another opening.
    He stepped through.

The rumbling increased and by now the vibration was so extreme that Marvin felt like the floor was going to crumble beneath him.

When he turned the next corner the crashing rumble increased yet again, like an inevitable locomotive pounding along steel tracks ready to obliterate him.

Marvin began to run. He ran and ran, ducking and bending and turning corners and racing down a long white hallway and he didn't know why, but he was running toward—not away—from the terrible screeching rumble.

He turned another corner and stopped in his tracks, his eyes wide, staring at the new unspeakable monstrosity before him.

The corridor had opened up into the biggest and largest and most cavernous arena Marvin had ever witnessed.

Like a Colosseum ten times bigger than the Roman classic.

But without bleachers.

Without participants.

A ring with no spectators.

Just Marvin Fischer.

Lining the inner circular wall of the towering colosseum was a singular, continuous white ramp with a railing that wound its way around the inner perimeter of the colosseum like a metal spring, extending many levels high. Marvin's brain rattled and his organs trembled within him as he stepped up to the curved railing that separated the donut-like platform on which he stood, a part of the coiling ramp circling the perimeter of the arena-like complex.

Marvin grasped hold of the cold railing with both hands and tried to make sense of the immense scene before him.

The sound was thundering.

The vibration staggering.

Like a perpetual earthquake.

Marvin's body throbbed and his teeth clattered. His shoes threatened to wriggle off his feet and run off without him.

When Marvin looked again out into the vast colosseum in front of him, he did not see what he might have expected to see.

Instead of a flat and wide playing field as its focal point, where games would be played, there was instead, in the center of the ring, beyond the railing and out of Marvin's reach, a gargantuan, monumentally wide clear tube, vertical and gleaming like crystal.

A colossal hurricane glass.

Consuming the entire center space of the colosseum.

The crystalline hurricane glass dove down through a giant hole in the floor into an endless chasm below, and reached high up to infinity above. Marvin stared in awful terror at the crystalline hurricane glass as he squinted and peered through it's thick and solid clear wall and tried to understand what was inside of it.

Inside of the hurricane glass was a swirling mass of cosmic energy, bright and searing and bursting with what seemed like electricity.

The mystical blue-white light flashed and blinked and flickered across Marvin's curious analytical face and eyes.

Was it a power source? A huge generator of some sort?

As Marvin looked closer, he could see that it was not one continuous stream of smoky flashing light that swirled within the glass. No, there were millions of tiny vaporous wisps, thin streams of bright gaseous swirls, some of them short, some of them long, hanging together, clinging and swirling and darting together in unison, round and round, at a thousand miles an hour.

And all of them seemed to be alive.

Like trillions of ocean mullet schooling in the Caspian Sea.

Swirling in perfect hydrodynamic efficiency.

But these were no ocean mullet, and this was no ocean.

This was a CYCLONE.

Booming, thunderous, and howling.

HERCULEAN.

The cyclone seemingly held each and every wisp captive in its magnetic grip.

What were those damned wisps?!

It seemed to Marvin like the wispy energy was trying to escape.

Shaking, Marvin let go of the icy railing and backed away.

THE TEMPEST IN GLASS

"Welcome, Mister Fischer. I see you have found my secret."

The booming voice almost knocked Marvin off his feet. He spun, frantic and desperate, looking up and around the immense arena, searching for the ominous caller.

"Who are you!?!" Marvin shouted into the air.

"You know who I am."

The voice was deep and toady and raspy, most wretchedly evil. Marvin circled and hobbled as he turned and turned, still looking for his enemy, his fear shifting to anger.

"Where is Antonio Valdez?!" Marvin shouted fiercely.

"Who?"

Marvin didn't believe the denial. He turned back to face the vibrating glass monstrosity. "And what's this? What is this thing!?!"

"Well Marvin, I wasn't planning on showing this to you," the booming voice echoed resignedly. "But sometimes even I get lost in my own maze. So now that you're here, welcome to the Cyclone of Captured Prayers."

67

AVENUE OF THE DEAD

Marvin broke into a sprint and dashed from the tempest in glass as fast as he could, stumbling over his own toes, his coordination still not fully restored. He wanted to escape, to get out of this place, to get away from the cataclysmic twister. The cyclone itself seemed to be laughing at him, and as much as it explained what had happened to his prayers, Marvin wanted to dismiss the cyclone as a nightmare.

Marvin finally reached the exit, where he found himself free from the sight of the cyclone, but once again a victim of the funhouse tricks of the whitewashed passages with its canted angles and tipping facades. The reflections and shifting shadows in the mind-bending labyrinth beckoned Marvin as he ambled through, this way and that, only to be lead further into disorientation and lunacy.

Marvin thought he was finally losing his mind.

He tripped his way down another corridor and was momentarily relieved when he realized the terrible vibrating and thunderous roar of the cyclone was diminishing. How he wished he could find that waterfall again, with its soothing mist and comforting cascade of refreshing peace. He would drown the damned cat. He wanted to lounge under the palms and hide and relax and gaze into the sky among the birds and forever unwind under a bright hot sun.

Clinging to the hopeful image, Marvin tore again down a hallway and bent around the twists and turns, hurdling shifty blockades and ducking beneath dropping ceilings.

Just as the place seemed to be closing inevitably in on him, Marvin's foot stepped onto something that rolled underfoot and he stumbled and sprawled headlong with his arms spread wide uselessly in an attempt to break his fall. But it was his chin that struck first, bashing onto the hard floor and sending him tumbling onto his side. Marvin lay there paralyzed for a moment, before his survival instinct activated and he rolled to his stomach and sprang to his heels. Fifteen feet down the hall, in the middle of the floor, was a dark and ovular object the size of a softball.

Marvin raced over to the obscure dark object and picked it up and turned it over.

It was a human skull, black as coal, smiling up at him.

Marvin hurled the skull against the wall where it burst to a cloud of ash.

Marvin turned again and found himself at the entrance of a large vestibule. Without logic or thought he dashed through the vestibule and stood now at the front end of another long hall, but this hall was different, much wider and longer than the rest that had thwarted him until now.

This hall was stable and static, free of the confusing and morphing architecture. Its broad walkway summoned him, yawning ready to swallow him.

Marvin stood stone still, panting and gasping at the new horror that now lay before him.

Yes—it was a long, highway-like path—an expansive white road some forty feet wide. Running along its entire length, on both sides, were gleaming white platforms with a rise of about two feet, extinguishing somewhere in the distance at the end of the avenue.

And laid out neatly along the white glowing platforms, about five feet apart, were skeletons, hundreds of them, dark and black like tar as the skull Marvin had just demolished. The skeletons on their display platforms stretched the entire length of the corridor.

There was something familiar to Marvin about the image, about the size of it, about the feeling of ancientness it gave him as he gazed upon the sight before him.

An echo of the ruins at Teotihuacán.

Erzok's Avenue of the Dead.

"Go ahead, my privileged guest," the booming voice returned. "Enjoy the walk. You've earned the grand tour."

Marvin hesitated, then moved ahead and walked down the center of the avenue, turning his head side to side at the skeletons as he passed them, the bones sprawled out on their backs with their arms crossed over their abdomens like mummies without sarcophagi.

"These are the remains of those who have come before," the sinister narrator continued as Marvin passed the unnatural spectacle of bones. "The remains of those experiments, those faithful dead religious humans whose souls I tried to steal."

Marvin continued to walk down the long avenue. He tore his glance away from the skeletons and focused on the destination straight ahead, which he could not discern, because it was nothing but a dead end, an ambiguous tall and solid white wall.

So he focused on the wall.

Anything was better than viewing the specters of death at his sides.

He moved decidedly through the space with an air of confidence even though he had none, the only soldier in this army of one, pushing through the cold wicked chill of the air. Marvin felt his heart hammering under his shirt, behind his tie. The place was like a refrigerator. No, it was a damn freezer. And for some reason, the sounds of some horrible fugue came to Marvin's mind now, something resonating, something he couldn't get out of his head. The ghastly drone of the flugelhorn, the foreshadowing of death by the baritone, the thumping heartbeat of the timpani, the torture of the haunting organ. All of it somehow creepily and miserably underscoring Marvin's experience here as he was a dead man walking.

As he neared the end of the avenue, Marvin took opportunity to quickly assess the rest of his surroundings. At the termination of the Avenue of the Dead, on either side of the dead end wall, were two more openings, one on each side. Marvin guessed the openings were access points to the maze of vexing hallways that he had already traveled, most likely connected to a vast network of moving tunnels that Erzok had presumably created as an elaborate security system to prevent access to the massive tempest in glass.

It had apparently been an accident that Marvin had stumbled upon the cyclone, an undesirable occurrence that Erzok would have preferred to avoid.

Presumably, knowledge of the cyclone's existence was privileged information.

But now Marvin had the humint.

Did Erzok not have total control of this place, of his own dwelling?

Erzok blathered on, "You see Mister Fischer, I have succeeded in capturing the prayers of those faithful religious for many generations. You have seen it for yourself now. The cyclone. There is nothing you can do about it, they will remain there forever. Trapped. Not even God knows they are there. He doesn't even know they exist. Doesn't even know his people tried to reach him in vain. All these feeble prayers you people pray, that you think get heard and somehow miraculously answered? Answers to prayer? Really? It's all coincidental. Happenstance!"

Marvin thought about it. Could it really be? All the people's prayers, captured before they had ever reached the ears of God?

All of them?

Surely Erzok had not succeeded in catching them all.

Or had he?
And if so, for how long?
For many generations, as Erzok had said?
For centuries?
Impossible!

Surely many thousands of prayers had made it over—escaped past the electric grasp of the tempest and found their way to God.

There had been so much testimony from believers! Testimony of answered prayers!

Certainly many had fired straight to heaven.
But what about those caught in the tempest!
How many of them were there? A million? A trillion?

Marvin continued walking and was snapped from his analysis as Erzok went on. "But even my capturing of the prayers was only a trial run. A test! A test for my ultimate goal. To keep God's people separated from him forever. You see Mister Fischer, it is the human soul that I seek to destroy, the human soul that I seek to capture, the human souls stamped by God that I must hold and keep from ever reaching their Creator. The soul is the ultimate prize. The ultimate victory over your pathetic God."

Marvin felt the skin on his forehead wrinkle as he frowned in anger. His teeth gritted with rage and the corners of his mouth turned down as he listened to the deranged monster prattle on.

"Yes, yes, Mister Fischer. I have yet to succeed with capturing the soul. Stop, stop right there."

Marvin found himself at the end of the avenue, thirty feet from the wall that was the dead end. The trail of skeletons on his right had ended a few feet behind him. But on his left, the skeletons continued, until he came to the very last skeleton in the line.

The final skeleton, black and dark and departed.

"Move closer to that one," the voice said.

Marvin, his brows tipped and his mouth tight, stepped up to the skeleton.

He forced himself to look into the voids of the eyes.
The crushed ribs.

The broken legs.

"Do you know who this is, Mister Fischer?" asked Erzok. "Come on. Guess! You're good at guessing. She died only recently. A couple of weeks ago, maybe?"

Marvin's respiration increased as he stared down at the skeleton in front of him.

And Marvin knew.

Of course.

He was looking at the remains of Rubi Maria Valdez.

Marvin kneeled down at the edge of the platform and stared in stunned bewilderment at the dry, dark bones stretched out before him. He placed one hand on the platform next to her foot, staring at what was once Rubi's beautiful face.

The voice droned on, "Madaki killed her, but I missed her soul. Slipped right by me! Almost had it! So close! It was my latest attempt at soul stealing, but I didn't quite succeed. You prayed for her, Marvin. Didn't you? For her safety? I'm afraid that prayer didn't quite make it."

How Marvin wished now that he were God. That he had the power to turn and destroy once and for all this horrible demon, the Prince of the Power of the Air, that had brought so much destruction and pain and suffering and death upon humanity.

If only Marvin were God.

If only he had the power of the orb.

Something.

He would end it all right here.

Right now.

But then something else caught the corner of his eye.

Movement to his right.

Marvin turned.

And he saw him.

It was Erzok.

Pure white and gleaming from head to toe.

His blazing eyes two gorges of deep orange fire.

Nothing like the myths.

Erzok must have emerged from one of the openings next to the dead end wall. He matched Marvin in height, thin and fit and calculated. Missing were the mythical tail and pointy chin, the curling horns and sharp fangs. Erzok's face was instead a perfect cut of superb masculinity, handsome as the finest actor. Gorgeous, sensual, and stunning. The most flawless rendition of a human face that Marvin thought possible. The zenith of creative achievement. Erzok's skin was brilliant white under a perfectly tailored one-piece suit of equally pure white. Even his shiny shoes were perfect white. In his right hand Erzok wielded a scepter, two feet long, intricately carved in white, tipped with a spherical black stone encapsulated in a quatrefoil cage of shining silver.

In spite of the misdirection afforded by Erzok's beauty, his presence was dominated by the unmistakable pulse of searing, invisible and unadulterated ancient evil.

The desolation in the haughty, ocherous eyes communicated only one thing.

Doom incarnate.

68
WE FINALLY MEET

"Hello Mister Fischer. We finally meet." The roaching voice was the antithesis of the visual beauty of the goblin. "I'm sorry I can't offer you any refreshment. I do hope you hydrated at the waterfall. In any case, you've saved me the trouble of trying the hard way again. You've given me a brilliant idea. Bring the humans *here*, and *then* take their souls. I should have thought of it centuries ago!" Erzok twirled his scepter like a drum major. "Forget the risk of having the souls escape from my grip at the moment of death, while en route to God. All the dreaded timing, the plotting, the selecting, the strategizing, the useless and worthless proxies and demons who can never do it right. Forget it all! Bring the people *here*!! It's so simple really, isn't it?"

Erzok shook his head and stepped closer to Marvin.

Twenty feet was now all that separated Marvin Fischer from the villain.

Was this white demon truly the greatest arch enemy in the history of humankind?

The pinnacle of evil?

The Satan of myth and lore and legend and religion?

"So," Marvin finally spoke. "What now?" He tried to maintain his poise, stressing intrepidly to keep the fear from his eyes, the tremble from his voice. "Kill me? Right here? And take my soul?"

"Oh no, no!" said Erzok. "Be patient, Marvin." He pointed his scepter at Marvin. "You have been a tricky one. Not even Madaki could stop you. The angels have protected you well. Until now. So rest assured, your actual death will be much more unpleasant than you could have ever imagined. But first there is something else I want you to see."

Erzok turned to the dead end wall of white at the conclusion of the avenue and moved to it. After several paces he reached the wall and, raising the scepter up and over his left shoulder, he fanned the wall with a swooping motion of the scepter and Marvin watched the wall vanish before his eyes.

Behind the wall that was no longer there was a gigantic and vast square chamber, twice the size of a football field, white and clean just like the rest of the architecture throughout this demonic place. There was no floor. In the middle of this immense space was a white rock pyramid, 400-feet square, suspended above nothingness, an invisible moat of air surrounding the pyramid. Across the great chasm spanned a single bridge connecting the Avenue of the Dead to a flight of stairs running straight up the front of the pyramid. One hundred stairs, cut sharp like the rest of the large towering mass, ascending directly up the center of the structure to its apex, where the pyramid was capped by a sprawling flat platform.

Front and center of the platform stood a single, lonely gray figure.

The figure was firm and motionless.

Who was it?

Erzok crossed the threshold of the newly revealed great room and walked onto the bridge. He crossed the distance and approached the base of the pyramid where the steps began their ascent. Erzok paused and turned to Marvin. "Come. Don't be afraid."

After a moment of cautious hesitation, Marvin crossed the threshold also, stepping onto the bridge. A quick glance up told Marvin that the ceiling here too had no limit. Marvin spanned the bridge and came nearer to the pyramid.

Marvin watched in stunned amazement as, lifting off his feet, Erzok floated above the stairs and made his ascent to the top of the pyramid with an effortless flair. Erzok's feet settled gently onto the pyramid's wide platform, just next to the lone and still and indiscernible gray figure.

Marvin watched Erzok cradle the scepter in its stand and then turn to look down at him. Marvin waited to see if he too would be airlifted to the top, but Erzok gave no accommodating sign. Erzok was going to make him walk the flight himself. So be it. With arms at his sides, Marvin began the march up the long stairway. Slowly and steadily Marvin climbed, cautious and deliberate, as Erzok watched in merriment.

At twenty steps from the top, Marvin stopped firm.

He looked again at the motionless gray figure on the platform.

Erzok smiled. Marvin continued up the rest of the stairs to the top, where he paused at the edge of the platform.

Marvin stiffened.

There, in the center of the platform, deep gray and hard and smooth, was a statue.

A statue of hard and solid cut stone.

It was Antonio Valdez.

Marvin stared at the likeness of the boy's young face, the hope in the eyes, the handsome smooth cheeks, the straight nose and firm chin. The slight step forward, the reach of the arm, the curl in the index finger.

The wave in his hair, the threads in his jacket.

The weave of his jeans, the laces of his gym shoes.

Every detail perfect.

Lifeless and entombed.

No… It couldn't be him!

Marvin felt the blood rush to his head. His eyes darted to Erzok, who stood pleased and pompous, admiring the rocky tomb of young Antonio Valdez. Marvin's eyes bulged and his lungs stretched. Screaming in rage, Marvin lifted his arms and stormed forward. He leapt and tackled Erzok like a linebacker. Erzok did not budge. He stood casual and unfeeling as Marvin beat Erzok's chest with his fists. Marvin's furious voice boomed through the hollow and massive chamber, bouncing off the distant walls, up from the platform, down the steps of the great pyramid and echoing down the length of the treacherous Avenue of the Dead below. Marvin could feel the swelling of his chest, the burning pain in his throat. His fists began to ache from the pounding. His knuckles split and bled. Repeatedly, endlessly, Marvin pummeled Erzok's face, the eyes, the teeth, the jaws and shoulders and belly, screaming and yelling and seething until he went hoarse.

Erzok stood unaffected.

Suddenly Marvin stopped the beating.

Marvin stood overwhelmed, panting, wheezing, bleeding, his mouth dropping, his eyes narrow like slits and his crystal blue eyes burning into the evil orange irises of the creature in front of him. Erzok stood still and impassive, watching his human victim stand feeble and conquered.

Erzok let the realization settle into Marvin's brain and then took a step toward the tall opulent stand where he had placed the scepter. Marvin watched Erzok lift the scepter out of its cradle, light glinting off its silver caged tip.

Erzok stepped to the statue of Tony. "It's too bad your friend Topiltzin isn't here to make a plea against human sacrifice."

With a sudden swivel of his hips and raising of the scepter, Erzok pivoted and swung the scepter hard and down upon the shoulder of the boy, smashing the rocky material in a crushing blow that shot slivers of shale exploding in every direction. Marvin shielded his eyes from the spray of shrapnel, ducking away from flying chunks and pebbles.

Opening his eyes and turning slowly back to where Tony had been, Marvin dared to look. There stood Tony, bewildered, his body shaking, eyes full of fright, free of his stony prison. Tony looked slowly down into his palms as he realized he was no longer entombed. Tony looked up, and when he saw Marvin Fischer—his best and most trusted friend—standing there in front of him, Tony burst forward in a rush of joy and thanksgiving.

"Mister Fischer!"

Tony crashed into Marvin's arms and hugged him deeply, pressing his head into Marvin's shoulder. Marvin wrapped his arms tightly around the boy and stroked his head. He muttered Tony's name and felt a deep paternal instinct and a desire to protect the boy at all costs.

Tony pulled away and looked down at Marvin's ragged clothes, the blood on Marvin's knuckles, the tremor in Marvin's hands. And the smile on Tony's cheeks melted into concern. Tony looked back up at Marvin's face and saw the quiver in the dry lips, the dreary and watery and sagging eyes, the evidence of pain and lost hope behind the once clear and crystal blue determination.

"Mister Fischer…" Tony whispered. "What happened?"

69

YOU WILL BECOME A TRUE BELIEVER

The cracking thud that struck Marvin's stomach knocked him sprawling backward.

Tony backed away in shock as three of Erzok's acolytes swooped in from the nether and crowded over Marvin's body, pounding him with their spears and staffs. The minion's bodies were as beautiful as Erzok's, but their faces flat and featureless. They said nothing and made no sound as they robotically struck the man on the floor. Marvin cried out in pain as he was beaten and kicked and punched by the portentous mob. Tony screamed in resistance and tried to leap to Marvin's aid, only to be held back by the powerful hand of Erzok as he watched the torture ensue.

Marvin grunted and groped at the floor, trying to crawl away from the executioners as they beat him and struck him. Blood spurt from Marvin's mouth as he rolled across the floor until he was kicked right to the edge of the platform, to the very top of the steps of the giant pyramid.

"Stop!" shouted Erzok.

And the three minions ceased their merciless beating of Marvin Fischer.

Erzok yanked Tony by the elbow and walked him to the edge of the platform to meet up with Marvin's battered body. Tony looked down in panic at his beaten and bloody friend. Marvin gazed foggily up at the boy through swollen eyes and a bruised face.

"Mister Fischer..." Tony's eyes welled and tears rolled down his cheeks.

"Antonio..." said Marvin, his voice hoarse and decrepit, "...don't ever give up."

Erzok scowled at Marvin's pitiful call to arms. Erzok bent down and snarled at Marvin, and through parted lips and gritted teeth Erzok sneered, "You stupid fool, it is Tony's soul that I will steal."

Marvin, seething weakly, his stare searing into Erzok, through bloody teeth, said, "You're crazy... you can't win... God will win..."

Erzok smiled and wagged his head. "What will you do? Pray for help? Good luck with that."

Erzok's laugh echoed throughout the massive chamber.

Marvin's lips clenched. His swelling eyes met Tony's fear, then closed in exhaustion.

Erzok, with cheer gleaming through his flaming eyes, said, "No, my humble hero. You will see. My victory is certain. You will become a true believer."

With that final statement, Erzok lifted his leg and kicked Marvin hard in the hip and sent him plummeting down the steps of the pyramid.

"NO!" shouted Tony helplessly.

Marvin's body tumbled and sprang and rolled down the steps of the pyramid like discarded trash until it bounced off the stairs and onto the smooth decline of the pyramid wall and slid down on the plane, until his body slammed into the base of the pyramid and came to rest on the deck just next to the bridge above the chasm.

Marvin Fischer lay on his back, wrecked and worn and listless and bloody and motionless.

He was still aware of his body.

He ached everywhere.

His brain tried to click.

He could barely see.

His eardrums registered the echo of Tony's crying voice from high above.

Barely conscious and his mouth limply agape, Marvin gazed cloudily into the infinity above, sensing the passing of breath faintly across his lips.

Fragments of delirious ruminations drifted through Marvin's battered mind. Shrouded in murky sensations and abstract pictures came the remembrance of Caroline's glad smile and twinkling eyes as they had come out from the old Episcopal Church together, sharing an umbrella on a rainy Sunday morning in Detroit. Caroline had had a particularly upsetting week on the police force, and had almost shot a young man in self-defense. But it was the mother of the perpetrator that had talked the young man off the edge, reaching into the most forbidden parts of the family's turbulent history, and he had put the gun down, and had fallen to his knees and sobbed in submission as Caroline's partner had slapped the cuffs on his wrists. Caroline Fischer knew in that moment that despite the troubled life of crime the young man had lived, somehow through it all his relationship with his mother had begun to heal, and this would be the beginning of a new life for them both, even though there would be jail time and a long bought of separation for the family. "Just like the minister explained," Caroline had said to Marvin as they'd walked closely together under the umbrella, the raindrops pattering softly above their heads, and as she'd dabbed her eye. "All things work together for good."

There was more to that passage, and to that sermon that the minister had shared that morning. But what had struck Marvin Fischer was the idea that there is some sort of reason for everything. Some purpose behind the hardship and the pain and the loss and the arduous and grueling experiences that life can often be, even in the best of circumstances.

The same ideas that Pastor Deckland Smith had claimed at Rubi's church.

How Marvin wished now that it was all true.

But it wasn't.

All things work together for good.

It was a false, insipid, and baseless proverb, a stale and trite pandering myth taught to flocks of wandering sheep who longed for hope amidst despair, looking for answers to why they had to suffer through aimless and meaningless and painful and purposeless lives filled with wounds too deep to heal, mistakes too great to fix, sins too deep to be forgiven.

Caroline had believed a lie. Even Gilgamesh had been wrong. Marvin's mission had been futile, a lost cause from the very beginning. There was nothing good about being trapped here with Erzok. Nothing good about Dante, Topiltzin, or Gilgamesh getting sucked away. Nothing good about Amina Karimova drowning in the cold brutal sea. Nothing good about Rubi Valdez dying in a senseless car crash, her skeleton rotting away here in Erzok's lair. Nothing good about Antonio Valdez entering his teen years without a mother. Nothing good about Deckland Smith's wife Shirley dying of pneumonia. Nothing good about Officer Garrison's prayers for his nephew going unanswered. Nothing good about Caroline Fischer getting crushed to death when the South Tower fell.

And nothing good about that infernal Saint Peter never showing up.

The tension in Marvin's body disbursed as he lay languid and sore and inert. Beneath misty eyes, Marvin sank into depression and accepted defeat. All hope and ambition washed away as his heart gave way to despair. His body would no longer answer him. He was too weak to be angry with himself for having fallen for the lie. For being so stupid as to trust in anything other than his own ingenuity. His own reasoning. His own intelligence and equity.

Rubi Valdez was dead and gone forever.

And her son Antonio was about to have his soul ruthlessly and brutally ripped away.

And there was nothing Marvin Fischer could do about it.

Not anymore.

The fight was over.

Marvin Fischer was finally going to die.

70

WITHOUT INVITATION OR SUMMONS

And then, without invitation or summons or explanation, into Marvin's anguished and groggy mind floated an image of Elizabeth Walsh's beautiful silver necklace, glinting in the golden morning sunlight of Marvin Fischer's office window.

The crucifix necklace.

The Christ, the Son of the Living God.

Could this Christ Jesus be Topiltzin's Hunab Ku?

Even The Great Nahmes, of whom Gilgamesh had spoken?

All one and the same?

The one God for all humankind, who wanted goodness and life for all creation?

The same one who had spread his arms wide for all humanity?

For Caroline?

Caroline Fischer had always prayed.

And she had always believed.

Even through the darkest of times.

Perhaps that was what Marvin Fischer had loved most about her.

~

As the inevitable doom and darkness overcame him, a few enduring electrical pulses fired and traversed the neurons in Marvin Fischer's brain, and his weak mind gave way to the composition of a plea. The bitter wall in his heart cracked and broke as anger washed away and his mind opened to faith. Perhaps one last prayer would somehow get through. And he began to speak out, to call out with a belief and a trust that he had not felt since former times gone by. And just before the moment his mind fell into subconsciousness, his dreams painted the presence of Caroline there with him, next to his cheek, praying with him, holding his hand.

And the words continued until his soul took over, and then when his mind was gone, came an interceding spirit—some soft power mumbling through his cracked and bloody lips, words trailing out in a long and continuous flow that no human or created being could have composed or understood or decrypted or interpreted or untangled.

As time stood still, Marvin groaned and growled and moaned, his mind now distant and remote and disembodied.

With closed eyes and his body destroyed, Marvin saw nothing, was conscious of nothing, and moved not a single millimeter. Small clear salty drops trickled from the corners of his eyes and down his temples, but he did not feel them. His mouth spurt and spat and burbled.

As Marvin lay in a coma, those unintelligible words phoned out in low whispers, reaching and searching and calling. And these quiet and secret vespers may have been filled with hope and joy as they yearned and begged, but then they finally ceased and yielded to destiny. Marvin murmured and whimpered as the remnants of strength left, and his tongue went still.

71

THE RITUAL

At the behest of some invisible force, Tony's feet swept abruptly out from beneath him. He felt a painful thump on his chest as his body was tipped violently and speedily backward and now floating prone. Erzok's orange and fiery eyes pierced into the boy's frightened face as the memory of the train attack flooded Tony's panicked memory and his wits stretched in helpless fear. Tony shrieked and groped into the air as his body hovered over the platform at the top of the pyramid.

Erzok calmly placed his white scepter in the opulent silver cradle near the stairway's top step, where, like three military lieutenants, his dutiful acolytes positioned themselves to watch over whatever ritual was about to be performed.

The freedom of movement Tony had in his arms only moments before was suddenly withdrawn as his arms and legs were restrained by the same force that had sent him supine in levitation, his captive limbs now held tightly as if tied down by chains and locks. "What are you doing!?" shouted Tony anxiously.

Tony's body hovered flat, four feet above the platform. With calm savagery, Erzok stepped closer, hands together in front of his waist, fingertips touching. "Antonio Valdez, son of Rubi Maria," Erzok began with pleasurable grim, "I want to congratulate you on being the first of many. Many in what will become a long line of faithful religious humans whose lives I will snuff out, and from whom I will tear souls to cast into eternal prison, in utter and permanent separation from God."

"What do you mean? What are you talking about?!"

"As I was explaining to your friend Marvin Fischer, I plan to steal your soul, young boy. I failed to capture your mother's, and, dead as she is, her soul has slipped away. But yours—yours will not. The pain will be severe, but try to be a big boy about it, you will make a name for yourself, for your experience shall go down forever in the annals of hell."

As Erzok spoke, an ugly gray cat appeared near the edge of the platform. The cat stood still on all fours, revolving its head, assessing the flat terrain, then focusing on the scene a few feet away. Now the scrawny feline silently walked toward the center where Erzok stood over Tony. The cat was wrinkled and smarmy and gruesome. Soon there was a companion, and then another, until ten cats now approached Tony in the center of the platform, coming in from all directions. The cats with their black and emotionless eyes crept closer, freakishly silent, confident and innocent and curious. Somehow, they seemed to already know their purpose in this most horrifying setting.

"What are those?" asked Tony, sweat beading on his forehead. "Those cats? What are they?!" Tony felt his body shiver with cold as fear shuddered through him.

"Those are the soul stealers, Tony. The *ket shees*. I had tried them on earth once or twice, in the eastern hemisphere. Sadly, they had no effect other than frightening a few of the locals. But here in my sanctuary, Tony, far from any possible interference from the spirits of good, they will succeed. Not even your God can save you now. Not even God can ever save your mother. And since your soul will be mine forever, I want it to be clear to you, Antonio Valdez, that you will never, ever, *ever*, see your mother again. Rubi Valdez's soul is gone, but yours will be mine, trapped with me for all eternity!"

"No! Stop! Stop it!" Tony cried. "You can't do this!!"

"Oh yes, I can young boy. I can and I will!"

Erzok stepped back as the spectral ket shees reached Tony.

And now there were at least 40 or 50 of them. They slinked and circled and strolled slowly and calmly around Erzok's victim. One of the ket shees jumped on to Tony's leg. Tony screamed in repulsed horror as another one jumped onto his stomach.

"Get them off me! Get them off me!! Make them stop!!"

Tony felt their sharp claws dig into his skin. A third ket shee jumped onto Tony's shoulder and began to lick his ear. Tony's mouth shot open wide as he screamed in terror at the demonic ket shees that would forever separate his body from his soul, as Erzok watched in brutal silence.

72
CHARGE OF LIFE

Marvin Fischer's eyes shot wide open at the shrill of Tony's scream. The bellows pounded from above and Marvin suddenly remembered where he was. Bewildered and dumbstruck, Marvin blinked his eyes and moved his limbs. His senses regrouped as energy and vigor returned to his body and his mind sharpened. He dismissed the desire to understand and retook command of his body. He rolled sharply over. With an easy pushup he leapt to his feet with a potency he could not explain.

Somehow and inexplicably, Marvin's body was charged with life. He had no idea from where the strength had come. The power of the orb had long gone. Mere moments ago, he had sworn he was already dead.

But he had a vague recollection of having said something as he'd lain there.

Babbled something.

Prayed something?

~

With renewed vitality, Marvin gazed up and saw the backs of Erzok's three acolytes high above on the platform. The minions were disengaged from him, their attention on something else.

Tony's imminent death, Marvin guessed.

Marvin navigated along the deck of the pyramid by the invisible moat with its chasm below, and reached the stairway. Quietly and efficiently, Marvin bounded up the steps two at a time.

Tony screamed again.

Marvin reached the top of the stairs and, staying low, peered over the top of the ledge and assessed. Two acolytes stood to Marvin's left, the third to his right. Forty feet ahead, Marvin observed Erzok standing near Tony's levitating frame, and the disgusting cats of terror crawling all over the boy's writhing body.

Marvin's brow wrinkled in fury and his lips tensed. Twice he clenched and opened his fists. He looked around, desperate for a plan. Wait—what is that? The opulent silver stand stood to his right, behind the third acolyte, cradling Erzok's scepter peacefully and expectantly.

What a magnificent stroke of good fortune! Perhaps Marvin could get hold of the scepter and use it to his advantage. A quick reassessment assured Marvin the scepter was his only bet.

Tony hollered again. In a rush of adrenaline, Marvin sprang from the top step and reached for the scepter. He lifted it from its cradle and winced. The thing weighed a ton. Marvin didn't care. With every ounce of muscle he had left, he pushed through the pain and hoisted the thing up.

Turning, Marvin set his eyes on the closest acolyte. Thanks to the lesson from Erzok himself, Marvin swiveled his hips and raised the scepter. In victorious wrath Marvin swung the scepter like a Louisville slugger, striking the acolyte on the right shoulder with a piercing crack.

The acolyte exploded in shards of flint.

Debris flew.

Nothing remained of the acolyte.

But now Marvin had blown his cover. The two acolytes on his left spun in surprise. Marvin moved to the closest one and swung again. Before the minion could get up his spear, he was hit in the jaw with the scepter and vaporized too into flying crumbs.

Erzok, hearing now the ruckus behind him over the ket shee's screeches, turned around to see what the clatter was all about. Erzok spun around just in time to witness the third and last of his acolytes receive the death blow from Marvin by means his own scepter.

Erzok's orange eyes flared in rage—and in his distraction—let Tony fall from his airy prison to land hard on the platform. The ket shees scattered, bounding and leaping and escaping, leaving Tony lying alone in the center of the platform, wincing in pain and fear.

Marvin, staring down at the crumbled remains of the acolytes strewn across the platform, turned now to face Erzok. Erzok closed the distance by zipping across the dais in a vaporous flash. Marvin charged, shouting fiercely like a Roman in battle, blue eyes blazing, cocking the scepter to swing at the approaching Erzok. Erzok raised a hand to block the speedy swing—and the middle of the white scepter crashed hard into his palm as his fingers clasped tight around it—and he froze in situ and instantly turned to stone.

There stood Erzok, hard as granite, a victim of his own magic, frozen in a dance pose with the scepter locked in his left hand.

Marvin stepped back in shocked amazement, gasping and breathing heavily and staring at the solid foe rendered impotent.

Marvin looked to Tony lying in the center of the platform and dashed towards him, slipping and skidding over the pebbly remains of the destroyed acolytes.

"Tony!!" shouted Marvin. He reached Tony's side, put his arm behind his back, and helped the boy sit up.

"Mister Fischer…" Tony gasped, his eyes red and bloodshot and wide in recovering fear. Tony gulped and flinched, feeling his stomach. "My stomach hurts!"

"Can you walk? We've got to get out of here!" Marvin coaxed.

Tony reached and urgently grabbed the collar of Marvin's shirt. "My mom's soul! Where is my mom's soul!?!"

"Tony, I don't know. We were too late!"

"God has to have her soul! We have to find her!!" Tony shouted fiercely.

But together they heard the sharp CRACK coming from the stairway. In unison, Marvin and Tony snapped their heads in that direction.

Erzok's right hand had cracked free of the rocky sepulcher, long gray hideous fingers twitching like the tails of scorpions. His wrist twisted and a knotty forearm moved and the elbow bent, and the rock split further up the grisly arm and fell away as the rock crackled.

A gruesome Erzok—the monster—was breaking free!

Marvin turned back to Tony and begged. "We have to go!" said Marvin. "NOW!!"

Tony looked again and saw the emerging Erzok and knew Mister Fischer was right. Marvin helped Tony to his feet and they rushed across the dais.

They'd have to pass by Erzok to reach the stairway.

Erzok's left hand cracked and his fingers opened. The scepter in his hand fell away and bounced onto the platform. The scepter rolled over the edge and cartwheeled down the steps of the pyramid, landing hard and solid at the bottom of the stairs and rolling to a stop.

The rest of Erzok's left arm—an abominable gray limb—burst forth from the stone.

Marvin looked ahead, gauging, as he and Tony neared the top of the stairway.

There'd be no time for the stairs!

"Come on!" shouted Marvin to Tony as they whooshed past Erzok. Marvin grabbed Tony's arm and together they leapt onto the flat and polished lateral face of the pyramid and rode the decline like a waterpark slide, skidding down on their behinds.

"Careful!!" shouted Marvin as they slid and twisted and sailed fast down the decline. "Don't fall into the chasm!"

Tony was the first to crash onto the perimeter deck. Marvin landed next and tumbled toward the edge, his legs sweeping and dangling over the chasm. Marvin hung on and groped. Tony jumped and clasped Marvin's arms, helping him back up onto the deck. Together they looked to the apex of the pyramid and witnessed Erzok thunder out of the remainder of his rocky tomb and flex with rage, the odious true-devil, the troll-like greyish ghoul fully revealed, his orange eyes searching.

Marvin and Tony bolted across the bridge. They passed the scepter resting on the floor and Marvin leaned to collect the heavy scepter, as Erzok spotted them and flashed down the length of the pyramid.

There was no time to run down the Avenue of the Dead. Marvin looked to one of the entryways to the maze and pushed Tony towards it.

"In there!!" Marvin beckoned.

Erzok flew toward them as they reached the entrance.

In a flash of calculations, Marvin dreaded the thought of reentering the mind-boggling labyrinth. But it was their only chance of escape. He hoped that the bends and twists of the shifting maze would shake Erzok from their trail and—by some miracle—they'd find a way out.

The whitewashed hallways were already dizzying and convoluted as Marvin led the way through the vexing maze.

"Tony, stay close!" shouted Marvin.

There came no response.

"Tony!" Marvin stopped and turned, scepter at his side.

The boy was already gone!

He'd lost him!

"Tony!!" Marvin shouted again.

Still no answer.

Marvin grimaced.

Now what?!

"FISCHER!" Erzok's voice boomed through the white shadowy halls. "Fischer!" The voice was sharp and seething with bloodlust. Marvin bent as the ceiling caved and he turned again to run. He never thought he'd be grateful to return to this horror-filled fun house, but this time it was working against his enemy. As powerful as the mighty Erzok was, he was apparently thwarted and trapped in his own creation.

Nervous sweat dripped from Marvin's temples as his thoughts went back to the boy. Would Tony find a way out?

73

THE FINAL RUN

Marvin ducked below a white cantilever and dodged a warping wall as he twisted and danced and leapt through the increasingly pandemonic craziness. As he raced between converging walls, Marvin's experience in these halls of doom had quickly encouraged a hatred for all things white. He decided that if he ever made it back to his plain white condo in Paradise Valley, he would make immediate plans to have it painted.

This place was a death trap. A killing machine not for the body, but for the spirit. Ceaseless, grinding torment that would slowly tear away every last fiber of reason and turn the will to mush. Marvin wondered how many angels had found their way here, on reconnaissance for God, only to be driven mad with paranoia and vaporized into oblivion?! Could Marvin possibly find his way? He cursed the tumbling tunnels of insanity as he began to slip and slide as if on ice, like a second-rate hockey player without skates.

And then his mind was numbed by the disturbing perception in his freezing feet. Marvin glided and slid to a cold stop and concentrated.

The hum was back.

And the rumbling vibration.

It meant only one thing.

The tempest was close by.

And as Marvin Fischer stood there panting in numb realization, he finally knew within his heart and soul and spirit what this was all about.

Marvin Fischer had to find that tempest!

And Marvin Fischer understood what he had to do if he ever got there.

Marvin kicked into high gear and raced and ducked and chased through the white walls of the maze with full determination and centrality of purpose. He ignored the corruption of his mind that the vicious and snickering hallways beckoned, the wicked and ferocious snarl in Erzok's menacing threats. Marvin batted away thoughts of delusion and madness and doused the fear.

The vibration increased.

The rattling intensified.

Marvin bent his mind and focused on the singular goal. His feet moved swift and sure and steady and he clasped the scepter now with both hands.

He was headed toward the single objective.

His single purpose.

And as Marvin rounded a curve and the wall opened up, his face went rave with fury.

There it was again.

The colosseum.

The Tempest in Glass — the Cyclone of Captured Prayers.

He'd found it!

Rumbling, crashing, swirling, piercing in its whistle.

Marvin again ignored the calls of Erzok's wild voice and raced up the ramp surrounding the cyclone. Round and round he circled, his gaze fixed on the swirling vespers within its cruel walls. He snubbed the fiery pain in his thighs as he persisted up the arduous incline. He had to make it to the top of the ramp, where Marvin hoped he'd be high enough to reach over the railing and come within touching distance of the crystalline cyclone's wall.

He was four levels up. Not close enough. He had to keep going.

The rumbling and ceaseless vibration became so severe that Marvin could no longer feel his pulse or sense his breath. The scepter became heavier. The cold was brutal. Marvin felt the sweat freeze on his temples. He continued upward.

He made it to the seventh level and paused.

The tempest continued up into infinity but Marvin could go no higher. He was at the end of the ramp.

He approached the railing and gauged the distance between himself and the outer wall of the tempest, strong and thick and solid and massive. Marvin looked up, and then down.

He could do this right here!

He reached across the railing toward the clear thick wall of the cyclone. Marvin guessed his fingertips were still a good three feet away. The cold was stabbing. The tremors quaking. It seemed the air itself was pulsating. Marvin stepped to the icy cold railing until his waist pressed against it. He lifted the scepter and swung it out over the railing. He vaguely heard a light tinkling as the tip of the scepter grazed the glass.

He had to get closer.

He leaned over the railing now, both arms outstretched, clutching the scepter.

He swung.

The scepter chinked and bounced off the wall of the clear crystal.

"Fischer! Where are you!?!"

Marvin's eyes darted around the arena, seeking Erzok's whereabouts. Marvin could not see him.

Erzok must have still been lost in the maze.

But Marvin knew at any moment Erzok could show up and stop him.

And it would all be over.

Each passing second was like lost gold.

Marvin looked again at the cyclone's wall.

He reached over the railing and swung.

Another chink and bounce of the scepter.

Marvin gritted his teeth. Still too far away. He didn't have the leverage or power in the swing! The scepter was too damn heavy! He looked and assessed and analyzed, then made his daring decision. He swung his left leg over the railing. Clutching the scepter with one hand and the railing with the other, he swung the other leg over. He locked his toes between the ramp and baserail.

Now there was nothing between Marvin Fischer and the cyclone except searing arctic gas and the deadly pit of the chasm below. He grasped the top rail with his left hand and hoped the sweat in his palm would not freeze his grip. With his right arm, he swung the scepter hard against the cyclone.

The scepter struck the wall with a resounding metallic thud.

Sparks flew.

But no effect.

For the fifth time Marvin swung and struck the defiant superglass.

The clash thundered its echo but still the cyclone stood firm, mocking his folly.

Marvin took another breath of the glacial air and checked his hold of the top rail. He was desperately afraid of losing his grip. But now he had to close out all distraction and again concentrate. Marvin summoned all his strength and focused his piercing blue eyes back to a very specific spot on the convex glass. He had to strike it hard and weaken it definitively. He lifted the scepter as high as he could and with a raging scream he swung across hard.

THUNDER BOOMED.

Light flashed and more sparks showered from the impact.

This time the crystal cracked like a sheet of ice on a frozen lake. Marvin's eyes bulged as he watched the fissure crawl and crackle up the glass to infinity. He looked down. The crack sliced on below, past his vision—but held.

Okay. Marvin lifted the scepter again. The next blow had to be perfect. There was no telling what might happen to the energy within, to the crystal wall, or to himself.

Just a little bit closer!

With Erzok's wailing and annoying voice resounding still nearer, Marvin pulled himself back toward the rail and wedged the scepter between the railing's balusters. He slipped the silk tie from around his neck and tied it tight to the top rail. He wrapped the other end of the tie twice around his left wrist and grasped it.

The extra length would get him six inches closer to the cyclone.

He reached for the scepter and picked it up and grasped it tight, its shaft cold as an icicle. The radiant icy wind of the cyclone froze the air. Marvin felt the skin on his face crackle from the stinging cold. His ears screamed. His lips burned. His head pounded and his bones quaked. His knee joints locked. His knuckles seared with frostbite. His eyes glazed. In a few seconds he would no longer be able to blink. He leaned and reached forward, stretching himself precariously out over the infinite chasm, one foot planted firm on the ramp, the other dangling over the abyss.

Now he was so close to the damn thing he could almost touch it with his hand.

His tie-wrapped left wrist screamed in pain from the weight it bore.

"FISCHER!!"

Marvin turned to see Erzok appear on the ramp!

It was now or never!

Marvin snarled with concentration, focusing on the fissure. Precision was paramount. He hoisted the scepter. He aimed at the fissure and swung hard, with what would now be the seventh strike. And in a blaze of sparks, the scepter smashed heavily and finally through the wall of the cyclone and Marvin knew he had victory. The fissure split like a break in a giant aquarium as the crystal wall ruptured with a deafening boom. Within milliseconds, the breach compromised the entire cyclone and the cracks spidered their way around the superstructure.

Marvin shielded his eyes and his eardrums ripped and his face sizzled as the explosion surged forth in a blast of massive pressure, and the wall blew out into a septendecillion pieces of crystal, and sharp slivers of the superglass flew out on all axes.

And out from the obliteration, millions of wispy vespers soared and swirled from their suppression as the colossal cyclone tumbled heavy and collapsed with a roar.

The downward draft sucked Marvin into the vacuum and he fell and spun out through the cascade of whirling debris, and the vespers shot up and high and bright like lightning bolts towards eternal freedom.

PART V

74

REANIMATION

It was dark. Marvin Fischer pressed his teeth together and churned the grit between them. After breath entered him, he coughed and spurted out the grit. Marvin found himself face down in packed sand. He sensed the hard mat beneath the length of his body and lay there for a full minute before trying to move. Then he creaked his head and rested it on his cheek. With the edge of his pupil he detected the moon, full and bright in the clear sky above. Obscure shapes and silhouettes popped against the midnight blue sky.

It was very cold. Marvin's teeth clattered.

Stiffly and painfully, Marvin curled his body into a ball and shivered.

Perhaps he was back in the black desert between the mesas, where he'd first entered the After Worlds. Marvin perceived strange shadows shifting before his eyes and he heard the wind bend. He was feverish. For a long time he lay in a cluster shaking. He ached everywhere and he felt distinctly alone. He remembered climbing the ramp and slamming the scepter into the cyclone. It had crashed like Jericho. The prayers had fired. He had fallen. Then what?

Marvin lay on the hard sand for several more minutes, trying to assemble his thoughts and reconstruct his experience. He had difficulty concentrating. His thoughts skittered constantly. Nothing gelled. Nothing came together. Nothing made sense.

After a little while longer, he thought he heard some shifting in the sand. There came the quiet snap of a twig, then more shifting.

Were they footsteps?

Yes... footsteps... steady and even.

Who ... ?

Marvin sensed the mystery visitor approaching from behind, then circling very close by. The footsteps stopped. The visitor plunked something heavy down on the dust near where Marvin lay. Marvin perceived the visitor crouching over the heavy object. Marvin craned his neck, straining to get a view through the dark.

In the hard blue moonlight, the visitor looked to be a man. The man pulled a blanket out from somewhere and fanned it out over the package next to Marvin. Now Marvin could see that the package gave the appearance of a body. A small figure. A boy's frame. The mystery man wrapped the blanket around the boy and tucked it comfortably. Then the man rested his hand on the head and rubbed it.

Hopefulness rushed as Marvin convinced himself the boy was Antonio Valdez.

Marvin's pulse quickened. The mystery man got up, rustled with something else, and moved beside Marvin. He knelt down and spread another blanket, thick and warm and heavy, over Marvin's curled body. The blanket smelled of the fresh hot sea in midsummer. The man reached for something else and brought a warm moist cloth to Marvin's face. He patted away the dried blood and the dust and the flakes of dead skin. Marvin felt a swell in his throat and his eyes became watery. He sniffled, tried to control his stuttering breath, and began to cry softly as the man dabbed Marvin's bruised face and head. Then the man took hold of

Marvin's right hand, with its swollen knuckles, split and torn under dried blood. The man massaged the hand gently with the warm cloth, then took hold of Marvin's left. Marvin curled tighter beneath the salvation of the blanket and pinched his eyes tight as the tears flowed from his face and he sobbed deeply and heavily.

The man rested a hand on Marvin's shoulder, then rose and moved away.

For many minutes Marvin lay there and howled away the distressed emotions from within his spirit as his mind and soul became cleansed with indescribable consolation. Finally, with a quivering jaw and through drenched eyes cooled by his tears, Marvin moved his lips to form words.

"Who are you?" Marvin whispered faintly.

The man cracked some twigs and small branches and placed them a few feet from Marvin's and Tony's resting bodies. He squatted and arranged the sticks and, turning to Marvin, he said plainly, "My name is Peter. Simon, Bar-Jonah."

Again the sobs burst from Marvin's mouth uncontrollably. His head bobbed and his body shook. His nose dripped and he swallowed hard and then wept some more.

As Peter finished his arrangement of tinder and kindling wood, he said with conviction and gratitude, "Marvin, you have done a marvelous and wonderful thing."

The fire sprang to life as Marvin cried. The flames crackled and blazed fast and high and sparks swirled upward into the blue. The soothing warmth met Marvin's face like a mother's touch. In the yellow light of the gleaming flames, Marvin fluttered his eyelids and opened them wide. With teary blurred vision he studied Saint Peter as he tended the fire. Peter appeared solid and corporeal. His hair was thick with curls, his face rugged and calm. He wore a sleeveless tunic tied at the waist, and heavy leather shoes. His easy movements and quiet expression exuded peace and certitude.

Marvin swallowed again and spoke. "I'm not dead?"

"No Marvin, you are very much alive." Peter got up and circled the fire. "Welcome home."

"I'm back ... on earth?"

"Yes," Peter smiled.

Marvin closed his eyes and coughed again and swallowed. "Rubi Valdez..." he said dimly. "We wanted ... to bring Rubi Valdez back to life."

"Yes, I know," said Peter empathetically. "I'm sorry, Marvin. Sometimes God can be disappointing."

Another tear streamed from Marvin's eye. He sniffled. "Why... why couldn't we find you?"

"Rest, Marvin. I know you have many questions."

"But..."

Peter threw some more wood on the fire. He circled it again and moved to Tony.

Marvin's eyelids fell shut as weariness overcame him. His emotions were spent and his body exhausted. He wanted to talk more with the good saint, but instead faded off into a deep sleep.

The clouds glowed hot pink when Marvin awoke to the sunrise winking over the far off mountaintops. He stirred and felt the crunch of pebbles by his feet. He was still covered by the warm blanket. The fire had gone out. He looked over to Tony, who lay sleeping just a few feet away.

Marvin rubbed his hands together. The torn and shredded necktie was still wrapped around his left wrist. He moved to undo it, and let it rest there on the hard sand. He patted it gently as if it were his hero. After another minute he sat up lazily, then pulled the blanket over his shoulders and looked at the spent coals in the pit. His face droopy and haggard, Marvin glimpsed around.

There was no sign of Saint Peter.

Marvin scanned the earth around the fire pit and observed the prints of the saint's leather shoes. He must have gone off.

Marvin breathed deep and sighed. The crisp morning air was cool and refreshing. For the moment he felt tranquil and at peace, enjoying the quiet stillness.

He didn't even crave coffee. He wanted a cigarette.

Marvin looked at the horizon and examined his surroundings. He recognized the character of the terrain as the Sonoran Desert of Arizona. From the vegetation he guessed they were somewhere in the arid part of the biome. There were low shrubs and velvet mesquite. The tall saguaro cacti stood sentry against the grapefruit sky. He did not know in which direction the nearest city might be. But he was back home, on familiar earth. Perhaps it was Saint Peter himself who had saved them and brought them back.

Swaying to his right, Marvin noticed now a full glass of water beside his makeshift bed, set on a flat stone, and a plate of what appeared to be three flame-cooked tilapia. A smile burst from Marvin's face. His eyes went to Tony. A cup and a plate had been set there for the boy also. Marvin turned to his water and drank it down. Plucking a fish from the plate, he crunched into the smoky meat. It was delicious, seasoned to perfection.

Taking another bite, he looked again at the fire pit and thought of getting up to prod the coals, but decided to put it off. He stretched and felt his face gently with his fingertips. His skin was tender and coarse. He had expected that his injuries would have been much more severe. He felt surprisingly good. He sat listening to the first sounds of the early desert. There was the sad call of the mourning dove, and a flock of grackles hooping somewhere in the distance and then fading. He watched a sparrow peek from its saguaro nest and fly off. A spotted whiptail scurried across the sand and plunged into a shrub.

Marvin finished the fish and looked down at the waking earth in front of his feet and at his sides. He arranged three small stones playfully in a row. If only his life could be so tidy.

He scanned the horizon again.

Still no sign of Peter. The saint had come and gone. Once again Marvin was alone to fend for himself. Bruised and beaten.

Left high and dry. Hanging in the wind. Now what? He wondered about the medium. The woman Amina Karimova, who had at first driven him to desperate impatience and then proven a dedicated companion, indispensible ally, the guide he needed by his side the whole way. Would she somehow be saved too? His heart burned over her and he was surprised at the feeling. He wished there was something he could do for her. But what?

"Hi Mister Fischer."

Marvin turned to the voice. "Hey buddy," he said.

"Where's Saint Peter?"

"He's gone."

"How are we going to get home?"

"We'll make a way."

Immediately Tony saw the food. He drank and he ate.

"He found my binoculars." Tony said with a mouthful, pulling the specs from beneath his blanket and examining them proudly.

Marvin squinted.

How … ?

Tony looked around and absorbed the brightening desert, took his last bite of fish, brushed his hands together, and sniffled. He sat up and pulled the blanket around him and gazed at the fire pit. "Mister Fischer?"

"Yes Tony."

"Do you think you might adopt me?"

Marvin had never thought about it. "I don't know," he said carefully. "What about the Tindals? Tom and Tiffany?"

"They're okay," said Tony moderately. "Are we going to start the fire?"

"I guess."

75

CONVERGENCE

They sat in silence for 30 more seconds before something on the distant ridge caught Tony's rapt and undivided attention. Tony sat bolt upright, intense and curious, his gaze fixed on the rise. "Hey," Tony pointed, "somebody's coming."

Marvin turned and narrowed his eyes. "Hmm?"

Tony grabbed the binoculars and tossed off the blanket. He stood up and looked and focused the specs. Not satisfied, Tony scampered to a boulder twenty feet away and climbed it for a better vantage point. Standing tall and alert, Tony raised the binoculars and refocused. "It's Saint Peter!" he shouted. "He's coming back!"

Marvin shifted. "No way."

"Yeah!" Tony smiled. "It's him! ... and someone else is with him!" Tony focused again. "It's ... I think it's Pastor Deckland... It's Pastor Deckland!"

Marvin stood up and quickstepped to the boulder. He held out his hand. "Gimme those."

Tony leaned and handed Marvin the binoculars.

Marvin held the specs with shaking hands and looked through.

Yes, it was Saint Peter, heading straight for them, with Pastor Deckland Smith close behind.

And then, someone else.

"Who's that other guy?" asked Tony.

"That's... that's Officer Garrison?"

Seconds later, others appeared over the crest, many others, following also behind the saint, more and more of them following in faithful assembled unison, flowing like cattle over the ridge and down the slope and into the sprawling valley, the huge group migrating right towards Marvin and Tony's little camp site.

"What are they doing?" asked Tony. "Why are they coming?"

There were hundreds of them now. The hundreds became thousands, fanning out far and wide, cresting the ridge and marching toward the rising sun with the good Saint Peter leading sturdily.

"Who are all those people?" Tony kept prodding.

Marvin adjusted the binoculars. He tried to recognize other faces, but they were strangers to him. Strangers of all ages, of all colors, of all ethnicities. Children, men, women, boys and girls in clothing of all kinds and types. There were rags and jeans, dresses and suits, saris and kilts, kimonos and hanboks.

A gathering from the world over, a melting pot, assembling here in this spot.

Why?

Marvin lowered the binoculars, his jaw skewing in utter perplexity. He stood mesmerized and let Tony grab the binoculars. The boy looked through again and beamed.

"That's amazing Mister Fischer! What is Peter doing?"

Marvin couldn't answer. He was dumbfounded, at a total loss for understanding. His heel ground in the sand as he turned and calculated, thinking and pondering. And when Marvin lifted his chin towards the sun, he saw now—

Over the opposite ridge—

Ahead of the brightening pink-orange sunrise facing directly Peter's crowd—

Another figure.

A singular figure, lone and bright and tall, arriving at the peak of the opposite rise on the other side of the valley.

"Tony ..." was all Marvin could get out as he set his hand again for the binoculars.

Tony stooped and handed them back to Marvin and turned, and now saw the lone figure.

"It's another guy Mister Fischer!"

Marvin raised the lenses again to identify this second figure. The figure walked calmly and assuredly and boldly towards them, still two hundred yards away.

The figure had long dark hair pulled tight behind his head. He wore a long white robe, bright and flowing and clean.

The face was plain and content and assertive.

And behind this new assertive figure appeared another crowd, equally large and spanning as Saint Peter's group. They followed this man, progressing straight down into the valley. The two massive crowds hiked through the valley, closing the gap between them. And that's when Marvin realized that he and Tony were at the epicenter of this grand appointment. The two multitudes of people were on a course towards mutual mass aggregation, poised to converge right where Marvin and Tony stood.

With each passing second, Marvin became more and more certain of this second leader's identity. It was a man whom Marvin had never seen before, but surely this man must be great.

The Great Nahmes.

Jesus? The Christ?

The gap decreased as the floods of people continued their procession across the valley. Then like a runner at the start of a track meet, one of the people near the front of Peter's group shot out and forward, running ahead and into the valley towards the oncoming group as the gap closed. It was a woman of about 30, smiling and cheering with her arms in the air and calling out someone's name. Immediately someone from The Great Nahmes' group bolted ahead to join the shouting woman and when they met they crashed and spun in each other's arms, laughing and embracing. And as more people from Peter's group began to recognize faces, they also ran ahead, towards the people led in by The Great Nahmes.

There remained only now about 100 feet between the converging groups and Marvin and Tony found themselves right in the center of it all and they knew that within seconds they would be flooded and overtaken by the crowds. Tony jumped off the boulder and stuck close to Marvin. Their eyes bulged as within seconds the lines of both groups broke and ran to meet, shouting with immense and overwhelmed joy.

Then came the full brunt of the collision when the crowd converged and the embraces boomed. Marvin watched the surreal scene and the reality of it hit him like a sledgehammer as he watched the loved ones reunite with hugs and tears before his very eyes.

Marvin's mouth dropped as he watched Pastor Deckland, smiling with his arms high, greeting a woman of about his age and their arms locked tight. Shirley.

And Officer Garrison, smashing into his nephew with a bear hug.

Saint Peter and The Great Nahmes met discreetly and without fanfare, shaking hands with a short hug and release. They spoke something to each other and then stood and watched with silent satisfaction, drinking in the fruits of their work and of their love.

Marvin put his hands to his head and spun on his toes, watching the grand reunion explode all around him, people with cheers and shouts of jubilant euphoria. Colors spun and sand flew at people's heels. It was a rendezvous of hope, a family reunification of colossal proportions, a fulfillment with tremendous implication.

Tony hopped up and down, trying to see above the people's heads. He jumped and leapt and ducked between the people, looking and searching. Marvin moved to Tony and slipped his hands around the boy's waist and hoisted him up and clutched the knees. Tony settled onto Marvin's shoulders and scanned above the heads, cupping his hands around his eyes to shield them from lances of sunlight. One by one he searched faces, calling and shouting.

"Mom! Mom!" Tony yelled. He lowered his hand from his eyes and squeezed Marvin's shoulder. "Mister Fischer! I see her! I see her! Over there! She's over there!"

Marvin tipped his eyes to see the direction Tony was pointing.

"That way!" Tony shouted.

Marvin sidestepped and pushed through the people and wound his way through.

"Mom!" Tony shouted.

When Rubi Valdez' expectant eyes saw her son, they flooded with tears and her face burst into a bright and wide smile. "Antonio! Antonio my son!"

Marvin ducked, letting Tony slide off his shoulders. Boy and mother crashed into each other's arms and spun and kissed and Rubi wept. Tony wiped tears, arms around his mother's neck, his smile unstoppable.

Marvin buried his feelings and ignored the wetness in his eyes.

Now Rubi Valdez turned from her son to face Marvin Fischer. Smiling broadly, Rubi put her hands around Marvin's neck and looked into his glistening blue eyes with deepest sincerity. "Hello, Marvin Fischer," Rubi smiled.

"Long time no see," Marvin nodded.

Rubi laughed as a tear rolled from her eye and then she pulled Marvin toward herself and hugged him tightly.

"Thank you…" said Rubi through tears. They held for a long moment as Marvin inhaled deeply and fought the feelings. Then Rubi released and looked and smiled at him again and wiped her cheek. "Thank you for praying for me," she swallowed.

"You bet," Marvin winked.

Then Rubi released herself from Marvin's gaze and turned back to Tony. Marvin moved off and looked around at the tearfest of swirling faces and sweeping smiles that continued all around him. He shook his head and smiled thinly and put his hands on his hips as he watched the party continue to rise.

The liberated prayers had been heard and answered ex post facto.

Those that died had been raised—and were now being returned to their loves.

Marvin laughed and kicked the sand and then lifted his head and his arms to the brightening sky and shouted out a single, booming call of triumph.

As Marvin lowered his arms and turned back to the earth and the crowds began to disperse and spread out into the valley, a fresh gust of morning breeze kissed his face, bringing the sweet scent of desert primrose. The flocks of smiling people wandered further away, into their new lives. Marvin turned. He lifted his gaze to the mountain peaks. The pink sky was giving way to clear pale blue. The realization struck him that the mission was over, and he was alone.

Again he felt the wind, stronger this time. Indifferent now. Void. Impartial. Empty of fragrance. Absently Marvin rubbed his hands across the dirty sides of his shirt. He took a deep breath as elation was snuffed and abruptly replaced with the pang of loneliness. The familiar melancholy overcame him. Another wisp of breath flowed through him, trying to cast aside the unwanted return to his old self. The solitary life, the one he had come to accept with forbearance.

With not a small amount of desperation he began to search the valley. Looking for her. His eyes hoped he would catch a glimpse. Any moment now, he'd see her, stepping over a low shrub, appearing from behind a saguaro. Surely Saint Peter and The Great Nahmes had not forgotten her.

Not after all this.

Could she be…?

Marvin turned again and—some distance away and seemingly from nowhere—emerged a lone woman. The lone woman wore an elegant silky dark sheath, as if dressed for the concert hall. Jet black hair. Skin healthy white. Lips red and exciting. The vision of stunning beauty.

The woman saw him. She smiled and began to cross the sand toward him.

Marvin's heart should have detonated. He always thought it would. His eyes locked with hers as she approached. The red lips parted into a smile, a smile he had seen—since that terrible day—only in his memory. The corner of Marvin's mouth twitched into a smile. Panels of emotion deep within flipped and tumbled and twisted in confusion. He had always thought her coming back would be impossible. He should have cheered like a fan at a stadium. He should have run toward her. He should have burst into tears of joy. After all this time, his prayer had been answered. But across the wasteland of the desert he had been looking for someone else.

Caroline reached Marvin and put a hand gently to his face, and with dreamy eyes she said, "Marvin Fischer, you look rough."

Marvin looked into the brown jewels of Caroline's eyes and smiled. Their hands came together. Now what? Within him there was resistance. Disinclination. Aversion. Objection? Caroline said something else. Softly. Tenderly. But Marvin did not hear the words. Then in the span of moments, he determined to stay the course. There must be no betrayal in his face. No evidence of regret. He must play the role of the man she had returned for. He shifted his shoulders to shake off the sting of disappointment. The aching of loss that is so much greater than the fleeting gratification of triumph. For a moment his eyes slipped over Caroline's shoulder and scanned the empty sands behind her. He met her again and said, "I don't know what color to paint the condo. And it needs greenery."

Caroline laughed and kissed him again. She slid her fingertips across his chest and touched his ragged shirt collar. "No tie?"

Marvin's eyebrows lifted. "That... is a long story." He looked down and noticed that Caroline held something cupped in her other hand. He sensed the doors of fate revolving. Immediately darkness swept him. He did not know from where the feeling came. There was no signal from the noirette in front of him. Swallowing the spear of dread, he tipped his chin. "What's that?"

Caroline brought up her hand. "Oh, I found this back there in the sand. Isn't it pretty?"

Caroline opened Marvin's fingers and dropped the small object into his palm.

Marvin's lips parted as breath pushed into him.

Glistening in his palm was a single, beautiful gold hoop earring.

THE END

AUTHOR'S NOTE

I find the subject of prayer to be uniquely fascinating. For millennia, people of all cultures and faiths have sought to communicate with a higher power, a supreme being, a great spirit, God as described in the Bible. Thoughts or spoken words are believed to be consciously transmitted by the human and then instantly known or heard by a greater being, in the hope that the human may find acceptance, peace, deliverance, healing, sustenance, enlightenment, salvation.

Over the last decade, to ascertain the role of prayer in people's lives, reputable institutions have conducted numerous polls. From *Pew Research* to *LifeWay* and *Barna* to *Gallop*, the subject of prayer has demanded steady interest.

Rather than exhibiting charts and percentages and statistics, permit me to distill the findings to their dramatic essence.

Substantial majorities of people from many faiths claim to reach out in some fashion to a higher power on a regular basis. While some claim to never pray, many pray daily. Others once a week, still others, once a month, or only when in need. Jehovah's Witnesses, Mormons, Muslims, Catholics, and Evangelical Christians seem to rank at the upper end in frequency, while members of other faiths claim a belief in reaching up also. Buddhists, Jews, Taoists, New Agers, etc., each in their own way.

Prayer is a global phenomenon, spanning all ages and genders and races, all countries, and almost all faiths.

(continued)

AUTHOR'S NOTE (continued)

For some, prayer is such a matter of routine that it has become rather un-extraordinary. But when one faces a time of crisis, a moment of intense fear or desperation, or when all hope seems to be lost, that is the time when one reaches up in the hope that some Ultimate Grace will shower down upon them and save them from whatever evil or natural disaster or undesirable fate stares them in the face.

Most people who pray claim that their prayers are answered *most of the time.*

Some say their prayers are answered *some of the time.*

And a few say that their prayers are *never answered.*

So, what happens to all those prayers?

In writing this novel, I combined my own experience with careful research, sketching with a heavy pen and much creative liberty. Its theology does not adhere to any specific dogma, but is instead an eclectic amalgam of tradition and hypothetical fiction, drawing from Christianity, spiritualism, archaeology, astronomy, prisca theologia, and the ancient myths of Mesoamerica and Mesopotamia.

The Tempest In Glass is written as entertainment, but it is a metaphor for my own voyage to understand prayer, the purposes of God, and the meaning behind some of life's most confounding circumstances. I do hope that you as the reader will find it thought provoking, and that some of its themes will resonate with your own experience.

For me as author, the writing has been a journey of surprising emotional release and spiritual evolution.

Dirk Eichhorst
August, 2020

ABOUT THE AUTHOR

Dirk Eichhorst grew up as a Baptist in the American Midwest. He is the founder and former president of *Cumberland Media Ministries Inc.*, a heralded 501(c)3 that specialized in producing promotional videos for Bible camps and churches. He served as Production Manager for *L. Plummer Communications* in Southfield, Michigan, and as a Video Director for *The Holy Land Experience* in Orlando, Florida. Dirk has worked freelance with *West Coast Media, Inc.* shooting business and broadcast, taught classes and seminars in the film arts, served as Membership Chair of *West Michigan Film Video Alliance*, and is an Accolade Award recipient for *Body Balancing by Tim Michaels*. Dirk's work has taken him across America, Europe, Africa, and Israel. He studied screenwriting and film directing at Columbia College Chicago, holds two General Studies degrees and a BA in Intelligence Studies from American Public University with honors. Dirk enjoys backcountry camping with his son Tobias, weight training, model building, and hauling ass in his Ford Mustang.

Photo by Melissa Bayer

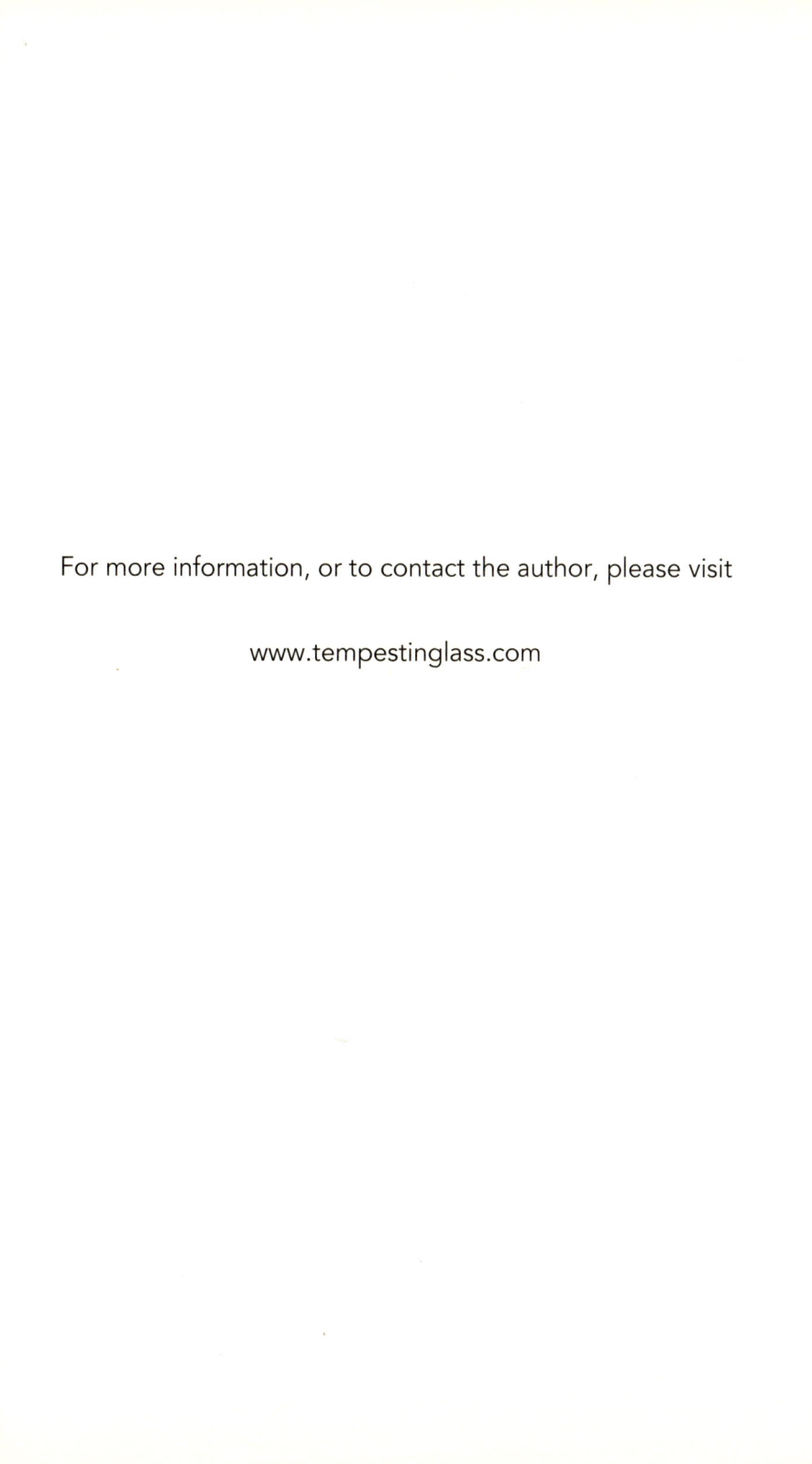

For more information, or to contact the author, please visit

www.tempestinglass.com